ODYSSEY

C. STEPHEN HICKS

First paperback edition 2025

ISBN: 979-8-9864844-2-6 (Paperback)

ISBN: 979-8-9864844-3-3 (Ebook)

Brought to you by Tomes of Kharazim

Printed by IngramSpark

Cover art by Therin Edwards

Map made in Wonderdraft

To all the wanderers in life.
Here's hoping the journey never ends.

May Death Find You Alive

Major Region of Sylvanna and Bordering areas

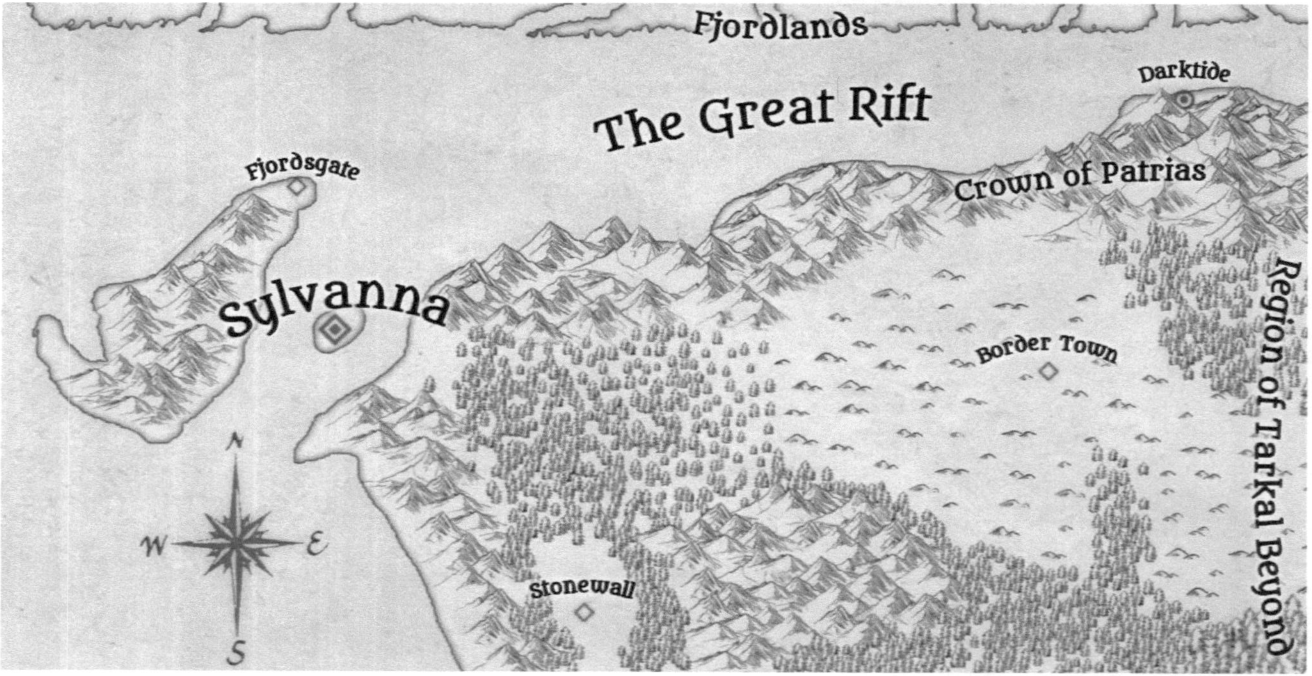

Part One

I departed my home a long while ago now. My original reason for leaving was to help a lost girl find her way, or at least partially. I had every intention of parting ways with her in Sylvanna, and returning to my mother, father, and sister. Now, I'm not sure when I'll see them again, but I think I am alright with that. Knowing my father, he likely thought I had quick feelings for this red headed hammer girl, but I don't believe I did. She is very pretty, and she has an energy that I'm not sure I could ever match, but she also hides a sadness. She has not told me what it is she seeks, but something tells me its something beyond our world entirely. She seems to have a hopelessness to her that I cannot remedy. I can only hope we can find a way to help her in the end. I certainly can understand sadness that cannot be helped. I thought that maybe she could fix what had been broken.

When it comes to feelings, I think I do have some for another. We found ourselves in a village outside Sylvanna, so filled with life I could hardly believe it, and very quickly, I seem to have been accepted as a kind of family member. These strange creatures seem enamored with me, simply because I did the right thing despite my fears.

That other woman...

Her features seem so rough, even more imposing in sheer body than the red-haired girl, but still a softness is in there somewhere. Frankly, she scares me, but I find I just want to know *her better. She is far my superior when it comes to fighting, and conversations with her make me so nervous I feel like I might pass out, but I can't help but look at her. It's not just a physical attraction either, because more than often, I find myself looking into those sharp red eyes rather than her muscled form. I've never seen eyes the color of red on black, they seem so angry, and so alive, and so interesting. Even now as we travel further than my life has ever taken me, I still want to know more about what is behind those eyes. I only hope she is willing to let me.*

I fear more violence is in my future. Already, I have seen more blood and death than I thought I ever would, even being a guard. I have also seen strange things. Things like out of a fairy tale, like storybook pages that have come to life. This world holds far more mystery than I ever would have imagined, and while I am interested and excited about that, I am also terrified. On this journey, so far from my home, I fear I will never see my family again. Even if I did, I hardly think they would believe my stories, especially my sister. She would accuse me of lying just to amuse her, even though I know my stories to be true and my companions know as well.

That is beyond my current future though, and I have far more important things to concern myself with. For now, I shall focus on the road before us, and perhaps on those red on black eyes, the eyes that so intrigue me, and perhaps will save me one day.

-Darion Woodsmark,
Knight of Sylvanna, Honorary member of the Shalti Tribe

1
REGRETS AND REMEMBRANCE

Seventeenth day of Commemorant, Year 1127

The late summer air hid a chill, the winds coming down from the northern lands biting into flesh, even with the warmth of the sun radiating down. The valleys around acting as a funnel, guiding those winds southward and through auburn locks. The crunching of loose dirt below leather boots furthered the condition of the lesser used path. The smell of crisp mountain air flowed like a great river from the cliffs above.

Erika walked along the pathway. Her bright red hair blowing lightly in the breeze, along with her cloak colored like the forest that hung loosely about her bare shoulders. She wore a metal breastplate that extended from her upper chest to just above her midriff, and a dark strapless shirt underneath her armor. Worn boots pumped with her otherwise bare legs under a tattered grey skirt that ran just below her knees. Her great warhammer rested in a two strapped sling, hanging from her waist just behind her thighs. The light tapping of it against her legs was a strange kind of comfort.

The young woman paused a moment and raised her unencumbered arm outwards, feeling for moisture in the air. The naked flesh wrapped in a winding crimson pattern not completely unlike a tattoo. Her bare skin tingled slightly as the warmth mixed with the cold.

No rain yet.

She turned over her shoulder at the long road behind her, remembering the wondrous spires of Sildenfeld to the south. Then she turned back to the longer road before her, and imagined what vistas still awaited her, along with the dangers they held.

The foliage here was mainly tall grass and weeds, with very few trees scattered across the valley. Because of this, she carried a thick bundle of wood from the last forest she had passed—for campfires—slung over one shoulder. A short time later, she began stacking some of the branches in a circle, then flicked a finger out towards it. Her appendage briefly caught flame, then transferred it to the stacked wood. She smiled, thankful for the convenient gifts she had been born with.

She sorted through her pack, pulling out various supplies she had purchased at the small village she encountered a few days before, the only settlement she'd encountered since leaving Sildenfeld. It was home to gaia elves, short creatures that only came just over her hip in height. They had long pointed ears and heads of varying colored hair, all of them very jovial and helpful to her. Many of them had crowded around her, marveling at her markings and auburn hair. They had begged her to stay longer, each one offering her their own backyard bath for as long of a soak as she'd like, as if it were some kind of friendly competition between all of them over whose she would choose. Erika simply couldn't bring herself to hang around for longer than she had to though, and quickly bid her farewells to the funny little folk.

Out of her pack she produced a handful of small traps, to catch rabbits and the like while she slept later that night. She fumbled with the ties slightly, still more used to a hammer and tongs than with strings and ropes. The most delicate work her previous life called for was with a small chisel and hammer, but even that came much easier than these tiny mechanisms that sprung to life when a small creature came too close. Eventually she had them tied properly, and set them out at various locations around her camp just as the sun set beyond the mountains, plunging the world into a sudden darkness.

She rested beside the fire, glad to be rid of her boots for a short while at least. She considered removing her compact breastplate as well, as the straps had begun digging into her shoulders and sides, but she waved the thought away. The slight anxiety that there might be something lurking at the base of these mountains overruled her normal preference to sleep bare, as well as keeping her on guard and restless as she tried to doze off to the sounds of nocturnal creatures.

She wrapped herself tighter into the dark green ranger cloak that she had been given by her friend, Teria, the enchantment working to keep her comfortable in the dropping temperatures of night. She checked to make sure her sizable warhammer was still next to her as well as the broadsword strapped onto her pack. She had much more proficiency with the hammer than the blade, but she had learned some, and still practiced when she found extra time to be confident enough in its use.

Eventually the night passed without any incident. She found herself jolting awake at the sound of one of her traps springing. A loud squeal echoing through the area, before being cut into solemn silence. She instinctively shot a hand to her weapon, though she missed the mark slightly, jamming her finger into the metal haft. She grunted and hissed as she shook her hand to rid the pain, instinctively grabbing the finger in her opposite hand as if her grip would keep it straight. She looked down at the reddening flesh and cracked fingernail and hissed again, biting down on the nail to keep pressure on it. She had broken her nails many times before in the forge, usually in worse conditions, but repetition never seemed to help the pain subside.

She dwelt on the thought, almost missing the regularity of the forge, but shook her head to remind her of the path she had chosen. She stared at the blade strapped to her pack for a long while, steeling her resolve simply in the sight of it. She sighed deeply as she rose to her feet, straightening her tattered grey skirt around her waist, while brushing off dead leaves and dirt. She decided against the boots for the time being, and stepped carefully through the field to find the traps she had laid. A scowl screwed up her face as she found only two to be sprung, and even more so that only one actually had any prey in it. The rabbit was motionless, not even a twitch escaping its body. After a while, and a few curses, the traps were dismantled and back into her pack, the rabbit hanging neatly from the side, awaiting a dagger to clean it and a fire to cook it.

She sighed at the thought of lamb chops from the local tavern in Valen where she had grown up, realizing how long it had been since she'd had the warm juicy meat. Her mouth watered uncomfortably before she took a drink from her water skin.

Where is another settlement? she wondered, almost aloud. Of course she knew not the answer to that question, as she lacked a map in her modest inventory of traveling supplies. She knew her destination lay somewhere far northwards of her home. A cleric back in Sildenfeld by the name of Valk had told her the way of her goal: Dragons in the far north, in her ancestral homeland of Máðir. Old world lore that hinted at the existence of her quarry, but not much in the way of exact location. Thus she became more of a wanderer than anything, trying not to measure her strides, for fear that she'd lose hope along the way. It hardly helped that she often lost track of which direction north was along that road.

⚔

Several days passed with the same routine. Walking, making camp, laying traps. She became thankful for the semblance of regularity though, glad of something more tangible to focus her mind on, rather than singing the various songs of her hometown's festivals to pass the time. The thought of those festivals led her thoughts to the night when her life changed forever. The night when a Daemon attacked.

The memories nearly brought tears to her eyes when she thought of the lost friends and the one she held most dear. Even if he was lost to her some time later, it was still in the same conflict with that Daemon. She had personally killed one of the four powerful Daemons that had found their way into the world, not counting the skeletal, and seemingly mindless thralls she had laid low in her flight from the initial attack.

She thought back to those desperate times which seemed so long ago, despite being only a year prior. She wished her friend

Teria could be beside her on this road. More knowledgeable and experienced as a ranger, she would have been glad for it all, if not just the other individual to speak with. Alas, Teria had lost a leg in the final battle against the Daemons, and likely would have been killed, were it not for Erika's sudden defense and the swift action of the field medics.

She paused on the road a moment, then began to wonder how long it had truly been since she had last been among other people. She mused that it was quite longer than she had thought, and was amazed at how far she had walked, and how many times she had camped almost out of routine alone.

She looked around, taking in the landscape that surrounded her for what seemed like the first time in a long while. The flat fields of the valley underneath the towering heights of mountains had been replaced with rolling hills and thick forestry all around. She looked back the way she came and found the mountains to be barely cresting the waning horizon behind her. She smirked slightly, amused by her wandering daze, but gritted her teeth and decided that it wouldn't happen again.

She looked off to the forest, and decided to make her way into the woods for a short time while the night was still a ways away. The canopy of leaves made for a refreshing jaunt, away from the hot sun. Shortly into the tree line, she found a thick brook with crisp and cold water flowing northwards.

Looking about, she decided it was probably time for a good cleaning, and began stowing her supplies beside a fallen tree. She had barely removed her breastplate when she heard a twig snap behind her. She wrenched the broadsword from its sheath on her pack and turned sharply, aiming the weapon towards the sound. A deer eyed her curiously from a fair distance away, seemingly sensing that Erika posed no threat to it. She cocked her head to one side, and glanced around again as she slowly lowered the blade. She breathed a deep sigh, then continued removing her armor and clothing. She unhooked the sword's scabbard from her pack and kept the weapon close to the banks as she ventured into the frigid water. She would much rather a hot bath in a tub with a rag to scrub her flesh with sudsing soap if she were to have her way, but there was something refreshing about a dip in a lake or stream, surrounded by endless nature. She was enjoying her journey, to a point at least, and it was nice to allow herself the occasional respite, floating in the serene brook for a while and taking in the peacefulness of the wood. The chilled breeze on her naked skin felt revitalizing as well, as she sat on the bank of the pond, her toes just inches from the water as she leaned back and looked up at the cloudless sky.

Some time later, she was dressed again and back on the road. She felt better now, and the enchanted ranger's cloak kept her still slightly damp body warm in the increasing winds. She let her auburn hair air dry in the breeze, letting the coolness to her scalp jolt her senses again. As she walked, she glanced into her satchel at the scarf given to her by her father's elven friend, Sárif. She figured she would begin to need it as she continued towards the much colder north, and the cloak's effectiveness began to wane. She still had time before then.

†̊ †̊

Later that night, she chewed absently on a caught weasel that she had prepared over her fire, gazing up at the stars above. She knew not many names of the constellations, but was able to pick out a few that others had taught her on her journey that year before. Some, the ranger Teria had shown her, others were by another. She bit down onto a tough bit in the meat as she fell into the thought. The reason for her pilgrimage.

The one lost to her.

"Irvine," she said aloud, though there was no one around to hear her.

She held few regrets in her life. Living by something her father had taught her of their Fjordling heritage. 'Life is lived in breaths, each breath ridding you of a regret, and once each breath has gone, there is no reason to think on it,' he had said to her a multitude of times.

She took a deep breath, then expelled it. Though she knew she could not expel this regret as easily. She blamed herself for what happened to Irvine. Though no one quite knew what had happened to him. During their final confrontation with the Daemon Zyrxak, a second entity had entered the battle. An Angelus of the old fables of the long past Daemon War. Strangely, the Angelus had proved nearly more catastrophic than the Daemon himself, before engaging Zyrxak in a melee. Irvine thrust himself into the conflict between the two ancient enemies, and in a flash of blinding light he and the Daemon were gone, the Angelus' body bloodied and dead on the scorched field. No trace was left of him or Zyrxak, save for Irvine's helm, which turned to ash a short while later, much to Erika's dismay.

Nothing in the encounter could have been changed by her, and she knew that fact well. She had expended much of her energy in the battle previous and could not muster any more strength to intervene in the clash. Still, she saw his disappearance as her fault and could not find the capacity to come to terms with it. It was especially devastating after she had realized how much he had cared for her, and how much she cared for him. She had only then realized the way he looked at her at the festival that night. At how he nearly broke apart when seeing her bandaged and healing from a harrowing incident with a beast of the wilds. Most difficult for her of all, was when he learned about her innate abilities, and how it so perfectly aligned with his strongest of fears. He had worked past his fear because of his feelings for her, showing just how strong his feelings were. She regretted not telling him of her heritage nearly as much as not being able to save him before his last decision.

She reached into the satchel that once belonged to him, and produced a small hard case. General Atrosby, the militant solider charged with the attack on the Daemon, had given it and Irvine's other belongings to her after her initial grief. He told her that Irvine wanted him to give her the box, but he hadn't the heart to ask her to open it.

Erika already knew what was inside. After having—to her embarrassment—snooped through Irvine's belongings during their time traveling. In it was a small emerald pendant that was a similar hue to her own green eyes. Irvine had evidently wished to give it to her as a more romantic gift, though he never had the chance to actually give it to her, raising yet another regret in her swirling emotions.

She laid it back into the pack, beside the letter Atrosby had given her upon her leaving of the city. Its tear soaked pages detailing how he considered Irvine a brother-in-arms, despite his initially harsh judgment of the young man. He wished her luck, and offered to provide her an escort, personally if she so wished, though she never responded to the offer.

She laid back, using her pack as a rough pillow, beside her removed breastplate that she had finally found the courage to doff. She massaged at her bare shoulders and slid her fingers beneath her tunic to rub at the spots that the armor had dug into, lulling herself to sleep with the motions.

2
STONEWALL

Erika awoke to the early morning light, the campfire smoking in its final breaths. She stretched eagerly, working out her tense muscles, and rubbed her thick shoulders. She brought herself to her feet and leaned backward to extend her lower back. She then leaned forward and took in a sharp intake of air as she found the evidence of a bootprint just outside of her rest area. She lurched forward into a crouch, fumbling for her pack and her armor. She suddenly felt naked and vulnerable, despite still being completely clothed. The possibility of another individual in the area making her heart race, anxieties regarding the shadowy cult that had released the Daemons in the first place coming to the forefront of her mind. Erika found the satchel and gripped her warhammer tightly, moving it behind her to a striking position.

Her other hand finally made contact with her breastplate, quickly taking it up and hurriedly strapping it to her torso, ignoring the pinch in the fleshy part under her left arm as she carefully stalked towards the prints. She rose steadily after deciding the individual had simply moved past her, though still uncomfortable with the arrangement that suggested they may have lingered for a moment.

She took a short breath, looking up and down the roadway. She found it darkly humorous how such a small thing could cause her such anxiety, wondering how she would have reacted when she actually had been fully naked at the spring the previous day if someone had happened upon her. She quickly gathered up her other supplies (taking care to make sure nothing was missing), and adjusted her armor straps to fit more properly. A short while later she was back on the road, walking with a bit more briskness to her step. She had a few thoughts of finding this individual and judging their character first hand. The pattern of the prints had unnerved her more than she was willing to admit.

As she walked, she began to notice more than just the boot prints that led from her camp area. There were deep ruts in the road, hoof, and claw prints, suggesting caravans leading the same direction she was as well as the variety of animals used to transport various commodities. Her thoughts of her would-be attacker suddenly drifted off as she smiled at the thought of another settlement. Even if it were just a small village, it would give her a chance to work her charms that her father had often praised her for in his blacksmith shop. She'd be able to sell the rabbit pelts she'd obtained along the way, and spend the money for some supplies and perhaps some other luxuries, if she had the extra coin.

She got caught up in the fantasies of the unknown town, warm meals and bathing in something other than a river, even if the cool water was refreshing. After a while, she started to hear the familiar ring of hammer on metal. It snapped her from her daydream and she focused in on the small town, some of the buildings towering up to two stories, with a small stone wall surrounding the outside. The smoke rising from chimneys and the sound of the forge sparked a warmth in Erika's chest, and her pace quickened, excited by the thought of seeing a town so much like that which she once called home.

Her excitement was quickly quelled.

Steel rang as the guards at the wall entrance drew their weapons, drawing a sudden stop and sharp gasp from Erika.

"State your business," one said, his eyes drifting over her with scrutiny.

She stuttered a moment, unsure of why she was receiving the harsh treatment. "I'm a traveler, headin' northwards."

The guards shifted at her accent, the other one speaking. "Who do you pledge allegiance to?"

"Allegiance?" she echoed incredulously. "I have no allegiance."

The guards firmed their stances and held their blades in combat ready positions, though the younger of the two seemed less sure. The first firmed his voice further. "No entry granted. Be on your way."

Erika took a slight step forward, which the speaking guard matched with a full step towards her, bringing his blade to bear. She nearly fell over herself as she backpedaled. She made no abrupt movement for her weapons, but still clenched her fist and teeth towards the two men. Then she changed tactics. Her left arm gripped lightly at her right elbow, and she bent one knee slightly, angling her hip to the side slightly.

"I'm just a traveler, weary o' the roads. Suren ye can let me pass through an' buy a few supplies?" she said, raising the pitch of her voice slightly like she used to do with unruly customers. She always found it awkward, trying to appear as innocent and feminine as she could, when she knew she could simply punch them in the jaw and yell a string of curses as they ran from the door. But she knew that this tactic would earn her less prison time in this situation, and perhaps the guards would take pity on her.

The one in the back eyed her up and down, seeing the mud on her boots and the tangle in her hair. He seemed younger than the other one, more sympathetic. He started to open his mouth, but was cut short before he could utter a sound.

"No entry!" the older guard bellowed. "I'll not repeat myself again, girl!"

Erika slumped, her hands falling to her side, and her hip pushing out more in annoyance than attempted ploy. The older guardsmen turned away and started back to his post, Erika jamming her fist up in a rude gesture towards him, gaining a stifled snicker from the younger guard. The poor sap got an armored slap to the back of his helmet, the metal ringing into the open air, as the first guard resumed his stance.

A whistle caught Erika's attention. She turned to the side to see a man of tanned skin and dark hair sitting cross legged on a blanket. He beckoned for her, and she shrugged as she made her way to him.

He was a strange fellow, dressed in thin robes rather than a tunic and trousers, and wore a brightly colored wrap around the top of his head, similar to a hat. He sat up against a tree, beside a considerable pack of traveling supplies, and other things that Erika could only imagine.

"What're ye wantin'?" she asked with a callousness.

He held up both hands in an act of surrender. "Absolutely nothing more than a conversation, my dear."

Erika narrowed her eyes, but knelt down only a short way from the edge of his blanket.

"Are you traveling from the south?" he asked. "I believe we are traveling on the same roads."

"And what's yer thinkin' there?" she said, raising an eyebrow.

"I believe I remember seeing you just the night before, I travel much during the night you see."

Erika's hand went to the sword on her pack.

The stranger's hands went up again. "Please! I am meaning no offense to you, and I offer apologies if it seemed I was being unsavory towards you while you slept."

Erika eased a bit. "So I saw yer prints outside my camp this mornin'?"

"Indeed," he began, trying to lighten the mood. "I was not meaning to rob you or anything ill willed. Quite frankly, and I admit this sounds strange, I was simply gawking at the beautiful woman whom I was seeing."

"Ye know it's not flatterin' to watch a girl while she sleeps," she replied with a growl.

"Yes, I am understanding of that, and I do offer more apologies for this. It is simply that I had never seen hair in such a color as yours."

Erika absently grabbed the thick lock to her side, glancing down at it slightly.

"All people, men and women I have seen since coming to this land have had dark hair like my own, or shades of yellow. I have never seen such a color in hair, and I simply was captivated by it in the moment."

She sighed slightly, brushing off her skirt. "And where is it ye find yerself from?"

The stranger pulled his sleeve up slightly, revealing his forearm and an intricate tattoo of strange markings. They almost looked like words of some kind, though Erika did not recognize anything offered by it. "My home is much further to the south, a great desert land full of sand and rocks."

Erika thought of the sand on the coastline not far from where she grew up, swimming in the ocean water when she was younger on day trips with Irvine. She imagined he was actually speaking of the continent to the far south, known as Haran, which she had heard various things about. Most of the stories were of how dangerous and inhospitable it was.

As if he read her thoughts, he continued. "However, there is no water in this land of sands, except for rare oases that mark settlements. We are craftsmen and shamans where I come from, and I come north in hopes to peddle wares of my home." She glanced to the pack beside him as she absorbed his story, and he sprang up to it, beginning to rummage through the inside. "Perhaps you are wanting to see my wares?" he asked with some excitement, pulling an assortment of tapestries and clothing.

"These are very popular among dancing girls where I come from. It nearly matches your hair," he said as he pulled two small, but brightly colored red garments from the bag. One looked to be like a thin halter, the other a short skirt, both made of a rather transparent fabric.

Erika balked at the items, staring at the tiny jingling metal baubles that hung all around them, and genuinely wondered if they would actually cover her at all. The top obviously seemed to be made for someone with a much smaller bust, and the skirt likely wouldn't cover her backside fully, even if she stood perfectly straight. Erika was certainly not the most shy of people, having worked in her old forge with nearly as little on as her father often did, but she was still unsure of walking around with this promiscuous outfit.

The stranger paused a moment, then hurriedly stuffed them back in. "Eh, perhaps not that. I offer more apologies, it is much warmer in my home, I am understanding of your confusion."

Erika wondered if he actually understood or not.

The stranger spent a time showing off his various goods to her, and some of it was rather interesting. The brightly colored tapestries of intricate designs, as well as the flowing robes that he said were more common among the everyday people of his lands, sharing in the bright colors and weaving designs as the 'dancing girl' clothing, as well as the relatively sheer fabric. Erika stifled a laugh when he mentioned that many people opted for little clothing—if any at all—during the hotter days, imagining the looks some of her friends back home if they were to hear his stories.

He paused again after a while, and looked to the setting sun behind Erika's back. She wasn't sure if he was looking more to the vista, or her silhouette though. After a moment, he blinked and cleared his throat. "I have not yet introduced myself, have I?" he asked rhetorically. "My given name is Kharim'akhala N'asheznemon."

Erika nodded. "I'll stick with Kharim if ye're not mindin'. My name is Erika."

Kharim made a seated bow, and smiled. "Your hair is as beautiful as the sunset, Erika, but not nearly as beautiful as your voice and name."

Erika smirked slightly, still holding some of her earlier callousness. "Ye say that to yer dancin' girls too?"

He smiled and shrugged, gaining a laugh from them both. As Erika began to relax, she glanced down and saw an intricate weapon with a wicked curve in its blade at Kharim's side. It had no scabbard and as a smith she doubted it could have a conventional one, considering its shape. She noticed the edge of the blade on the inside curve, similar to a sickle or another harvesting tool. It had no crossguard, and the handle appeared to be made of glass, with a constantly swirling dust inside.

Kharim brought a hand down to the weapon, and slid it behind himself slightly.

"An unsavory weapon." he said with some ire. "Though you seem not the stranger to weapons."

He motioned towards her pack which was now laying on the ground beside her, and she nodded. "I used to be a smith where I'm from. Not smithin' these days though."

Kharim must have noticed the sadness in her voice, because he returned to his jovial tone. "Of course! I should have been knowing! That is the reason for your very muscle arms!" he said with a laugh and an upward display of his own considerably built arms. The sleeves of his robes fell to his shoulders as he did, revealing more of the intricate tattoos, some of which seemed to be akin to magical sigils she had seen before. He quickly returned the garment to its original position though, as if embarrassed by the markings.

She smirked again as she stood, stretching and unintentionally flexing her own muscles he had spoken of. Kharim applauded her, and began packing his bag, then folding the blanket he sat on.

"Leavin' so late?" she asked, looking to the setting sun.

"Indeed," he grunted as he stood, stowing his strange weapon behind his pack. "Remember, I am traveling greatly by nighttime. Also, it seems your beauty has gained you another who wishes to speak."

Erika looked to where he motioned to see a young man walking tentatively towards them, dressed in simple clothes and town shoes. After a moment, she recognized him as the younger of the two guards that she had interacted with earlier.

Kharim tapped her shoulder, then held out a bracelet of small stones and gems. "A gift for you," he said, and pressed it into her palm before she could protest. After a moment, he shouldered his considerable pack, and made his way into the forest.

Eventually, she turned to the patient newcomer. "Friend of yours?" he asked. He was a handsome young man, with a clean shaved face and short dusty brown hair.

"No, just met 'im," she replied.

He seemed to lighten slightly. "Oh. Well, anyway, I was wondering if you had a place to sleep for the night?"

She eyed him and brought out her arms, motioning to the ground around her.

"I see," he said, somewhat deflated, like the conversation hadn't quite gone like he expected it to. "Well, my family can house you for the night, if you'd like."

She shifted her weight, jutting her hip out in another annoyed pose. "No entry," she said in a mocking way of the other guard she had met.

"I know, and I will probably get in trouble for it, but you seem nice, and I don't think you're here to hurt Stonewall," he said somewhat sheepishly.

"Why would I hurt yer town?" she asked with an exaggerated shrug.

The young man stuttered. "How long have you been traveling?"

†ｐ

Kharim watched as the fire haired woman disappeared into the small town that had rejected him, along with the young guard. A smile drifted across his face knowing that she had found a way into the town where he had not. His road had been long, and he hardly expected room and board at this point. He was no stranger to being turned away, and was not surprised in the least when the guards had done so. He had mostly stayed on the roadways and in the wilderness of this continent and its Regions, as the locals called them, so he was uninformed when it came to the politics that surrounded them. He was hardly surprised that there was threatening conflict. Conflict always threatened everyone, even if they didn't like to admit it. How would things have progressed if that intriguing woman he had just met decided to bare her considerable hammer in his direction?

He had confidence in his own ability, but those markings that spread across her skin, those were filled with magic. It was unlike any magic he had ever experienced either, older, more primal in a sense. So far, Kharim had little experience with any mages on this continent. For all he knew, she would turn into some kind of feral beast and tear his throat out with her teeth before he ever had the chance to raise his blade. He had read of individuals with transformation abilities like that. He hoped he wouldn't find out if there was any merit to those tales.

Kharim paused at the roadway, pulling a thick cloth from his pack and draping it over his shoulders. This place had amazingly cold nights, even by his own desert standards. He still couldn't shake the habit of traveling primarily in the dark hours, even if the sun was not nearly as harsh here as it was in his homeland. Alhough, he felt he had to keep alert even more while traveling. Trees could hide much above his head where sand could not, and the thought of creatures diving down from the boughs made him nervous.

Shouting from a ways off caught his attention. There was a time when curiosity would have drawn him in blindly, but those days were long past him. Kharim had been through far too much, and nearly been killed far too many times to abandon any kind of cautiousness now. So he left the road and carefully picked through the brush, blade in hand. That woman seemed enough of a goodly person that he felt somewhat ashamed at the wicked weapon that he could hear even now.

Greetings again, are you going to hide me from more souls? Or are we going to cut something?

The hairs on the back of his neck stood on end at the chilling sound which as far as he could tell, no one else could hear. He was sure everyone in the vicinity could hear the shouting just ahead of him.

"Gods above, this beast doesn't stay still does it?"

"Move over there! Pull that chain!"

The voices were rough, masculine. The bodies and faces matched the sounds as Kharim came into view of the torchlight. A group of six men and one sol elf, all in ramshackle clothing and armor. Each of them carried at least an arming sword, the elf held a full broadsword. Among them were three carts drawn by horses, each one having a large cage set into it with a myriad of shapes inside. Slavers. A concept Kharim was unfortunately very familiar with. From his understanding, bandits of this variety were rare on this continent, but deplorable people always existed somewhere. On the edge of the torchlight, two of the men were wrestling the restraints of a large creature, standing three times any one of the humans. Kharim was unsure what the creature was, but it was obviously in pain from the manacles around its wrists and neck. After a moment, the elf waved his hands in the air, his light yellowish hair flashing a strange hue of orange as he groaned. "Just tie the damn thing to that thicker tree over there, or something. It's obviously not going to sit where we want it," he started to turn away. "Daemon's breath, if it wasn't so lucrative to sell the things alive, I'd just say kill it now."

Kharim narrowed his eyes, raising his blade to the side and willing it to activate. It responded with a hiss and a strange kind of laughter as the shadowy wisps escaped the handle. He stepped into the clearing a moment later, blade at his side, but not yet in a threatening posture. His sensibilities demanded they admit to their crimes. "Greetings," he said clearly, drawing the attention of the seven individuals. "May I ask what you are all doing so late in the day? Your shouting is causing all manner of unrest."

One of the men scoffed, drawing a small club with metal reinforcements from his belt. "What we're doing is none of your business, outlander," he said with a rough voice, waving the club threateningly towards the Haranian. "You'll just be turnin' around and forgetting you ever saw any of this."

Kharim scowled at the little man. "You are obviously not the leader. Please shut your mouth and be sure it remains so."

The elf at the back smirked, crossing his arms and leaning back just slightly.

First came the man's angered shout, as he lurched forward and swung the club up in a predictable arc. Kharim wasn't there when the stick came back down, and that's just what it was in the hands of this thug. A simple stick. Kharim seemed to vanish from the man's view, spinning around him in what looked like a blur to everyone else. The razor edge on the inside curve of his sword came up underneath the man's throat, dragging him back and around. He let out a squeal of fear as he spun around, Kharim returning to his original position, only now with the man at his mercy before him. The rest of them, save for the elf, quickly had weapons to their hands. "Perhaps the leader there can specify the operation," he said from behind his captive, making him flinch. "This one presumes much of an outlander as he says, perhaps I am wishing to join some kind of job, yes?"

The elf stepped forward, raising his arms outwards in a gesture of friendliness. "A simple trading caravan, that's all. We trade in high price commodities."

"Specificity would help me, I am new to your language." Khrarim barked, as his patience thinned.

With a nod, the elf continued. "We track down people who have failed to pay debts, thieves, or other criminals, and sell them to those whom they owe."

Kharim suppressed a groan. He grew tired of all the fancy speech. "So you are slavers, yes?"

"That would be an accurate term," the elf conceded with an elaborate shrug.

"Thank you for your sincerity," Kharim breathed, and that was the last of what the little man in his grasp heard. The drag of the blade through his neck nicked at his spine and he fell lifeless to the ground. Dark sand poured from the man's rent throat, but not a single drop of blood.

Delicious... the voice cooed in his mind. *Not satisfactory, give me the rest.*

One of the men to his right side yelled a curse, starting to raise his crossbow to loose the loaded bolt, but he never got so far, as a black arrow sped cleanly through his skull and dropped him with a thud. The prisoners in the cages started screaming and crying in terrified waves.

"Damn!" the elf hissed, drawing his broadsword.

Kharim never held any love for the chaos of battle, but strangely, the confusion of the men drew a wry grin over his lips. A warrior looking as if he were made of shadow burst forth from the brush, his arms sprouting blades. One of the men with a sword drawn cried out in surprise, barely getting his weapon up in time to ward off one of the wicked strikes. At the other side, another black shadow warrior with a bow slung three more arrows in quick succession, though less accurate than the one that killed the crossbowman. The elf ran to the side, one hand over his head as if it would ward any projectiles. Another with a sword rushed at Kharim, who seemed to be lost watching the elf's retreat. The slaver's expectation was shown to be folly, as the man hit nothing but air. The Haranian, with preternatural speed, whipped around the back of the assailant and with one clean thrust the blade was into his back. Pain washed through him, quickly replaced by a cold nothingness. Black tendrils of sand sprouted forth from the handle of the blade, squeezing between Kharim's fingers and draping over the attacking man's shoulders. Kharim removed his blade as the dark sand enveloped the man completely. He gave one last shudder before turning with a savage posture, and leaping for his comrades.

Against the opposite side of a wagon went the elf, huffing from the sudden rush. Everything started happening so quickly, his mind could hardly keep up. To the side he watched as one of his fellows, named Moris, frantically tossed his chain whip around and through one of the shadowed warriors. He couldn't help but gawk at how similar to another comrade, Kieran, that specific warrior looked. Luckily, Moris angled his whip just right and wrapped it around his attacker's neck. With a quick jerk, the blades on the whip tightened, and bit deeply into the thing's neck, laying it low in a puddle of the dark ooze that it seemed to bleed.

Before either of them could celebrate though, the Haranian outlander seemed to appear just before Moris, running him through with that strange blade of his. The sol couldn't tear his eyes away as that horrible darkness wrapped around Moris' head, prying his mouth open and gouging into his eyes. Within moments he stood there, another shadow warrior at the bidding of their attacker.

He turned just barely in time, and dodged away from another of the creatures, this one wielding a pair of daggers. The sol twisted around, hacking with his broadsword and knocking one of the weapons free from its grasp. Taking the opportunity, he reversed the momentum and used all his strength to cleave through the thing's head. Black liquid sprayed across his face as he ran around the side of the cage wagon, only to see Piren groan in agony while he was lifted from the ground, the creature with the arm blades holding him high in the air before savagely jabbing his blades into Piren's gut several more times. Before Piren's boots even touched the ground he was stabbed another six times, each hit accompanied by the horrified cries of their prisoners.

The sol leader had nowhere to go, it seemed. His last comrade Loran, fell when the bow-wielding creature slashed his throat with one of the bladed limbs of his bow. The Haranian man stepped out easily into the middle of their camp, an outstretched hand calming the aggression of the black warriors. The elf huffed angrily, and made a rush for the human, and apparent source of the dark warriors.

He could still salvage all of this. Surely?

In a blinding flash of sparks, his weapon came apart before his eyes. The front half of his blade fell to the ground with a *thump*, and he was left with naught but the hilt in his hands. The Haranian held out his arms in a similar way to how the sol had done not long before, a mocking gesture.

"One last chance, hmm?" the man said to him, dropping that strange curved weapon to the ground beside him.

The creatures backed a step from him, his once friend among them, still holding his chain whip. The elf grew angry, pulling out a pair of cestus from his pouch and starting to strap them over his hands. The thick leather gloves were studded with metal at the knuckles and were a popular armament among fighters in Patrias. Every Haranian he had ever heard of balked at true hand to hand combat, so his confidence began to grow. "Last chance, and those things go away, yeah?"

Kharim shrugged. "Better yet, you kill me, they are yours."

After a quick glance at the strange onlookers, and back at the caged wagons of whimpering and weeping captives, the sol licked his lips.

That could work.

In a flash he rushed forward, hands held up to block any incoming attacks, before he lashed out with a jab of his left and a hook from his right. The Haranian dodged the first, but the wide hook caught him on the side of the jaw and sent him out to the side. The elf was hardly content to let him breathe, and dashed forward again. He landed several more hits in a short span, each one heavier and more confident than the last. The outlander bled from his lip, nose, and from a nick on his forehead. The dark red of his blood shimmered in the firelight.

Though while his brazenness in the fight grew, the sol's spacial awareness shrunk, hardly noticing that he was chasing his opponent in a tight circle. The strange annoyance on the Haranian's face made him pause, just enough.

"You should have gotten me away from the blade," Kharim said, his voice almost sounding mournful. With a quick dip, the weapon was retrieved, and a quick extension of his arm drove it through the sol's throat.

The black sand took him as well.

Kharim relaxed his posture, removing the blade from the elf's flesh slowly, as the last few traces of sand escaped into the new revenant. With a deep exhale, he shook himself from his distraction. At his bidding, the black warriors quickly broke the manacles free from the large ogre and Kharim made a sweeping gesture to the creature. "Away with you, you are free."

He wasn't sure if the ogre understood him at all, but it at least lumbered off to the north and west. Next, he freed the captives in the wagons, offering them clothes from his pack as most of them were either naked or only covered in scant remnants of clothing. His dancing girls clothing and the rest seemed to have come in handy after all, even if he wasn't truly being paid for it. Not that the wares were anything more than a convenient story to tell when prodded about his trek northwards. The people were understandably nervous as they filtered out of the cages, giving him a wide berth after taking the clothing he offered with reverent bows.

"Do not go to the town over that ridge, they are wary of outsiders and you are wearing clothes of Haran now. You will find more luck away from there," he said to them when they were all dressed and drinking from the water skins of their dead jailers. They took the supplies and horses of the slavers, after one older man took some charge, leading them off to the east. Kharim took another heavy breath after they were gone, picking up his mostly empty pack and holding his blade out to the side.

The warriors had grown bored, three of the revenants disappearing into the brush as the elf with his cestus fell into nothingness. He considered chasing them for a moment, but shook his head. He had always been able to dismiss them in the past. Why should these be any different? In any case, the farther he was from them, the weaker they were. So he decided the best course would be to simply make distance from the creatures, until they ultimately fell out of range of his blade and returned to it.

3
STRIKE IN THE NIGHT

Darion can pick whoever he chooses!" the female voice said sternly.

The male replied. "But if she's from the outside, it puts the family at risk!"

"You should be proud of your son, she's a beautiful young woman!"

"A beautiful young woman who might bring problems for his position!"

"If his job is more important than a gorgeous young lady like that, then he shouldn't have that job!"

"And where do you think she's possibly from? Who do you know that has tattoos all along their face and head?"

The contest of voices continued in the small, but cozy, home that Erika found herself in. Darion, as she had come to an acquaintance with, sat next to her on her right, scratching the back of his hand and bouncing his leg nervously. Across from her, was a young girl, likely less than half her own age of twenty-four. Erika found herself plagued by the stare the girl gave her. Those piercing blue eyes digging into her own green orbs. Occasionally, that dagger gaze would wander, following the crimson marks on Erika's skin down to her chest and where they disappeared beneath her strapless tunic. Erika became suddenly aware of how much skin she was showing while under the girl's scrutiny, doing her best to discreetly lift the garment higher over her breasts, though that only seemed to draw more attention to her bust. Although tattoos were not uncommon among the Regions—the girl's mother actually had some ink displayed on her arm just below her sleeve—she imagined the curious child's first question would be along the lines of, 'Do your tattoos cover your whole body?'

The actual words from her made Erika stumble in her seat.

"Are you and my brother going to get married?" she asked, with a deceptive innocence.

Darion squirmed in his seat, and turned a shade of red much brighter than Erika's hair. Erika simply shifted in her seat, taking a small sip from the cup of tea that was given to her.

"Yer brother and I are just good friends," she tried to reply casually, exaggerating her words a bit to appease the young girl.

She grinned almost evilly. "He likes you. I think he wants to kiss you."

Darion's leg began to bounce with more fervor, until Erika jammed her hand under the table and gripped his knee with such force that Darion nearly cried out. "I assure ye, yer brother and I are just friends."

Darion nodded. "She's just a friend Jess. Nothing more. I met her when I was working one time."

Technically not a lie, Erika noted. So she continued the story without a missed beat. "I'm a smith, and I repair 'is armor and stuff. After he fights the monsters."

Jess's eyes lit up. "I bet you tend his wounds too, don't you?" Erika wondered if the girl had sneakily read some lewd romance novels, considering the strange sparkle in her eyes.

"No, no!" Darion cut in. "The clerics do that. Erika doesn't dress my wounds."

Erika nodded, trying to convince this determined little girl that she had no romantic intentions with her brother.

Their mother and father walked in a moment later, both sitting on opposite ends of the rectangular table to Erika's left and right respectively. Silence ensued after, Erika suddenly kicking herself that she had missed the end of their supposed 'private' conversation, that she might know their intentions.

"Well, dinner is nearly ready," Darion's mother, Minora, chimed in, breaking the quiet atmosphere much to Erika's relief.

Not long after, Erika and Jess had helped set the table with steaming bowls of pork stew, complete with potatoes, herbs, and spices. Erika hesitated to begin eating despite staring hungrily at the well seasoned meal, but Darion's mother insisted she eat, that she couldn't possibly have a guest without feeding them. She gladly obliged, happy to have a warm meal other than dry roasted rabbits. The flavors brimmed from each bite, spices tingling her lips, the broth warming her whole body. She found herself thanking the gracious family more times than any of them could count.

"Now then, lass," the gruff older man named Garol spoke after the bowls were cleared, and the conniving young girl was ushered to her bath. Erika began to shift in her seat, unsure of where the man was taking the—until now, casual—conversation. "I know that you're not actually my son's lady friend, despite what my wife and daughter seem to think."

Erika nodded, slowly taking in the man's voice and patiently awaiting the inevitable question she could feel coming.

"So, why are you here?" he asked with a sigh.

Erika looked to her hands, absently tracing the crimson patterns with her thumb. She took a deep breath. "I'm a traveler, as I'm sure ye've come to understand. I come from the south, Sildenfeld."

Garol took a deep breath of his own, nodding his understanding, but allowing her to continue.

"Just over a year ago, a Daemon came to my hometown further south still, and burned it down in a single night. We ran from the town to Sildenfeld and garnered the aid o' the military there, and eventually slew the Daemon." She paused a moment, and tried to control her breathing as she recounted the story, even in a shorthand fashion. "I'm headin' to the north lookin' for my own answers to things," she finished, choosing not to divulge the full reasons for her pilgrimage.

The older man scratched his beard, and Darion ran his fingers through his hair, obviously stressed. "So there are Daemons," Garol said after a long silence. "I had hoped the rumors were false."

"There are more?" Erika asked, a panic in her voice.

The man nodded slowly. "Madness has swept the lands, lass. Territories at war with each other is on the table again for the first time in two decades, all because of confusion and supposed conspiracy."

Erika knew some of the history of Patrias, though the tumultuous time of war was primarily ending when she was just a babe. Wars broke out between regions due to differences too many to count. After enough blood was spilled, each city became its own self government under the shared Regional Treaties. The surrounding villages and towns were brought into official boundary lines decided upon by the Region Council, who also decided on shared infrastructure within the Regions. Each individual state was given free reign with regulations and institutions unique to their climates, as well as military and religion. With the united continent, wars were thought to be a thing of the past.

"If your story is true," Garol began again, interrupting her thoughts, "then the continent is in for some serious trouble. Territories fighting amongst themselves, only skirmishes so far mind you, while Daemons muck about, causing the real mayhem. Things could become worse than they used to be."

She nodded, understanding the implications. Darion still sat, bouncing his knee more and staring at the table. Erika didn't bother stopping him again.

"You need to be careful boy. Bringing in outsiders at a time like this is a bad idea."

Darion looked up finally, seemingly not taking a breath. "But she needed help! I couldn't just leave her outside in the woods!"

Erika tried to cut in, but Garol seemed to forget she was there for a moment. "I don't care how pretty the girl is, Darion, these times call for caution above all else!"

"I didn't do it because she was pretty!" Darion defended, his father opening his mouth for another shout.

Erika slammed her hand on the table loudly, immediately turning a shade of red at her actions as both of the stares came back at her. "I was the ignorant one. I thank ye all for yer kindness and the wonderful meal."

The two men's gazes softened, both looking apologetic.

"I'll be takin' my leave now. I thank ye again for yer hospitality," she said with a finality as she stood. She made her way to the door and began sliding her boots back on. A moment later, she felt a calloused hand on her shoulder and looked up to find Garol.

"Please, stay the night. I understand your feelings and I apologize for my outburst. I am simply trying to protect my family."

Erika stood, one foot still bare, and nodded her understanding.

"You seem an honorable woman," he said as he began to walk away. "You can share Jess' bed, too big for her anyways."

Darion watched as his father stepped loudly through the hallway to the living area and looked back to Erika. He seemed about to say something, but shook his head and walked into the hallway after his father. Erika slipped her boot back off, then stood and stretched, bunching her hair up with her hands behind her head while taking a deep breath. Things had gotten a lot more complicated. Her mind swam with how much she had possibly missed in her ridiculous amount of time in the woods, getting lost every other day when she should have just been walking in the same damned direction the whole time. She rubbed at her bare shoulders, thankful for the longer respite from her packs and armor, but trying not to get too used to the relaxation. Eventually she followed the pair into the living area, Darion whittling at a small chunk of wood while his father talked to Erika about nothing in particular.

⚔ ⚔

Erika laid in the darkness of the small room, Jess slightly kicking in her sleep. She simply stared at the ceiling, trying to take as little room as she could beside the young girl. Her gaze came up towards the door at her head when Darion quietly entered the room, laying in the bed on the opposite side of the room. She wondered what he and his father had discussed after she had retired. The small house actually had decently thick walls, so hearing conversations in other rooms wasn't really possible. She stretched her arms upwards and rested her head over them, trying to discern her course of action for the next day.

Rain began to fall against the roof above them just as Erika began to fall asleep, waking her fully again. She sighed quietly in frustration, not wanting to wake the soundly sleeping girl beside her. Jess had started to snuggle up to Erika's side sometime during the night without her noticing, now resting her head on Erika's breast. She smiled slightly, amused by her new little friend and her many antics. Darion's position changed for what must've been the thousandth time, his sleep seemingly even more restless than her own. The rain continued to make pattering sounds on the rooftop just above her head, as she absently stroked Jess's hair. Even if she weren't actually sleeping, having a rest in a soft bed with a warm blanket was good enough for her. It was all much better than trying to take cover under a tree in the rain, which is where she figured she would be if the Woodsmark family hadn't taken her in.

A moment later, Darion sat up in his bed. He rubbed his left shoulder slightly, then turned, not realizing Erika was awake until she offered him a smile through the dark room. His eyes seemed to harbor a sadness in them though, and her smile quickly faded. He started to open his mouth to say something, but was suddenly cut short as a bell began ringing in the distance. His tired eyes shot open and he quickly dove onto the floor, startling Jess awake, who immediately jumped further onto Erika's chest and hugged her neck as if her life depended on it. Erika sat up as well, holding the girl but also frantically trying to keep her tunic up through the spooked flailing of the child.

Darion emerged only a moment later bearing a small leather chest piece and a sword, with an expression of urgency. Erika stood up, easily carrying the small girl with her in her muscular arms as she asked quietly. "What's happenin'? Is that the alarm?"

The young man nodded with a grim expression. "Call to arms, something more than a forest beast is attacking."

As if on cue, the door to the small room burst open, Garol sporting a full raiment of mismatched armor pieces and a broad axe. "Time to go boy!"

Darion nodded as he was already to the door before his father finished his statement. Erika began to pace the room briefly, trying to calm Jess, who dug her head into her chest violently. Erika could feel the warmth and wetness of tears soaking the front of her tunic. She started stroking her hair again and whispered to her. "Everythin'll be alright little one, I need ye to go with yer mother though. I'm to be helpin' with yer brother."

The young girl reluctantly nodded as she was handed off to her mother in the hallway, Erika rushing over to the door side to jam her boots back on.

"What're you doing?" Garol asked.

"Goin' to help ye," she grunted as she wrenched one of the boots on "Ye aren't for trustin' me fully, and I understand that. So let me help ye."

The older man stared at her as she finished pulling her boots on and matching his gaze defiantly. He chuckled a bit, nodding his understanding as he grabbed her hammer and handed it to her.

⸸

The rain started to pour. The streets filled with mud, threatening to slip any who came through unprepared. Erika, Darion, and Garol jogged through the torrent towards the source of the alarms. Windows shuttered and doors locked all around them, as the citizens who didn't take up arms began to prepare for the worst.

"What's the worst ye ever get?" Erika called out, not caring who answered.

Darion replied quickly. "Normally? Stray jordhaks, or gryphons. A bad day? Bandits or orkish barbarians."

"Or Daemons," Erika muttered under her breath, genuinely hoping that wasn't the case.

Eventually they found themselves at the walls, guards were yelling commands that Erika couldn't quite make out, bodies shifting all around. One guard caught a glimpse of Erika's increasingly wet hair, matting to her face, back, and shoulders, raising an eyebrow at her. She only hoped it wasn't the guard she had dealt with the evening before. She felt a hand on her back, as Darion ushered her forwards, silently confirming that fear.

"Keep moving," he whispered in her ear, pressing a little harder.

The rain was a full wall of water, blocking any visibility outwards to the source of whatever threat was coming towards them. Erika saw what she was sure was a motionless body, a flash of crimson reflecting in the dim light of the moons over the clouds, dripping down their chest. She felt her stomach fall as she realized that the throat had been cut, not by beast, but by blade.

Garol's back slammed roughly against a higher section of the wall, cupping his hands below him in a crouch, to which Darion responded by jumping forward. Garol hoisted his son onto the side of the wall and he peered carefully over. Erika held her breath, waiting for his report.

"I don't see anything. Wait, there's something—"

His voice cut short as an impact hit him, Erika gasped in a mouthful of rainwater as she saw the red spatter erupt from him. Garol roughly caught the young man who sputtered his own blood for a moment before screaming. "What in the Seven Hells?"

Erika choked out of her stupor, relieved that he was still alive, then leapt onto the wall kicking off of Garol's shoulder. She dove over the wall and landed hard on the other side to find the strange creature that had struck Darion. Its body seemed to be made of pitch, but had a constant motion to it. It was human in shape and stature, wearing what appeared to be a tattered black cloak. It seemed to chuckle slightly, slinging its weapon to the side, tossing the fresh blood into the rain. The long bladed whip jingled in a macabre way as it danced back and forth.

"Right," Erika said, unsure of what this creature was. She dashed forward, kicking up a fresh patch of mud and losing some momentum before she even began. She swung her hammer, but the creature stepped easily back and out of reach. It slung its whip outwards and Erika ducked, glad that her hair was matted to her mostly bare back, for fear it would have caught in the sinister weapon.

It whipped again, and again, Erika narrowly dodging or leaping over each strike and trying to angle herself for another swing. In her closer proximity, she believed she could see a broken and jagged face in the dark form, balking at its grinning demeanor. She slipped in the mud and fell backwards, straight into a large puddle as it slung around for another strike. She rolled to the side, narrowly avoiding the weapon as it slammed into the ground, but was unable to dodge the backswing. The tip of the bladed whip slashing into her right shoulder and cutting deeply. She felt the warm liquid flow from the wound and down her arm, but gritted her teeth against the sting. She brought her weapon around and swung it again, this time the creature seemed too preoccupied with her blood dripping from the whip to notice the strike. The hammer's head connected solidly with the side of its leg and it exploded outwards in a shower of black dust, the creature falling to one side as Erika reached to grapple its weapon hand.

Garol and Darion dropped down on her side of the wall, blood still flowing from the side of the young man's face where he was struck. They rushed to help the young woman in her struggle, but were held at bay with the whip waving wildly outside of their grappling match.

She hooked the head of the hammer around the creature's wrist and yanked it back, its other arm coming around in a left cross. The blow hit Erika square in the jaw and she squealed in pain and surprise before jamming her boot down on the wrist that held the weapon and smashing the haft of her weapon into its off hand, knocking it aside. Just as Darion started to make his way over to try and help her, Erika slammed her hand onto what appeared to be the throat of her adversary and willed her innate abilities to manifest. Darion nearly fell backwards as the dim area suddenly burst into light, a blazing fire raging along Erika's left arm. Her hand and forearm immolating in a massive red flame and her flesh rendered into obsidian, cracks of magma forming a spiderweb of lines along her flesh. The immolation extended along her arm all the way up to her shoulder as she pressed harder downwards. The creature howled an unearthly scream, wracked with pain as the molten attack melted through its shadowy exterior. The head separated from the shoulders and the body fell limp, suddenly turning to dust under Erika's knee as she fell to her side.

She regained her footing a moment later as her two companions rushed to her side, though Garol was a bit slower, both wide-eyed in awe at her abilities.

"That was amazing!" Darion said, still shaking his head in disbelief.

Garol's head continued to eye the surroundings, unsure of the battle's finality.

Erika grinned sheepishly as she glanced down to her blazing left arm. A moment later she heard a twang of a bowstring, and lifted her hand as quickly as she could, one arrow slicing across her left cheek and side of her neck, another shattering to splinters on her hardened flesh.

"There's more!" she grunted through the pain and dashed off quickly. This time, the two men kept pace with her. She felt something warm, but she knew that was likely the blood flowing down her right arm and her neck, the latter draining into her already soaked tunic and flooding down her ribs. She glanced at Darion's still bleeding wound with some concern, but knew nothing could be done about it while the creatures still moved around them.

Further to the side, where the forest edged closer to the town, several guards were engaged with two more of the creatures. One, was the culprit of Erika's newest wound, sporting a wickedly curved bow that he loosed two or more arrows from at a time and the second was a larger, more burly creature with blades jutting from his arms.

The guards had just arrived to confront the strange invaders, yet many were already unmoving around the area. Arrows jutted from heads and chests, some pinned onto trees, while others lay with visceral slices through their throats or midsections.

Erika rushed into the fray with abandon. She raced for the bowman, who seemed to be picking off men that were too far away for its companion to get to. It turned to her, bowstring pulled, and she dropped low into a slide, swinging her hammer to the side. It leapt over the strike, but Erika used the momentum to right herself and bring herself back to her feet. The creature waited to loose its arrows until she stood again, the two missiles flying towards her. She sidestepped one, but slung her still immolated fist outwards in knowing she had no hope to dodge it. The black arrow shattered into dust against her knuckles and she started forward again while it retrieved more arrows from its hip.

Darion slinked up behind it quicker than it could recover and brought his blade in a slash across its lower spine, causing the creature to lurch forwards. Garol was on it in an instant, and as it bowed forward, the man brought his axe upwards and cleaved the thing roughly. He missed its neck squarely, but separated one shoulder and its head from its body. The creature exploded into dust and its weapon fell to the ground.

The battle seemed nearly won. Erika snapping to the last creature as the rain sizzled onto her immolated limb. Darion looked like he would pass out from hyperventilating, his eyes wide and darting around. Garol grabbed his son roughly though and dragged him into the next fight.

She watched as the team of father and son began their strategic front. Darion slipped to the side as Garol brought his axe to bear, the creature locking one arm blade with the steel of the axe. They struggled in a contest of might for a moment, before the other bladed arm came out and slashed at Garol's belly. He dodged narrowly, but took a light gash across his side. Darion came from the back and stabbed his sword cleanly into the creature's hip. It didn't seem to notice, slashing back across and snapping Darion's blade in two, with a shard still lodged in the creature. Darion sustained a cut to his arm in the strike, dropping his weapon from the shock of it, but managed to catch it with his off hand. Two other guards in full gear rushed forward, bringing long pikes up and jamming the creature's side with the weapons. Garol slashed downwards onto its leg, causing it to fall from the severing blow and Darion recovered enough to slam his broken weapon into its shoulder. It struggled a moment more before falling to the side and bursting into another shower of dust.

Erika relaxed her stance, and released the immolation on her arm when she heard someone call "All clear!", and looked up to see Garol lifting Darion into a tight embrace, the latter looking like he was about to vomit.

"What in the hells are you doing here?" a familiarly gruff voice called, causing her to flinch. The same guard that had stopped her at the gate and the same one who had noticed her before making it outside, stomped through the mud towards her. His face was screwed up into a scowl, the likes of which she'd never seen, even on her own father when he became furious with her over sneaking out to see Irvine after he returned home late one night. She started to defend herself, but he continued to cut her off. "No entry! My word as a wall guard is final! How did you get in?" he demanded.

Garol stepped forward. "I took her in to my home, Jhon. She's my responsibility."

Darion looked like he might fall over, expecting to take the blame himself.

"You are bringing outsiders into all of our homes, Garol!" Jhon shouted back. "There are wars starting everywhere! What if she's an enemy agent?"

Garol slammed his foot down, staring down at the slightly smaller man. "That outsider just saved my son!"

The area quieted suddenly. The only sound was the heavy rain that fell among them all. Erika had trouble keeping her eyes open with the fall of water down her face, but she felt obligated to stand attentively. The cuts at her neck and shoulder stung in the rain though, making her fight a grimace the whole time.

"We took her in because we trusted our own judgment, and I'm damn well proud of that judgment!" Garol continued, causing Darion to take pause at the reference towards him. "She single-handedly destroyed one of those monsters and was a great aid in felling a second! I hardly think her spying is a primary concern right now!"

Jhon retreated just slightly, and looked back to Erika. He seemed to regard the wounds that she had sustained, then looked to the fallen around him. He set his jaw firmly, turning sharply. "It would be a first for your son to have good judgment," he spat at him, though he was looking at Darion while saying it. "She's your problem Garol. Just don't drag the whole damn town with you."

The remaining combatants began to vacate the area, now that the spectacle had subsided. Teams joined up to carry the dead and wounded back to their homes and the local temple. Erika simply stood there, unsure of how to react to this new development. Garol stared off towards where Jhon had stormed, his shoulders bouncing up and down with his angered breaths. Darion stepped forward to her, cautiously reaching a hand to rest on her unwounded shoulder. "Are you alright?" he asked quietly, his voice shaking.

Erika started to feel her emotions break. Tears began to well in her eyes which, thankfully, melded with the rain around her. She had inconvenienced these people, then they defended her, and now he asks if she was alright. The situation brought a lump to her throat and blocked her voice, she tried to reply but couldn't choke one out. She simply nodded, absently wiping her cheeks and wincing when she brushed the slice in her flesh.

"Come on, lets get you back and clean up those cuts," Darion said, carefully ushering her towards the town again.

Garol whirled around and Erika was suddenly very scared that he might strike her. His features hardened for a moment, but then he stepped forward and hugged her tightly. "Thank you for everything you've done. I am sorry."

Erika couldn't stop the tears now, she could only hope that Garol didn't feel the warm of them against his chest. She returned the embrace, nodding her head in the only response she could muster.

"If anyone asks, you're part of my family now. You are no outsider," he said, determined to defend her against the entire town if he must. The way he brandished his axe going back into the town surely made it seem like he was ready to strike down any who accosted her at Jhon's behest.

4

Grim Shades

The winds of the Fjordlands were strong at all times, though they were harsher when the first signs of winter began to show. Even in the autumn months, the ground was covered with a blanket of snow that made traveling difficult for anyone not of the continent. Most of the native Fjordlings took this time to stay inside their homes, whether they be permanently built or simple hide tents.

The former was the case for the Guluran Clan. Their brick and mortar homes stood strong against the powerful winds of the cliffs that hung over the world. Now however, they were under the threat of more than inclement weather. A large tribe of orks had taken up residence not far from them, a gathering bigger than any tales had ever told. Orks held a natural ability to adapt to and resist whatever conditions befell them, and they had begun threatening the clan's homes. They could be a neutral or aggressive creatures, but rarely friendly. These seemed more bloodthirsty for some reason that the Guluran people had no time to ponder.

The sea of yellow hair inside the meeting hall was aflutter with tense conversation. Every member of the strong Fjordling clan was on edge, wondering what the days would bring, and if they could withstand the coming storms. The younger members were full of fervor and optimism, sure that they could defeat any adversary that came to them. The elders, with much more experience in violence, knew what a prolonged war with the orks in the winter could mean.

The head of the tribe was a large barrel-chested man with golden locks that fell past his shoulders. His muscled arms lifted in the air, and with that, all the conversation came to a halt.

"Jorthgar speaks!" his wife called across the crowd, silencing the last few whispers with the guttural native tongue.

"We must find a plan of defense for when the orks arrive!" Jorthgar called. "Our strength alone will not win this battle. We must be clever, outwit the creatures."

Ideas began sprouting from the crowd of blonde clansmen.

Charging the orks under cover of night, though the snows would likely freeze them.

Abandoning the town and then crashing back upon them when they arrived, though they worried the orks would use their own homes as defense.

Surrounding the opposing army, though their numbers would dwindle before reaching half their circumference.

An older man stood, slamming his walking staff into the wooden floor. "We should leave! Our ancestors walked these fjords easily, we have grown weak!" The room fell silent at the elder's accusations. He spoke of a time long past, when the people of the Fjordlands were nomadic. That was a time before the *Bløt Herja*, a time that even their eldest were too young to remember. "We must become strong again, through the glory of the Almother, we must follow Her guides! This must be a sign from Her! A sign that we must leave our built homes and become one with the wilderness again!"

As if the wilderness was answering him, the door of the hall burst open, sending with it a rush of the bone chilling wind from outside. Snow cascaded into the first stretch of the hall, several young men leapt to their feet to secure the door but froze when a large black bird swooped through and landed on the wooden planks.

Murmurs began spreading through the room again, though now even more hushed. "*Drathra*," they said, the Fjordling word for both raven, and for death. All eyes watched the eerie animal, as it stalked carefully further into the room, letting out an ear piercing caw that made the even burliest of northmen jump from their skins.

A heavy footfall came soon after. A woman with thick leather boots stepped into the warmed hall. She wore tattered black clothing that covered her muscled frame loosely, a coat billowing from below her waist in the violent winds from the outside. Her head was wrapped in a thin black cloth that did nothing to hide her similarly black hair. With a tilt of her head, the light caught her dark hair in such a way that made it look a sickly crimson, as if it were dyed with blood. Her sharp eyes held an otherworldly crimson hue, surrounded in a dark ink splatter that made the red of her eyes stand out even more. Her bare arms were covered only in fresh scars.

"Svartur," muttered another elder in the back. "They are all supposed to be dead."

The woman seemed to smirk slightly, but her angular jaw still appeared set in its violent expression. She took a step forward, baring a massive blade nearly as tall as she was, with a hooked tip and a thick cross guard. A metal ring sat on the pommel, holding a chain that swung lightly from the movement.

"I shall kill the orks," she said, her low tone sending a chill down the spines of her audience as she leaned on the guard of her sword. "I shall be your blade."

Jorthgar stepped through the crowd to stand over the woman, although she was not much shorter than him. "How can we trust you? Were you sent by the Almother?"

"Mortia," the stranger answered, causing everyone to recoil at the name of the Goddess of Death. Even if she did not fit in their beliefs, the name was still known and feared at most times.

"What stake does Mortia have in this?" the elder from before called.

The woman shrugged. "Perhaps she doesn't want all of you cluttering her passage."

Her casual allusion to their deaths sent another chill though the room. One young man found the statement more annoying than threatening. He dashed to the front of the room and moved his chief to the side, throwing his fist into the air towards the woman's face. It never arrived. The woman's hand flashed up in a gout of black smoke and caught hold of the young man's eager strike, and before he could react, her elbow snapped down to her hip, taking his fist with it and violently dislocating his arm at the shoulder. The young man fell to his side promptly after.

"The orks die at dawn," the woman stated flatly and turned for the door. Several steps into the snow the door shut, barring the view of her form melting into more black smoke.

The world turned dark around her, with a whispering wind that blew her coat and headband in twisting directions, though it no longer held the same biting chill of the Fjordlands. The landscape became broken and the light in the sky was gone, replaced by eerie pale blue glimmer shining through cracks in the ground. No snow came here, but the air was still cold. As frigid as death itself.

A figure leaned up against the building, a dark and broken reflection of that meeting hall from the physical world. A tall and gaunt man with long black hair and a wide brimmed hat. He sat up slightly, straightening his waistcoat and adjusting the scarf around his neck. A rapier bounced on his hip as he walked towards the woman who had just appeared before him. His similarly crimson eyes flashed at her.

"Mortia will not be amused at you offering your help to them," he said, his voice coming out in a smooth tone that irritated her to no end. "Mortals aren't supposed to know about Shades, dear Vaerisa."

Vaerisa turned to him after offering a scoff to the empty isles around her. "And yet, I hear rumors that you are close to meddling in the southern lands yourself, Craven."

Craven gave a low bow, sweeping his hat out in a wide arc and letting his long hair fall around his face. "Alas, my quest is sanctioned by the Matron of Death herself. She asked me personally to do this for her."

Vaerisa groaned, hiding the nervousness she held knowing the task he was about to be off on. "I care not who your quest is for. Only that I may satiate my rage. Be on your way Lord Wraith."

"Very well. Do be careful, wouldn't want you getting hurt," he replied teasingly. "I'll be gone for some time, I trust you'll do well in my absence."

Vaerisa did her best to ignore him as he walked away, but he called back and made her flinch. "One day you will have to retrieve one as well. You will not come into your own until you do."

A moment later, his form melted away and drifted along the winds. Craven was a much stronger Shade than she, much more powerful than any of the Shades had ever been. She knew that, and knew to heed his words when they came. Still, his voice caused irritation—and often fear—to rise in her chest. She wanted nothing more than to strike him where he stood, in the vain attempt to shirk this new life she had been given. This would come with grave consequences from the Matron, so she simply stood attentively at his presence.

She perched herself atop one of the crumbling buildings, facing the direction of the ork encampment in the physical world. One leg hanging off the side of the rooftop. There she waited. Despite her aggressive demeanor, she held her arms close in an attempt to ward off the fear she felt, trying her best to simply forget the Lord Wraith's words.

5

HEALING WOUNDS AND FURTHER VIOLENCE

Upon arriving back at Darion's home, Minora immediately set to Erika's wounds. She took her into the back room where Jess was splashing lightly in a large tub. "Such a little runt, demanded a warm bath after you all left," she said as she, nearly forcibly, stripped Erika's armor and tunic and began searching her for injuries other than the obvious ones. "Though I suppose she was simply worried for you three and needed a distraction."

Erika glanced over to find Jess staring at her, now that she was bare to the waist. she wondered if the small girl was staring at her bloody cuts, scars, or perhaps at her markings. In any case, the girl seemed fascinated, diverted from her playful bath, eyes exploring her form.

"You've seen much more battle than this, it seems," Minora commented, gently running her fingers across the three large scars that ran diagonally across her back. The smooth touch against her naked—and slightly sensitive—skin sent tingles along Erika's spine. After a short time, she had thoroughly cleaned the open cuts and gathered up her garments to wash them. "Go on then, get in the bath," she said as she beckoned for Jess to vacate the tub. "The clerics give us special salts for the water that will heal you."

Erika removed her boots and dropped her leggings to the floor, scowling at the amount of mud that had caked onto the legs, before handing them to Minora. Jess was soon out with a towel wrapped around herself and hugged Erika, pressing wet hair into her bare stomach tightly. "I'm happy you're back, and safe," she said before running off to get dressed.

The door shut after that and Erika took a breath, walking over to the mirror to examine herself personally. Her jaw on her right side was thoroughly bruised already and would likely take a time to heal even with magic salts. Her upper arm bore a decent laceration, but nothing severe enough to blemish terribly once it haled. And lastly, she examined the left side of her face, wincing as she touched around the deep wound where the arrow had sliced through her cheek and continued down her neck nearly to her shoulder. Of them all, she thought, that one would surely leave an angry scar.

She sighed, then stepped across the room again, her bare feet making soft sounds on the wood beneath her. A spare thought crossed her mind of how she had just been wishing for a hot bath while on the road, before she stepped into the warm water and lowered herself down to where only her face was in the air. She gasped sharply and her eyes went wide as her wounds began to burn fiercely, the salts beginning to take effect, or so she hoped. She lay back for as long as she could take it, then sat up in a more comfortable position, though she was dismayed at how cold the air above the water was. She could hear the rain continuing outside and wondered how long it would persist, genuinely not wanting to travel in the rain.

After rummaging through her personal supplies that she'd thought to grab, she began to carefully shave her legs—having a warm bath to help in that small task was a blessing in itself—while she ordered her priorities for the next day. A map was a definite needed thing, along basic supplies as well. She could use a new rope, as hers was beginning to show some wear from her continued knot practice. Maintenance tools would be nice, but she wasn't sure she could afford them. Her blade upkeep tools she had brought from home were starting to show their age. Although she hardly used the sword, she still tended to it compulsively. If she had only used them on her dagger, they would not be as worn down, but her emotions wouldn't allow her to leave Irvine's sword unpolished.

The door creaked behind her, interrupting her thoughts. She lurched forward into the water reflexively, her legs splashing into the water and her back immediately growing cold from the open air.

"Sorry," Darion said. "I was just dropping off some extra clothes for you, we didn't know what you had."

Erika glanced back slightly, he was looking vaguely in her direction, but his eyes seemed unseeing. Sadness poured from him, making Erika's chest hurt slightly, despite being submerged in the healing water.

"Thank ye, Darion. I'll be out of yer family's hair in the mornin'," she promised, wishing to alleviate the young man of his negative thoughts, as she assumed they were because of her.

He nodded and placed the stack of clothes on the small bench by the door. Erika laid back again as he closed the door, considering the implications of the night and the strange creatures that attacked them. She used a small cup to idly pour the hot water over her skin, making for nice little floods of warmth as it flowed over her. Eventually she shook her head and returned to raking the prickling hairs from her legs with her small razor.

† †

The next morning came quickly and with less sleep than Erika had hoped. The rain had finally stopped, the noise from outside becoming more quiet. Erika carefully slid from underneath Jess, placing her back onto the bed and covering her. She kissed her forehead with a smile, then quietly as she could, got dressed into her traveling clothes that were thankfully able to dry by the small fire in the shared bedroom.

She failed to notice as she was changing that Darion wasn't in his bed.

In the dining room, she gathered up her satchel and breastplate, strapping it to her chest as quietly as she could. She reached into her pack to bring out a small parchment and a marking stick, meaning to leave a short note to the family that had cared for her. She nearly squealed when a voice called out from the other side of the table.

"Don't bother," Darion said, startling her. He was dressed in his leather armor with a pack slung over his shoulder. "I've already spoken with my father, he understands your rush. Jess will be sad to have missed you though."

Erika eyed him through the dim room. "And where are ye going?"

His eyes perked up, meeting hers. "With you."

She couldn't help but scoff slightly. "No, no. Ye're not. My road is my own."

"I've already made my choice to see you to Sylvanna, at least," he said, tightening the bracer on his left wrist.

"Why?" Erika asked, spreading her arms out wide. "Ye've no reason to come with me."

"I have all the reason I need."

She raised her eyebrows, expecting more of an explanation, but he set his jaw and offered none. She let out a sigh, finally convinced that she had no hope of arguing with him.

"Let's go get some supplies first. I don't know about you, but I definitely need a map," he said, stepping past her towards the door.

"I thought ye were only to see me to Sylvanna?" she asked with suspicion.

Darion shrugged. "Maps never hurt, I'm no courier after all."

He paused a moment, looking at her. She noticed his dull blue eyes still held a sadness to them, but not like the previous night. He stared at her for a long while and she felt herself starting to flush slightly, until he finally said, "That bruise looks terrible," and walked through the door.

She brought up a hand to her cheek and felt the tenderness, not sure whether to be offended or amused by the comment.

† †

The morning came quietly, though slower than Vaerisa would have hoped. She slowly appeared on the roof of the hall in a dark haze as the sun crested over the eastern plains. Her eyes squinted, bothered by the sudden light, but she could still see the march of orks. Tribes of the creatures usually only reached around two score at most, the force before her proving to be multiple tribes joined together. Clan colors showed clear lines between the ranks.

Several of the Guluran clan stepped lightly out into the thick morning snow, staring out at the oncoming orks with bravery. Though the Shade could see the fear behind those eyes. She heaved herself forwards, landing with a rough crunch on the white landscape below. Several of the Fjordlings jumped back in surprise, not realizing her overnight perch.

"Wait for their ranks to break," she said in a dark tone, but loud enough for the organizing defenders to hear. They let her step forward unhindered. Out into the open dale she stalked, her blade resting casually on her shoulder in an obvious display of aggression.

The icy-blue skinned orks slowed, while a particularly large one broke through and faced the much smaller woman. His bulging muscles carried him to an intimidating eight foot height, but still Vaerisa stood in defiance. The great ork scratched his lip beside one massive tusk as he eyed her quizzically. She wondered with a slight smile if she could break that lower jaw and force the tusks through his eyes.

"We come for the yellow hairs!" he called out in his rough grasp of the Fjordling language. "They hunt on our claimed lands and kill with no reason!"

"And here you are to slaughter in return. An eye for an eye?" Vaerisa asked, interrupting the ork's rationality.

Hesitation filled the air as the orks failed to charge, and the Fjordlings awaited the newcomer's next move. This was all Vaerisa needed. "You've come to fight. So fight!" she shouted, before vanishing into a black smoke. A heartbeat later she appeared next to the ork, her blade diving for his chest in an arcing swing. The ork brought his own sword to bear and was able to duck under the strike while deflecting it with his parry. Vaerisa grinned wildly.

Shouts began to ring out as the force made way for the sudden duel, cheering for their champion and insults to their opponent. Their deadly dance was wild and furious as the ork maneuvered his weapon with a strength unrivaled but the dexterous woman was much faster, her own greatsword twirling and swinging in blinding routines.

The ork saw a chance after one spin, thrusting his free hand outwards, grabbing her by the upper arm and lifting her free of the ground below. She responded by swinging both legs upwards and wrapping them around his head, twisting her hips with a strength that he had not expected. He flung himself forwards into the soft snow to avoid the hard lock, Vaerisa releasing her hold just as he did and flipping deftly back to her feet with a flourish that caused the crowd to pause in their cheers.

She angled her sword back around but the champion spun in his prone position and kicked the flat of her blade, throwing her wide. His own blade came in much faster and ran through her midriff, erupting from her upper back in a sickening splash of crimson that painted the surrounding blanket of white.

The ork smiled as he stood, driving the blade further up and lifting the smaller woman off the ground. He knew the strike to have easily severed her spine just down from the base of her neck, though he puzzled at her still strong grip on her weapon. He looked up to her face, the dark splashes around her eyes growing a deep red, accentuating her eyes. Her smiling face dripped a thick gout of blood. An expression of terror spread across the ork's face.

"Give me more," she said, halfway between taunting and pleading. She gripped the cross guard of his sword with her left hand and pulled, sliding the metal through her flesh even further and closing the distance between herself and the icy-skinned ork. "Make me feel *something!*" she shouted, the ork flinching both at her voice and the stomach-churning sound of the metal slowly grating through her body, across her bones.

The ork slung the blade wide, throwing the woman off it in another spattering of lifeblood. He was even further unnerved as she twisted and landed on her feet in a slightly crouched position, the bloody grin still wide across her angled face. "What are you?" the ork breathed, though it was his last.

She vanished from sight again, appearing next to the ork. She ran up the length of his blade and swung her own around with a fervor, cleanly separating his head from his shoulders. She stood atop the body as it fell to the ground with a *thump* in the thick snow. All around her was silence, halted only by the whispering wind flooding through the stunned crowds.

Vaerisa inhaled deeply, the wound in her stomach quickly stitching back together and reforming her muscle, tissue, and flesh. Her eyes looked to the mass of terrified orks, all holding their jagged weapons with unease. She smiled once again. "Give me more," she said, her eyes alight with rage.

She surged forward in a shadowy haze, matching it with an even deadlier dance, her great blade twirling about and wreaking havoc upon the opposing forces.

A leg separated from its hip.

A gash torn through a rib.

Another through a shoulder.

Heads landed unceremoniously in the snow beside dismembered limbs. Weapons reached her occasionally but the orks were unnerved further when she seemed to step into their strikes, causing a deeper wound than they had originally expected to inflict.

What frightened them more than her willingness to be struck, was her laughter. It rang out across the field in disturbing waves, intensifying with each slain enemy and each blow that she endured.

Moments later the ranks of the orks broke, allowing the Guluran clan the chance to rush forward with battle cries to meet the shattered horde, though they ran a wide swath around the woman and her whirling blade.

Craven stood easily atop one building, watching the spectacle of Vaerisa in her bloodlust. He worried over her. Over her intense pleasure in the heat of battle, and her reckless usage of her Death given abilities. He could see the anguish in her eyes, threatening tears even now. She laughed to fight back that flood of misery. The world was changing, he knew, and it needed justice more than ever now.

Only this, was not justice.

He vanished a moment later and began his long walk southwards.

6

A Place of War

The pair were out of the town by sunrise. Darion trailed behind the strong pace of the young woman, already feeling homesick. His parents would have to explain to Jess why he was gone. He genuinely wondered what they would tell her. She already believed he was smitten with this girl, so she'd likely believe he ran off with her to get married or something even more frivolous considering her imagination.

The thought made him groan unintentionally, drawing a sidelong look from the auburn-haired woman. He quickly waved his hand in front of himself to dismiss her, to which she shrugged and continued walking forward. He found himself watching her, the sight of her distracting him from the fact that he was abandoning his family and his position. The large and defined scar on her back was a common thought that plagued him after accidentally seeing it while she was in the bath the previous night. He wanted to ask her about it, to know what creature could have possibly caused such a devastating wound, and where this horrible creature was currently. His own embarrassment stopped him though, knowing that to ask would be a full admission of his wandering eyes while she relaxed in the bath. If she knew that, he worried that she'd think ill of him and demand he leave her at once, or even worse, hit him with that large hammer or her burning fists. Just the barest edges of the scar on her shoulder blade could be seen above the strapless tunic she wore, but he didn't think it showed enough to warrant a question over it.

He started wondering what this girl possibly thought of him in the first place and what she assumed as to why he was so willing to accompany her to their ruling city of Sylvanna, although he had full intentions to accompany her further still than even that. His father had talked to him the previous evening, the topic spanning more onto Darion's own depression, and how this girl was an opportunity for change. She was a traveler and he was a resident of the Sylvannan region, giving him full knowledge and understanding of how to move through any settlement in the area. Her being barred from his small town of Stonewall was already a testament to the growing turmoil across the continent but was to be expected for being a border town, even if the more southerly Region of Sildenfeld was no opposition to them.

He watched her tie her locks behind her head with a leather strip, her muscular arms flexing in the early morning sun caused Darion more than a little jealousy in regards to his own—much less defined—musculature. The crimson markings on her skin was also a cause for wonderment at the woman. He assumed it had something to do with the incredible abilities she had displayed the previous night, flushing her arm into flames and using it to great effect against the strange attackers. Similarly though, he found himself intimidated and afraid to ask her anything.

† †

The air steadily became colder, while the forest became thicker around them. The sun peeking through in shafts of light that pierced the leaves and fell to the earth below. The companions stepped lightly through the shaded glade, happy for the respite from the punishing sun on their necks, but also put more on guard by the multitude of angles they could be attacked from.

Erika gripped the haft of her warhammer just under the head while holding the strap of her satchel with her other hand. Her emerald eyes glanced to and fro, dancing between the trees. Her ears perking at each slight noise she heard. Darion however, seemed much less concerned with their surroundings.

"You alright Erika? You seem on edge," he prodded lightly.

She failed to look back at him, still leading by several feet. "Just watchin' fer anythin' that might do us harm."

Darion shrugged, attempting to offer some comfort. "There usually isn't anything around this area that attacks anyone. It is a common trade route between Sildenfeld and Sylvanna."

Erika wasn't put at ease by this, stopping suddenly. Darion, being too distracted by the sights of the roadside, didn't see her stop and promptly ran into her. He jumped back with haste and began apologizing profusely, seemingly distraught over the slight bump. Erika silenced him by jamming her hand around his mouth and squeezing at his jaw, the sound of his exhales resounding loudly off of the space between her thumb and forefinger.

"I'm not all that calmed by 'usually'," she growled, motioning to a clearing not far from them, where a massive creature sat passively against a thick tree in the sunlight that bathed it in warmth.

Darion's eyes went wide and he began to scratch at her hand, begging her release. She obliged after a moment and wiped the moisture of his breath onto her skirt. "That's an ogre!" he hissed aggressively.

Erika simply nodded in reply, as she took a half step forward.

"We can't possibly fight it!" he pleaded, unsure of how far this strange girl would take this encounter.

Erika's eyes set on the creature's steadily rising and lowering torso, she slowly set her satchel to the side of the road and steadied her warhammer in both hands. "Can't be any worse than the things from last night. Besides, if we don't kill it now, another traveler may be fallin' prey to it," she said quietly, taking another step forwards.

Darion nearly fell over at her bravado, but set his own pack beside hers nonetheless and drew his blade as quietly as he could. She was careful of her steps, knowing that most creatures varied in how deep their sleeping was, but resolved to rid the road of the snoring monster. Couriers were usually to dispatch any dangers on the roads for the less equipped travelers that walked them, and despite not being a courier, Erika knew the world was missing one of its best. So, she had decided to do some work in his stead, at least until she could return him to his duty. Unfortunately, her companion was not so careful of his step, Erika startling when she heard a long dry twig snap behind her. The ogre's snoring came to an abrupt end with a disgusting sucking sound that echoed through the clearing. Its tiny eyes came down onto the two, frozen where they stood, watching the great being as it came to realization of what was before it.

The ogre lumbered upwards to stand on its wide feet, measuring a full fifteen feet and easily cresting the tree tops around it. Darion loudly yelled a curse as he dashed to the side, leaving Erika right where she wanted to be in the first place. The creature brought its right fist down towards her in a lazy punch, easy enough for Erika to time her own strike. She kicked her warhammer up in an arcing uppercut, gaining momentum and crashing into the ogre's knuckles. She felt one crack, as her weapon sunk into the otherwise flat face of the fist, awkwardly bending one finger inwards and into its palm. The staggering strike caught the ogre off balance, giving her partner ample time to rush in and slice into the back of the monster's knees.

The two strikes in near tandem caused the ogre to lurch in both ways at once and howl in pain at his wounds. Darion crouched to the side, awaiting his next opportunity to strike, but instead pausing dumbfounded at the woman's sheer strength. She sidestepped another punch, the ogre's fist crashing into the soft earth below. She reversed her momentum, throwing her legs in the opposite direction and sending her shoulders in a whip-like fashion back to the creature. Darion felt his stomach churn suddenly as the hammerhead connected with the outside of the ogre's elbow, cracking it to bend in the opposite direction with a horrible snapping of bones and tendons. Before Darion could recover his senses, the fiery woman was already to the creature's shoulder as it doubled over in screaming pain. She brought her devastating weapon around again, smashing its flat edge to the ogre's left temple and ending the creature's pain forever.

Darion summarily vomited to the side of the tree he crouched next to. The sight of the crushed skull and massively ruined limbs caused his stomach to tie in knots. Erika threw her hair back with an arm, her chest rising and falling with lightly labored breaths. After a moment to confirm the thing was dead she began to wipe the blood from her hammer, looking over at Darion with some understanding. She was similarly repulsed the first time she had fought a more humanoid creature after leaving Sildenfeld. A skirmish with a band of goblins that had ambushed her on the roads, their eyes looking more human than she would have liked, their screams echoing in her mind for days. She had also vacated her stomach involuntarily after the last of them lay dead at her feet and the adrenaline had started to fade. She understood that it was a necessary evil on her path, and those goblins would have done worse to her or others had she not slain them. After retrieving their packs, she made her way to him and crouched next to him, placing a hand on his shoulder and offering him a warm smile.

"How can you just walk away like that?" he asked with wide eyes.

She sighed, glancing to the side. "I know that I'm needin' to. I can't be lingerin' over every little thing on my journey."

He didn't seem to digest the answer well, but accepted his pack from her and cleaned his blade of the bloody streak it had gained. She turned to him, cocking her head to the side in confusion. "Ye're a guardsman, hadn't ye seen death before?"

He swallowed hard, trying not to look at the ogre's crushed face "Of course, but I was still somewhat new to the job. It's a small town, not much happens there. That, and the other guards always struck the killing blows against any bandits or the like."

She nodded, but returned her gaze again. "What about the things last night?"

"Those things didn't bleed, not really anyway. No life in their eyes, which means I don't have to watch it leave," he explained, his gaze locked on the ogre's one intact eye, devoid of any life just as he had said. "Even still, I almost vomited last night."

Erika grimaced, understanding his logic and remembering how he had looked when his father took him into his embrace after the battle. She began to walk back to the roadway, wiping errant strands of hair from the sweat on her face. Darion trailed behind her after a moment of making sure his stomach wouldn't turn inside out again.

†‡

Sands whipped through the air as the crimson sky shifted with every passing moment. The strange and unknowable realm known as the Sands of Conflict were ever changing and ever deadly. A figure sat atop a stone and carefully examined the lance that he held vertically in his hands. He often spoke to the jagged weapon, though no reply ever came.

"Still no answer?" a gravel toned voice asked him from not far off, causing him to flinch.

He shook his head in reply. "Not that it matters to you much."

The second figure gently floated towards him. A skeletal visage with a cracked skull that bore only one horn where there once were two. The formerly imposing sight of Zyrxak seemed to grin at his companion.

"Now now, Irvine, there is no reason to be that way."

Irvine's shoulders slumped as his gaze fell to his legs, where the armor of the Dragoon spirit had become more cracked and worn. Sections of the armor fell away from him at times, though he had no feasible way of reattaching them, so he left them where they lay. This place was strange indeed, Zyrxak having explained that time moved erratically here, hence the rapid healing of the wounds that he had sustained in a fight that seemed just a few hours prior. The Daemon insisted that the skirmish was likely several months in the past and that the world had moved on completely, without either of them. Even wounds he received from battles here healed incredibly quickly, and he had seen some of the same combatants more than once, despite laying them to rest with the Dragoon's spear.

He reached down and helped the shin plate free from his left leg, the metal falling unceremoniously into the sands. His bare flesh beneath was heavily scarred, he could feel nothing that touched the flesh. One of Zyrxak's monsters had melted the skin from the appendage like acid, doing similar damage to his right hand up to his wrist. Both were now healed, but still not quite the same, Irvine finding it difficult at times to maintain his hold on his weapon.

"I suppose your Dragoon friend said nothing about the properties of the spell you enacted?" the Elder Daemon asked him, causing Irvine to grimace.

"No, they did not. Only said that given the circumstances, it was the only way to save my home and the people I cared about," he replied, wondering why he was even speaking with the monster that was the root cause of all his issues.

"Well, hopefully you killed that damnable bird," Zyrxak chuckled, referencing the Angelus that had joined their clash and brought about what very well could have been the end of Irvine's world altogether. He raised a cracked hand to his head, shading his one intact eye socket from the light above them, speaking casually. "Oh, incoming."

"What?" Irvine asked, but before he could react properly, the missile that Zyrxak had just witnessed came crashing down and impaled the young man through the chest, flinging him from his seat and slamming him to the ground. The Daemon watched the spear vibrating from its impact, with some amusement, as Irvine lay motionless in the sand, his eyes wide open and staring into the endless red sky.

"You should really pay more attention, I am trying to help you here," Zyrxak said coyly, unconcerned that his only companion had just been fatally pierced. "I suppose I'll just count grains of sand until you return."

7

The White Carmino

The road to the city of Sylvanna was long and winding. The hills becoming more aggressive as the pair began their ascent into the mountainous region that approached the Rift. Erika paused for a long while as they crested a hill, looking up at those high spires where several long jutting structures that looked like massive ribs reached upwards to the cloudy sky. Darion told her of a legend about a mythical Titan that had died there, his flesh turning into the mountains they saw now, leaving only his bones behind. They certainly looked like real bones from this distance, but Darion shrugged at his own tale. "None of the rest of the skeleton was ever found though. No skull, no pelvis, no femurs, no..." he trailed off as he walked ahead of her.

The indigenous creatures of the lands caused them little issues and Darion had thoughtfully brought along a crossbow that allowed them better meals besides rabbit. Although he quickly regretted tracking a wounded deer through a thicket, instead meeting an irritable porcupine on the other side. Erika spent the better part of that evening picking the quills from his neck and shoulders. They were both grateful that none hit very deeply, or worse, his eyes.

She often found herself looking into reflective pools next to the rivers and streams they passed, eyeing her newest scar with annoyance. The pink and healing flesh stretching along her jaw and down her neck where the strange assailant had sliced her with his arrow. She let out a heavy sigh.

Darion stood off to the side, looking like he was wanting to ask her something but couldn't find the words.

"What's on yer mind, Darion?" she asked after watching him squirm for a while, with some idle amusement.

He made eye contact with her and started scratching the side of his neck idly—avoiding the porcupine pricks—while mustering his voice. "What is the scar on your back from?"

She raised an eyebrow, Darion beginning to stammer an apology.

"Why d'ye want to know about my worst scar?" she tried to avoid expelling any sign of her emotions regarding the claw marks across her back.

Darion seemed to calm at her second question, recomposing himself and clearing his throat. "I've never seen such a wound is all. Honestly, thinking about it more, it starts to make more sense why you're able to go through battles so nonchalantly."

Erika sighed. Looking to the ground for a moment, before finally speaking. "Scars are a common thing fer me it seems. I made a lot o' mistakes on my first journey from home. I paid the price in a lot o' blood," she began, gently raising the bottom of her tunic and rubbing at the tooth scars, where a jordhak had nearly crushed her in its mouth. "My best friend was a courier, and on that first journey, I realized how much he went through every day he was away. I'm still not as good as 'im out 'ere, but I'm tryin' my best."

She tried not to wear the sadness outwardly too much, but she didn't figure it was working very well, especially as her accent intensified. Darion spoke quietly, seemingly in an attempt to reason with her, or maybe himself. "I'm assuming that your friend died somewhere along the way and you blame yourself." Erika didn't answer him, but still he continued. "Nothing that happened was your fault, Erika. Bad things happen, we can't always control things like we want."

He didn't seem to realize that he was stepping closer to her, but she did. She lashed out at his last words, grabbing his shirt roughly and jostling him until he made direct eye contact with her. "Don't ye be consolin' me when ye weren't there," she warned, tossing him back slightly and retrieving her supplies. She shouldered her satchel as she walked away, pausing several yards from him and calling back. "Not meanin' to be ungrateful Darion. I just don't want to talk about it."

Darion stood by the river, watching her leave as he realized a crucial fact. She was in an entirely different world than he was, and he felt more out of place with her than he ever did as a member of his town's guard, yet he could understand her regret better than he could put into words. He gathered his own supplies, sparing a short glance back in the direction of his hometown. "Distance," he said quietly. "Making distance."

Finally, he jogged off to catch up with her.

Erika thought on her interaction with Darion at the riverside as they drew away from the location. She felt some guilt, having never lashed out like that at anyone before, even if he had irritated her to a degree. He seemed to be trying to fix her life, without knowing even the base amount about it. In her frustration, she ended up tying and re-tying her hair up nearly a score of times as they walked, never being able to get it comfortable enough to leave. Each time she finished tying the leather strap around her thick shock of hair, she would walk a few steps, then groan loudly whilst violently tearing the leather down. Darion began to ask what was wrong each time, but was quickly turned away by Erika's thick hand coming up flat to him. After a while, he gave up and simply let her grumble and retie her hair. Erika tried not to think about her ranger friend or how many times she had scolded her. 'Tying your hair back over and over won't make the problem go away, sweetheart.' Teria would often say, though it served little else than to frustrate Erika further.

She looked at him with some contempt when he was distracted. He reminded her of Irvine in certain aspects, although he seemed to lack in traveling experience and often relied on her for certain solutions. Having him along strangely caused her thoughts to drift to Irvine, as she often found herself picturing his long brown hair and dull blue eyes that held an attractive sharpness to them whenever he would look at certain things. She remembered that they often took on that sharp appearance when he would look at her. The sadness over his absence turned to anger and frustration more than anything, finding herself violently breaking twigs or other objects she'd pick up. Things had been so much easier when she was just walking alone, even if it was slow and circling at times. At least she wasn't constantly filled with thoughts and memories of Irvine as she dazed.

Darion suddenly spoke. "So, who was this friend of yours?"

She took a long time to reply, but eventually replied. "Irvine." Darion glanced to her expectantly, but found her scowling visage looking dead ahead of them. "He's my best friend. The one I'm searchin' fer, the one..." she started, only to give up on the words, drawing a puzzled look from the young man, but accepting nonetheless.

After days of traveling, the pair found themselves nearing the island city of Sylvanna. Guard towers became more prevalent in the mountainous passes, and the two were ushered through after Darion displayed a set of papers that declared him as a Sylvannan native. Erika found all of it strange, and wondered if the turmoil across the continent had truly become so bad as to warrant such defensive behavior. After the latest guard post they started off across the wide and long bridge that led from the mainland onto the large island that Sylvanna was built upon. The expanse of the city sprawled ahead of them, past a great wall and further upwards. At the very center of the city, and its highest point, was a towering cathedral that Darion told her was the home of the ruling monarch, Queen Stacia Sylvanna, who was said to be an aloof woman with a dark sense of humor.

"What are your plans after Sylvanna?" Darion asked just after leaving the checkpoint, glancing back to make sure none of the guards were giving them odd looks.

"Keep headin' north," she said, without looking from the road before them. "Maybe take up a small job or somethin' to earn a bit more coin, I'm startin' to run a bit low. But straight north after that."

Darion chewed his lip, wondering if this girl truly meant to go past the Great Rift, thinking her crazy on one hand but drawn in by the promise of unseen lands on the other. She stepped resolutely forward, gaining a quickened pace from him as well for fear of being left behind.

"What kind of work are you thinking? Maybe I could help out?"

"Easiest. Maybe a bit o' smithin'. That's what I grew up doin', so maybe I could give a hand fer a couple o' days," she replied, holding up a muscular arm and pantomiming a hammer strike motion. "Then again, I'd honestly prefer somethin' that pays a bit more, an' can be done in a quicker amount o' time."

Darion's mind drifted, speaking his thoughts aloud. "Quicker money would be some rather unsavory work, which I wouldn't peg you for." That drew a glare from the Fjordling and he hastily continued. "Or, some mercenary work. Maybe some delving into a ruin or something. There are quite a few dwarven sites around Sylvanna, and despite the best efforts of the dungeoneers, none have been fully explored. At least, I don't think they have."

Erika brought a hand to her chin, thinking on the options. She knew dwarven mechanics could fetch a hefty price, especially if they were still functional. Though diving into the ruins could be treacherous due to the same strange automations that were so valuable. She recalled a story Irvine had once told her of a dwarven construct that had escaped a long abandoned mine on one of his routes and how it was one of the few things that he had actually run away from. There were many unpredictable and dangerous things that the dwarves made so long ago.

Getting into the thick walls of the city was interesting enough, with Darion concocting vague reasons as to why a citizen of the Region was carting around with an outsider, but Erika didn't dispute him on any of it. She even resolved to act as his wife-to-be if it got them into the city, just as long as no one expected them to be too hands on with the act. She figured she'd simply say it was part of her Fjordling culture to keep a healthy distance from her betrothed until after the ceremonies, and at least none of the Patrian soldiers would be able to dispute her. She found herself going so far as to go over the Fjordish language in her head, despite having not spoken it since she was several years younger in her father's house. Alas, nothing ever came to such a measure and she was given free passage into the city after what seemed like hours of hazing through the gate watch.

Adventuring and mercenary work was its own commerce in most cities and Sylvanna was no different on that point. The Regions had a well-traveled countryside, full of individuals and parties searching for fame and fortune. Adventuring was a dangerous but lucrative opportunity for many to find a way in the world. Only just a year before, Erika would have never believed herself foolhardy enough to actually walk into such a guildhouse, considering herself much more suited for one of the craftsman guilds instead. Now however, she found herself looking up at the Adventurer's Hall in the heart of Sylvanna.

The sun fell low behind the guildhouse and Darion hurried her inside, hoping to be able to pick a job for the next day before the guild closed for the night. Inside was a lavish waiting area with comfortable chairs and couches with the colors of Sylvanna draped over them, blue and green fabric hues contrasting with the orange glow from outside. Across the sitting area was a sol elf behind a massive wooden desk that spanned nearly half of the great chamber. The tall man looked over the desk at them, his back hunched in his chair over a stack of documents. He straightened and gave an audible sigh, motioning the pair closer. Erika twirled around as they approached, admiring the building and its comfortable aura, despite the reputation of such guilds that she had always believed before.

Darion stepped to the desk and greeted the elf who, even when seated, nearly looked the young man directly in the eyes. "We're passing through and were looking for a bit of work before continuing on our way."

The sol elf and the Fjordling behind him both gave Darion a look with a raised eyebrow, although Erika was simply observing his choice of words and wondering why he said '*we* are passing through'. The elf reclined a bit and looked the two over. "Well, we are clean out of mercenary work. The border lines are full up, dealing with the incursions from Tarkal, but if you wait a few days perhaps someone will give up or die and a spot will be vacant."

Erika tried to hide her look of panic at the mention of what sounded to be an all-out war between Regions while Darion did his best to distract the elf from her failed attempt. "Perhaps something a bit more local? We're moving northwards on our journey, and I'm afraid we haven't the time to help in a border dispute."

The elf scoffed, both of the humans noting the sarcasm in his voice. "Border dispute, indeed. Very well then, just the two of you?"

At the pair's nods the elf deftly thumbed through a stack of documents, searching for something, periodically glancing at the two, as if he were sizing them up and trying to find a job that wouldn't kill them. Erika shifted her weight and tried to focus on the comfortable looking seats again, put off by the demeanor of this elf who was the only other she had met besides Sárif—and his stories of his aash mate who had sadly been killed—back in Sildenfeld.

A moment later he retrieved a thin binding of documents, handing it to Darion to read. As he looked over it, Erika used her slight height advantage to glance over his shoulder at the print. One of the nearby forested passes was home to a lumber camp, but had been vacated due to creatures that attacked. Now the camp needed to be reclaimed.

"Why has no one taken such a simple job?" Darion asked. "Isn't the Region at war? A lumber camp should be an urgent thing to win back."

The sol elf reclined in his chair again. "Sylvanna is not officially at war as of yet. Alas, the pay is too low for most parties to take on. A simple pair should have no issue completing it, and less hands to fill with coin as they say, yes?"

Erika scowled, looking at the bottom of the paper and finding the truly measly reward of one hundred gold aurums. "Right, and there's no way to bump that price at all?"

The guildsman raised both eyebrows now, his hair flashing a streak of white as was common in the elven features when they experienced sudden or intense emotion changes. "You think you two are worth more than that, Fjordling?"

Erika stood defiantly, jutting out her hip and shouldering her warhammer. "I know we're worth more than that. I've polished weapons fer more."

"So you're a craftsman, not a fighter?" the elf replied, caught in the fiery girl's negotiations.

"Once a craftsman, still havin' the skill, but havin' a bit more of a hankerin' for violence lately," Erika said with a slight grimace, the hanging threat more than obvious.

Darion stepped back lightly, unsure of how far Erika was going to take it, but after a short pause the elf began to look very tired. The sun outside was well past set and he kept looking at the doorways, seemingly hoping no other passerby would come through them. Eventually he rubbed his temples and stared at

Erika's hand, which she had pressed on the desk, shoving the parchment back towards him.

"Very well, I have a different bounty for you," The elf responded, slipping out a separate paper and sliding it in front of Erika.

Erika wore a smug expression on her face after noting the much higher reward on this document, happy that she still had her knack for haggling. "Very nice doin' business with ye."

She signed her name onto the forms and sauntered off towards the door, Darion watching her jovial hip sway with amusement. The woman almost looked like she would start a giddy little dance. He similarly signed his name and shot a smile at the elf who looked as if he would slam his forehead into his desk, but instead simply waved his hand towards the door, practically begging the two to leave. Darion turned to find Erika rubbing a hand across one of the blue pillows, only to scowl when it apparently wasn't as soft as she was expecting. He smirked at her and motioned for them to depart.

They made their way through the streets, looking for a suitable inn that had rooms available, while also having a reasonably populated dining room as well. "No diners mean bad food," Erika reasoned to Darion, which he accepted with a shrug.

Most taverns they passed had drunk patrons even this early in the evening stumbling from the doors that would call out to the pair, who would either laugh at them or ignore them altogether.

"You're in better spirits now?" Darion commented as she waved to one of the drunks who summarily passed out on the cobblestone after trying to wave back.

She whirled around and clasped her hands behind her back, her warhammer bouncing on its sling behind her thighs. "Glad to be in a settlement again. Got less than stellar reception at yers."

Darion grimaced. "You have my apology for that. I'm glad we're doing alright here at least."

"Nothin' fer ye to apologize fer," Erika said, peeking into a tavern window and motioning for them to go inside. She paused a moment though, stopping him and taking a moment to find her words. "I'm sorry fer shovin' ye around by the river. I know ye were just tryin' to help."

He nodded, looking into her green eyes and seeing the trueness of her apology. "I'm sorry for prodding where I shouldn't have."

The two reached an understanding then, and headed into the tavern and inn by the name of *The White Carmino,* referring to the small ferret-like creatures that were commonly kept as pets among more well-off families. The interior was dimly lit with lanterns all around, four out of the ten tables occupied with a variety of patrons. A woman came over to the table they sat at shortly after, giving them a friendly smile while asking their orders.

"Easy meal an' a room fer the night," Erika said, smiling sweetly at the woman.

Darion started to protest, digging into his coin pouch to purchase his own room, but Erika stopped him. He felt his face begin to get hot, not fully understanding what was happening. When the barmaid stepped off to get their food and mark down their room, Darion leaned low to the table, unintentionally hissing at his companion. "I can get my own room!"

Erika smirked at him, flashing her eyes coyly and running a finger down a bare shoulder. "What? Shy?" She openly laughed at his fluster, entertained by the shade of red that his face ran at her comment. "No worries," she explained. "We already technically shared a room at yer house. I'll take the floor, and we save money to boot. I've fallen out of an inn bed before, so I'd rather just start on the ground."

Darion seemed to deflate on the table, laying over on it even after their food was brought to them. Simple pork slices with an assortment of vegetables. Erika was just happy to again have something that wasn't rabbit or otherwise over a campfire. She took her time eating, savoring every flavor and bite. The only distraction from her happy meal were the other patrons of the small tavern. Rough looking men who gawked at her hair, something she was used to by now, but these seemed to be gawking in a different way. Darion threw sideways glances while he gnawed on a carrot, trying not to make eye contact but also trying to be watchful in case any of them moved towards their table.

Erika scowled slightly, as if the attention soured her food. The owner behind the bar gave the men a look while he cleaned the wood, but none of them seemed to pay him any heed. One of them stood, and Erika let out a sigh. Darion reached a hand under the table and set it on his sword hilt, hoping against everything that he wouldn't need to use it. Erika turned in her seat to make eye contact with the burly man as he stepped over to them.

"Strange sight this is," he began, leaning his weight on their table. "Girl looks like she could lift five of you." His gaze pointed at Darion, breath stinking of alcohol but eyes looking clear enough to be fully aware of his surroundings.

"Aye, I likely could," Erika answered before Darion could utter a word, drawing a laugh from their intruder. She glanced curiously at his hand, noticing that he had an extra knuckle on the edge of his hand, though the finger was missing. She tried to reason that it was a birth defect, and not what her mind jumped to immediately.

"She fight your battles for you too boy?" he remarked, still talking in Darion's direction. "Not sure you're equipped to handle a woman like that."

"Delron!" the owner of the tavern behind the bar yelled out, making the large man's shoulders slump. "Stop bothering my other patrons! Back to your table."

Delron growled at Darion again, before finally stomping back to his table and roughly sitting back down. Darion breathed a sigh of relief, but Erika kept watching him, her eyes narrowed into small slits and her brow furrowed. Images flooded into her head of the ordeal in Sildenfeld the previous year. The entire root of the Daemonic incursion lay in the six fingered clutches of a cult known as the Abyssal Hand. Before leaving Sildenfeld on her pilgrimage, the resident head cleric Valk, had warned her that they may not have seen the last of the Daemon obsessed organization and that she should be careful on her journey. The fact that this man had a finger missing from his otherwise full-fingered hand was unusual at best.

Her thoughts were interrupted when the owner placed a pair of heavy wooden mugs on their table. "An apology for his behavior."

Erika waved her hand. "No problem. I'm used to bein' harassed. Comes with the looks," she winked with a wry grin.

The man shook his head and shoved the mead closer. "I insist. Half off your room too. Delron is a nuisance, and I know I should kick him out, but I still let him in every night. Please, it's the least I can do."

Darion carefully slid the mug closer to himself and thanked the owner. Erika sighed and eventually conceded to him. Still, she couldn't find the same amount of enjoyment from her meal after that. The sweet mead doing little to dispel her suspicions.

8

Death in the Dark

The night seemed endless. Erika lay awake on her bedroll, stretching her arms over her head to ease out the tension in her shoulders. Her mind filled with unease at how things had unfolded. The Abyssal Hand was the entire reason she was on this journey in the first place. Their efforts released the Daemon known as Zyrxak upon the valley that she called home. Just as the evening of the harvest festival had become euphoric for her, dancing with Irvine, possibly even leading to more, the Elder Daemon attacked and destroyed the town in the same night. The memory was a conflicting one for her. On one hand, she spent nearly her entire time at the festival with Irvine and she suspected that he had purchased the emerald pendant on the same night. The joy of the memory threatened to bring tears to her eyes.

Their flight to Sildenfeld began shortly after Zyrxak attacked, the journey causing their relationship to become even closer, yet she could not be completely happy about the memory. Many people that she knew or grew up with had perished in the initial attack, or fallen victim to Zyrxak's horrible devouring. Not long after, she gained the one that she considered to be her best friend besides Irvine, Teria the ranger, although she also endured grave injuries in the battle with the Daemon and his summoned underlings. Worse still, Irvine was ripped away from her in the final battle, after the Angelus Wystaea had joined the fray and all looked truly hopeless.

All because of the Abyssal Hand.

She found herself balling her fists in her thoughts, the muscle tension worsening the condition of her weary shoulders. She brought her hands down and rubbed under the straps of her nightshirt, trying to work out the knots to no real avail. She sighed quietly, careful not to wake the soundly sleeping Darion above her in the bed as she sat up and looked around the dark room. She carefully took his whittling knife out of his loose grip, sheathing the little blade. She smirked at him, finding it endearing how often he practiced his hobby craft, though somewhat less so when he fell asleep with the blade above her.

The sound of a door shutting in the hallway made her jolt, eyes suddenly wide open. She carefully slid out from her bedroll fully and cracked the door open slightly to find the burly Delron walking down the hall.

Why is he in an inn if he lives here? she wondered. Before she knew what she was doing, she began stepping down the hallway herself, not even bothering to change out of her scant night clothes. She followed the man as stealthily as she could, creeping down the stairs behind his stomping boots. Out of the tavern they went, the dining room dark and vacant, into the streets of Sylvanna. The cobblestones were lit poorly by occasional lamps on the sides. The darkness allowing even Erika to conceal her pale-skinned complexion, while also keeping track of the suspicious man.

Even still, she suddenly became keenly aware of her position The cold stone under her bare feet and the breeze that sent chills through her loose shirt and shorts that hardly covered her thighs at all. She was already too far to turn back now, reasoning that if the man was up to anything, she'd catch him doing it now of all times.

Into a side alley he went while she followed, suppressing the slapping sound of her bare feet against the cobbled street as much as she could. Her stomach plummeted from her gut though when she rounded the corner and lost sight of the man. Panic set in as she looked around frantically, trying to discern where he had gone. After a moment of finding nothing in the pitch-black alleyway, she turned back to the street, wondering if she had somehow missed him dashing back out.

She didn't see him come from behind her.

Erika tried to scream when he grabbed her left leg and hoisted her back, but his other hand clasped over her mouth and muffled the sound into nothingness. He held her sideways in an awkward position, feeling like her other leg would dislocate from him jerking her around.

"Now what are you doing following me girl?" he growled in her ear. "Strange tattoos you have, they supposed to mean something to me?"

Erika glanced down past his meaty hands and saw the markings down her torso and arms. Her legs were bare of them—save for her right foot where she had immolated for the briefest of moments once—but even her face bore the pattern. She realized that the power would be her only way out of this. She stopped struggling, causing a satisfied grunt from Delron. She closed her eyes and focused, willing her body to heat in an area where she had never tried before.

She had always avoided immolating her legs, but she saw no other choice here. She knew a full body immolation would burn her clothes and leave her naked in the middle of the city, so she had to focus as best she could. Her left leg flared to life, flashing a brilliant orange in the dark alleyway and blinding Delron briefly. The light was the least of his worries though, as he dropped the young woman to the ground after her burning leg scalded his hand nearly to the bone. He staggered back screaming as she recovered from her impact on the ground. She faced him resolutely, her left leg still burning to just above her knee.

"What kind of Daemon are you?" he yelled.

She grimaced, looking at his amputated sixth finger on each hand. "Ye should know yer Daemons."

The man seemed to understand her recognition as he backed away into the alley. She stalked closer, her immolated foot burning scorch marks into the ground below her and illuminating the once dark corner.

"No! Please, I'm done with that life!" he pleaded, suddenly very afraid of her. "I was a member of the Abyssal Hand, yes, but I fled! I cut off the finger that they forced onto me with their black rituals! I'm just trying to make a new start here!" His face paled almost instantly as his mind went elsewhere. "Did they send you to kill me?"

Erika straightened her back, her leg slowly cooling and returning to her natural pale-skinned appearance, curving crimson markings lingering where the Ignis power had touched. She softened her gaze, beginning to believe the man now that he was pleading for his life. She took a deep breath. "Look, I'm sorry I was suspicious of ye, and I'm sorry for burnin' ye. I'll pay a cleric to heal ye."

Delron seemed to brighten slightly, happy that she had come to an understanding and that she wasn't an assassin after his life. He began to walk forward when a hiss rang through the air. A chill ran down Erika's spine sharply and quickly, the air seemingly dropping to a freezing chill in an instant.

She watched him with widened eyes as he choked, grasping his hands to his throat but to no avail. She looked on in horror as his head rolled from his shoulders without a single drop of blood. His body fell to its knees and then toppled forward, while the head landed on the ground with a sickening slap. Erika stood frozen in the alleyway, her limbs feeling as if they were encased in ice and she was unable to free them. Icicles stabbed through her lungs and a frozen claw gripped her heart, which began to beat faster and faster. Moments later the head slowly began to melt into sand, scattering in the wind.

She looked past the corpse and into the shadows further down the hallway. The darkness seemed to move and contort, watching her the whole time. She suddenly felt very exposed and uncomfortable in the alleyway, more so than being in the middle of the street in such little clothing, but she couldn't will herself to turn and run. She thought she saw a shadow lash out at her and she instinctively immolated her right arm, forming a ball of flame in her palm and slinging it into the darkness. The black visage vacated with the bolt of fire as it flew through the air and impacted with the stone wall on the opposite side, fizzling into nothing.

Erika didn't wait to see if there was anything actually there or if it were just her imagination, as she was already running back to the tavern. Her legs pumped furiously beneath her, her feet slapping harshly on the stones. She didn't stop until she was back inside the doorway. The owner, Thrane, as he had introduced himself earlier, sat up from his chair behind the counter where he had dozed off. "Everything alright, Miss?"

She tried to nod, but couldn't in her panic, swallowing hard and wrapping her arms around herself.

"You look like you've seen a ghost," he said slowly, starting to stand. "What're you doing walking around town like that?"

She waved him off and started for the stairs, not realizing how erratic her breathing was until she spoke. "Sorry, I don't know what had gotten into me. I'll be back up in my room."

Sleep never came to her. She simply lay in her bedroll, the fabric pulled tight against her chest as she stared into the darkness of the room with tears in her eyes. Her body still shaking from the harrowing experience.

†┠

Kharim fell back further into the alley, his chest heaving and constricting in pain. He was unsure how much of the anxiety was his and how much was being fed into him by the sword he held tightly in a grip like death itself. He stepped hastily to the street, watching that beautifully feminine form disappear around the corner. The weapon flooded him with fear, especially as he looked at that bare leg of hers, painted in red markings where there had been none before.

Away! Away! The voice screamed in his mind, sounding so terrified, like nothing before. *Elementia Blood will destroy us! We are not strong enough!*

He spared a glance down at the lifeless body of the man he had just decapitated, the head completely melted away and the soul consumed by the blade he performed the deed with. Even if he was truly a *former* member of the Abyssal Hand, he was still guilty of their crimes by association. Kharim could suffer none of their kind to live, it was simply the way of things. None could be done with the life of the accursed cult, not truly. The stains of the Abyss on his blade were proof of that, black liquid that seeped upwards in defiance of gravity. Even besides that, his attack against the fire-haired woman was proof enough of his guilt, even if the girl had truly stunned and frightened Kharim in her display of such magic. At least now he knew the answer to the intriguing puzzle of those markings on her body.

72

Unless, the voice cooed along to its own musings that Kharim hadn't been listening to, *we simply kill the Elementia!*

"No!" Kharim hissed aloud, hurriedly glancing around for fear of any passersby. "She showed me kindness, I will not be her killer."

Weakness! If you have not the stomach for the duty you must do, we will simply find another!

"And what is that duty, truly?" the Haranian glared at the flat of the weapon as he held it at an angle, his own reflection in the metal painted with glowing golden eyes. "Do you truly seek to aid me in my quest, or are you steering me in such a way as to sow your own chaos?"

The long silence filled Kharim with anger. He wanted nothing more than to simply toss the blade away, perhaps in the waterways that surrounded the island city of Sylvanna, so that none may know the words of this wicked sword ever again. He could simply carry out his grim task without the damnable thing. The drunken laughter of a pair of men walking down the street distracted him from his internal debate, the two arm in arm and both grinning stupidly. In a flash he was at the rooftop above the scene of his latest killing. The two stopped with a severe lean, one glancing into the alleyway and hiccupping loudly.

"He hasn't got a head," the one said, his stupor seeming to fade at the grisly sight. "We need'ta call the knights!"

The other began laughing hysterically, apparently thinking his companion had made some delightfully amusing joke. Kharim simply shook his head as he stood, stalking away down the rooftops and sliding his weapon back into his belt. The sands in the crystalline handle roiled as if in a horrible storm, but it whispered nothing more into his consciousness. The silence proved more comforting than before, but Kharim still considered a way to rid himself of the cursed thing. "It is good she has made it this far," he mused, looking in the direction that Erika had ran, though he worried over how much she had seen of him in his grisly task.

† †

The next morning, the pair began leaving the city limits and heading to the eastern forest pass. Erika was happy that Thrane was not working the tavern floor. Instead, the barmaid, Selia, served them breakfast. She really didn't want the man to confront her about rushing back into the tavern doors wearing as little as she was last night. She wasn't sure what she'd tell him in excuse, or Darion for that matter.

Darion asked multiple times why their pace was so brisk on their way from the city, but gave up after a short while. Erika began to wonder if everything the previous night had simply been a vivid nightmare after checking the alley where she had fought Delron briefly, only to find no evidence of the encounter at all—besides the small scorch marks on the ground and opposing wall. Even despite the lack of proof, that same eerie chill she had felt crawled up her spine making her shiver in the warm daylight. She walked with an intense determination, trying to resist the urge to glance all around them, as if the thing that had killed Delron would swoop in and decapitate her as well.

Out of the walls they walked across the great bridge to the east, their pace not slowing even when they reached the forest's edge. The hinterland neighboring Sylvanna was a lush and rich place, filled with deep shades of green that Erika had never seen, even on short trips into the Sildenfeld forest with Teria. Darion, similarly, was entranced by the unusually thick wood all around them, finding himself whirling more than once at every motion and the intense feeling of being watched. Erika's previously nervous behavior was replaced by a wonderment akin to a small child, though she regained her composure upon seeing Darion's amused face when he happened to look her way.

Darion retrieved the bounty papers from his pack, looking over the rough depiction of what was titled as, 'The Devil of the Wood'. He let out a small groan at the description, several too many usages of the terms 'horrible' and 'terrifying' for his liking, though the lowermost text detailing a reward sum of four hundred aurums was plenty exciting.

"What do ye think the creature actually is? And why is the bounty so high?" Erika asked, looking over his shoulder at the rough sketch on the parchment. She traced the curving horns, hoofed feet, and thick tail of the naked creature.

Darion shrugged as he rolled the parchment up and stuffed it into his pack. "I suppose it doesn't matter much. Gold is gold, and I'm doubting we need to worry much as long as we can do the job."

The Fjordling girl eyed him, finding herself absently rubbing underneath her tunic at one of the tooth-mark scars on her midriff. "Suppose someone asked ye to do a job, and was payin' a massive sum o' aurums fer it. Yet, ye found the job to be one that was meant fer ye not to return."

"That would be greatly unfortunate," Darion answered without hesitation, unknowing of the reason behind the question.

Erika sighed. "Let's just be careful, alright? I don't like to be regrettin' things."

⚔

Their exploration into the forest became silent, save for the natural surroundings and their own footfalls. Eventually they found themselves upon a large lake, no doubt running into a river that eventually met the great Sylvannan canal itself. The water before them was crisp and cool with a shining blue gleam to it. Erika knelt down and tested the water, finding it wonderfully refreshing. She took the opportunity to fill her waterskin with the cool liquid.

Darion stretched his arms over his head, looking out and across the expanse. "Fancy a swim?" he said, a jovial tone in his voice.

Erika eyed him from her kneeling position. "Feel free to strip down and have yerself a grand time. I'll be workin' while ye play, and take that shinin' reward fer myself."

"And if I were to just push you in?" Darion asked with a raised eyebrow.

She stood and brought a hand up, immolating it in an instant. "I may just fear drownin' and accidentally scald ye with boilin' water."

The young man conceded her point with raised hands and allowed her to pass. Her smirk being the only thing to save him from believing she actually meant him any harm. "Mayhaps later, a swim might be nice," she said coyly as she started to step back into the forest. His eyes lingered on the gentle sway to her, before he shook his head and returned to the lake. His casual viewing was suddenly caught off guard by a flash of peculiar red on the side of the lake, just to his right. He squinted his eyes and brought a spyglass up from his pack to get a closer look.

Crouching down by the water was a strange creature indeed, red skin with cloven hooves at the end of its muscular legs. A thin tail whipping about with apparent mirth as the creature brought its four-fingered hands filled with water to its face and taking a deep draw. Two long curling horns extended from the creature's brow, its eyes were completely black, though large and emotive of its happiness in the cool water that dripped from its hands and onto its bare body. Darion chuckled incredulously when the creature turned forwards a bit, and it became obvious that it was a male and had all the obvious parts that marked it as such.

He fumbled with his other hand to retrieve the bounty paper from his pack. The gawking and searching was suddenly halted when the spyglass shattered, his vision through it going dark just as the creature perked its vision towards him. He jumped back at the sudden blackness and looked to his tool to find a large arrow protruding from the end of it, stopped only by the arrowhead catching on the inside of the tool as it grew smaller to the one end. He looked back up to find the creature scrambling up the shoreline and running back into the forest, Darion following suit and nearly falling over backwards in his sprint.

"Erika!" he shouted, hoping that she hadn't gone too far.

⸸

The Fjordling paused in her hike, turning back towards the lake where a swim actually sounded wonderful, considering the enchanting coolness, but she knew they were pressed for time. Darion darted into sight and grabbed her by the upper arm, his hand unable to completely envelop her considerable muscle. He dragged her with his sheer momentum and continued his sprint further into the forest.

"What're ye doing?" she called to him, her long legs barely able to catch her falling body with each massive stride as she struggled to adopt the pace. The forest become a complete blur around them, yet still Darion did not stop.

He spoke in between breaths. "I saw it! The Devil of the Wood! It's running from us, but something else is defending it, I caught an arrow in my spyglass!" He held up the destroyed tool, the long shaft topped with dark feathers jutting out the front of it, as if in a strange pride.

Erika broke free of his grip and began pumping her own legs underneath her to keep up with his pace, drawing Irvine's blade from its sheath. "Might be the reason for the price, eh?"

Darion similarly drew his own blade and he nodded, starting to understand her point from before.

9

The Heathens

Through the forest they ran, on and on, weapons bared and ready. Dodging low branches and leaping over fallen trunks, the pair intent on finding the whereabouts of the elusive Devil of the Wood. Darion hurriedly explained the appearance of the creature, Erika questioning him with a sputtering laugh. "Ye're sure it was a boy?"

"He had all the parts!" he called back with just a bit of fluster. "I just wish I saw what had shot the arrow." He glanced down at the shaft protruding from the ruined spyglass. The wood was dark color and the fletching was from a bird that was native around the northern parts of Patrias, known as a Spider Catcher. The birds were notoriously rare to find though, and even harder to capture. They seemed to have a sense for when danger was near, even more than most wild animals.

Eventually the two broke into a clearing and were suddenly surrounded by a group of rough looking men. They came to a halt, both of their chests heaving in labored breaths from their flight. After a brief pause—both parties looking over one another— one stepped up to Erika, past Darion who froze completely in his tracks. The man had a red cloth tied around his neck and a multitude of scars decorating his face, making jagged lines in his oddly neat beard. His hair hung around his ears, leaving his sharp eyes in clear view, those eyes looking her up and down. His body was wrapped in a thick leather armor, though Erika could see the chain mail underneath the myriad of cuts and abrasions in the material. A sword lay sheathed on one hip, while a dagger rested on the other.

"Look here, what a beauty," he said crassly, whistling at Erika's more feminine features that showed through her raiment. Several others of his group laughed and eyed her similarly.

In turn, Erika simply angled Irvine's longsword between herself and the man, unsure of how to proceed here. She jumped slightly at Darion's protesting call when a massive brute of a man came up from behind him and lifted him by the back of his shirt.

"Looks like she's taken boss, not sure this one'll give her up so easily," he said, laughing at Darion's attempts to break free.

She got a better look now at the total of six in their party, each wearing a red cloth around their necks. Joining the one who approached Erika was the muscular man who held Darion aloft, a smaller man in a crouch on a tree stump, one with small hat armed with a crossbow, and two in matching hoods, one with a wide bladed axe and the other with a hammer rivaling Erika's.

Erika knew that any sudden movement would probably cause this group to leap on them and slit their throats. She could remember a similar group of rough looking individuals, when she was nearer the age of Darion's sister, who had come into her father's smithy. They had to be forcibly removed by her father and Irvine's uncle when he was still a Guard Captain. That day was the first time she remembered seeing blood wrought from violence.

The first man leaned forward, getting uncomfortably close to Erika's face and took a deep breath through his nose, like he was catching her scent. "What is such a sweet young girl like yourself doing out here?"

She swallowed as discreetly as she could, trying to ignore his leering expression coming down on her. "We're here fer a bounty. Devil o' the Wood."

"Oh? An accent too, not from around here?" he asked, backing off slightly as his eyes drifted down to her breastplate. "Your friend sounds more or less local. Never met an exotic woman before." The man crouching on the tree stump giggled weirdly and whistled a catcall.

Erika wanted nothing more than to kick this man straight between the legs, but she worried that Darion would be thrown into the group of them and torn apart if she did. The leader once again interrupting her thoughts. "Well, it just so happens, that we are here on the same bounty, what a coincidence, eh?" he extended a hand suddenly towards her. "Name's Hargreave. Mayhaps you'd join us? Share in the bounty. We're a colorful bunch, but not nearly as colorful as you dear...?"

"Erika," she answered, trying to hold her scowl back.

"Erika," Hargreave echoed with a grin. "How wonderful to meet you. Bull, put the boy down, they're coming along."

The large man promptly dropped Darion, who scrambled away to his own sword that had fallen from his grasp. He retreated against Erika and she carefully placed a hand on his lower back, trying to signal him to calm down.

"So," Hargreave continued. "Did you two happen to see anything out there? Could scare someone, charging in with weapon's drawn like that, or hurt yourselves."

Erika held his stare as he again stepped past Darion and roughly ran a gloved hand across her cheek and chin, pausing on the fresh scar that she wore on her neck. His head tilted at the sight a bit, before returning to her emerald eyes. "Looks like you know your way in a fight. A bit more and you'll be as pretty as me."

The rest of the band laughed at his jest. The more diminutive looking man crouching on the stump with a twitching eye, twirled a dagger as if Hargreave was offering for him to make her 'pretty' like him. Hargreave waved his hand at him to calm his demeanor. "No need to scare the poor girl, Fink, I think she's wanting to come with us, maybe even join up. I'm sure she'll earn those scars in due time. I'll have to find a scarf that shows off that pretty neck though."

Erika shrugged as casually as she could and carefully walked behind the leader of the band, but still holding the sword in her hand. Darion followed suit shortly after, glaring at Bull, who offered a broken smile in return.

High above them in the treetops, a pair of red eyes watched the situation transpire. They were soon joined by another pair of eyes, the two speaking in an eleven tongue that whispered through the leaves in hushed tones.

"I don't think the two mean ill," the first offered.

"You struck true with your arrow," offered the second. "They came running in an attempt to find you, weapons drawn."

"Be that as it may, they are not with the first band," a chill ran through the trees. "We may yet have to aid them."

The second groaned quietly. "You always have to help the strays."

"As if you've never found a softer part in your heart on more than a few occasions."

⚔

Erika stepped lightly abreast Hargreave, his eyes seemingly always on her. Alhough if he were watching her for an attempted attack or simply imagining her in less clothes, she could not tell. Either way made her blood boil and made her want to strike the man more with every passing moment. She held her anger though, passing a casual glance over her shoulder periodically to make sure that Darion was still following her lead in the situation. Her thoughts swam with tumultuous emotions. She would gladly beat any one of these men into a bloody pulp with a moment's notice, but she knew that not a single one of them would hesitate to kill her just the same.

Darion had mentioned discomfort at their killing of the ogre before Sylvanna, and she had been able to slay goblins before then. However, this bunch was very much human. Not a single ogre, goblin, or Daemon was among them. Erika wondered if she'd even be able to follow through if she was required to kill one of them.

"What are these markings? Tattoos from your homeland?" Hargreave asked, running a hand down her arm and lifting it by the wrist.

Erika quickly pulled away from him but nodded, lying in her explanation. "Aye, marks me as a fully-fledged woman."

The man chuckled, eyes obviously lingering on her hips. "And a fully-fledged woman you definitely are."

81

She felt a shudder surge up her spine as she felt the man's eyes look her over again, conceding to plant her fist in his face if he did it again.

"More time for that later though, love," he said coyly, moving a branch out of their path and motioning to an area with apparently heavy foot traffic judging from the state of the plantlife. "Bolt! Check it out for us will you?"

The thin man leapt forward, the one with a crossbow strapped to his back and a thick quiver full of bolts on his side. He began looking over the area in a crouch, studying the prints in the trampled foliage.

"Bolt? What kind of stupid name is that?" Darion asked with a smirk, gaining a light slap to the back of the head from Bull.

Hargreave turned to him. "Ah, I suppose I hadn't done any real introductions yet, have I? My apologies." He turned to the rest of the group, naming each one of them in order. "The big guy is Bull, as you know. The one with the crossbow is Bolt, cause that's what he uses, obviously. The shaky little guy with the knife is Fink, he's our little rat. Lastly, the two in the hoods are our resident twin brothers, Axe and Hammer."

"Guess ye like to keep everyone straight?" Erika mused, looking around the group as they nodded or puffed out their chest in response to their name.

Hargreave laughed at her remark. "You could say that. Quite honestly it just softens the blow when they die, right? No matter the name though, we make up The Heathens, as we like to be called."

Axe and Hammer shrugged at the comment when Erika glanced at them. Bull and Fink were busy playing some kind of strange word game, and Bolt was still looking over the markings in the soft ground.

"More than one," he said a moment later, pointing at separate sections of the grouping. "Looks to be a common crossroads, but these are all different. There's a large set there, but then a smaller set here. The smaller set is more fresh, so unless the creatures can get smaller, there's much more than just one. Not all cloven hooves either, not sure we're the first on their trail. Lot of 'em are barefoot though."

Hargreave stood over them, watching each of Bolt's motions with interest, before smiling at the rest of the group. "Well, more than one creature, means more than one bounty, right? Even more to split with our new friends, Spitfire and..."

Erika smirked slightly at the dubbing of 'Spitfire'. Darion crossed his arms and looked expectantly at Hargreave, who seemed unable to think up an apt name for the young man.

The man waved his hand to the side and grinned. "Hey, I haven't seen much of you yet, maybe when we get into a scuffle we'll find out what your name will be, right? Blade or Sword seems a little simplistic for you."

Darion muttered under his breath about Axe and Hammer, increasingly perturbed by the band.

The group continued on after Bolt decided on a direction that would lead them closer to these creatures. Hargreave now taking up the rear of the group and pulling Erika by the waist alongside him.

"Now don't you worry, sweetheart. I give everybody nicknames, and while I was truthful about it making possible deaths easier to handle, it'd be a shame for the world to lose such a pretty face. So, I'll be sure to keep you out of harm's way," he said quietly, patting her on the backside and stepping ahead of her.

Erika felt her body heat start to rise, and was shaken from her thoughts only by the audible steam rising from the bare skin on her arms. The crimson patterns that covered her flesh beginning to flare to life and brighten. She turned away trying to calm herself, running her hands over her face and through her hair. It took all her focus to will her body to cool, still finding the task exceptionally difficult this time. Eventually she regained her composure and stepped off to catch up with the band of mercenaries that still held Darion in the middle of their march. Thankfully none of the Heathens seemed to notice her magic starting to activate with her anger. Hargreave simply glanced back at her after a bit and leered down her legs again. *That certainly doesn't help,* she thought.

† †

Much time passed and the talkative group had eventually fallen silent. The thicker depths of the forest starting to cause them some issue when it came to navigation of the winding paths around the massive trees that only became larger and larger. Just as they were beginning to lose hope of finding their quarry, they finally found it. Darion recognized it as the same creature he had seen at the lake, red skinned and with a naive look in its youthful face. Its large black eyes went wide as it saw the group coming towards it, especially as Hargreave's chiseled features curled into a wicked smile.

The *twang* of a crossbow sounded out as a bolt flew through the air, whistling as it drew closer to the creature. It turned to try and run but the missile caught it in the back of the thigh and it fell unceremoniously to the ground, reaching back and cradling the bleeding wound.

Erika grimaced at the display, but was unsure of what she could do. She was ready to slay this creature up until just a moment ago when she saw fear in its eyes. The goblins and ogre only held rage and blood lust, causing her no issue when it came to battling and killing the monsters. This supposed 'Devil of the Woods' was nothing more than what seemed to be a helpless child.

Her new companions didn't bear the same sympathy, as they began rushing forward, weapons bared. Hargreave stalked forward slowly with a hungry look on his face, a look that caused Erika's stomach to rise into her throat. Darion was nowhere to be found, she realized, and just when Erika realized he was missing she found him rushing ahead and meeting the head of the charge. Her expression changed from disgust to shock in the blink of an eye, as the young guard pulled his gambit.

Darion ran as hard as his legs could carry him, diving in front of the raging plow of mercenaries to cover the red skinned creature with his own body. He whipped his sword around furiously, slamming it against the oncoming attack of Axe with all his strength. His arms became numb as soon as Bull's greatsword came down, deflecting it into a tree root to the side. A burning pain shot through his leg when Fink jammed a dagger into the side of his thigh. "Back off, kid!" Hargreave roared. "Gods, I might just call you Dumbass at this point."

Erika watched for only a moment, before catching on to what was happening and steeling her resolve. She ran up behind Hargreave and kicked him in the back of the knee, causing him to buckle. It had been many years since she had used her bare hands to fight anyone. She quickly readied herself for the inevitable pain in her knuckles. Hargreave barely looked back to her before her fist met his jaw squarely in a right hook that sent his head twisting horribly and his body falling to the ground. She spat a curse at him and grinned wildly in her victory and satisfaction, only damning the fact that she hadn't thought to pull a weapon before attacking him. She grabbed Irvine's sword from her pack as she began running up behind the rest of the group to try and aid Darion in his failing defense.

Before she arrived, the forest around them exploded into motion. Dark figures fell from the trees in graceful pounces and whipping wicked bows into action. Bolt jolted in odd directions as arrows sprouted from his back, one going cleanly through his neck with a bloody splatter. Erika halted in surprise as he slammed onto the ground, his head cracking against a raised tree root. One of his wide and lifeless eyes was discolored red, matching the spattered greenery around his corpse. Fink narrowly dodged several of the arrows and quickly dashed behind Bull, who similarly turned and ran. Several arrows nicked his back, but none made full purchase through his thick muscle. Axe and Hammer disappeared shortly after, quickly grabbing the unconscious body of Hargreave as they fled.

Just as quickly as it began, the battle was over. Erika stood stunned at the scene that seemed to play out before her heart finished another beat. Darion laid to the side of the naked red-skinned creature, who gripped at his pierced leg while watching the young man with an attentive gaze. Darion clutched at several wounds across his body, breathing heavily and looking unaware of his surroundings. Erika was instantly surrounded by the newcomers and she quickly recognized their ebon skin, carmine-colored irises on black eyes, and silvery hair. "Aash elves," she breathed, several of the warriors exchanging looks at her recognition.

The group stood in a stark contrast to the one aash elf she had ever heard of, F'Skar, the mate of Sárif in Sildenfeld. The short haired elf had bore numerous robes and was weak of body, causing his eventual departure from his tribe as she knew from stories Sárif would tell her. These however, stood bare to the forest, some wearing only loose coverings such as loincloths. Each of them stood at least a full foot taller than Erika, sporting thick musculatures that were easily on par with her own toned body.

Their hair draped down their backs, some loose and others braided, a few nearly to their thighs in length. Three in the group of nearly twenty bore glittering markings that drew a curious glance from Erika, which was interrupted by the tip of a spear being aimed just under her chin. Her hands shot into the air, trying to prove her intentions to the amazingly skilled group that had freed them of their captors in a battle that had lasted seconds. She winced when Irvine's sword hit the soil, regretting even pulling it out instead of her warhammer.

One of the elves stepped forward, a beautiful female with her long ashen hair tied into a single thick braid that dropped to the middle of her back. A shimmering pattern of crimson wove around her shoulders and down to her elbows, while also extending around her back and onto her bare sides. Her muscularly feminine form was barely covered by a loincloth and a crossing wrap that covered her breasts, several pouches and two axes with strange runes carved into the blades decorated the belt around her waist. She grabbed Erika's wrists with a strength even greater than what she was expecting from the stern looking woman, tying a leather strip around her wrists to bind them. The only surprise that came to her was the intense heat that radiated from the woman's skin, not immediately unpleasant to the touch but much warmer than any living creature she had ever come into contact with.

Erika didn't resist, instead watching as another elf approached Darion's shaking form. This one was a male, wearing a simple loincloth as well. A beautifully verdant design ran from the tops of his shoulders, around the sides and back of his neck, and reaching up to border his shining red eyes. He wore his silver hair mostly loose, save for a few thin braids around the sides, the strands shifting to the side as he leaned over the wounded man. With not a word, he ripped part of Darion's trouser leg where Fink had stabbed him, inspecting the wound as Darion himself seemed about to pass out. Erika watched with curiosity as he retrieved a small coffer from a pouch on his hip and drew a pitch-colored cream, spreading it over the deeply bleeding wound.

Another elf, not bearing any of the sparkling markings, came forward and took the small creature that had led all of them here and lifted him into his arms. He was careful as to not aggravate the crossbow bolt that protruded from its leg. The elf that tended to Darion lifted him off the ground and the group was led further into the forest, the large female guiding Erika by the arm.

† †

Hargreave shot up with a string of curses, causing the remaining members to jump up as if they were under attack again. The scarred man rubbed his jaw where Erika had struck him, grinning wickedly while glancing around. "Damn, she really is a Spitfire. Bolt?"

Bull shook his head, Hargreave simply nodding his understanding. He stood a moment later, gathering stock of his surroundings and grinning again. "Well, looks like we've got work to do. There's still a bounty, and I think Spitfire and Loverboy are about to steal it out from under us.

The remaining members all nodded their agreement, starting off in search of their lost prize.

10

The Aash Elves

Erika marveled at the open space between the thick arboreal wall, a great open plaza of sorts made entirely from dense wood and foliage. Homes were built into the sides of the massive trees around them, and the entire area was lit only by spare beams of sunlight that glittered down from the thick canopy of leaves and branches far over their heads. Aash elves made their way to and fro all around, all varying greatly in appearance and sizes, the smallest children coming only to Erika's knee in height, save for the babes held close to the breasts of a handful of females that disappeared into homes at their arrival. Most wore less clothing than the warriors that they were led in with, while even more were completely bare as some stopped and watched the oncoming procession. The temperature of the place seemed raised considerably, Erika being reminded of the heated flesh of the hand still gripping her upper arm that likely permeated their home at all times due to how many of the warm bodies there were, as well as how isolated the clearing was.

Out of the corner of her eye, Erika began to see more of the red skinned creatures emerging from the homes as well. Most of them were much larger than the one that had led them here, leading her to suspect that he was younger. They all similarly wore very little clothing, though any that did appeared more tattered and haphazard than the deliberate aash coverings. Many of the creatures bore obvious wounds as well, a female's arm slung from her neck, a male's leg wrapped in a bandage with a tight splint against it while he leaned heavily on a crutch. Erika found her brow furrowing further with each of the creatures she found.

Eventually, she was led to a large open tree on the far edge of the sizable clearing and was relieved of her belongings by another female warrior that had accompanied them. The way she took Erika's things didn't strike her as aggressive, so she didn't protest even when Irvine's satchel was taken from her. The one that gripped her by the arm handed away Irvine's sword to the other, which caused Erika to look after it wistfully, the blade covered with soil from where she had dropped it. Moments later, she was guided to sit on the ground in front of the great tree. The female that had been guiding her the entire way sat next to her, crossing her legs underneath her and making herself comfortable.

Erika started to question, but was unsure if these elves could understand Patrian. She was answered a moment later when she spoke without looking at her.

"I am to guard you," the muscular female said, her voice deep but pleasant. She leaned on one knee, sitting most unladylike Erika noticed with idle amusement. "You seem to be very strong, so I am to guard you, because I am considered the strongest of my tribe."

Erika nodded her understanding, not wanting to seem hostile in any way, even accidentally. So, she sat calmly on her knees for what seemed like ages. Not far off, she could see a very wide room in an open tree where Darion had been laid out and stripped of his armor and much of his clothing. The male elf with the green markings tended to him with bandages and more of the black cream. The area was swimming with the dark-skinned elves now, Erika finding herself smiling slightly at the sight of all the silver hair and red or purple hued eyes. There was a subtle peacefulness to the place, and the general positivity everyone had was infectious. Her gaze eventually met her guard once again and her eyes drifted down to the glittering red markings on her dark flesh. The designs curled around her arms and down her considerably muscled back, eventually reaching down and hugging her rib cage on either side. The aash woman grimaced and raised her hand to Erika's jaw, forcibly turning her to face forwards to the tree before them. "They are none of your concern," she said harshly, causing Erika to blush slightly from her unintentional staring, not that any of them seemed to mind their bodies being on display. Erika wasn't sure she'd ever seen so much naked skin.

Eventually, the curtain of the tree before them shook open. A much smaller, older, aash elf hobbled forward, barely held by her twisting cane below her. She wore thick robes that extended up into a hood that hung low over her head, contrasting greatly to the rest of the scantily clad elves but more familiar to Erika from the tales of F'Skar while she lived in Sildenfeld. The elder stared at her with shaking eyes and eventually flopped down on a low stone that she used for a stool, putting her on equal level with the Fjordling.

They sat and stared for a long time, Erika trying not to blink as she looked into the woman's faded red on black eyes. Erika's eyes barely caught a shimmer of blue in her mostly covered silver hair, something that Erika knew to be a sign of happiness in the only other aash she knew of, though colors could be different for individual elves. Finally, the old elf spoke.

"Untie her hands," she said with a thick accent, motioning with her cane. The one who sat next to Erika seemed to hesitate, but obliged nonetheless. The elder smiled, another streak of blue flashing through her hair. "What brings you to us, young one?"

Erika rubbed her wrists where the leather had chafed slightly while she thought on an answer. "I'm headin' northwards from Sildenfeld. My companion and I stopped to try and earn a bit o' money, and accepted a bounty that led us out here. The bounty was fer that one," she said, pointing towards the red skinned creature who began screaming just then, as the elf with the green markings ripped the broken crossbow bolt from his leg, causing Erika to wince slightly. "I can see now that our bounty was misplaced," she added.

The woman next to her seemed to relax slightly, seeing that Erika wasn't an immediate threat. She leaned back in her seated position, her shoulders tightening as she rested on her arms while Erika did her best not to stare at the elf's firm abdomen and sides. The elder thought for a long while, making direct eye contact with Erika once the Fjordling finally looked back up.

"You say you come from Sildenfeld?" she asked slowly.

Erika nodded eagerly, and pointed to her satchel against another tree not far from them. "Aye, in my bag, there's a scarf. It belonged to F'Skar, he was an aash too."

A male elf retrieved the leather satchel at the old elf's call, depositing it to Erika. The female warrior tensed slightly, seeming annoyed that the elder granted this outsider her belongings so easily. A moment later, Erika produced the beautifully intricate scarf with colorations of red and gold, symbols across it seeming to spark interest and amazement to any of the elves who were watching the exchange.

"And what of F'Skar?" the elder asked.

Erika's expression darkened as she recalled the fate of Sárif's mate. "Sadly, he was killed in a conflict that occurred late last year."

The old woman seemed to shrivel further, tears rimming her dim eyes as well as the eyes of the female who sat next to her, Erika noticed. They composed themselves quickly. "I am very sorry to learn of this tragedy. F'Skar was my brother, as well as the uncle to your handler, F'Lessa, and her brother F'Skal," she said, motioning to the one that sat beside her and the apparent healer that still tended to the wounded pair. The former simply nodded, bringing a hand up to clear her eyes, flashes of purple streaking through her thickly braided hair.

"You're F'Skar's family?" Erika asked, F'Lessa nodding slightly. "I'm very glad to have met ye all then. I sadly only heard stories of 'im, from Sárif."

The older aash woman seemed distracted suddenly, Erika wanting more than anything to try and comfort her, but was unsure of how to do so. "I am F'Tara," the elder finally spoke again. "I am the standing shaman, archdruid, and leader of our tribe. The Shalti welcome you into our midst, Erika of the Fjordlands. Your father and his friends were an interesting group, my niece and nephew were only children when they came through this very wood."

Erika's eyes widened a bit. "How did ye know my name and heritage? And ye knew my papa?"

Before she could answer, it seemed F'Tara was asleep on her stone stool. F'Lessa leaned back further, uncrossing her legs and extending one off to the side, drawing an unconscious glance from Erika. Her thigh seemed nearly as wide around as both of her own. "She's the shaman. She knows things just from looking at you," she explained, seeming suddenly very casual in her demeanor. Erika raised an eyebrow at her, impressed by her distinct lack of an accent when speaking in the Patrian language. F'Lessa's eyes looked up to the thick canopy high above, squinting from the spare sunlight peeking through as she let out a deep sigh.

"I'm sorry about yer uncle," Erika said, her hand reaching slightly towards the elf.

"How was he?" she asked plainly, not moving.

Erika watched her eyes, and spoke slowly. "I understand he was happy. Sárif spoke very fondly of 'im."

F'Lessa smirked slightly and met her gaze. "And you never met him?" Erika shook her head, making F'Lessa chuckle. "Nothing for you to be sorry for then. I hadn't seen him since I was small."

"Well, I'm sorry ye never got to see 'im again," Erika offered. The stern elf seemed to soften a bit and smiled at her.

"Make yourself at home. I doubt your friends from before are finished chasing our guests," she said, motioning to the red skinned creatures who still spectated the newcomers, especially Darion, who was starting to stir. She stood a moment later, and Erika strained to look up at her great height from her sitting position. "Let me know if you need anything. Me specifically, don't bother anyone else."

She stepped off a moment later, her bare feet making hardly a sound in the soft ground. Erika watched her leave and then leaned back on her hands, smiling at the elder who had begun to snore slightly.

† †

Darion sat under the wide open cavity in the massive tree, holding a small cup filled with a bitter tasting liquid. The elf, F'Skal, who had been in the middle of tending to him when he had awakened from his wound-induced sleep, had told him it was a medicinal drink that would help him recover his strength. Everything had been a shock at first. Last he had been fully aware, he was defending the small red creature from the Heathens and figured himself likely to die for it. Then, he was suddenly awakening to a strange place he never could have imagined. He was thoroughly perplexed to see he was surrounded by many of the red skinned creatures. Survatri, he learned them to be called. Runaway slaves of the Daemonic Dominion of Wrath in the Seven Hells, and were now being harbored by the aash elves. The one he had saved was coming closer to him now, a smaller specimen and not fully grown as he could see in the features and proportions of the male and female variety not far off.

"Brother?" it said quietly, as it had taken to calling Darion after he had saved it. "Are you needing anything?"

Darion let out a deep sigh and looked at the small creature with a friendly smile. "No Vati, I'm quite fine. You should be getting some rest yourself, getting shot in the leg isn't any fun."

Vati seemed to sadden slightly, as if upset that he could not serve Darion. "Yes, it is not fun. Daemons hurt us more. Bad men hurt you more."

The once guardsman looked into the dark, featureless eyes of his new friend and sighed again. "Well, you're safe here, with these elves."

"Yes! Elves are good. Vati is glad that Brother thinks so too," he said, brightening again.

Darion couldn't help but smile at that face, no matter how alien to him it looked, especially not after he had so comically looked through his clothes that were set to the side. Vati seemed fascinated by his shirt and trousers, though he had mixed up which was to be worn on the torso, and which the legs. He knew these creatures were technically Daemons themselves, although he couldn't help but see them as innocent creatures that wouldn't hurt anyone. Eventually, Vati limped off towards a group of other survatri children, and began playing a little hand game with them.

"That one has taken a liking to you," came the soft voice from behind him. His healer, F'Skal, came into view. His muscular frame shining in the low sunlight as he set down a tray of various creams and balms. He sat next to Darion, who couldn't help but admire the glittering emerald markings that spread from his upper back and onto his neck and jaw. Darion had always heard of these elves as being dangerous and savage, their lack of 'civility' as some were apt to say. How untrue all of those statements seemed now, as he watched the intriguing folk that made their way through the small village of trees. He figured a bunch of humans had once seen a group of the naked elves rout a group of armed soldiers or a large beast, and brought back a story of terrifying dark elves in the wilderness.

Their behavior was incredibly efficient, no quarrels or arguments breaking out, and every task was done with a smile on their faces. Besides a few wandering individuals, Darion had only ever seen the one sol elf at the bounty guild. He found them to be truly beautiful creatures, not a one of them looking like they couldn't keep pace with a sprinting deer.

"Are you alright?" F'Skal asked, startling Darion from his thoughts.

He stammered for a moment, feeling embarrassed that his gaze had lingered for so long. "Yes, I'm fine. Just admiring your home is all."

The elf smirked slightly, bringing a leg closer to himself where he sat. "Must be quite different from your own home."

"It is. They are all so involved. In my hometown, everyone is so caught up in their own business that they don't give a damn about anyone else," he said, thinking back to some of the gruffer members of his town.

"In aash tribes, we are all one," F'Skal explained. "There is always a helping hand, and anything done for the good of oneself, is for the good of the tribe. All are eager to help all."

Darion couldn't help but laugh at the thought. "If only. Where I come from, if it doesn't benefit you, there's no point in doing it. I'm honestly kind of jealous."

F'Skal looked to him curiously. "I am jealous of you though, and your freedom to walk the world."

"Freedom to follow that one more likely," he answered, motioning to Erika who was currently having her hair braided by an aash woman and a couple of survatri children. "Dad said to escort her, but I'm unsure of who's doing the escorting."

"You are her mate?" the elf asked as he watched the young woman, causing Darion to nearly choke on his bitter drink.

"No, no. She's just a friend," he explained quickly after regaining his voice.

The elf's thin eyebrow raised. "You have no interest in her?"

Now Darion hesitated, bringing a chuckle from F'Skal. "It's not that I don't have any interest in her. She's beautiful. Her bright hair, and those green eyes. But I think she's got someone else," Darion finally said. "I don't think I could keep up with her even if I tried to anyway."

F'Skal sat back slightly, continuing to watch the Fjordling now that the elf had finished braiding her hair, and was now holding a looking glass up for her. "I think I understand," F'Skal said, giving a shrug. "Well, perhaps you will find a mate elsewhere then."

Darion whirled on him. "And do you have a mate, nosy elf?"

F'Skal laughed again. "A mate I have not. I am dedicated fully to my duties as a healer. That, and no females have seemed to take an interest in me. Nor do I have the interest in males that my uncle had."

Darion found himself staring at the elf's handsomely angular face and attractive features, wondering what was causing a lack of interest in such a man. He found his answer when F'Skal pointed out his twin sister, F'Lessa. Her incredibly beautiful frame only interrupted by what seemed to be an expression of perpetual anger in her angled eyes. She would soften slightly when she met with F'Skal or Erika, but Darion suspected that she was the reason the other females kept their distance from her brother. He was only just becoming friends with F'Skal, and he already worried that the massively muscled woman would beat him to a pulp.

His thoughts became interrupted when F'Skal stood suddenly and jogged off to meet a male elf who had just climbed down the side of one of the trees, another setting off up the side of the bark with incredible speed and agility. Darion heard him ask something in their native tongue, the other elf stretching his arms over his head and flexing his back, angling his completely bare body in such a way that made Darion flush suddenly and glance away, opting to watch the elf climbing up the massive tree.

F'Skal returned after a short conversation with him, and nodded to Darion. "Seems you two came at the best possible time. There's a storm coming, and it looks rather large."

Darion continued watching the elf as he climbed, until he disappeared into the treetops far above them. Nothing made a better watch tower than these trees, he figured. He nodded to F'Skal and regarded Erika as she stepped lightly towards them, her bare feet making soft sounds in the ground below her.

"Feelin' better, Darion?" she asked, then turned to the elf beside him. "Ye're F'Skal, right?"

The aash nodded and smiled warmly. "And you are Erika, ward of my sister."

Erika nodded back, looking over her shoulder as if nervous about something. F'Lessa appeared at her opposite shoulder and leaned over the smaller woman. "You're not bothering my brother, are you?"

Erika squealed at the elf's sudden voice, barely stammering a reply. "I was just sayin' hello is all!"

F'Lessa grinned at her as she straightened her back, Darion finding himself staring at the powerful woman as she crossed her muscled arms. Her neatly braided silver hair gleamed in the sunlight, with a pale yellow streak running through it, all alongside the intricate shimmering markings. He quickly looked away when her gaze met his. Her expression hardened, the yellow streak turning a strange color between red and pink, before flashing away entirely.

Erika broke the silence as her head snapped between both of them quickly. "I've been meanin' to ask, what are the markin's on your bodies?"

F'Skal explained past F'Lessa's half-hearted protest. "Gem dust that amplifies our natural abilities and skills."

Both Darion and Erika's heads cocked to the side, still confused. F'Skal chuckled before he continued again. "I'm sure you've both noticed that we aash elves wear significantly less clothing than what I'm sure you're used to seeing."

"Or none at all," Erika interjected with a giggle as a pair of rather well-endowed women passed by with nothing between them and the air around them. Darion followed her gaze and quickly averted his eyes, his face reddening.

F'Skal nodded with a light smirk. "This is because our bodies are much warmer than other creatures and it is uncomfortable for us to wear much more than this, even in winter. As such, we are able to undergo a ritual, where shattered gems and crystals are ground into dust and spread across our skin."

F'Lessa continued for him. "The dust melds into the flesh from the heat of our bodies combined with that of a sauna we create for the ritual. The latent magic within the crystals seeps into our bodies, giving us special abilities we would not normally have. For example, my brother has the dust of an emerald on his shoulders and head, which allows him greater perception and skill when it comes to healing."

"And my sister is painted with the dust of a ruby, which greatly increases her already considerable strength," F'Skal finished, to which F'Lessa raised her left arm to show the dust glittering in the light, extending underneath her crossing wrap and down her ribs.

Darion sat back and placed his cup on the ground beside him, staring perhaps a bit too long at F'Lessa's arm. He broke away once he realized his eyes moving down the limb to her body where her crossing halter had shifted off of her slightly. "That is very interesting, and rather incredible if I may say," he directed towards F'Skal.

Erika placed her fingers to her chin in thought. "Sárif never mentioned anythin' like that on F'Skar."

F'Skal raised his hand slightly to garner her attention. "Unfortunately, our uncle was born with a rare affliction that caused his body to be extraordinarily cold by aash standards. This meant that he was constantly wrapped in our thickest of robes, and commonly stayed inside due to the chill rain we experience. He would have—quite literally—frozen to death on a warm summer's day. This also means that he was unable to undergo the ritual to be painted with the dust," a slightly saddened look spread over his face. "I suspect that if he had been able to, his hands and arms would have been dressed in amethyst, considering his love for artistry."

The two humans jumped when a crack of thunder resounded through the glade, rain beginning to pour through the thick treetops, like the bolt had split a hole in the sky enough for the water to fall freely. F'Lessa stood in the rain, seemingly unbothered by it as light steam started to rise from her dark flesh. Conversely, Erika dashed under the cover of the tree to stand beside Darion and F'Skal. F'Lessa chuckled lightly at her sudden flight, but her eyes flashed to the entrance of the glade when another elf shouted out. All of them were rocked from their feet when an even louder sound crashed outwards, shrapnel flying through the village and several of the dark elves being flung wildly from the force. Erika and Darion looked on in horror as the closest to the blast were separated from their limbs, and others were impaled with flying pieces of debris. F'Lessa was off in a heartbeat, padding through the mud and rallying the warriors.

Darion started to stand, wincing from his still lingering wounds, while F'Skal urged him to sit down.

Erika stood again and looked out to the exploded entryway of the peaceful village. She scowled when Hargreave's laughing visage came into view. The rest of the Heathens flooded into the glade and took the opportunity of surprise to begin cutting down any elves and survatri that were in range. Erika's rage began to boil over and, without even realizing it, her arms immolated up to her shoulders with a flash of light, startling both Darion and F'Skal. Hargreave scanned over the chaos and then met eyes with Erika. That wicked grin spread across his face.

11

BLOOD AMONGST THE TREES

The massive man was once known as Orak, but now he was known only as Bull. His greatsword was larger than any that most had ever seen and his strength was unrivaled. He was able to punch through solid wood doors, and had been known to cave heads with a clap of his great hands, but today he tested his strength. Bull lived for this kind of test, one where death was on the line, where it was him or them. The dark elves were also large and muscular, and were able to hold their own against Bull, but still he was able to best them. Their ranks fell around him and his broken smile was wide, as he believed himself the better. That smile faltered slightly when he heard a call that he couldn't understand, and all the elves began to fall away from his intrusion.

Once they cleared, only one stood before him. An incredibly muscled female, her flesh seeming to steam in the cold rain that fell around them. Across her shoulders, upper arms and her rib cage was a strange red marking. *That marking must mean she is their best warrior,* Bull thought to himself, growing even more excited.

Bull wanted nothing more than to fight her. His gapped grin returned to his face as they stared at one another.

F'Lessa's silvery braided hair had begun to come loose in the madness that followed the sudden siege, and now lay matted across her face. Her normally silver locks held solid streaks of red, bleeding down the strands and manifesting her fury. This giant of a human in front of her was of the same height as her, but this did nothing to deter her resolve. The massive man threw his greatsword to the ground and raised his thick arms in an obvious challenge to her. She obliged and threw her own axes to the mud below. Words need not be spoken between warriors.

Bull began his charge.

F'Lessa matched his speed, but with much greater ferocity.

††

Vati was terrified, not only for the second time since he had escaped the terrible realm of the Seven Hells, but somehow the second time in the same day. The violent humans that had chased and wounded him were back again and he was scared that he and his kin would be taken once again to be used as slaves. He ran through the corridors of trees in a desperate attempt to flee from the men, tripping over his wounded leg and falling into the sloppy wet ground below. He didn't know where the others of his *zelak* had gone and he felt so impossibly alone in that cold stream of water from the sky. He slowly pushed himself up from the mud as a cackling laugh resounded above him and his dark eyes rose to find a thin man with shaking hands holding two jagged daggers. Vati remembered this one, and how he had cut Brother in the fight before.

Fink bent down and grabbed the creature by one of his horns after jamming one blade into the soft earth below.

"You look familiar," his raspy voice breathed into Vati's frightened face, and Vati felt tears falling down his cheeks. Their warmth mixed with the cold rain.

††

Darion watched the chaos break out, cursing the Heathens for being able to find them so quickly. He scanned the battle as it progressed. Hammer and Axe folded into a large group of the Aash elves, while F'Lessa faced off with Bull. Erika had run off to meet Hargreave he knew, while Bolt was most definitely dead from the furious arrows, leaving only one of the Heathens missing.

"Fink," he said with panic shaking his voice. He looked around hurriedly, finding no sign of the rat, nor a sign of Vati among the survatri who were taking shelter in the small infirmary. His stomach dropped in his gut.

He dashed with all his strength to grab his sword and search for the little one that had begun to call him Brother.

⚔

Erika ran into the middle of the battle, dodging around the rushing elves who mostly went to one side. Her gaze fixed on Hargreave and his laughing face. Hargreave too, made eye contact with her as he watched her approach. He deftly moved around any elves that attacked him and countered them viciously with his blade. Holding up a finger towards Erika for every aash that lay dead beside him. Her rage increased with each additional digit he raised.

She made off in a sprint towards him, balling her fists together and focusing her energy into a small orb of flame, slinging it with all her might towards the sadistic mercenary. He dodged to the side, the bolt sailing past him and deeper into the forest, but Erika didn't expect to actually hit him with it.

Hargreave turned back to her, shock and surprise contorting his face. He twisted around and brought his blade around in a slice, but it was slapped aside by Erika's hardened hand, her opposite arm lashing out into a straight punch towards him. He dodged awkwardly, not expecting her to deflect his sword with her bare hand, and she took the opportunity to sweep her leg under his. With a sputtering cry, his leg was ripped from under him, sending him cascading into the mud. Before she could strike downwards though, he was rolling backwards and back onto his feet in an instant.

"Seems those markings don't just signify you as a woman after all. I've heard stories about your kind. I have to say though," he said, noting the Ignis magic that flowed from her flesh and angling his sword tip at her in a diminutive stance. A wry grin came across his face. "You are even more stunning when you're angry, Spitfire."

She screamed out at him and lashed out further, their duel having only just begun.

⚔

F'Lessa ground her heels into the mud at the last moment as Bull threw his right fist forwards. The more agile elf dodged underneath and to his side, swinging her left arm inwards to connect with his ribs. The massive man let out a pained exhale, but came around for another strike just as quickly.

The two muscled combatants traded blows for a while, Bull connecting strikes on F'Lessa's sides and jaw, while her own strikes landed similarly. Each hit making loud percussive sounds past the drowning din of the rain, but both took each strike in stride and their furious battle continued. The other aash around knew better than to get in the way of the fighters, finding a way to blockade against any of the intruder's allies instead.

F'Lessa gritted her teeth together and slammed a quick series of punches to his abdomen, then quickly spun around to dodge his two-handed blow. Around she turned and used her momentum to sling another strike into his back.

Bull recovered from the attack and turned with a smile on his face. She lunged again, but he caught her fist in his hand. Her opposite arm came in just after, but was met with the same. They stood in a locked contest of strength for what seemed like eternity, her hair coming fully loose from its braid and matting to her face and shoulders. Steam rose freely from her flesh now as her body temperature rose, adrenaline and blood pumping furiously through her corded muscles.

Bull grinned wickedly, speaking with only a little difficulty through the strain. "You'll all fetch a nice price somewhere."

F'Lessa screamed in rage, activating the magic bestowed upon her by the shaman's ritual. The ruby dust in her flesh brightened with her call and flared to violent life. Her skin heated further, and Bull could feel her knuckles alone nearly scalding his palms. Her body size seemed to increase suddenly, as she threw her arms out wide and took his hands with them. She whipped her wrists around and gripped his forearms, snapping his arms out and twisting down, pulling both shoulders from their sockets. Her grasp crushed through the bones where she held, and to Bull's horror, his left arm ripped away at the shoulder adding a quick shower of blood to the torrent of rain. The sound of a long and agonized howl filled the air, before F'Lessa released his intact arm and slammed her palm into Bull's chest, sending him flying off the ground and crashing into the mud.

F'Lessa stepped forward, her chest heaving from the fight. Her free hand wiped a streak of blood that had come from her lips and nose as she dropped the severed arm from her grasp. Bull was struggling to his feet, having trouble breathing through the shock. The powerful strike had surely broken several ribs, not to mention the searing anguish that spread from his severed limb. He looked up with gasping sounds escaping his throat, and he knew fear. He was able to angle himself up on his knees, before cradling his remaining demolished arm in his lap and mumbling incoherently in a native tongue from the eastern Regions. She growled as she stepped towards him, a massive wall of steam obscuring her ebon flesh.

"We'll fetch no price for you," she said to him, moving around his torso methodically. She wrapped one arm around his jaw, her other hand on his head, and exhaled slowly. With a violent twisting motion, Bull's neck shattered with a sound like a twig splintering against a tree's trunk, his body falling motionless into the mud below.

⚔ ⚔

Axe and Hammer were right at home, dancing around each other and batting down elves left and right. Blood slung from their weapons at the edges of their deadly spin. Hargreave was off having his fun with Spitfire, and the two of them wanted to return to his side and aid in beating her down. The two relished the thought of capturing the young woman and holding her captive for a few months. Torture was a particular love of theirs, and when it was to repay a person who crossed the Heathens, it was all the sweeter. The two of them had been with Hargreave the longest and knew how he could get when he was angry with someone. They only hoped they could join in with him for Spitfire's punishment.

F'Skal loosed two arrows quickly into the middle of the grounds. Though he wasn't surprised when the two mercenaries were able to avoid the shots. He leapt from his perch and welcomed the two into battle. They exchanged a look, before charging at him with their weapons bared. F'Skal was much more nimble than them, easily dancing between their strikes, parrying blows with the thick limbs of his bow, and slapping them with it as he passed. Their boots slid in the mud slightly at the end of every charge, both becoming obviously frustrated with the tenacity of the elf. They exchanged looks each time he evaded any damage from either of them, continuing with even harder, more aggressive routines.

Much to their dismay, other elves had been bolstered by the staggering that F'Skal had provided. The brothers quickly found themselves on the defense soon enough, and as a group of three kept them in guarding stances, F'Skal glanced over to see his sister ending her own battle not far off. Axe and Hammer became desperate when they saw Bull fall lifeless to the ground, their resolve only barely held up by Hargreave's taunting voice from the front of the village. However, they quickly came to realize that their initial chaos was spent, and their strikes reflected that.

After moving back in, F'Skal easily sidestepped Hammer, grabbing hold of the warhammer's shaft and guiding it into the leg of Axe. He buckled under the pain and swung his axe out in reaction, but F'Skal was faster, planting both hands on Axe's shoulders and vaulting over him. Axe couldn't stop his strike. He could only watch as his weapon cut into his brother's leg, nearly amputating it fully.

Both knew their breaths to be their last. Hargreave had finally led them to doom.

Hammer nearly passed out from the sudden shock of the blade driving through his bone, but Axe stood again, shaking on the partially dislocated knee where the hammer had struck him. He charged in, nearly falling forward with his own attempted momentum, to swing the bloodstained axe towards F'Skal. Before the strike met its apex, F'Skal was inside the arc, gripping the man's hand hard. He drove a long dagger underneath Axe's jaw, the blade finding a smooth track underneath his skull. Hammer stared at the weapon's handle showing under his brother's chin. F'Skal kicked over the falling corpse and brought the heel of his foot across Hammer's cheekbone, crushing the invader to the ground. Another of the elves was the one to finish him. F'Skal stood as the rain fell over him and breathed a heavy sigh. He was never happy to take a life.

††

Fink enjoyed carving lines into this creature's flesh. With how many were in the village, he didn't figure the depreciation of one's value would matter too awfully much. The screams that it made were much more worthwhile to the sadistic little man. Pain was such a lovely thing, but he wasn't terribly used to it himself, which he realized when a burning pain shot through his leg. He looked down at the sudden sword tip in his thigh, turning back to find the young man that Hargreave had termed as 'Loverboy' and he suddenly felt a strange fear wash through him.

Darion looked down at the small man, unable to contain his wincing. Rage was in his eyes. Vati lay nearly unconscious next to him, with a horrifying number of thin lines across his flesh, each oozing a bright orange ichor. It seemed Fink was even less than a rat. Darion ripped his blade from his leg and brought it down in an arcing cut, but Fink was able to deflect it with the dagger still caked in Vati's orange blood.

Fink scrambled out from under the strike that seemed to exhaust the guardsman, dashing as quickly as he could away from the seemingly crazed man. His progress was halted however, when a swarm of the red skinned creatures blocked his path. He turned, finding more of the beasts blocking the way behind his assailant as well, and he began to panic. Where he was once elated at how many of the devils there were, now that same number broke his spirit down tremendously.

Darion finally recovered, and looked around to the multitude of survatri around him. He smiled softly, then returned his attention to his opponent. "Nowhere to run, Fink, no one to help you. Just give up and we'll work something out."

Fink didn't seem interested. In a mad dash, he slung a dagger out towards Darion, who was able to slap it harmlessly to the side. In his desperation he lunged for Darion's unarmored ribs in one last gambit, hoping to take advantage of his opponent's surprise at the flung weapon. Darion saw the movement and at the last moment he twisted around, trading his weapon to his left hand and grabbed Fink's wrist to neutralize the blow. He continued the momentum and before he realized what was happening his blade drove through Fink's right eye, gouging through and bursting from the back of his skull. Fragments of the bone quickly sunk into the mud while a mélange of red and orange pooled beneath them.

Fink's quickly dead grip lost hold of his dagger and it fell to the ground with a dull *thump*. Darion stumbled backwards, shoving the lifeless rogue with his hands, but was caught by several of the survatri before he tripped into the muck. Fink lay back on the ground, the longsword tip jammed into the soil and propping him up in a macabre position, before gravity slowly drew him down the length of the blade with the sickening sound of air escaping the bloody wound. Darion turned from the survatri and vomited into the mud, the cascading rain washing away the refuse with the pool of Fink's blood.

⚔

Hargreave danced furiously with Erika, his gusto only rising with her rage. He knew early on that he could only dodge her flaming hands and while he couldn't pause to fully understand it, he had plenty of time to strategize against it. His resolve began to wane though, when he caught a glimpse of Bull's head snapping horribly to one side, then Axe and Hammer falling to their knees. His assault of chaos was fading, and he no longer had the advantage here. A short while later, a group of the survatri rounded a corner and threw the carcass of Fink into the open plaza.

Panic set in now. His smile fading into a grimace. He dodged Erika's punch and twisted around, kicking her square in the back before dashing away into the forest. Erika lurched from the attack but was after him in a flash.

Into the forest they ran, Hargreave leaping over fallen trees and blinking through the blinding sheets of rain. Erika was right on his heels and it was all Hargreave could do to twist around trees to try and shake her pursuit as Erika started to tire from the mad dash and her immolation began to fade. A glimpse of Hargreave's grin to the side filled her with renewed vigor and she decided on her reckless strategy.

With cooled hands she hiked her skirt up as far as she could, flushing both legs into flames up to the middle of her thighs. The darkened area brightened as she felt the power flooding through her lower body. She kicked off in a shower of scorched earth, amazed at the speed with which she ran. Hargreave glanced behind to find her closing in on him in an impossible leap and nearly cried out before ducking to the mud. Erika sailed over him and slid across the ground on her back. She screamed when she saw the cliffside just as she slipped over the edge, barely catching onto a tree root. Her legs returned to their normal state as her skirt fell back to her calves, whipping in the wind that flew through the ravine.

Hargreave stepped to the side of the cliff and stared down at her. "What a shame!" he taunted. "You almost got me too. Unfortunate things didn't turn out differently!"

Erika tried to avoid looking down, her mind flooding with memories of her trek down a mountain with Irvine during her last journey. She had discovered her intense fear of heights that day, and this was doing nothing to help that fear. Through the intensifying rain she could make out the sound of Hargreave unsheathing his blade once again. Her heart pounded in her breast as fear gripped her mind, unable to shunt the thought of the agonizing drop below her.

"You know, I was actually rather fond of you, Spitfire," he started, looking around for any pursuers, and then back to her. "You would have made a great addition to the team, and now that I'm seeing those abilities you're hiding... well I'm sure I came up with a good name for you at least!"

She did her best to control her breathing, however the knowledge of the distance below her and the hostile man above her made the task seem impossible. She groaned as Hargreave continued, just as much at his grating voice as it was at her own fatigue from hanging as she was.

"Look, girl. I would love to just say I could simply walk away here, that everything will be like nothing ever happened," he crouched down now, holding the edge of his sword over her knuckles threateningly. "But, you've left me without my Heathens, which means I'll be out of work for a while. That, and a personal insult to my pride with your little stunt earlier today. I'm afraid I just can't leave things as they are."

"Ye're the ones who attacked!" Erika shouted back at him. "If ye had just left things alone, all o' them would be just well and fine!"

She screamed as the blade slowly dragged across the tops her fingers, Hargreave standing once again and angling the tip towards her. "You seem to be misplacing the blame in this situation here, girl."

Erika looked up at him, tears warming her face from the fear and the stinging pain in her fingers as her blood dripped down the length of the blade in the rain. A rage built in her eyes, fire engulfing her arm again. "Ye mad bastard!" she shouted, heaving herself upwards with her immolated hand that began melting through the root.

Hargreave jumped back slightly as she flung herself back up to his level, his sword coming straight up with her ascent. She felt the searing burn as the blade jammed into her left hip, the barest pained groan escaping her lips. Her right arm immolated to the shoulder as her feet planted on the solid ground again. She twisted around him and slammed her flaming palm into the side of his face, drawing a scream from the man as the strike threw him hard to the side. In his intense drive to get away from her, he wasn't careful of his own footing and stepped fully over the cliffside.

Erika gasped horribly as his blade wrenched from her side, but took grim satisfaction as he fell into the great ravine with the left side of his face blackened from her attack. No scream ever came, and she reasoned it was likely a last ditch effort to retain his sick dignity. That, or she did more damage than she had thought with her final strike.

She collapsed to her knees a moment later, driving her hand under the waistline of her skirt and clutching at her bleeding hip, her breathing coming in labored gasps, her vision becoming darker. Moments before she lost consciousness, she thought she could hear Irvine calling her name.

⸸

"Erika!" Darion shouted, desperation beginning to take hold of him. F'Skal slapped his shoulder a moment later, pointing to a shape hunched over near the cliffside. Fear gripped his heart as he saw her form, crumpled into the mud, but was relieved when F'Skal shouted that she still lived.

He watched as the dark-skinned elf carried her back to the aash village. He looked around for any sign of Hargreave, finding none. Darion was unsure if that was a good thing or not.

"You care for her?" F'Lessa asked to the side of him, startling him from his thoughts.

Darion looked to the woman, who stood a full head over his own height. Her body was covered in bruises and small rips where Bull's fists had torn her flesh. Her upper lip was split, and still dripped blood nearly as intense in color as her eyes. Those eyes locked onto his in a hard stare, causing him to recoil slightly. The two of them were the last two in the area. The rain had started to slow and he briefly became distracted with the way her loose hair stuck to her body.

"Answer the question," she said sternly.

He jumped again, swallowing hard. "I would like to believe that we've become good friends."

She shook her head violently, her silver locks dragging across her skin in the light rain. "That isn't an answer to the question I asked you."

Darion stared into her deep knowing red eyes, and grimaced. "Yes, I care for her, but she is not the one for me. Is that a good enough answer for you?" He recoiled slightly at his own aggression, hardly meaning for his tone to sound so harsh.

F'Lessa held his gaze for what seemed like an eternity, the only sound around them was the raindrops filtering through the trees and Darion nearly ran from her in fear of an outburst he felt was coming for possibly giving the 'wrong' answer. He held her gaze nonetheless. She hugged her arms to her breast in a more feminine motion than what Darion would have expected from the more masculine seeming of the twins, her eyes falling away from his.

"I see," she said finally as slight blue streaks ran down her hair, and Darion could almost find a sadness in her eyes but was unsure of where it came from. After a while, she tentatively stepped away from him, back towards the village where repairs and healing were the only tasks of the evening. Darion followed after her, watching her long silver hair as it swayed free of her back, only to be stuck to her skin again when another shower came down on her from the trees, hardly seeming to faze her. The blue streaks continued, almost intensifying as she walked away from him.

He suddenly, and desperately, wanted to know the meaning behind the color.

†††

The rain continued to fall over the ravine. The river at the base filling more and more with every drop. The lightning flashed and small animals that had found shelter on the riverbank suddenly dashed away, believing their relative safety to be destroyed. A motionless form lay on the rocks, blood mixing with the waters in a swirling display. A deep gasping inhale scared away the last few creatures that still lingered, as the form was motionless no more.

Hargreave slowly pulled himself onto the land further, closer to his sword that was jammed into the softened earth. The crimson stain of Erika's blood slowly drifted from the gleaming metal. The side of his face was disfigured horribly, and he could no longer see out of his left eye. He felt his own saliva dripping from the deadened muscle of his jaw, but he couldn't linger on that. The water was rising quickly, and he knew he would drown in his condition. He clawed his hands through the mud, crawling closer to his blade. Several ribs were broken and he was careful to avoid worsening his state, but knew he was dead anyway if he slowed.

With a groan that echoed through the ravine, Hargreave dragged himself out of the clutches of death.

12

Vindication and A Respite

rika awoke slowly. The sunlight peeking through the trees and reflecting in the lingering rainwater that stuck to the branches. Her eyes squinted up at the smiling face of F'Skal, the emerald dust around his neck and face glowing as he used a small mortar and pestle.

"Be gentle," he urged. "You were hurt rather badly and your body has not fully absorbed the medicine. Hargreave's blade grated against your pelvic bone, I only just finished removing the fractured splinters."

She complied after finding the striking pain in her hip when she tried to sit up, opting instead to slowly lift herself with the healer's aid. She looked down at her lower half, covered only in a loose sheet that left her leg and hip exposed. Her upper half was covered in a crossing halter similar to the one F'Lessa wore. The deep stab wound in her lower abdomen was covered in a black substance that seemed to melt into her skin. As her senses awakened, she felt the slight stinging sensation that came with it. Around her were a multitude of similar beds, all housing elves or survatri who lay wounded and healing.

F'Lessa stood against a wall not far from her. "Your clothing is folded away underneath you. I took the liberty of washing them."

Erika smiled and thanked the elf, adjusting the aash clothing that she wore while graciously taking a small stack of pillows from F'Skal to lay back on. She thought back to Kharim and his 'dancing girl' clothes that he showed her and the similarities to the minimal coverings these elves wore. Although she couldn't deny the fabric was comfortable, despite how little of her skin it actually covered.

"Where's Darion?" she asked, looking around the small open area that was walled away from the rest of the village.

F'Lessa clicked her tongue. Before Erika could inquire about it, F'Skal answered her. "He is in the process of helping our people with the repairs. As well as the removal of the fallen."

Erika's face darkened. "How many did ye lose?"

The woman stalked closer to the exit and leaned out slightly, seemingly looking at something. "Twenty-four of our people have returned to nature, most from the initial explosion and ensuing surprise attack. Nineteen are still wounded and in varying conditions." A moment later, she leaned back into the room, her brow furrowed from whatever she had been looking at.

"I'm sorry," Erika said quietly, tears starting to well in her eyes.

F'Skal leaned forward in his seat, gingerly applying more of the dark substance onto her hip. She gasped at the burning sensation that spread across her leg and abdomen, resisting the strong urge to grab at his hands and the exposed skin around the wound. "None of this is your fault," the healer said as he worked. "Even if you and Darion had not been there, the mercenaries would have found us regardless."

"It was the survatri they were after, and our people would have fought them when they eventually found us." F'Lessa added, though the words did little to stop the tears that ran down Erika's face and onto her skin.

F'Skal gently put his fingers under her chin and directed her gaze towards him. "If you place blame only on yourself, you will inevitably crush yourself under the weight of guilt."

Erika blinked at him through her watery eyes, and tried to nod. He continued to apply the medicine to her wound shortly after, Erika obeying his instruction to lay back with a never ending string of grimaces. She kicked her right leg in response to the pain several times, threatening to toss the sheet off until she grabbed at it. F'Lessa shortly left the room with a slight nod to her brother.

"Ye two are close," Erika observed, trying to distract from the sensations.

"She is lost without me, I'm afraid," he said, leaning closer to her to carefully place a small globule of the substance. Erika winced as she felt his fingers push the stuff inside her wound. "Though I know her to be kind and warm on the inside, she just does not know how to easily show it to anyone."

She noticed the sadness behind his red on black eyes as he exhaled and leaned back. He noticed her watchful gaze a moment later and met it with a warm smile. "I apologize, I'm sure our clothing must be a bit strange to you. Humans generally wear much more as I understand."

Erika ignored the sudden change of subject and looked down at the crossing fabric that came much farther above her midriff than anything she had worn before. "It is a bit odd, aye. I don't mind though. I appreciate yer hospitality with it. An' it is more comfortable than I was expectin'."

"Thank F'Lessa, not me. It is technically hers. Though she was muttering something about having to adjust it so much," he quickly added. "Er, I wouldn't take that in any negative way against your bust."

Erika laughed. "No, I understand she just meant I'm smaller than her overall."

F'Skal stood from his stool and started to step off, placing a warm hand on Erika's shoulder. "Let the black moss set on the wound, but don't cover it. It will become uncomfortable, but after it has melded with your flesh it will accelerate your natural healing quite a bit. You should be walking by this afternoon. Just call if you need anything."

A moment later, he was attending to another of the wounded, and Erika was left alone. She looked down to her bare left leg, now covered up to her mid-thigh in the swirling crimson patterns that marked her Ignis abilities. Her eyes eventually moved to the hole in her hip, now caked generously in the strange moss substance that F'Skal had dressed it in. Thoughts drifted to the previous year, when she had lain in a similar state, only having just sustained the wound to her back. She looked down again at the aash clothing, feeling the fabric of the pillows behind her, musing that the garment covered little of her back or the scars across it. She brought a hand back over her shoulder to feel at the rough skin where the Daemon's claw had raked across her. Strangely, thinking on the wound brought thoughts of Irvine again and the need to see him that she so desperately held.

She looked around at the medical ward, the open-air environment soothing as the sounds of the repairs started to sound clearer from outside. She wished she could share this sight with Irvine, and all the sights she had experienced since his disappearance, as well as what she suspected she would see on her continuing journey to find him. She wished for the sight of him more than anything else, as she struggled to picture the exact shade of his eyes.

† †

Darion was unsure how to aid in the repairs of the gateway, especially when a group of elves stepped forward and began a strange ritual. Save for occasional ornamentation, each of them were naked—not that it surprised him at this point in the village. On sections of their exposed skin, they bore intricate painted patterns that were distinctly not the gem dust that he had learned of the previous day, all in a variety of colors and styled in intricate designs. They lit small bundles of dried herbs, drawing sigils in the earth below the shattered wall, and chanting in a tongue that he did not recognize as the elvish he normally heard spoken through the village. The warrior woman F'Lessa joined them nearby, but seemed to only observe their practices.

He stood back at the suggestion of another elf, watching in awe as the foliage before the elves began to grow and rise into a wall just as thick as any other that protected the village. Every so often during the process, his gaze drifted to F'Lessa, sitting on her knees, back straight with her hands resting on her bare thighs. Either she didn't notice his lingering eyes, or she was doing her best to ignore him, but he couldn't tell which was the case.

A passing elf paused next to him, a young girl who introduced herself as Y'Skara. She was a pretty elf, about Darion's height which caught him strangely off-guard. "They're called druids. They hold the ability to harness the magic of the natural world, which they harness with the markings," she said from beside him, her body heat radiating onto his shoulder as she edged closer without his realizing.

What all that entailed, Darion could only wonder, but he was glad that the repairs on the exterior walls were so swift. The girl lingered, her eyes—purple on black—drifting up and down his body with a slight grin, as if his being dressed was enticing to her, as opposed to her converse lack of clothing. Darion nervously shifted away from her, trying his best to give a friendly smile and nod back to her while doing his best to not let his eyes wander down her naked side, the ceramic pot she carried doing little to hide her curving flesh. He startled when F'Lessa loudly cleared her throat and caused the young elf to jolt as well before shuffling back to her own duties. Darion faced forward again, trying not to notice when Y'Skara kept throwing idle glances at him over her shoulder.

Rebuilding the homes and collecting the shrapnel from the attack was another issue that he was much more able to help with. However, as he collected the shards of wood and fallen weapons, he found an audience around him. Several of the survatri stood idly by, none directly impeding him. Eventually, Vati approached him, covered in bandages, and embraced him in a tight hug. The creature, including his small horns, only stood to Darion's chest.

"Brother saved all survatri," the small creature said.

Darion smirked at the hyperbole.

He startled, when as one, all the surrounding kin broke out in shouts. "Savior of survatri!"

Darion was quick to drop the items he had collected, and was off trying to quiet the praise. "I didn't do anything, I was just trying to help."

"But in helping, you became their hero," a feminine voice said, Darion turning to find F'Lessa with a bundle of wood cradled in one muscular arm over her shoulder. She stepped closer to him, causing a strange panic in his gut. He started to backpedal furiously, nearly tripping over Vati who was still clinging to him. The imposing woman stood only a breath away from him and he found himself fearful of what she would do next. His fears were subverted when she placed a hand on his shoulder and smiled only slightly. "You did very well, and the survatri appreciate it. Enjoy their praise now, since I doubt it will be long before you two depart."

Darion cocked his head slightly, finding another hint of the slight sadness in her last statement. Although, before he could muster a reply, she was walking away again, her hair streaking that same blue. He found his gaze locked on her as she left. Vati distracted him quickly from the lingering thoughts, as he continued to embrace him with as hard a grip as the little creature could muster.

† †

After dusk had fallen over the village, the elves showed even more hospitality. A full feast was prepared, and the newcomers were encouraged to join them in their celebration. Erika was able to move again, though her pace was greatly slowed by her still healing injuries and she occasionally required assistance in moving around. Darion found himself flushing slightly at the sight of her in the aash clothing, despite all of the elves in even less around them. However, he was quickly distracted by the sight of her bandaged hip underneath the loincloth and the much more numerous scars that were no longer hidden by her usual garments. He swallowed hard, thinking about how she must have gotten all those injuries and what kind of things she must have faced.

She sat next to him with some difficulty, finding it easier to sit with her left leg extended outwards. She was only able to ease down with the help of Darion and a couple survatri, who were all too happy to help her sit. Darion constantly checked on her to ask if she needed anything, but she waved him off every time.

"I'm injured, not helpless," she scolded him with a grin. "It is amusin' how the survatri are dotin' on ye more than ye're dotin' on me."

He smirked at the truth of the statement, glancing up to find Y'Skara sitting on her knees on the opposite side of the spread from him, a small smile on her face as she eyed him. Darion felt his face get warm, as he struggled to focus on his food under her gaze. After a while, the girl looked above his head before quickly averting her gaze downwards to her bowl.

F'Lessa sat on the other side of Erika, who still seemed dedicated to being her attendant while she stayed in the elven settlement. Darion quickly looked away from both of them, unsure why F'Lessa had made him so nervous suddenly. F'Skal was found taking a few bites and then retreating to the ward where his patients occasionally needed some kind of aid. The siblings explained to their guests that the feasts were commonly held after trials were overcome. In this case, the attack from the Heathens was considered a trial for the entire village, and thus warranted a feast to celebrate their victory.

It all sounded similar to what Erika's father used to tell her of the Fjordling culture, and their battle-centric society. F'Lessa continued to detail that anything could be a trial, including storms or even simple hunting trips. Several of the elves came and greeted the two humans, congratulating and thanking them. Some even welcomed them as honorary tribe members, though F'Lessa told them that only the elder shaman could technically bestow that honor. Eventually the elder F'Tara joined them as well, and spoke highly of the two and their defense of a place that was not their home, but welcomed them to consider it their home from then on. F'Lessa then explained, with a smile towards Erika at least. *"That,* was your true admission as honorary tribe members."

Erika smiled genuinely at the sentiments, truly hoping she could visit this place again after she had found Irvine. Darion was similarly touched by the words of welcome and encouragement, if a bit uncomfortable at the constant attention between the survatri eager to aid him, Y'Skara's occasional glances, and F'Lessa's intimidating presence. He slumped his back every time a survatri would refill his drink after he'd taken the smallest of draws from it.

The night wore on and eventually things were cleared away, the members of the tribe began returning to their individual tasks or retiring to their homes. F'Skal brought beddings for Erika and Darion. While Darion helped F'Lessa and some others to pack away the wooden bowls and cups to be washed the next day, F'Skal redressed Erika's wound.

"You should be walking easily tomorrow, just don't overexert yourself," he assured her once he was finished, helping her retie the aash cloth around her waist. They set up the beddings on the side of the medical hut, that way she would be within distance of F'Skal if she experienced any pain during the night.

She thanked him as he walked away, though he soon returned with her belongings. He also handed her a pouch that was heavy with a slight jingle to it. She looked inside to find the bag to be filled with gold aurums. She looked to him and stammered a response.

"Please, do not worry yourself over it," he said with a smile. "Those are the coins that we found on the attacker's bodies. We aash have no use for the currency, so we wanted you to have it."

She looked down at the pouch again, and he began to walk back inside his workplace. "After all, is that not the reason you two were out here?"

Erika paused at the comment, feeling a wind rush through the village and over her skin. A handful of survatri sat nearby a small fire, waving their hands around in some odd game, or perhaps their own celebration. She sighed heavily, stowing the coin pouch in her pack. Things had turned out well, all things considered. Once again, she idly rubbed at the tooth-mark scar on her bare midriff. She decided she was glad they took the 'Devil of the Wood' bounty, even if all the devils they had found were human.

† †

Darion placed a stack of the bowls onto the wooden table, breathing a sigh of relief that they were the last of the dishes. He turned to leave, but immediately stumbled backwards when the imposing form of F'Lessa appeared at the entryway. He unintentionally slammed against the table, knocking several bowls to the ground. She simply eyed him as she set down a stack of cups onto a neighboring table.

"Do you fear me?" she asked plainly.

He felt as if the room became much warmer, though part of him rationalized that it was because of the high body heat that each of the elves had. Another part of him knew that wasn't the reason. She stepped closer to him and he felt his heart nearly leap from his chest as he tried to back away further, but found nowhere to retreat to.

"Answer the question, please," she said calmly.

Darion hardly noticed the addition of 'please', feeling a sweat break out on his brow as he struggled to look up and meet the tall woman's gaze. He became painfully aware of their height difference now as she continually closed in on him. "No, I don't fear you," he finally choked out.

She stepped back slightly, crossing her arms over her breast and narrowing her eyes at him. "Why do you act this way whenever I am around, then?"

He found it easier to meet her gaze now, though his heart still raced in his chest. Her hair was returned to its neat braid that fell over her shoulder, the evening glow of the village reflecting off her skin in a rather pleasing sight. "I'm not sure of your meaning," he admitted.

She clicked her tongue and threw her head to the side, whipping the braid to the opposite shoulder. "You humans confuse me," she said coldly as she turned to the side.

"Are you sure that it's humans that confuse you? Or just me?" he said with a slight grin and chuckle, though that faded when he realized his words.

Her eyes flashed back to him. "Are you are attempting to flirt?" she asked with wide eyes.

Darion could do naught but hold his hands up in surrender.

He tried to explain his meaning, but was interrupted when a survatri woman came into the room with a handful of utensils and became excited at the sight of Darion. She rushed forward and grabbed the young man's wrist after depositing the woodware, and dragged him back into the village proper. Darion drifted past the aash woman and brushed against her side.

F'Lessa paused for a long while, staring at where he had been. She brought a hand to her arm where he had grazed her, and took a long sigh. His flesh felt so cold to her. "Perhaps, it is just you."

⸸

The village was quiet after night had fully set in, the sound of wind rustling through the trees met only by an occasional drowsy cough or uncomfortable moan. F'Lessa kept her brother company while he redressed a wound that had reopened on another elf in the infirmary. Her eyes locked on the form of Darion just outside, sleeping deeply after being forced to play an amusing game with the survatri—involving a strange ball they had crafted from deer leather—before retiring.

"So, what is going on?" F'Skal asked in their native tongue, drawing a stitch tightly against the flesh of his patient.

Her eyes darted away and began surveying the ward, watching all of the other medically inclined elves as they toiled away with the wounded. The emerald dust on the most proven of them sparkling in the low light, though he could see them clearly as day with her elven eyes.

Her brother chuckled as he snipped the string away. "Ignoring me helps you none."

"Do we actually have to accompany them?" she asked him, beginning to allow her more sensitive side to show just slightly.

"Aunt F'Tara urged us to go. Destiny awaits those two somehow, she saw it in her visions," he said as he cleaned his tools. "Who are we to argue with fate?"

F'Lessa groaned quietly. Only moments before had they returned from a meeting with the shaman F'Tara, who had told them that she had a vision during the battle. The trance seemingly tied to the intense emotions exuding from the two defending humans. Much to F'Lessa's seeming annoyance, she had informed them that she and F'Skal were to accompany the pair on their journey.

"Personally, I am looking forward to our departure. I have wanted to see what was beyond the bounds of our home for quite some time. I was always jealous of our uncle for being able to see more of the world," F'Skal continued, taking a drink from his tea. His sister sat cross legged on a stool, her focus shifting wildly. "Do you not like them?" he asked as he sat across from her.

"No, I do. Erika is an interesting girl, and I look forward to fighting alongside her," she said, taking a long pause.

F'Skal stared at her intently. "And what of Darion?"

She turned to him, and for the first time since their uncle had left for his new home, he saw tears in his sister's eyes. "I don't know. I am confused about him."

He smirked slightly despite himself. "Are you attracted to him?"

The look in her eyes flashed as if she was stabbed through the chest, a streak in her hair running pink for just a moment. "I...," she stammered, looking suddenly desperate for something to do with her hands.

F'Skal waved her away, not willing to force her to break herself over her own tumultuous emotions. "I understand. Now, dear sister, what is stopping you?"

She stared at him and blinked, looking as if she was stabbed once more. "He is human!" she nearly shouted, quickly quelling herself.

He shrugged at her. "It is not unheard of. Our uncle left to spend the rest of his days with a sol elf."

"But was still elven!" she reasoned. "And both of them were male, engaging in a relationship that was purely for their own happiness."

"What are you getting at?" he asked, lowering his gaze.

She was nearly standing now, her posture wavering between aggression and vulnerability. "They could not have children!"

F'Skal looked up to his sister, whose eyes were suddenly wide and expressionless. After a moment she realized she had stood up and slowly sat down again, unable to find words. He simply smiled and took another drink.

"Half-elves do exist. Young Y'Skara seems interested in him as well. She seems very interested in exploring the possibility of interracial relations," he chuckled into his tea cup, teasing her. "You always show your true thoughts once I get you a little worked up though."

"I don't know what I want F'Skal," she said, starting to breathe more regularly now. "He seems to be such a good person, and..."

"And you are attracted to that. His handsome face as well as his good heart," he said, nodding at her.

She looked to him again, finally making eye contact with him, a streak of orange running through her hair now. "So what am I to do?"

F'Skal smirked. "Well, unless you mean to keep him in the village for the rest of his life—and are prepared for the long battle against Y'Skara's girlish charms—I suggest you ready yourself for tomorrow's journey."

She watched him motion to his own bag, already packed, and then glanced to Darion again.

"He already said he has no romantic intentions with Erika," he encouraged. "Her quest seems centered around another, and he understands that. So perhaps you should do the thing that makes F'Lessa happy, for once."

"And if her quest proves fruitless?" she replied, attempting to fight his logic.

He chuckled again. "You do fail in your perceptions at times. The way he looks at her, is not of romantic intent to begin with."

F'Lessa looked at him questioningly.

F'Skal leaned forward slightly, locking stares with her. "He looks at her how a brother looks to his sister. He sees her as a friend, or sibling," he said, putting a hand against her cheek which she leaned into, appreciating the support.

She looked back to Darion's sleeping form again as he tossed slightly, narrowly missing Vati who curled beside him.

Her brother leaned back in his seat again, raising his tea to his lips with a smile. "So, do the thing that makes F'Lessa happy."

PART TWO

I came to this land long ago, under a pretense of violence. My home was razed by Daemons, summoned by an unnatural cult. My people were slain, thoughtlessly and without remorse. My own sister was torn to pieces before my eyes. I was left for dead in the unforgiving sands of my home. In those sands though, I found a dark salvation. A blade that spoke to me, and told me of ways I can destroy those who had destroyed me.

I had not realized that this blade raised restless spirits around me, even when I did not call them. That it killed just as thoughtlessly as those I sought to slay. That poor red haired girl. I never meant her harm. I wish we could have met under different circumstances. I wish I could have lived differently. Had my rage not blinded me to the truth of my own actions.

My old belief teaches that even for the lost, there is salvation. Even for the murderers, the thieves, the liars, and the cheats; even they can find peace. All who pass from this world are given another chance to find happiness, away from the temptations and hatred.

This place is much different though, and their Goddess of Death is strange. She judges by the life that was lived, and the heart that beat within their soul. The people here seldom speak her name, and she has few followers considering the worshipers of their many Gods and Goddesses. A stark contrast to the one deity my people held before them, lifted ever higher by the Jaquar-al-quarak and their machinations.

Just the same, these people live in peace. They may have their tribulations and their squabbles, but they are normal folk, who lead normal lives. Many are taught combat at an early age, both with other peoples and with the savage creatures that roam our land in both the day and the night. We are adept at using many tools, from harvesting, to hunting, to killing. These people though, they master a single tool, or a single manner of tool; they focus on the farm, or the hunt, or the kill.

Many of my people would have called them weak, jesting after slaying them with their blades and taking their fertile land for ourselves, were it not for our sacred lands keeping them tied to its shifting landscape.

I have heard of another realm, only in sparse text and hushed words of priests who discuss these mythical Dragon creatures. The 'Sands of Conflict' they call them. Full of sand, rock, and blood. How akin to my home that all sounds. A painful mirror held up to my culture that I cannot shatter, for fear of proving who I am.

I pray to the Spirit, that I may find that salvation that is referred to in the ancient texts, that I myself preached unto my people. I wonder though, if I am too far out of touch from the Spirit, and only this land's Mortia may take me.

-Kharim'akhala N'asheznemon,
Exiled Priest of the Sands of Haran

13
DEPARTURE

The next morning came and with it, Erika and Darion's departure from the aash village. F'Tara sincerely thanked the two of them for their help in defending the village against the Heathens, wishing them well upon their journey. Darion turned a shade of red when the survatri collectively paraded out to bid him farewell, all with tears streaming from their black eyes. None more than the youngling Vati, as Darion was forced to endure the long embrace that the small creature held him in. Erika mused that he didn't seem to mind that much though, and actually began to believe that Darion would miss the diminutive Daemons just as much as they would miss him. She also noticed when the young elf Y'Skara kissed him on the cheek as she passed him, flushing him even more. Erika had to stifle a laugh, especially at seeing Darion's flabbergasted expression.

A short time later Erika approached F'Lessa, holding the aash garments that she had worn, while the elf looked at Darion's parade with a slight scowl. "I'd be happy to wash 'em first if ye'd like."

The aash woman shook her head. "No, I was actually planning on letting you keep them. Especially since you should still be letting that wound heal in the open air."

Erika looked down at her skirt that the elf motioned to, and flushed slightly. "Well, as comfortable as they are, I admit I'd feel a bit strange walking back into Sylvanna wearin' such clothes."

They were joined by her brother now, who lifted two bags over his shoulders. He promptly handed one to his sister and smirked at the auburn-haired woman. "Why is that? We'll be walking into Sylvanna wearing such clothes."

"What?" Darion said immediately, turning towards them and pulling Vati to the side with him. The little Daemon made an excited noise as his hooves left the ground briefly, before coming to rest as Darion continued. "You two are coming with us?"

"Indeed," F'Lessa said flatly, dropping her axes into her belt.

F'Skal smiled despite his sister's brusque behavior. "F'Tara tasked us with accompanying you."

Erika blinked hard and shook her head, gesturing wildly towards them. "But ye're the village healer, ye can't leave, and ye're the strongest!"

"Others are strong as well," F'Lessa said.

F'Skal following her. "And I am only one of the healers."

The two humans exchanged glances, and looked back to the elves, who continued checking their traveling supplies.

F'Skal met their gaze a moment later. "The elder knew how much we wished to see the outside world ever since our uncle departed, and knows that this is our best chance."

Erika wasn't sure how much she believed him, something in his tone sounding like he wasn't letting on fully. She disregarded the thought for the moment and nodded. Soon after, the party of four were out in the forest surrounding the aash village, heading back to the west and towards the city. Erika still pondered what the true reasons for the elven twins accompanying them was, while simultaneously happy for not having to say goodbye to two very fast friends. She was also glad to be on the road with more than just Darion for a bit more varied of conversation. Their marching order leaving the forest made up of her and F'Lessa walking abreast of each other, with Darion and F'Skal walking similarly behind them. This brought her line of thinking back to Darion inevitably though, and his original statement of accompanying her to Sylvanna.

When does he plan on heading home? she wondered, glancing back at the young man as he conversed with F'Skal. She shook her head free of the thought and continued on, limping occasionally from the sudden pains from the still healing wound, F'Lessa lending a warm hand any time she stumbled.

"You really should change out of that skirt," she said, motioning to Erika's increasingly tattered garment. "My clothes would be sufficient, and would give the injury air to breathe."

Erika smiled and nodded to her. "I suppose I should. I'm not one to show off my hips much though, and yer loincloth does plenty o' that."

F'Lessa simply rolled her eyes, but smiled afterwards to soften it. "You humans are such strange creatures."

"On the topic o' that, do we need to get ye and yer brother some warmer clothes fer the northlands?" Erika asked. "If yer plannin' on accompanyin' me all the way there that is."

The aash woman nodded. "We do plan on traveling with you for the foreseeable future. You are a friendly face in a world of unknowns for us. However, we will likely have no need for any new clothing. Our body heat will keep us plenty warm, even if we were to be naked in the snows. Although, since you humans are so strange and generally react negatively to the natural form, we have cloaks to wear in the settled areas, so we do not draw so much attention."

Erika snickered at F'Lessa's jeering tone about the 'prudish' humans as the elf glanced behind them at their companions. Erika raised an eyebrow when F'Lessa flushed before whipping back around and slumping her shoulders slightly. Erika followed her gaze to find Darion, who was walking several feet behind the elf, staring into nothingness, his eyes blank. F'Skal seeming to simply be enjoying the scenery around them.

"What's the matter?" she asked her.

F'Lessa shot her a sidelong look, with streaks of pink running through her tight braid. She hushed her tone considerably. "Is he not starting at my backside? Even if I were wearing nothing, isn't that still considered rude?"

Erika had to stop herself from laughing. "He's likely not meanin' to, love. He looks off, lost in thought, rather a lot. Ye get used to it after a while."

"What is it that he's thinking about?" she asked, daring to glance back again.

"I 'aven't the slightest idea. He's got a family back in his hometown, maybe he misses 'em?"

She noticed another change in the elf's features, a slight scowl that she almost seemed ashamed of. "A family you say?"

Erika kept watching her as she replied, narrowing her eyes just a bit. "Aye. Mum, dad, an' a little sister. They seemed quite the happy little bunch."

The elf almost seemed to sigh in relief, which led to Erika entertaining other thoughts. F'Lessa seemed suspicious of the young woman's sudden smile but she similarly didn't inquire about it, which Erika was glad for. She doubted she could stop herself from laughing over the strange situation now that she started to realize why the elf Y'Skara had always hurried away or averted her gaze from Darion whenever F'Lessa arrived, as well as why F'Lessa had worn that scowl after the younger elf had kissed Darion's cheek. She tried to imagine Darion and F'Lessa as a couple, hoping the aash didn't have some strange mind reading ability that they hadn't yet mentioned. The rest of their walk was in relative silence, save for F'Lessa's scolding of Erika every other time she limped due to her wound.

† †

The hall was dim, hidden from the midday sun beating down outside the doors. Maral, the sol elf attendant, took a deep breath as he started sorting the papers from the previous night's clerk. Many bounties had been turned in it seemed, while others were still pending arrival. He shifted through a small stack, glancing down to a specific contract that caught his eye: The Devil of the Wood.

Neither party that had accepted that job had returned yet and he began to regret giving it to the young pair of humans that had come in a few days prior. Part of him had hoped that the 'Heathens', as they called themselves, would be amicable and accept the two into their group. Then again, they didn't seem the friendliest of characters, save for their more charismatic leader, Hargreave.

He had become unsure of many things in the past week or so. Several people in the city had turned up missing, some even being found murdered in the streets. He recalled a recent killing just the previous night, a woman who had returned home from the tailors that Maral lived near, had been slain in her own living area. The accounts he heard from the knights were grizzly indeed. It was all he could do to rid his thoughts of the woman lying in her home, butchered beyond recognition, the furniture and walls painted with her blood.

He shuddered slightly, and started to reach for a small bottle of medicinal herbs that he had been given to ease his anxiety, but was interrupted by the doors swinging open. The two young humans made their way in, accompanied by two tall individuals clasped in long cloaks.

"I'm sorry, but unless your friends were on the bounty, they will not be eligible to be paid. *Officially* by the guild, that is," he said, knowing that they would likely split the reward as soon as they left the hall.

Darion stepped forward. "Actually, we are here to announce our resignation from the job."

Maral raised an eyebrow and glanced to the two newcomers who stood quite a bit taller than their human companions. Their hoods eventually came down and his eyebrows shot up at the sight of the two aash elves. "I see, and why is that exactly?"

"'The 'Devil of the Wood', as it was misnamed, is a harmless creature," he said confidently. The elf began to speak again, but Darion wasn't finished. "Besides the fact of it being completely innocent, I understand that you cannot take the bounty down due to my claim of that alone. *However*, I am contracted to inform you—as per the bounty we agreed upon—that the Devil of the Wood is entirely too dangerous to approach, due to the existence of the aash elf settlement."

Maral looked down to the contract, and to the small area towards the bottom that stated a list of special terms. "You mean to tell me that the Devil of the Wood is under the protection of the Shalti tribe?"

F'Lessa and F'Skal nodded in unison. Maral was speechless for a long while, glancing from the pair of aash elves, to the two humans, and finally to the bounty page before him.

"We would all be happy to sign," Darion said as he placed both hands on the desk, leaning towards the elf slightly.

Maral shook his head to break his daze. "Of course. If all four of you would be so kind. I'll have the papers in to the guild masters as soon as I can."

Darion was the first to sign the papers, and as he did, Erika looked to F'Lessa, who seemed to have an amused smirk across her face. When she turned back, Darion was handing her the quill for her to sign next. After the two elves had signed their own names, the four were out of the guild hall, albeit empty handed.

"I apologize that you two were not able to claim the reward," F'Skal said as they walked through the streets. He was careful to keep his cloak tight around him, converse to his sister who seemed to hardly notice when her cloak drifted open. "The pouch we had given you with the money from the mercenaries seems greatly insufficient considering the coin that was offered."

Darion shrugged. "The money those monsters had is plenty to buy us comfortable lodgings for the night and supplies for the journey."

Erika stepped in front of the group, halting them and eyeing Darion. "And when're ye plannin' on headin' home? I'm sure Jess is missin' ye by now."

He paused a long while, taking a deep breath and looking her in the eyes. "I'm not going back to Stonewall yet. I know that you weren't very excited on having me as a traveling companion in the beginning, and I understand why."

She raised an eyebrow at him.

"However, I think I can do some good things out here. I helped save an entire group of creatures that are newcomers to our world as a whole," he said, referencing the survatri. "I think I can do more too. Wherever you go, trouble seems to follow, and I think I can help quell that trouble."

Erika looked to the two elves, who seemed impressed by Darion's conviction. They both shrugged. She breathed a deep sigh and stepped to the side, allowing Darion to pass.

"And besides, I'm a native to this Region, Miss 'never been out of my hometown before a year ago'," he teased as he walked away.

Erika gaped at his audacity for a moment, shaking her head as the twins passed her by with amused chuckles.

They eventually found lodgings at *The White Carmino* once again. Thrane welcoming them back, and commenting on their new companions. "Never thought I'd see an aash elf in my tavern, let alone two of them," he said, prompting the twins to exchange a glance. "No quarrel from me, mind you! Make yourselves at home and let me know if you need anything."

Erika slumped slightly, remembering the night before they had left and the strange occurrence that had happened in the alleyway nearby. She stepped over to the bar, flagging Thrane to her. "Anythin' interestin' happen while we were gone?" she asked carefully, still unsure of what she had seen.

The tavern owner wore a sad look suddenly. "Well, there's been a string of killings unfortunately. Delron was one of the first. The burly man that was messing with you the night you and your friend were here."

She nodded, expecting the news about Delron but not the other murders. "Have they any suspects?"

"Eh, I only hear bits and pieces from the knights that drink here, which are few if I'm honest," he explained. "Hard to say though, and a lot of the corpses are hard to identify. Delron for example, they found his corpse, but never found his head. I actually was able to tell them who it was just from the body. Found only a few streets from here."

Erika nodded again, grimly, and expressed her condolences before heading back to the table, Darion had retrieved drinks from the barmaid and accompanied her. Both of them paused a moment, Darion looking flustered, as both of their elven companions had shed their cloaks. "What happened to not drawing attention?" Darion asked towards F'Skal, though his eyes kept darting back to F'Lessa.

"He said to make ourselves at home," F'Lessa said, as if it should be obvious.

Erika laughed with their two new friends at Darion's agitation, but she was still distracted. Thoughts flooded her mind on what could be doing these things, but was unsure of anything. She shuddered when a crack of thunder brought a new rainstorm over them.

⚔ ⚔

The rain beat down once again across the city of Sylvanna and the sun had set. Neither of the moons could be seen this night though, for the rain clouds had obscured everything into eerie darkness. Maral was approaching the last few hours of his work now. Finally he would be done with this desk, and heading back to the comfort of his own home. He was good with documents and clerical duties, however, he was not so good with the rough kind of individuals that usually made their way through the great doors before him. He was always uncomfortable around the general crowd that this hall attracted, but the young woman and her group were an exception. Despite their haggling, they seemed like decent people; and if they had befriended the Shalti tribe, then that spoke all the more of them.

His aash cousins were a callous bunch in his experience, though he had only had meetings with them a handful of times. Their state of dress—or lack thereof—was appalling to him for one, although he understood the biological reasons as to why they wore so little. Their attitudes were another thing, despite their somewhat shorter life spans they were able to attain just as much strength as their sol counterparts, if not even more. Likely their hard lifestyles, away from the comforts of modern society, caused much of that.

He heard the double doors swing open with a crash and he sighed disdainfully, expecting Taggar to relieve him whilst already inebriated. The man was an insatiable day drinker and Maral could not condone him coming to the workplace in such a state. He glanced up as he resolved to turn the issue up with the guild masters, but instead found a familiar—if unexpected—silhouette.

Hargreave.

"Ah, yes. Hargreave, the leader of the Heathens," he said, barely looking away from his work. "I'm afraid the bounty that your group accepted has been revoked. Another party arrived earlier today and informed me that the creatures are under the protection of the native aash elves of the Shalti, and Sylvanna has very strict laws regarding that tribe, as I'm sure you know."

He jumped when Hargreave slammed both hands onto his desk, splattering water and blood across his papers. He looked up to find the mercenary in a truly horribly state. The entire left side of his face was burned and disfigured, his eye missing completely. Blood dripped down the haggard man's bare hands, flowing with the wetness of the rain that had soaked him.

"Those damnable bastards were here already?" he growled, in a manner most uncharacteristic of the suave man Maral had seen before.

The elf stared up at him in horror, his eyes wide and locked onto the man's one good eye. "What happened to you?"

"I need that reward, elf," he snarled in response, inching closer to the clerk. "I need an advance on that reward, you'll have the Devil of the Woods, I'll kill the damn thing myself. All of them."

"I'm sorry Hargreave," Maral stuttered. "The reward has been revok—"

A sickening gasp escaped the elf's mouth, interrupting his speech. Hargreave easing his broadsword further into the flesh of his neck. "You talk too much. Damn elf," he said, the tip of the blade now scraping against the stone wall behind the desk. Lighting flashed and Maral's vision went dark, though his eyes still hung open.

⚔

The party purchased two rooms in *The White Carmino* that night. One for the girls and one for the boys, they reasoned. Erika stepped into her and F'Lessa's room uneasily, her mind still on the recent killings, and the fact that she was witness to the first of them. F'Lessa immediately dropped her loincloth to the floor, her crossing halter quickly atop it. Erika respectfully turned away from her as the aash began cleaning herself with a washcloth.

The elf woman laughed slightly. "You humans, so afraid of the body. I for one feel much better without that confining cloak."

"I'm not afraid of the body," Erika argued. "Just tryin' to give ye yer privacy."

"I don't need privacy to simply bathe, Erika," she said, moving into Erika's view. "What are you afraid of then? You've been on edge since we arrived in this area of the city. Even I've noticed, so you can be sure my brother has."

Erika averted her gaze again, although this time it was not due to the aash's nudity. "Strange things seem to follow me is all."

"Then we'll investigate the 'strange things'. Often times in the forest, things appear to be unknown in the dark of night, yet when you lay eyes on them directly, they are shown to be mundane," F'Lessa said, placing a warm hand on her shoulder.

The young woman was hardly comforted by this, her thoughts still flashing to the dark presence she had felt in the alleyway not so far from where she now sat. She was happier than she would let on, that F'Lessa was so close to her. Eventually she relaxed more, looking to the wooden tub of water at the edge of the room. Erika shrugged, figuring the two twins among a few others had seen her bare, so she stripped down as well before sinking down into the warm water, sighing contentedly. F'Lessa sat on a stool next to the bath, folding her cloak and clothing, engaging Erika in light conversation while she relaxed. The elf seemed to want something with which to distract her own thoughts as well.

In the next room down the hall, F'Skal had similarly cleaned himself and now sat in a small chair to the side of the room, using his mortar and pestle to reduce a strange black plant into a fine paste.

"Comfortable now?" Darion asked with a raised eyebrow, turning back after the elf finished cleaning himself.

F'Skal chuckled. "Rather, yes. Aash elves are generally uncomfortable wearing clothing, as I have explained to you. So when relaxing we generally do so in the most comfortable way possible. Don't you usually bathe without clothing?"

Darion glanced at the tub in their room, and shook his head slightly. "Yes, but generally not with others in the room," he said sitting on another chair. He pulled out a small piece of wood he had started working on and his whittling knife, wanting something to do than just sit there until they decided to sleep.

F'Skal idly smirked at his shyness, but did not press further. They both fell silent, occupied by their respective tasks.

"Are you alright?" he heard the aash ask a while later. "I heard the story from one of the older survatri. You are not accustomed to killing, are you?"

The memory of Fink's lifeless eye staring at him made his stomach churn. He started to make for the bucket at the side of the room, but as he cleared his mind the nausea passed. "No, I'm not. Erika is much more adept at that kind of thing."

"She has been traveling longer than you, and through more dangerous territories. Though I would think it has at least something to do with temperament as well," he reasoned.

"Yes, I suppose she has all of that. I have only made my way through the Region on carts or horseback. Always with a company of guards or my family at minimum," he explained slowly, carving off a large chunk from the wood. "I'm not sure I'll ever be comfortable with death."

He turned to F'Skal after a long pause, noticing the emerald dust glowing on his temples and down his neck. It quickly dimmed, and he returned to his medicine with a shake of his head. "I apologize. My markings allow me more precise sight, and I confess, I was using it to search you for tells."

"Tells?" Darion asked, confused.

The elf breathed deeply. "Yes, tells. Small twitches in the muscles around someone's eyes when they are talking about something that scares them. Or a thin layer of sweat when they lie, perhaps a flush in the face when they are embarrassed or looking at someone they love. I commonly search for these things, because I find them interesting, and I like to believe they help me be more personable."

Darion nodded his understanding. "Not everyone is so obvious though. Elves have those colorings in their hair that change with their emotion, but not all humans are so easy to understand."

The elf chuckled again. "Indeed, and just like humans, some elves are better at hiding their true emotions as well. Unlike my sister, who's hair streaks with every passing feeling, I have had nary a change since I was a youngling. Difference in temperament, as I said."

"Difference in patience as well perhaps? Though I admit I do not understand what the colors mean, I have seen them in her hair quite a lot," the guard offered.

F'Skal nodded in amusment. "Yes, she does lack patience as well. Likely a good thing that you do not know the meanings in the colors. They differ for each individual elf, and many view it as an intimate thing for another to know their colors. Anyway, I do hope my prying did not upset you."

Darion waved his hand in front of his face. "Of course not. Honestly, you seem like you'd try and help me with my issues rather than just silently observe them."

"Only if you wish for the assistance, my friend," F'Skal replied.

The night grew loud with the pressing rain, but the rooms became silent. All four of them finding sleep alongside their new friends, as they awaited the next dawn.

14
RUMORS ON THE WIND

The next morning came with just the barest of rainfall against the windows of the inn. Erika sat up and stretched her arms over her head. F'Lessa greeted her from the middle of the room, already up and doing exercises. The aash elf had heated the bed even better than a warming pan, and without the worry of scalding should Erika accidentally touch her. The warm bed and the freedom to sleep without clothing for the first time in a long while made for quite the restful night for Erika. Even her loosest of tunics seemed to strangle her in the middle of the night at times, so she was happy to have one fully relaxing night, even if she had to deal with some chastising from the aash over her initial hesitance. She sat for a while in the bed, watching F'Lessa go about her routine that she had previously seen in the village. Eventually, the two of them dressed and packed up their things, making their way into the hallway just as Darion and F'Skal were. They bid their good mornings and descended the stairs into the main room where Thrane went about his duties, waving them to any of the open tables. Shortly after sitting, Thrane brought them all meals that consisted of eggs, bacon, and a small bread roll to their table.

Amusingly, the two elves had starkly contrasting reactions to the meal. F'Skal happily began eating the food, commenting to Erika, who sat across from him, how much he enjoyed the varying flavors of every piece. F'Lessa however, spent several minutes picking at the items with her fork and watching her companions eat with a slight scowl. The yellows of her eggs jiggled awkwardly as she stared in near horror. Eventually, Darion reached across the table and explained what they were and what she could expect from them. Erika noticed slight golden streaks running through the elf's hair when she glanced up at Darion, though the young man didn't seem to see them or her gaze. F'Skal met Erika's glance and grinned, saying nothing.

"What did you all normally eat in the forest?" Darion asked, laughing lightly as he thought of the soups and simple roasted meats at the festivities. F'Lessa's hair had streaks of pink as she suddenly flushed at his laugh.

F'Skal was quick to interject. "Mostly venison and eggs—that were plenty scrambled—among other forest flora and fauna. Mushrooms are common, as well as oats that we grow in the village. Once, I obtained the meat of a cerotae through a trade of medicinal herbs with a traveler, though my sister was quick to shun the unfamiliar meat."

Erika considered the large herd animals that bore a single horn on the edge of their nose, commonly farmed in all the Regions. "Ye'll need to get used to the cero meat, love," she said, motioning to F'Lessa. "It's one o' the more usual meats in the towns."

A softer color of blue ran through the elf woman's braids, Erika looking to F'Skal who explained with a barely hushed whisper. "Disappointed."

He was met with a slap on the arm from his sister. "Don't tell them my colors! I can't help it."

She seemed to deflate onto the table slightly, staring at her mostly full plate while her hair now flashed orange.

"I'd be interested to know," Darion offered, causing F'Lessa's hair to alternate between pink and orange, making for an interesting show. "I don't have much experience with elves, and I'd love to know more about you."

F'Lessa peeked up, expecting to see him looking between the two of them, but her eyes widened when she met his eyes directly.

She practically slammed her head back onto the table and put both arms over her head to try to hide the flashing colors. F'Skal and Erika heartily laughed, while Darion grinned at them, obviously not fully understanding the situation. He glanced back down at F'Lessa, unsure of her sudden erratic behavior from her previously stoic nature.

Their mirth was interrupted a moment later though when a man burst into the tavern with a crash. "Thrane! Did you hear the word?"

The owner turned to the newcomer, still wiping off the countertop. "I haven't been out of the building since yesterday, Quill. So, no, I have not."

"Tarkal has an Angelus!" the man blurted in a panic.

Erika dropped her utensils loudly and stood suddenly, jostling the table. "Where?"

Quill looked to her with surprise. "The Region of Tarkal, it's east of here. Sylvanna is at war with them, don't you know this?"

"Details man!" Thrane interrupted. "Give me more details. She's not from around here."

F'Skal eyed the man suspiciously when he gave Erika more of an alienating look than he and his sister had ever received around humans, but Quill answered quickly. "The morning news just released, I got here as fast as I could after. Word is, Tarkal summoned an Angelus to aid in their fight against us!" he approached the counter and asked with a shaking voice. "Does this mean that their Region is more righteous than ours?"

Thrane took a breath. "Could be nothing more than rumors. And if the Angelus chose that blasted place over us, then they've chosen wrong."

"More like Tarkal's choosin' wrong!" Erika shouted, drawing the two men's gaze again. "The Angelus are nothin' but damnable monsters, too busy slaughterin' the masses to know the pain they wrought! They're no better than Daemons!"

Darion and F'Skal worked to try and pull her back down in her seat, both taking notice at the tears that had started down her face despite her determined expression.

"You'll be sent to the Hells for that!" Quill called back, Thrane trying futilely to stop him. "That's the kind of talk that will lead us to ruin! What's with those markings all over you anyway? You a Daemon yourself?"

"I'd rather go to the Seven Hells than the damned Ten Peaks! At least I know how to kill the bastards down there!" she shot back, flexing an Ignis marked arm towards him. "Maybe I am a Daemon then!"

F'Skal stood quickly, holding his hands out to both combatants. "Perhaps we should all take a breath, yes?"

Quill only then took notice of the strange outsiders. "What's a savage doing here?" he said, looking to Thrane.

The owner had worn an expression of disdain since the other man's mention of Erika's markings, throwing an acknowledging nod to the elf and the Fjordling. "They're paying guests, Quill. I'm not to turn away a customer, no matter their heritage."

The man seemed to take this information poorly, scoffing and making for the door. Erika took a step as he stared at her, lighting her hand in flames and clenching it into a fist. His pace increased as she did, and Darion genuinely wondered if he would send authorities after them next.

"My apologies, that's now twice you've had to deal with a rowdy regular," Thrane said. "I do appreciate you keeping your fire down on both occasions, miss. My tavern has quite a bit of wood in its construction."

Erika sat back down, her hand fizzling back to normal and her face contorting as she came to her senses. She nodded her apology, staring at her food. F'Skal returned to his seat across from her, and thanked Thrane for his kind words.

"How did you know about her?" F'Skal asked a moment later, continuing after the owner shot him a look of confusion. "You mentioned heritage and looked to me, as well as her."

He tapped his arm, signifying the markings. "She's an Ignis Blood. My wife was a Terra, her markings were green."

Erika sat back up slightly, taking sudden interest in his story.

"She passed away three years ago unfortunately. We never had any children to continue her legacy. I regret that more than anything.

"Our condolences to you," F'Skal said, bowing in his seat. "It does make sense that you are able to spot the other elements though, thank you for the explanation."

"Well done for noticing the recognition," Thrane replied with a beaming smile. "And don't worry about Quill, he's just worried about Tarkal. Skirmishes are far from here though, and no official statement of war has even been made, so I don't think we've anything to fear for a while."

The four returned to their meal a moment later, Darion watching F'Lessa as she finally ate the food freely, albeit slowly. F'Skal was the only one to see that she ate in the exact order that Darion had: first the bread, then the eggs, and lastly the bacon. He worried about her, and her passiveness in the interaction. F'Skal knew she was nervous when it came to humans, and was unsure of their laws and customs. Her face was painted in frustration, while her hair flashed shades of light red. Erika was distracted completely though, pondering the implications of another Angelus finding its way to her world and the catastrophe that had come with Wystaea.

⸸

Irvine awoke with a scream. Zyrxak quickly shoving a skeletal hand outwards to quell his outburst.

"Do you want to be killed again?" he whispered harshly.

Irvine sat up fully, and looked around, seeing the dead sands around them while he brought his breathing back under control. "No, not especially."

Dying was an unpleasant experience to say the least. Unfortunately, it was a concept that he was no longer unfamiliar with. The Sands of Conflict bore a harrowing curse for every creature that remained in it, and Zyrxak was quick to inform him after the first time he had been slain. He had lasted quite long, considering his injuries upon first arriving here. Irvine eventually fell to a lanceman behind a warrior that he had defeated only seconds before.

"The merciless Gods that lord over these plains are sick creatures by *my* standards," he said in a strangely sympathetic tone towards Irvine, who had just awoken from his first death. "Anyone who resides in this place is expected to fight and expected to die. But here, the dead do not lie. Instead, they rise a time later, as if nothing were amiss in the first place, and are expected to charge into battle once again."

Irvine had tried to take the knowledge as comforting in a way. Now he sat in the sands, freshly awoken from his seventeenth death. The last time he had a longer conversation with Zyrxak, an errant spear had hit him in the chest, marking his fifth. He could only wonder if he was keeping an accurate count.

They had avoided the ongoing conflicts that occurred across the landscape for much of their time here. To Zyrxak's credit, he was exceptionally good at dodging the armies that constantly battled in this awful place. The Daemon leaned close, and observed the thin line across the human's throat from his latest demise. "Well, that one is going to scar for sure, and rather badly I'd say."

Irvine groaned. Another drawback of the place was that the injuries he sustained lingered. The mad sol elf he had battled this time had slipped inside the reach of his lance, slitting his throat before he could react. Irvine could feel the blade dragging across his spine, darkness and the warm sands overtaking him just after. Such things should not be known sensations to the living.

The worst concept of this place was that every time he awoke, it was to the Daemon that started everything negative in his life.

How he wished to see Erika's beautiful face framed in auburn hair at least one more time. She had been one of the only reasons he remained living in his hometown, and he always looked forward to seeing her smile and emerald eyes when he arrived home in Valen.

Not anymore. Here there was only violence, and the Daemon.

He brought a hand up to his throat and felt the open flesh that was quickly stitching itself back together. It was an uncomfortable experience, one that he always hated to endure.

"Thinking about your wench back in the realm of mortals?" Zyrxak inquired sardonically.

Irvine looked to him with an expression of pure malice. "She is no wench, Daemon. And I can think on whatever I choose, thank you."

The specter scoffed, sending a bone shard cascading from his rib cage. As it fell, the chip violently convulsed before swiftly blowing away in the harsh winds of the realm. Zyrxak spared it an irritated stare as was it sent away from them before speaking. "Indeed. However, you may wish to keep your thoughts on the situation at hand, unless you'd like to die more?"

"And you can offer no aid against the denizens and their madness?" he shot back accusingly.

"If I were to die in this plane, I have no guarantees that I would return like you. I know the properties of this realm when it comes to mortals—humans, elves, and dwarves—like you. However, when it comes to Elder Daemons like myself, I have no idea," a wicked smile spread the skull's jaw unnaturally. "I sometimes wonder if that Dreadnaught Angelus was transported here alongside us, and was summarily ripped to shreds by a raving band of orks. How delightful that would be to witness."

"Considering the final clash of the battle, I have reason to believe my lance beheaded the thing. Though I sometimes wonder what would have happened if I had reversed the weapon."

Zyrxak gave him a look feigning offense at the casual comment towards his life, but quickly turned away when he heard something approaching. "Appears to be that raving band of orks I was speaking of. Try not to die this time, hmm?"

Irvine used the butt of the weapon to heave his weary legs upwards, taking a long inhale of the foul air around him as he prepared himself for the inevitable battle.

How he truly missed Erika. Her warm touch seemed like an unattainable heaven.

15
The Inquisitor

The party began leaving *The White Carmino*, planning on heading northwards to the far reaches of the Sylvanna Region, to the port town of Fjordsgate. The morning sun had already risen to a decent height, and F'Skal urged them all onwards to not leave the city any later. His dismay turned to frustration and confusion when the companions were suddenly surrounded by city guards outside the tavern.

Thrane stepped out with a determination. "What's all this then? You harassing my customers?"

"They are your customers no longer, as they have left your establishment," a scantly armored but well-dressed man replied. His dark brown eyes flashed in the early sun, looking as if he hadn't slept in a while. He looked to be purposefully straightening his back, like he was used to a slouch. Even still, he stood slightly under Erika's height. Short blonde hair topped his head, though he brushed it back several times with his hand, seeming annoyed with its refusal to stay back. "This group is under arrest for potential involvement with a murder and is to be questioned. Either you come willingly, or we will be left no other choice than to use force."

Erika's face paled as she watched the scene play out around her, Darion quickly stepping in front of her and the rest of his group. "What murder? We've only just arrived in town last night, who could we possibly have murdered?"

"Surrender your arms and kindly walk with us," replied one of the armored knights, his face obscured by a thick helmet. "We don't want to call upon violence any more than you."

Reluctantly, the group turned over their weapons. Their arms and belongings were placed onto a cart that accompanied them back down a familiar path towards the guild hall they had visited the previous evening.

In time, they arrived at the building, which was now flooding with guards and knights clad in the blue raiment of the city. The mass parted for the thinner man as he walked into the hall, giving him a definite air of authority. As they came closer, Erika let out a gasp when she saw the lifeless corpse of Maral, pushed against the wall in his chair. His eyes were still open, drying in the morning air. Blood had cascaded down his entire front. starting from his throat, some having spattered onto his desk as well. Darion quickly shoved past the guards and exited the building, none moved to stop him upon seeing the look on his face. He arrived at the entryway and began heaving just outside the door and out of sight of the bloodied desk. After a moment, F'Lessa convinced the guards to let her go after the young man to help, while Erika and F'Skal stayed behind.

"The boy's reaction does not tell me much, but yours does," the officer said to Erika, walking slightly around the desk and staring into her face as she looked at the body. "You knew this elf, yes?"

She nodded, hand clasped over her mouth as she purposefully looked away from the corpse.

"Inquisitor, the witness just confirmed that this was the party that she saw last night talking with the victim," one guardsmen said to the officer.

"Inquisitor?" F'Skal asked.

The thin man stepped back around the desk. "Yes. Inquisitor Marq is my full title, I suppose I had not introduced myself properly. I am sanctioned by the Queen of Sylvanna, and the Regional Council to investigate any, and all, crimes against the city or the Region itself, as needed. If the mystery is too large for the local forces, I am to step in and fix what is broken."

The elf nodded his understanding. Erika reminisced to her one time meeting Inquisitor Bael in Sildenfeld several months before her departure, though she had not been as intimidated by him as she was by Marq. She glanced to the side and saw a human girl, likely just younger than herself, standing to the side. Her face wet from the tears that still fell from her eyes. She looked back to Marq with a panic, realizing the implications fully. "We didn't kill 'im!"

"That's what I am sincerely hoping," he said dryly, looking back at the corpse.

F'Skal stepped forward, the green markings on the sides of his face and neck beginning to glow brightly. Several guards stepped forward, but halted when Marq held a hand upwards. "What do you see, elf?"

"I recognize the wound," he said.

"Not helping your case," Marq sighed, his tone still flat. The knight that had stayed close by stifled a laugh.

The aash elf stepped back and motioned to Erika. "Lift your skirt."

She immediately flushed a bright red, glancing to all the eyes that were on her. "I'll do no such thing, F'Skal! What're ye thinkin'!"

"The blade that killed this man is the same that stabbed you in the hip," he explained, pointing down to her wound, though it was still covered by her skirt. "I dressed it several times myself. It was the blade of Hargreave that killed this clerk. You can see the same patterns where his blade tip was jagged from use. Well, perhaps you all cannot see that."

Erika's face fell from embarrassment into dread. "Ye can't be serious. Hargreave fell into the ravine."

"What am I missing here?" the Inquisitor asked, glancing between the two.

F'Skal and Erika then recounted the sequence of events that brought them together, as well as the downfall of the band of mercenaries known as the Heathens. Marq stared at them both intently as they spoke, digesting every word. Erika was unnerved at how he never seemed to blink or acknowledge them, though she somehow knew that he was understanding their story with greater ease than most would have.

While they spoke, Darion finished his vomiting just outside the doors. He could feel F'Lessa's warm hand on his back and was genuinely touched by her concern.

"A shame. Was a good breakfast," he said with a grim smirk, pulling a small rag from his pocket and wiping his lips. "I'm sorry."

She gave him a sympathetic look but quickly glanced away, her hair streaking a light orange color. "There is no reason to apologize. Although, I am confused."

He straightened his back and looked up to the taller woman expectantly.

"Didn't you say you were a guard in your hometown?" she asked, her eyes much softer than he had ever seen them. The red on black was still sharper than any human's eyes, but there was something else that seemed different in them.

"I was. Though I was somewhat new to the occupation. I was better at the rules and laws aspect than I was at the violence."

She nodded her understanding and started to look back into the hall. He tapped her on the arm causing her to startle. "You can go back in with your brother. I'll be alright by myself, I'm sure these fine men will keep a close eye on me."

A few guards shifted around them, confirming his point, but F'Lessa shook her head and looked to the ground. Her hair streaks now running a light pink "No, I'll stay and help you."

Darion smiled slightly, though he was confused about her sudden concern for him. He could hear the conversation inside, as Erika recounted the tale of her final encounter with Hargreave, and how sure she was that he had been killed.

"But you didn't see his body?" Marq asked, Erika shaking her head.

"Strange things do happen, I suppose," F'Skal offered.

The Inquisitor scoffed. "An understatement, I assure you."

As the room continued shuffling around, Inquisitor Marq leaned against the table, though he was careful to avoid the crimson splashes. "So, if your suspicion is true," he said motioning to the perceptive elf. "Then we have a third killer on our hands."

"There's three?" F'Skal said, disbelief lining his tone.

"The first group of killings were incredibly clean, no blood and no heads. Only bodies."

This evoked the memory in Erika of the night before they departed for the forest, though she did not say a word.

"The second set of corpses came that same night, though much more brutal and seemingly random. Now we have this, also brutal, but with a motive," he said solemnly. He looked to Erika and she noticed the colors of his eyes brighten to a brilliant golden color. "Tell me, girl, that no one in your party committed any of these crimes."

She found herself inexplicably drawn to those glowing eyes, and said clearly. "We've only done what is right, defendin' the aash elves in the forest, and ourselves. We did not kill any o' these people."

The Inquisitor closed his eyes, blinking hard several times before nodding. When he opened them again, his eyes were returned to a dull brown, but horribly bloodshot. Erika couldn't help but wince at the obvious pain the Inquisitor was feeling. "Thank you. Let them all go, Carmine," he said to the knight that stood next to him. Carmine nodded without so much as a word and allowed the group to pass out the doors. They collected Darion, F'Lessa, and their weapons, before starting back towards the center of the city once again.

"So who actually did this?" Carmine asked after the party had departed.

Marq took a long draw from a flask before stowing it into his jacket. Carmine scowled slightly as he drank. "This Hargreave individual is certainly a suspect, even if the witness only saw them, and not him. More digging will have to be done, though I have an itching suspicion that those four are not finished with whatever did this. I'm not sure we'll be able to solve this one ourselves."

"You Delved into her, didn't you?" the knight asked him.

"I did."

Carmine took a breath. "Just be careful, Sir."

✝✝

Kharim made his way through the alleyways of the city, preferring to keep a low profile in the light of day. His eyes sagged slightly from the many sleepless days and active nights, but he kept to his task. This city was getting messy, and the multitude of deaths that he had not caused was very worrying. Perhaps he was allowing the ghosts to run a little too freely. The streets crawled with guards, and he had seen the Region's Inquisitor leaving *The White Carmino* with Erika. He regretted involving her—even inadvertently—but knew that she was already intertwined with his own fate. He only hoped to never cross her path under negative circumstances, although he knew he wasn't helping himself in that regard when he purposefully chose to rest outside the inn he knew she was staying at. The blade's voice in his head screamed at him to leave every time he saw her but still he stayed, worried that she had seen too much of his grim task those nights before.

"Out of the way!" a gruff voice called from the side. Kharim narrowly dodging around a shove from the man.

"It is rude to be so rough with strangers," he replied calmly.

His scold was met by a strike from a sword. Kharim deftly brought his weapon to bear and blocked the blade with a ring that echoed through the alleyways. "It is also rude to strike at one who has offered you no quarrel."

Hargreave growled at him, the still bloody blade shaking against Kharim's blocking sword. "I don't have time for you."

Kharim raised a suspicious eyebrow, and flung his blade wide, slinging his opponent away. "What are you searching for?"

"None of your concern, now leave! Forget you ever saw me, or I'll kill you too."

"Your wounds appear grievous. Perhaps you should see a healer?"

"I'll have time to heal later. I need to kill someone, so kindly move aside!"

"Explain who it is you are to kill, and I will consider moving," Kharim shot back, parrying two more strikes to the side. "I will not be easily deterred, and I believe you may have more blood on your hands than even I. *Literally* at this very moment, so I imagine the authorities will be happy to side against you."

Hargreave slouched, clutching a hand to his side where he had taken the brunt of his fall. His one good eye darted around the alleyway and weighed his options. "A woman with red hair crossed me and left me for dead." The recognition in Kharim's eyes sparked an interest in the mercenary. "You know this woman?"

The Haranian nodded slowly. "I believe I do, though I suspect she will not stay here much longer. Perhaps we can assist each other?"

"I'm not interested in a trade," he replied angrily, wanting nothing more than to be done with this interaction.

Kharim smiled slightly, unnerving Hargreave with its callousness. "That is a shame. I cannot allow you to hurt that woman, so I'm afraid I'll have to insist."

Before Hargreave could react, the strange man in the robes was upon him, his face only a breath away from his. A searing pain shot through his body and he realized that this man had bested him in the blink of his one good eye. Kharim had brought his sickle-like weapon upwards, stabbing it underneath Hargreave's ribs, pushing it up into his chest cavity. The world became colder than anything Hargreave had ever experienced, as he believed his life to be leaving him.

"Do not worry," Kharim said, as if reading his thoughts. "You will not die."

Hargreave's form slowly melted into a fine powder-like sand and grafted onto the blade. Each grain slowly made its way down the metal and into the glass handle where his sand met with the rest of the chaotically swirling particles.

The weather began to make a turn for the worse in Sylvanna. The rain fell harder than ever before, but Kharim was unbothered by it as he stood alone in the alleyway. He relished in the rain, so rare and sacred in his home.

16

Tumultuous Emotion

The rain continued around the companions as they walked. Erika and the elf twins relatively fine in their cloaks, though Darion grumbled in the continuing rainfall that soaked him to the bone. F'Lessa offered multiple times to give him her cloak, but he refused each time, especially after a pair of locals under an awning gave them strange looks when she absent-mindedly lifted the fabric from her scantly clad body at one point. Eventually, Erika darted into a small general store and purchased a dull grey cloak for him, which he took gladly but declined putting it on at the time.

"My clothes are already soaked, it'd be pointless to use this right now," he shrugged in explanation.

F'Skal chuckled. "What a drawback to your human customs."

"Still helps when someone tries to gut me, hanging around you lot!" Darion shot back.

"Then simply don't be there for the gutting," the elf continued, still laughing lightly. "Moisture dries from skin much faster than fabric, even with lower body heat."

Erika watched the two in amusement but noticed F'Lessa in a seemingly dour mood not far off, her braids streaking alternating colors of orange and purple. They walked across the great bridge on the north side of the city and towards the northwest island. The rain persisted, becoming more and more biting as they went along. The winds from the bay north of Sylvanna hardly helped either, tossing the torrents in occasional heavier gouts when a sudden strong gust would burst through.

"What's the matter?" she asked the aash finally, confident that the weather would obscure their voices.

In reply she was dragged back by the arm, allowing the two males of their party to ease ahead of them. F'Lessa's expression cracked into concern, her silvery hair following suit into a darker orange color. "Don't humans easily become ill after cold rain?"

"I suppose?" Erika said, unsure of her meaning.

F'Lessa sighed dramatically, speaking as loudly as she dared. "Well then, Darion should avoid the cold rain! He'll get sick going on like this!" Erika stopped in the center of the great bridge and stared at her elf friend. F'Lessa stopped a few feet in front of her and turned back to her. "What is it?"

"Ye care for Darion, don't ye?" she asked carefully, finally revealing her suspicions.

F'Lessa flushed and her hair streaked a hot pink furiously. "I simply do not want him catching any illnesses! He would slow down our progress if that were to happen, and..."

Her speech trailed off when Erika began laughing heartily, likely her deepest and most genuine laugh since before she had lost Irvine. Everything suddenly came into full clarity after F'Lessa had been acting so strangely around them. She almost kicked herself in the leg for not completely understanding sooner. Even F'Skal had been alluding towards it. As he and Darion turned around to investigate her laughter, F'Lessa made a strange squeaking sound for a woman of her size and threw the hood of her cloak over her head. She turned away from Erika and stormed past the two men who were exchanging confused looks. Erika caught up to the two as they both started to question her, but Erika waved them off. "Nothin' to concern yerselves with."

The remaining length of the bridge was walked in relative silence. F'Lessa walked ahead of the group with her hood still drawn, F'Skal and Darion walking abreast and occasionally speaking. Erika fell to the back of the group, looking back to the city periodically.

She knew Irvine had been to what was commonly called the *City of Water* before on his courier missions, but she wished deeply that she could have seen it with him for her first time. Much of her time traveling after joining with Darion had been questioning what Irvine may or may not have seen in his own travels. She wondered if she walked the same paths as him, wondered if their feet fell in the same places, and wondered what he had been thinking when traveling through these locations. Part of her hoped that his thoughts had been of her and wishing that she would join him on his travels. Though she assumed with how often he had declined helping in her father's forge, he likely would have thought it uncouth to invite her along on his occupation.

How foolish that boy could be sometimes.

Erika had to remind herself that he was no longer just a boy. He had grown so much, in such a short period of time. She was always just focused on her friend in Valen that often went out of town that she hadn't noticed how much of a man he'd become in the meantime. She hadn't often dwelt on how long his trips had been, the trials he had overcome, or the experiences he had, until she left their hometown for the first time as well.

How foolish she could be sometimes.

Ahead of her, Darion stared at the cloaked form of F'Lessa, genuine concern washing over him heavier than the rain above them. "Do you think she's alright?"

F'Skal sighed, understanding his sister's plight immediately when she had walked past them as he had seen the intense coloring in her hair. He understood her conflicted feelings, but he was starting to believe that her feelings for Darion were beginning to win out, and if she continued on like this Darion would begin to understand as well. F'Skal wondered what could happen then.

"She is unused to humans," he replied finally, conceding in the partial lie. "She is simply coming to understand her own feelings about things."

"Is that why her hair has been flashing such brilliant colors?"

F'Skal eyed his friend slightly. "You like the colors?"

"How could I not?" Darion laughed slightly. "They are beautiful, and the way they light up her entire face, it really compliments her dark skin and makes for a very appealing sight."

The elf found himself grinning maniacally, though Darion didn't seem to notice. He started to feel a slight bit like a troublemaker, though he couldn't help himself. "And how do you feel about my sister as a whole?"

"Well, she's a very kind person. My initial impression was that she's just very gruff, or maybe even outright hostile, but she is similar to a stuffed toy my sister had back home."

"Oh? How is that?"

"Well, the toy was supposed to resemble a royal gryphon, and while it did to a certain extent, the thing was outwardly terrifying. I used to have nightmares where it would chase after me through the streets of my town, Hellsbent on killing me," he explained.

F'Skal continually raised his eyebrows as the story grew more strange. "And this describes my sister, how?"

"That's the funny part. The gryphon toy was so scary at first, but then I witnessed my sister wake from her own nightmare in the middle of the night. The way she clutched onto the thing, it painted it completely differently. Instead of looking scary, it actually became very fierce and protective. Soft on the inside, but willing to do anything to protect her."

F'Skal watched Darion as he recounted the tale, his eyes still transfixed on F'Lessa. "I think I understand. Like your sister's toy, my sister is very intimidating, or even scary on first meeting. However, after you get to know her, she is revealed to be a very kind being that will do anything for those she cares for."

Darion nodded, looking up to the elf with a sigh of relief. "That's exactly what I mean! I am so glad I explained that so it didn't sound strange."

The aash closed his eyes, then looked forward to his sister again as he chuckled. "Not strange at all."

† †

With time, the rain subsided and the party crossed onto the northwestern island. F'Skal opted to remove his cloak for a while to air out the cloth, while Darion remained in his soggy state. He was convinced by F'Skal to remove his armor and outer layers, leaving him in a simple shirt to dry out somewhat better. Erika was likely the luckiest of the four, having an enchanted cloak that stayed resiliently dry for the most part, leaving her to just wring out her auburn curls.

The trek was still long to the port town of Fjordsgate and it seemed that Darion was starting to near the end of his rope when it came to navigating his home Region. The best they could do was follow the road, which was winding at best and rocky at worst. The incredibly uneven landscape proving to be a tiring walk for even the two elves who boasted greater physical stamina than their human companions. At one point Erika wondered aloud as to how any carts could possibly get through the pass, to which Darion explained that most cargo was taken into the city via smaller boats that could easier navigate the narrow waterways around the island.

The days they spent traversing the tumultuous terrain found F'Lessa using her gem dust given abilities to clear away their rest areas with great efficiency, moving entire fallen trees or boulders. Her feats of strength were always met with a light applause from Erika and Darion. Her hair would initially flash pink in her embarrassment at the attention, but eventually turned a beautiful golden color after she realized the compliments for what they were. From there, Erika and F'Skal would set up their campsites, Erika using her abilities to start their fire with ease.

Whilst they prepared their camps, Darion would scout around the area, taking note of any wild animals that may take unkindly to their presence, while also hunting for a good dinner. One such evening, Darion had scored such a large buck that F'Skal lamented they did not have a cart to carry the leftovers. Darion still smiled as he cleaned the creature, knowing that they could likely fetch a good price for the pelt and antlers. He considered they would have to stop for a while so he could tan the hide though, so it wouldn't become foul before they had a chance to sell it.

F'Lessa sat on a small log watching him intently as he carved through the creature a fair distance from the camp. Her eyes tracked his movements as he separated the pieces and organized everything neatly. She particularly noticed that his hands were caked to his wrists in the animal's blood, although he seemed rather unfazed by any of it, even the less than pleasant smell.

Darion glanced up to her intent stare, causing her to stammer an apology with a quick flash of pink through her hair. He only smirked at her. "Darion, why is it that you are alright with butchering this deer, but you've vomited twice at the sight of gore since we've met?" he asked for her, not particularly mocking her voice in any way.

She nodded to the question, admitting that he had correctly guessed her inner thoughts. Her hair started to run pink again, though she was quicker to draw the hood of her cloak that she had not bothered to do away with since leaving Sylvanna—which was strange behavior according to F'Skal.

Darion paused, his bloodied hands resting to the sides while he looked upwards and took a breath. "Death is a concept that I am well acquainted with. I helped my father hunt and clean animals from an early age, so this is practically muscle memory for me. The death of a person though, is a little different."

F'Lessa looked up again, meeting his eyes from under her hood. "How is this deer any different from the mercenary you killed in my village?"

"The deer supplies many things to us. Its meat and certain organs are used for food. Other organs and antlers can be used for tools and materials. While the pelt can be used for blankets or clothes," he said, the elf nodding to each point. "While I am sad that I had to kill the creature to obtain these things, I regret killing that bastard, Fink, more."

"Why is that? He was a monster that was only interested in torturing the survatri and collecting money for their heads," she pondered, her tone darkening.

Darion spoke again, this time without pause. His words and tone caused F'Lessa to recoil slightly. "Because death was too kind for him. He should have been held accountable for his actions, but instead, I killed him. I lost my stomach because it was the first person I had killed, even if he was a monster on the inside."

F'Lessa deflated as she watched the young man continue his work. She couldn't come up with any more words after that. She saw pain in his eyes and her chest started to hurt, feeling that her words were the cause.

"The blood seems different when it belonged to something that had emotions and thoughts like me," Darion continued after a while, allowing F'Lessa some respite. "Sounds stupid coming from a once-guardsman though, I know."

"Certain feelings cannot be controlled, it seems," F'Lessa said, alluding to more than Darion could know.

Erika watched the two with an interest, especially since she had begun to see a resemblance in F'Lessa to herself. Similarly, she was completely smitten with Irvine, and the young man had seemed absolutely unaware of it. She eventually came to realize that wasn't the case, albeit too late for her liking. Perhaps Darion, as well, was not as clueless as he seemed. F'Skal hardly paid attention to the interaction, spending his time preparing his medicines and turning the sections of meat that Darion had already given him in the pan over the fire.

"It seems so obvious now," she mused, speaking in little more than a whisper. She knew the elf would hear her.

F'Skal just grunted in response, adjusting his sitting position. He retrieved more herbs to grind down after wiping the mortar into a small pouch and cleaning off the pestle similarly. Erika puffed her cheeks out at him, rolling her eyes as she sat back.

"Do not think that I disapprove," he said finally, garnering Erika's attention once again. "I simply wish she would just get on with it."

"How do ye mean?"

He sighed. "She is normally a very prompt individual, completing everything in life with haste and time to spare. However, she has never even entertained the idea of a mate, and as such, I don't think she really knows how to go about it."

Erika smirked now. "Well, I'll tell ye from my own experience. I wish I would've just said somethin' sooner."

"And that is precisely what I think she should do," he replied quickly. "She has no more reason to think that he has any interest in you, so I don't understand why she does not simply tell him how she feels."

She ignored the mention of his possible interest in her, shifting her weight slightly. "Perhaps she's worried that if he were to turn 'er down, the rest o' the journey would be strange or... awkward?"

F'Skal paused a moment, looking to Erika, and then to the pair still seated a ways from them. Erika quickly adding in. "Not that I think he'd turn 'er down! That'd be foolish, I don't think I've ever seen a woman so beautiful."

"You are quite beautiful yourself, Erika," he said, causing the young woman to blush. "Though by the same token, I wouldn't expect him to make his decision based on her physical properties alone. He seems much too complicated for that."

"Aye, I suppose ye've a point there. Time will tell then, I only hope she works up the courage to tell 'im," she said, laying back in the grass and staring at the moons and the stars above them, the clouds finally making way for fairer weather.

† †

The dark of night was much more comfortable in the physical realm. The well-dressed man easily shifted through the southern exit of Fjordsgate, none of the posted guards taking even slight notice of him, despite his casual jaunt through the portal. He tipped his hat to the town with a smile—though he knew no one would see his salute. He was getting closer now, despite the long walk through the realms to arrive here. Vaerisa was likely still enjoying the slaughter in the Fjordlands and hunting more orks, but now was time for a more delicate situation. He could feel the stirring in the Veil even from here. It came from much further south still, but seemed to be moving northwards as well in a meandering way. The chase had begun it seemed, and he knew that the less time he spent, the more pleased his Matron would be. Where was the fun in that though?

Any thoughts he had entertained of being quick in this expedition were ultimately dispelled when he felt a new disruption. The Veil was the thin curtain that lay between the world of the living, and what was known as 'The Isles of the Dead', a place that he could pass through freely. However, this was not a disturbance in that curtain, which felt akin to a cold breeze or a ripple in a pond.

This, was a shockwave.

Given the current circumstances of the world, he believed this likely to be something from the Seven Hells. A scowl spread on his gaunt face, knowing that this would complicate things immensely. Daemons had apparently been popping through left and right in the world of the living, ever since the Sundering.

"If that damned Angelus hadn't butted in last year, none of this would be happening now," he sighed at his helplessness for the world state.

Matron Mortia had sent him for the one disturbing the Veil, but he knew she wouldn't mind a few dead Daemons or Angelus along the way.

17

Thief

Another morning came and the four rose diligently, with Erika the latest to wake from her slumber as was usual. Darion began commenting on the fact but she shot him a glare that quieted him. She turned mocking Irvine's voice. "Ye sleep in incredibly late fer a blacksmith."

None of her companions could understand the significance more than the obvious jeering at her weariness in the morning. She rubbed at her eyes, annoyed that she had such a hard time waking up sometimes.

They all packed their belongings in silence while Erika made sure that the fire was completely doused. Suddenly, F'Skal dumped his entire bag of supplies, making the other three startle at the sound. "Where could it have gone?" he said frantically.

"What's gone?" Darion asked.

"My mortar and pestle, I had set it beside myself to dry overnight from the herbs I had ground," he said, his concern increasing.

Darion seemed flustered. "I didn't see anything during my watch last night."

Erika and F'Skal both looked to F'Lessa, who had taken the first lookout shift. She widened her eyes and flushed slightly, her hair alternating between pink and red. "I was keeping a tight vigil! I am appalled at your doubt!"

"Then it has to be around here somewhere, right?" F'Skal said, searching in the underbrush near them.

Erika had a sudden sneaking suspicion and checked her own satchel. Her heart rate quickening when she noticed the absence of the small jewelry box that Irvine had intended to give to her. "Anythin' but that!" she called out involuntarily, drawing the attention of the other three.

Similarly, Darion found his whittling knife missing, and F'Lessa was unable to locate her cloak.

"What could possibly have taken them?" Darion said, breathing a sigh of exasperation. "F'Lessa saw nothing during her watch, and I saw nothing during mine! Not even goblins are so sneaky as to not raise even a perked ear."

His statement was met with nods, but no propositions for an answer. Eventually, with their heads hung low, they felt they had no choice but to continue their journey without their belongings. None were more distraught than Erika, who began kicking herself for not leaving the trinket with Teria in Sildenfeld as she fought back tears. The only of them that seemed completely unbothered by the missing items was F'Lessa, who, despite the heavy autumn chill, had no issue without her cloak.

Onwards they marched, all keeping an eye open for whatever may have stolen their items. They sat for a rest when midday came around, all of them chewing on rations and taking draws from their water supplies. Conversation comprised of Darion explaining the Region holidays to the two elves, and what they had missed with the Harvest Festival. Erika kept quiet for that recounting, despite adding extra tidbits to other holidays earlier in the year. F'Lessa listened with interest, but F'Skal seemed still irritated over the loss of his medicinal tools. He was commonly more comfortable preparing medicines than just simply sitting still during their rests, his hands wringing together without anything to work on.

As they began to leave from their rest, their problem continued even further.

"Has anyone seen *my* cloak?" Darion asked, looking around the small area that they had rested in, finding no sign of the garment they had just recently purchased.

The group collectively shook their heads, and though F'Lessa was in no hurry to find her own cloak, she was suddenly very worried about his. "We'll surely need to find that!" she said. "The weather is getting colder, you'll need it to avoid a chill."

Erika and F'Skal exchanged an amused look, but agreed that the two humans would need to keep as warm as possible as they did not have the same comforting body temperature as the two elves. "Darion could always just get real close to ye when it gets colder," Erika jeered, making F'Skal stifle a laugh and causing F'Lessa to shoot her a bewildered expression. Darion didn't seem to notice the comment, too busy looking around at the forest that surrounded them.

Their biggest continuing issue was that they had no clues to go on, and no signs of anyone coming and stealing their things. However, as they began walking again, Darion thought he saw something in the forest next to them. A strange shape that disappeared from the edge of his vision just as quickly as he had noticed it.

†⸸

Craven made his way southwards still, the day pressing on and the sunlight becoming increasingly more irritating, despite the heavy cloud cover. The realm around him began to shift, a sardonic smirk spreading across his face at the realization that he was being pulled back into the Isles of the Dead. Moments later, he stood on a barren hill overlooking the scattered dark islands lit only by the greenish glow from beneath them. Without hesitation, he bowed deeply when a figure stepped lightly in front of him. She was dressed in long flowing robes of the darkest black, her raven hair draping down to her legs, her eyes covered by an ornate crown that almost appeared made of bone. Below her clasped hands, she held the chains of a thurible that exuded a gentle smoke, smelling faintly of jasmine and sage. The thin robes outlined her shapely feminine form as a wind whispered across the Isles, rippling the fabric, carrying the laments of the dead with them.

"Greetings to thee, my Queen," Craven said slowly, all emotion erased from his face.

"Well met, Craven of the Endless Waters," she replied, her pitch-colored lips unmoving with her words but curled in a slight yet voluptuous smile. "I trust thine quest proceeds with naught in the ways of tribulations?"

Craven stood a moment later after he felt her cold slender fingers draw sensuously across his shoulder, though she appeared to not have moved her hands from the chains she held. "No, Matron. Although, I fear that may no longer be true for much longer. I have sensed a disturbance, not just in the Veil, as I expected, but in the Walls as well."

"Indeed. The Walls hath become weakened upon the Sundering. The work of the Elder Daemon, Zyrxak," she confirmed, causing Craven to take some pause at the name. "Worry not, my love. Thou art not one to be disheartened, I know well."

As she stepped lightly around him, he glanced down to her bare feet peeking from the edges of her robes. He was unsure of what to say, as he always was when she called upon him. Moments later she was behind him and quietly walking away.

"Matron?" he called after her, meeting her delicate features as she turned back to him. "Will I have the strength to rid the living realm from this blight?"

A chill ran down his spine when her black lips curled into a more defined smile. The Isles vanished from around him, her form drifting into smoke with the rest of the realm. His gaze fell to the ground again, as he found himself returned to the world of the living. His question was more out of habit than actual curiosity. Even if he knew the answer, Matron Mortia was always so vague.

⸸

Through the remaining course of the day, more items had gone missing, including one of F'Lessa's axes and the crossing halter that Erika had been given by the aash elf. Moods soured as things disappeared, but the troupe carried onwards. Darion found himself scanning the tree line, searching each time they discovered lost belongings for the shape that he had seen. Indeed he had found it again, but only in fleeting glimpses. He still could not get a good look at the creature, if it truly was a creature at all. He began wondering if he was going insane looking for something that was never actually there, yet still he searched. Several times, F'Lessa would ask him what he was looking for, but each time he would wave her off or simply use a small animal as an excuse. She didn't seem to believe his simple lies and he never expected that she would, even if she did nod her head and leave him be whenever he made them.

He was unsure what had changed in the elf to suddenly check on him so often. He had understood her to be Erika's 'attendant' in the aash village, but he was unsure if she was continuing with that role or not. Now it seemed like she was more his attendant than anything. He certainly didn't mind the attention from her, even if her size was a bit startling when she'd suddenly appear alongside him, as well as that scrutinizing gaze she commonly gave him. He nearly laughed aloud when he thought about the fact that he was intimidated by Erika when he first met her, but now F'Lessa was much worse of the two. Perhaps some of that lay in the fact that she had killed Bull with her bare fists, a man that had easily lifted him by the collar of his shirt. He appreciated the softer look she would sometimes give him infinitely more, most times having to forcibly rip his gaze from her red eyes when she would look at him that way. *I wonder if I've become her attendant,* he found himself thinking, since he was the one commonly teaching her about human culture, foods, and customs.

His thoughts were interrupted when he glanced up to find that the booklet F'Skal commonly scrawled notes into had fallen on the ground and was slowly moving off the road into the tree line. The land sharply cut downwards in a deep slope shortly after the edge of the highway, obscuring Darion's sight line quite a bit. The notebook moved as if being pulled by some invisible strand, adding nothing but strangeness to the uncanny scene.

"What in the Seven Hells?" he muttered, only the perceptive ears of F'Skal picking up on the quiet words. Darion was already off, his blade flashing into his hand and following the booklet into the forest.

F'Skal stammered a shout to the girls, but felt forced to follow his friend down into the uneven grounds below their current smooth road. Erika and F'Lessa only realized a few moments later that both of them were away.

Incredulity washed over Darion as the notebook in its sudden flight had actually taken literal flight, and was increasing in speed.

He wondered if he should wait for the others, or if the others even realized he was missing yet, as he hadn't actually said anything to anyone before dashing off to give chase. What if the creature doing this was something he couldn't handle alone and he had just abandoned his only chances of survival on the road? His mind swam with thoughts of error, but he did his best to shove them out, if only to keep focus on the small handbook that was increasingly hard to see between the trees.

Far behind now, Erika's stomach had dropped in nervousness at the prospects of what they were chasing after. F'Skal had shouted out from somewhere ahead, his enhanced eyes seeing what was happening. "Something is being taken from us! As if from an invisible thread!"

Those words suddenly evoked more poor memories of the previous year. In the final battle with Zyrxak, she and Teria had fought a Daemon of Lust in the fields outside Valen. The creature employed the use of spidery strands to puppet soldiers against their wills and murder their kinsman. In another sick use of its power, it had removed Teria's leg from her body, ending her career as a ranger and nearly ending her life. It had taken all of Erika's strength to finish the Daemon off, and she only hoped it wasn't another one of those creatures that was pulling their belongings on a thin thread as bait into a larger web of lethality.

She couldn't focus on her concern though, as she struggled with the uneven ground that led down the small mountainside they had been traveling on. Her fear of heights had not affected her much as they descended, likely due to the trees that filled the space. Now however, she was nearly falling down such a sheer slope that she wondered how trees actually even thrived here. She found herself struggling with every single fallen trunk, every spare boulder, and every patch of loose earth. Her screams and squeals did nothing to slow the aash elves ahead of her, carried easily down the ridge on their shapely muscled legs in pursuit of Darion and the suspected culprit of the thefts. Several times she found herself rolling uncontrollably down the hills, becoming dizzied in the spinning landscape, only to stop when she hit a rock or a tree trunk. She was happy to hit on her armor plates for the most part, though she did her best to focus enough should she need to immolate an arm to stop her chaotic tumble. Unfortunately, she soon lost track of her aash friends and eased down to a sitting position on a rocky outcropping a few feet from the next lower level, searching for movement but finding none. She breathed a low groan of exasperation at the disappearance of her companions, but relieved in the respite and the opportunity to catch her breath. She knew them to be capable and rational enough to avoid a fight if it were too much for them. For now, she waited for any sign of them, not wanting to become lost herself. With a sigh, she rested her hands on the cool rock behind her, idly swaying her legs off the small ledge.

Darion continued running. As he followed the booklet around a tree, the thing took a hard turn. He skidded to a stop, kicking multicolored fallen leaves and dirt away from his boots as he did. He looked up to find a creature just under his height that appeared akin to a goblin: drooped pointed ears, angled chin, and jagged teeth, with wrinkles and cracks running the length of his ugly face. The creature was grey as stone, with bright gold eyes that pierced through Darion like a spear point. It stared at him as its clawed hands gingerly pinched a grasp on the notebook.

"That's not yours!" Darion wheezed, barely lifting his blade to the creature that he recognized from the silhouette in the forest that he had seen before. "And I'm willing to bet you've got several other things that aren't yours as well."

The thing looked at the booklet between his forefinger and thumb, and back to Darion in confusion. "Is it not? I do believe there is a certain rule called 'finder's keepers', yes?"

Darion raised an incredulous eyebrow at him as he struggled to catch his breath from the chase. "You quite literally just stole that from my friend's bag!"

"You seem to be more confused than me, my boy!" the goblinesque creature replied with a shrug. "I was simply taking a stroll through this lovely forest, and this interesting little trinket just floated into my hand, such a curious thing!"

Darion cocked his head to the side, unable to understand what the creature was reasoning, but was saved the trouble when he heard his companions skidding down the hill. He turned around the tree to find F'Lessa coming just ahead of her brother, a concerned look painted her face. Her braided hair flashed orange streaks behind her as she held her one remaining axe at the ready.

"This creature is the culprit," he said to them, pointing his sword tip behind the tree. Through his friends' confused looks though, he glanced back to find the thief gone. "It was just here!" he stammered with a curse, twisting around madly in his search for what he had only just been conversing with.

His spinning became more and more furious, his mind swimming with guilt and confusion until he was abruptly halted. F'Lessa held his shoulders tightly for a moment before putting her warm hands to his cheeks and leaning down to look him in the eyes. "It is not your fault," she said in a firm, yet gentle tone that brought him back to matters at hand. Darion's already racing heart felt like it skipped as he stared into her beautiful face, her calloused hands still holding his. "We believe you that there was a creature and we will find it. You did well."

A short while later, F'Skal peered around the area, his gem dust glowing radiantly as the magic amplified his sight. "You said it appeared goblin-like?" he asked.

Darion sat on a small stump, sketching a rough likeness of the thing on a spare piece of parchment he had. "Yes, though it had skin like stone, or at least colored so. Much bigger as well, his head came up to my chest." He returned to his hasty sketch, suddenly distracted when F'Lessa leaned closely over him to take a look at the page. He jolted as the soft warmth of her breast pressed on his shoulder, her breath wafting across his neck. His face flushed as he tried to keep his eyes on the paper in his hands.

"Gods! There ye all are!" Erika exclaimed, causing all three of them to startle. F'Lessa's silvery hair drew across Darion's cheek as she rose suddenly, only causing his face to warm further.

"Where've ye been? What's happened?" Erika continued.

F'Skal was the first to answer, while Darion tried to refocus on his sketch. "There was a creature, it stole my notebook with some kind of magic, pulled it straight from my bag and into its claws. Darion found it, but when we arrived, it disappeared."

Darion held an expression of shame for a moment, until F'Lessa patted him gently on the shoulder. "Fortunately, it appears to be heading northwards, just like us, or at least following us. So, we'll be able to confront it again, and perhaps barter for our belongings back."

Erika regarded her words, though she didn't care for the idea of trying to barter with a thief for things that it had stolen from her. With a sigh, she looked back the way they had come. "Well, should we be headin' onwards then?"

F'Skal nodded, and joined her in the trek upwards to the road they had previously followed. F'Lessa lingered, watching Darion as he meticulously scrawled on his parchment. "Darion, please don't blame yourself for this," she said softly, her hands clasped behind her hips. "Let's get back to the path."

She waited only a moment longer, as Darion didn't seem to acknowledge her words. She sighed quietly, resisting the urge to pull him along by the hand and started after F'Skal and Erika. She just hoped that Darion would be soon behind her.

† †

Craven watched the group as they discussed what that had stolen their property. Avarice Daemons were hardly the most dangerous of the Legions, but they were troublesome and slippery. He himself took more interest in this curious party though, two humans and two aash elves, and one of the elves seemingly infatuated with one of the humans. A grin spread across his lips, amusement filling him and thoughts of how he could garner some aid with this company. First, he needed to prove his own worth.

He set off, quickly and quietly as a breeze, melting through the shadows, up the slopes and back towards the road he himself had just been traveling southwards on. He could feel the presence of the Daemon, but not exactly where it was. Luckily, he knew the way to draw the creature out. When he arrived on the roadway, he made sure to keep ahead of the group he had found, retracing his steps northwards once again and finding the right spot for his gambit.

After a short while, he found it. With a flick of his wrist he sent a globule of darkness onto the middle of the roadway. The black smoke around it coalesced and solidified into a music box, the small trinket sitting just barely open and resonating a muffled song in its chimes.

"Surely the Daemon cannot resist such a treasure," he mused quietly to himself as he promptly leapt onto a tree branch above the road. Now all that was left was to observe.

18

Avarice

Erika pondered the events that had transpired, and given Darion's description of the creature, she no longer suspected it to be a Daemon of Lust. She knew it to be a Daemon of one of the Seven Circles, however she could not remember which that it belonged to. Teria had given her extensive lessons on the various types of Daemons, and while she remembered some, she had not been able to retain it all, regretting her common dozes during the lectures with the woman as she paced in her wheeled chair. This one didn't seem to be of the more outwardly violent variety such as Wrath, Pride, or Envy. It did cross her mind that it could simply be a Sloth Daemon, but the thought was quickly discarded when she considered how quickly the creature had vanished from Darion's sight.

Leaving only Gluttony and Avarice.

One of the former had been a combatant against their forces in the battle with Zyrxak and she had heard that it had caused Irvine some considerable harm. That and the reports mentioning the thing being amorphous and ooze-like in appearance made the strongest possibility being an Avarice Daemon. It made sense, considering all of the seemingly random items that had been taken from them.

What would a Daemon possibly want with a jewelry box with an emerald pendant? Erika thought causing her to seethe with frustration and further her drive to find the creature and reclaim what was rightfully hers.

To her continued irritation, her companions seemed to be considering ways that they could barter for their supplies and come to a peaceful resolution with the thieving sneak. "Better to just kill the damned thing," she muttered under her breath as she walked. The wonderful experience she had with the survatri in the aash village was surprising and amazing, but it was far from enough to erase the memories of the previous year.

As they moved further, her mind drifted from the subject of the Daemon, and onto the weather. It was getting significantly colder and the leaves in the trees were beginning to fall heavily, long after changing into the colors of autumn. She knew that some of the temperature drop was due to their trek northwards, but much of it was still because of the lateness of the season.

"Darion," she called back, drawing him from his conversation with F'Skal. "What day did we leave Sylvanna?"

He thought a moment "I believe it was the twenty-eighth," his expression darkened as he continued. "Commemorant is over, we'll have to take extra precautions during the nights."

"Shite," Erika muttered as her face soured as well, though her reaction wasn't completely due to the coming monthly festivities or beliefs. "Superstitious, Darion?" she said, trying to lighten her own mood.

"Not especially," he replied quickly. "Just wanting to make sure everyone is safe is all."

"I'm confused," F'Lessa cut in. "What is so bad about nights during the month of Hallowden?"

"Superstitions about ghosts," Erika explained, stopping in the road and giving her a flat look.

Darion broke off from the group and threw his arms up in the air. "There are legends and stories about the Veil—the barrier between the world of the living and the world of the dead—becoming very thin when Hallowden comes around. I've never heard proof of otherwise, so I don't feel like taking chances."

Erika rolled her eyes, but F'Lessa extended a hand towards Darion. "There's nothing to worry about Darion, we will be careful. Maybe Erika just has other issues with the month?"

F'Skal narrowed his eyes at Erika when she exhaled sharply, and he suspected his sister was closer to the truth than she knew. A nagging part of his mind demanded to find out in that moment. "What is your other issue with the month, Erika?"

The Fjordling stared at him as if he had shot an arrow at her with no warning. Before she could answer, Darion called out, startling them all from the suddenly tense moment. "There he is!"

The three turned to find the suspected Avarice Daemon thief crouching in the middle of the road, a massive wicker basket tied to his back. He clawed irritably at a small object on the cobbled stone.

The creature nearly fell over as the troupe rushed up to him. "What is wrong? Can I help you?" he asked, almost in a panic.

"Give back what you stole!" Darion yelled with a force that surprised all of them.

"I am afraid I do not know what you speak of," the Daemon replied. "I have not stolen anything, I only carry what I have found."

Erika bit back a curse, but wasn't able to contribute before F'Skal stepped in. "Then perhaps we can barter for some of those items, if you'll be so kind to show us your wares."

"Metlox is my name. I do not believe any of my belongings are directly for sale, but perhaps we can come to some kind of agreement," he said, pulling the heavy looking wicker basket from his shoulders and placing it on the ground as if it weighed next to nothing. His gaze continually flashed back to the object in the road, a small music box that echoed a faint but muffled tune.

The contents inside were somewhat visible, Erika spotting some of their belongings quickly, such as F'Lessa's axe, and the clothing that she had given her in the village. "What use could ye possibly 'ave fer a woman's halter?" she asked accusingly as she pointed to the garment.

Metlox looked taken aback suddenly, like she had insulted him. "What use do you have for all the things you carry? Perhaps no use now, but later you may have a use for them."

"I've got a use fer this hammer right now, ye'll be sure o' that!" she growled, stepping forward before F'Skal yanked at the straps of her breastplate and pulled her behind him.

"It does seem as if you have happened upon some items that we've lost, and if there was a way we could obtain them from you again, we would be much obliged," he said after Erika finally stopped struggling against him.

The Daemon's face curled into a smile. "Perhaps we could play a game for it then? I do dabble in a bit of magic, and can make things interesting for some coin."

"How do you mean?" Darion asked, keeping a hand on the hilt of his weapon, but not drawing it.

"Simple, really! Just wager one of those shiny aurums, and then you'll obtain an item from my basket," he answered, snapping his gnarly clawed fingers. The holes into the wicker basket suddenly went dark, Metlox stepping slightly to the side and seemingly trying to ignore the music box that he was having trouble picking up just earlier.

"For example, you simply pay to play the game," he continued, snapping his fingers on the opposite hand, causing the basket to flash gold before a worn old shovel fell from the top of it. "And you win something, though I do not think you need this." He made a weird face at the thing as it landed on the ground by his foot.

Darion glanced to the two elves while Metlox casually tossed the tool back to the top of the basket, where it promptly disappeared. "We have money to spare," he said quietly to his companions. "I'm sure we could win back our belongings, right? Even if it is a bit of a gamble."

Erika had to resist the urge to groan, sure that the Daemon wouldn't play the game fairly, but knew that Darion wanted to avoid violence if he could.

The group—excluding Erika who had retired to a nearby tree stump—agreed to the terms of the game and began their trials with some success. F'Lessa was returned her axe and Darion's cloak was won shortly after, the aash woman breathing a sly sigh of relief at both. Everything else up to that point was consistently odds and ends that had no pertinence to them. One turn they received a small hooded lantern with no oil, another time a broken crossbow bolt, and then a half of a chair that had been cleanly sliced in two from top to bottom.

Erika began to tire of Metlox's game, much preferring the option of just beating the Daemon down until he returned their things, though her companions seemed more interested in earning their belongings back in the unsavory game. "Just because the survatri are nice, doesn't mean all Daemons are," she muttered under her breath.

The sight of the Avarice Daemon's grin made her blood boil and her internal flames start to heat her flesh. Yet she had no chance to act upon that rage as a newcomer suddenly appeared behind the Daemon. Dressed in a grey waistcoat and a jet black jacket. The gentlemanly looking individual grinned wider than the Daemon ever could.

Metlox's grin vanished instantly into an expression of terror.

Erika stood and started forward, but didn't even see the man draw his thin rapier. The strike was precise and clean, piercing into the Daemon's large skull and protruding from the other side before any of them realized how close the newcomer was. Metlox's head lurched to the side from the sheer force of the attack, the barest of pained groans escaping his gaping mouth.

F'Lessa and F'Skal drew their weapons in a flash, but the man simply raised his hands in surrender. Darion fell backwards with a startled yelping curse, heaving slightly from the sight of the brutality.

"I mean you no harm," he said in a smooth baritone. "It only seemed as if this rabble was giving you trouble."

Metlox's corpse began to fall, the light from his eyes faded and his skin even more stone-like now. As he fell the man retrieved his weapon with his opposite hand in a smooth motion, slinging it to the side, spattering golden-colored blood onto the stones below. The group looked on in shock, careful of the stranger even as he sheathed his thin blade into its scabbard and once again raised his hands. "I'm sure this Daemon has stolen something from you?" he said, stepping back and kicking the wicker basket onto its side, spilling its great many contents. F'Skal scowled as he quickly surmised from the ensuing avalanche of objects that they would have long run out of money before obtaining their belongings again.

Erika grinned slightly despite herself as she stepped forward, watching as the Daemon faded into a gold light that stretched into the sky. A sure sign that the Daemon was dead and sure proof that this individual understood as well as she did as to how dangerous the creatures could be. "And who might ye be? A Daemon slayer?" she asked.

He let out what seemed to be a genuine chuckle and replied. "A slayer perhaps, but not specifically of Daemons. My name is Craven, and for now I am a simple traveler, Daemon slayer no longer. Now that the Daemon is dead, that is."

F'Skal helped Erika gather their belongings, Craven also lending them an aiding hand in sifting through the various items that spilled from the basket. He also offered that they could sell some of it in town to regain the coin that did not reappear when Metlox was slain. Darion claimed Erika's tree stump, gripping his arms around himself and having a general look of trying not to lose his last meal. F'Lessa draped his returned cloak around him, and after a brief consideration, wrapped her arms around him in an attempt to comfort him. Darion hardly noticed her warmth or tenderness, his eyes locked on the spot where Metlox had fallen, although the corpse was no longer there.

F'Lessa found herself even more drawn to him despite his weakness with death, and for some reason, had a strong desire to protect him from just that. "Everything will be alright," she said softly, bringing his head to gently rest on her breast while stroking at his hair. "I'm sorry things ended the way they did."

Erika glanced back to them, as Darion held his head under the cloak to try and bury his face in one hand, F'Lessa simply holding onto him with a sad expression. Erika smiled slightly, but it turned to a grim scowl when she considered that her own happiness was somewhat at his expense. Eventually, she found the jewelry box and snatched it from the pile. She turned from the group and peeked slightly into the container, just to confirm that the contents still lay inside. She breathed a sigh of relief when she caught the glint of the emerald wrapped in silver. She quickly stowed it into her satchel, making sure to bury it under the other contents and continued helping to find the rest of their items, happening upon F'Skal's mortar and pestle next.

"So ye said we could sell some o' this and get some extra aurums?" she asked the newcomer. "The next town up is Fjordsgate, right? We could sell it there, an' maybe get passage to Máðir with the coin?"

Craven seemed to perk up slightly. "Oh, you're heading for Fjordsgate?"

F'Skal and Erika looked up to him, nodding in unison at the query.

"Ah, I am afraid the port town is closed to the general public. They would not let me through the south gates, I have a hard time thinking they'll let two aash elves in even with their human companions," he continued. "Perhaps we could stick together for a while longer? Head back south to Sylvanna and perhaps make our way to another port? I'm heading to the northlands myself."

Erika sighed heavily at the news, but nodded. "Aye, that'd probably work fer us. Ye seem plenty capable a fighter, though do forgive if we have one o' our own do the watch fer the nights."

"But of course," Craven said with a smile. "I wouldn't expect a new group of traveling companions to trust me implicitly upon our first meeting. If it makes you any more comfortable, I can make my camp elsewhere for the nights. Simply traveling with others would be wonderful."

F'Skal was quick to reply. "No no, please stay close by when we camp. Safety in numbers, as my father commonly says."

Craven smiled and nodded at the elf, though F'Skal was wary of the stranger, unsure of the truthfulness in his words. His trust further wavered when they departed south on the road. He glanced back at the music box that Metlox had been trying to pick up, still laying in the road, before it faded into a wispy black smoke.

† †

The party of five spent the remaining hours of the day on the road back towards Sylvanna, stopping only when Darion volunteered to hunt a deer for their dinner, though F'Lessa had to help him retrieve it when he was having trouble lifting the animal from where it had fallen between two downed trees. When they prepared it that night, Darion was unable to eat his entire portion due to a lack of appetite. Erika eyed him as he gnawed on a piece of meat, knowing that he was likely still fixating on the death of the Daemon from before. He had a hard time eating for a while after she killed the ogre and after he killed Fink, even if he did do well at hiding it in the village. F'Lessa seemed even more doting on him than she had in the last few days, Erika figuring that even she could easily see what was bothering him.

Craven was locked into a conversation with F'Skal, as the elf continually asked him more and more questions about many disparate things. The latest of which being his choice in weaponry.

"I am able to use plenty different types of tools when it comes to combat. Daggers, broadswords, axes, bows, all of them are sufficient when it comes to battle. The rapier, however, has a certain elegance to it I find. It always spoke to me since I had first come across it," he said between his small bites of venison.

F'Skal listened intently, but Erika noticed the narrowness of his eyes and the sharpness of his brow. "I see, and have you had this particular rapier for a long while? Or is it a new commodity?"

"Hardly new," Craven answered with a chuckle. "I have had this beautiful work of art for a great many years now."

F'Skal seemed satisfied with the answer, but was already working up a new question. He lost the chance to ask it when Craven held up a hand to him after wiping his mouth. "Perhaps we should forego the questions for now? It seems one of your human companions is not feeling quite well, and I cannot help but wonder if our banter is bothering the poor boy."

Darion glanced up at the mention of him, his eyes cold and empty, but his brow angled into anger and annoyance. F'Lessa flew into a panic, her hair flashing orange hues as she struggled to think of a way to distract Darion.

"I have many things I could say right now," Darion said past F'Lessa trying to garner his attention. They were the first words that Erika had heard from him since before Metlox had been slain. "However I do not think any of them would do any good."

Craven smirked. "Signs of a sound mind, good to hear. Picking your battles is a good thing to do, especially when you do not know much about your enemy."

Erika snapped her gaze back to Darion, her stomach dropping when she saw the look in his eyes change at Craven's goading. "Curious choice of words. You picked a battle with a Daemon that the average person does not know much about. Honestly, I'd say that the only one here that truly knew anything about that creature was Erika." F'Lessa's eyes went wide, flashing to Erika who similarly was shocked at Darion's sudden divulge of information. "So why is it, that you suddenly just appear and slay a Daemon that we were simply playing a game with in order to retrieve our belongings?" Darion finally finished, seemingly unaware of anyone or anything around him besides Craven.

The man in black's smile widened further. "And do you play a game with the common thief that stole your coin purse in town? Or do you turn him into the authorities and have him hanged?"

"What if he were a starving child who needed money to purchase food?" Darion shot back.

"Then the boy is delusional and should simply steal the food," he leaned forward and put a hand on his knee. "Your reasoning ties circumstance into the treatment of the thief, to which I say: this thief was a Daemon. If the thief were a malicious man who could not be steered into a proper direction, the average person would have him executed by the guards. If it were the boy, they may give him a handful of coins and a slap on the wrist. The Daemon is closer to the malicious man on this scale here. I did the world a service, I did you *all* a service as you had no way of fairly winning your stolen goods back."

Darion slumped back. "Lives aren't so simple for one man to dictate."

"Daemon lives are different, they chose that when they wrought genocide against this world," Craven said with a finality, his smirk having fully disappeared into a hard expression that gave all of them pause. "Fair is fair, eye for an eye."

Darion started to speak again, likely with a defense using the survatri as an example, but F'Lessa moved to snatch his attention away. She placed a hand on his knee and leaned between him and his opponent, her other hand caressing his cheek. Erika couldn't make out what she said to him, but knew that it was at least in an attempt to be comforting to him. She had some hope that F'Lessa could work out her feelings for him, but now that Darion seemed to have something around to hate, he seemed so distracted that she doubted he'd be able to provide an answer at this point even if she did work up the nerve to confess her feelings. She sighed deeply when she saw how Darion's gaze seemed to go through F'Lessa, rather than see how she was calming him. Erika finished her own meal in silence along with the rest of the group. Even F'Skal ceased his continual questions and ate in relative peace, though he still watched the newcomer with scrutiny. He quickly volunteered for the nightly watch, if only to keep an eye on Craven.

19

Hallowden

The days passed with ease on their trek back to Sylvanna. The cooler weather blowing down from the north with forceful gusts that made Erika's stomach swim when they again walked alongside the cliffs of the northwestern island. F'Skal spent most of the journey either on his own or alongside Erika, leading to casual conversation—to distract her from the heights—about her home Region or jests about his sister and Darion when they were not in earshot. They found the pair to be commonly outside of their speaking range and walking together. Occasionally they would stop alongside one another to gaze at the scenic mountains above them to their west or the gaping cliffs to their east. The latter vista was accompanied by the tumultuous waters far below, crashing against the rock with the irregular rhythm that Erika came to know from the tides.

She reminisced briefly over the trips she and Irvine had sometimes taken to the shoreline not far from their home. Days spent in and beside the water. She had always felt so far from home when they took those trips, taking solace in Irvine and his extensive traveling experience, even if the coast was only a few hours from Valen by foot. How far and out of reach those waters seemed to be from her now. Irvine even more so.

She began to wonder if she would ever see him again, and how changed both of them would be if they ever did find one another. She touched a hand to her face, realizing that he had never seen her with the Ignis marks up to her head, outlining her eyes and curling over her cheeks. He had kept a small painting of her in his satchel to remember home on his journeys, making her wonder if he would prefer how she looked back then. She looked down at herself, suddenly becoming aware of how much she had gone through. All the new markings and scars. Would Irvine even recognize her anymore?

Her thoughts were interrupted when she felt a warm hand on her shoulder. She glanced up to find F'Lessa's concerned face staring down at her.

"You feeling alright?" she asked.

Erika smiled weakly and nodded. "Aye. I'm just, feelin' a bit down is all."

F'Lessa drew her in to an embrace, lightly brushing her fingers through her thick auburn hair. "You'll find what you're looking for. We'll make sure of it."

Erika turned her head to keep from suffocating, but the warmth did make her feel a little better. She realized she hadn't begun hugging her new companions as much as she had some of her old friends in the Sildenfeld Region. She decided to try and remedy that going forwards.

Darion stepped past them, smiling at the small bit of Erika's face that peeked out from between the dark elf's breasts. "We're nearly back to Sylvanna now. Guess we'll get to partake in some of the Shadesfall festivities, eh?"

Erika slumped slightly in F'Lessa's arms, causing both her and Darion to give her a confused look.

"What is wrong with this festival?" F'Lessa asked, pulling away from her and holding her shoulders at arm's length.

"Nothin' is wrong with the holiday itself," Erika started, "besides the ghost stories havin' scared me a bit as a girl."

Darion piped in again. "So, there is something else that's got you dreading this month? You've been scowling at every mention of Hallowden since I mentioned it the other day."

"It's my birthday," she conceded after a long pause. "I never liked sharin' with the celebration o' the dead 'cause it used to frighten me, as I said, an' I don't remember ever spendin' a birthday without my papa or..."

"Him?" Darion continued for her, Erika confirming with a nod.

He sighed quietly. "And I'll guess you're more upset about the latter not being around for your birthday?"

Erika's silence was the only answer he needed, F'Lessa giving him a grim look. He started back down the road, looking back to them. "Well, maybe we can treat you to a good birthday in his stead, hm?"

F'Lessa placed her hand on Erika's back and ushered her forwards, where F'Skal was watching them. Just to the side, Craven stood at the edge of the precipice. Erika shuddered when she noticed that only his heels sat on the ground, the toes of his boots hanging out over the cliff. A look of sadness washed over his normally charismatic face. He stepped back easily as they approached, giving them a smile before continuing down the road back to Sylvanna.

⸶ ⸷

Finally, they arrived in Sylvanna after once again traversing the great northerly bridge. The regular green and blue standards across the city were now joined by candles and lanterns that burned strong even during the mid-afternoon hour. The five glanced around as children chased each other in ghastly costumes and streetside bards played eerie tones on strange instruments that were only used during the season in addition to their regular fare. Craven smiled and stepped forward, tossing several gold coins into the violin case of one that bordered the plaza. The bard thanked him with a quick jig and an increased fervor with his bow. Erika couldn't help but grin at the liveliness of the place, encouraging each of her companions who were trying to improve her mood just earlier that day. Although F'Lessa and F'Skal seemed gloomy simply due to the cloaks that they had once again donned to not raise attention in the city.

Their effort at a low profile was short-lived, but not due to them.

Over the music came a strong feminine voice. "Craven? Is that you?"

F'Skal heard their new companion curse lightly.

The party turned collectively as a figure made her way through the small crowd. She wore a beautiful form fitting gown of black and orange, fit for the season, and wore a similarly colored mask that looked more at home at a masquerade ball. Her blonde hair, though silvered with age, danced across her bare shoulders as she moved across the cobbled stones on her heeled shoes hidden by the hems of the skirt.

"I'm sorry miss, you must have me mistaken for someone else. I'm afraid I have one of those faces that people seem to recognize as others, you see," Craven quickly said, tipping his hat to obscure that very face.

The woman sighed sharply and removed her mask. "Cut the act, I know it's you."

The crowd collectively gasped and fell to the ground in deep bows, Darion similarly dropping to one knee in an instant. Leaving Erika, F'Lessa, and F'Skal dumbstruck at the situation, as the woman stared intensely at their new companion, who similarly did not bow.

"For Gods' sake, you really made me take off my mask in public just to get your attention?" she said harshly.

Craven smiled uneasily. "My apologizes dear Lady, I have been away for quite some time."

"Fifteen years is *quite* some time," she retorted.

"And might I say, you have grown only more beautiful with time," he said, obviously trying to win with flattery.

"And you look exactly the same," the woman said flatly. "Come with me, and bring your companions with you."

She turned to the crowd that still sat in deep bows around her. "Everyone please, disregard me, and enjoy the festival to its fullest!"

Craven carefully stepped forward, ushered on as two knights appeared at his back. The rest of the group was similarly moved forward, Darion breaking out in a sudden sweat.

"What's goin' on?" Erika asked him in a hushed tone.

He looked to her and the two aash elves, his face pale. "That's Queen Stacia Sylvanna III. The reigning matriarch of my Region..."

Their eyes widened at the revelation. "We've nothing to worry about then, right?" F'Skal said optimistically.

"I suppose that depends on what the Queen wants with Craven," F'Lessa answered grimly, watching as he walked directly behind the regal woman, suddenly flanked by nearly a score of fully armored knights.

† †

As they made their way through the city they were met with bows all around, the people falling to their knees at the sight of the Queen. She held a firm stance as she walked, but seemed to be somewhat annoyed at the entire situation. Erika simply gawked at the display, unused to a Monarchal government. In Sildenfeld, the city was run by a council of people that represented each of the social classes and guilds, though this city was much larger than the leading settlement of her home region.

After walking up several sets of stairs that connected the different levels of the city, they found themselves in a wide plaza with a large fountain in the center. At the center of the fountain was a statue of a woman sitting on the ground with long shapely legs to one side, her face cast upwards to a flagpole that she gripped onto tightly which bore the standard of Sylvanna. Erika paused a moment, her eyes glancing back and forth between the nude statue and the Queen that led them on. The resemblance between the two was strange and uncanny. Her attention was broken away soon after as they arrived at the doorstep of the massive cathedral that sat on the opposite side to the statue's back. It reached high into the sky with looming towers adorned with stained glass windows, all of their small group—save for Craven—craning their necks at the spires as they were led inside. The interior was well lit with chandeliers and wall sconces, the main hall decorated with various tapestries and draperies that celebrated the season. A multitude of guests stood inside around tables and standing areas, all creating a hum with their conversations. Erika had hardly seen such a gathering of people, and definitely not one that seemed so incredibly formal.

"If I had known I'd be at the Royal Sylvannan Court when I had left home," Darion began, shrinking at the great hall. "I'd have brought my uniform."

"Nice way o' sayin' we're all underdressed?" Erika asked.

Darion replied with a nervous laugh and a motion to their elven companions. "Some of us more than others."

F'Skal glared at him from beneath his hood, but even he could see that they were incredibly out of place here, nearly nude under their cloaks in a veritable ballroom of well-dressed men and women.

Queen Sylvanna stepped into the middle of the room and called out with a powerful and practiced voice. "Ladies and gentlemen, I apologize for my absence. I had wished to see the revelry from outside the Cathedral as well."

She was met with a wave of laughter around the room, though the group all wondered how much of it was genuine.

"I have brought with me however, several esteemed guests," she continued, waving her hand to the band of newcomers, who were then shifted forward by the knights. Darion started muttering a string of curses, F'Lessa and Erika both eyed him, surprised at his tongue.

"What are your names?" the Queen asked them quietly, interrupting Darion's panic. "Quickly, the crowd is waiting on your introductions."

A moment later, she stepped forward again, this time holding Darion by the arm. "Darion, guardsman of Stonewall!"

The audience applauded him, despite his less than stellar attire. Next, she brought Erika. "Erika of Valen!"

The droning applause continued, making Erika flush at the intense stares she got from the crowd. Queen Sylvanna then grabbed both aash elves by the hands next and lead them forward, two knights lunging forward and yanking their hoods back. "F'Skal and F'Lessa of the Shalti tribe!"

Lastly, she grabbed Craven by the arm. "And finally, after fifteen years away from our fair city, Craven, has once again graced us with his presence!"

As the knights ushered them out of the center and closer to an exterior wall, F'Lessa replaced her hood over her silver hair as it streaked wildly with shades of pink and orange. Her brother walked just in front of her scanning over the crowd and watching everyone's reactions, his emerald dust glowing as he took in the details. They arrived in a corner of the room where none of the guests seemed to congregate. Darion resumed his nervousness, looking as if he would scream when a familiar face suddenly stepped over to them.

"Inquisitor Marq, wonderful to see you again," F'Skal said, breaking the silence as the thin man made his closer.

He was still dressed in his Inquisitor uniform, but seemed even less at ease than he had been at the murder scene where they had last met. "You know, if I had known you were friends with the Queen, we may have had less of a rocky introduction," he said coolly.

"It seems we've a mutual friend is all," Erika replied, nodding towards Craven as he approached them. F'Skal raised an eyebrow at the sudden spark of recognition in Marq's eyes when he looked to the man.

"Well, what a wonderful party," Craven said with his customary smirk, looking to Marq and smiling wider. "Ah, Prince Marq, wonderful to see—"

"*Inquisitor* Marq," he shot back before Craven could finish his sentence. Erika exchanged shocked glances with her friends as he continued speaking to Craven. "I had no idea you were returning."

"Neither did I," Queen Sylvanna said, startling Darion, F'Lessa, and Erika. "I see you've met our guests already, brother?"

Marq smiled warmly. "Yes, we have had the pleasure of making acquaintances just the other week, actually. I hadn't expected to see them again so soon though."

"How wonderful. Would you mind entertaining them for a short while? I have some private matters to discuss with Craven," she said, lightly clasping her hands in front of herself.

"Surely things can wait, Stacia? Perhaps I can socialize with both of you for a while," Craven interjected, trying to take the lead on the conversation, but the siblings seemed to know his game perfectly well.

"I would be delighted to entertain our guests," Marq interrupted again. "Perhaps if they plan to stay a while, they would enjoy borrowing some formal wear?"

"Perfect idea, dear brother!" the Queen replied with a flourishing smile. "The matters I need to discuss with Craven are sure to take a while, so I'm sure the guests would love to wash up and enjoy the festivities."

She grabbed Craven by the arm once again and guided him to the large doors at the back of the room and just up a small flight of stairs.

"Please, follow me to the washrooms," Marq said in as cordial of a tone as he could manage, though one did not need F'Skal's perceptiveness to notice the annoyance behind his eyes.

† †

Into the great hall above the wonderfully decorated foyer stepped Craven, guided by the arm of Queen Sylvanna. The knights behind them shut the great doors, and once they closed fully she violently swung him before her. The late afternoon sun bathed in through the ancient stained glass that depicted a nymph rising from the water, the very same nymph depicted in stone just outside the Cathedral.

"Where have you been all these years?" she screamed, confident that they were alone.

Craven shrugged. "Here and there, you know how it goes."

She stepped forward and gave him a forceful shove with both hands, causing the dark man to step back ever so slightly.

"No," she continued shouting. "I do not know how it goes!"

Craven watched her, sadness filling his eyes as she began to flush with the exertion. He glanced to that stained window, the nymph's face causing him a pain in his chest that he could not describe.

"You were always there, Craven! Always!" her voice began to crack. "Always there to watch over us! Marq and I, Mother, and all the others!"

"I had other business to attend," he said quietly, almost fearing a higher octave.

"Drought on your other business!"

Craven flinched at her rare curse.

"What about us? You didn't even come to Mother's funeral!"

"I couldn't."

She cursed again, louder and more foul, reaching down and drawing Craven's weapon from his hip. He did nothing to stop her, and made no move of surrender.

"Answer me, Craven!"

"And if you do not like the answer?"

They stood in silence for a long while. Craven wishing nothing more than to avert his eyes from the tears that streamed down her beautiful face. With a scream she rushed forward, executing routines of rapier work that Craven knew well. He had taught them to her.

A string of curses came from her lips as he dodged every strike, every slash. Her hair whipped from its tight bun, falling over her face with every attack. They continued the strange and violent dance for several minutes before he sidestepped her mad rush to stand idly behind her. She turned quicker than he expected the blade poised for his throat.

With a wave of his hand the rapier dissipated from her grasp in a dark smoke and reformed in his hand. He slashed outwards, cutting through the upper left edge of her dress just under her collarbone and made lightning quick stabs towards her legs. She backpedaled furiously, the blade never touching her flesh. Wide holes opened in the fabric of her skirt, as her whole dress began to droop from her bust just slightly from another cut on the right side of the bodice. Finally Craven ceased his affront and threw the weapon to the ground with such force that the stonework cracked where it impacted.

Her chest heaved as she stared at him, her loose hair matting to her face where her tears had dried.

"What are you, Craven? This is not the first time I have seen you demonstrate abilities like that."

"There is more to this world than anyone should know, Stacia," he said quietly.

She scoffed, motioning to the stained glass high above. "Our own city is built on the myth of a water nymph that rose from the sea and built the First Cathedral."

"There is more to that story still, than anyone knows."

She started for his hands. "Then teach me! Show me what we have lost."

Craven pulled away sharply. "I cannot do this for you, Stacia. As much as it pains me."

For another eternity they stood there. Craven stared into the stained glass and Queen Sylvanna gazed into his longing eyes. She groaned with frustration, bashing his shoulder with her fist and starting for the door. If he hadn't felt as numb as he did, that punch may have made his shoulder ache.

† †

Inside the large bath hall, F'Skal was hard at work scrubbing his dark skin with a soapy washcloth. Darion on the other hand had barely begun to undress.

"Something bothering you?" the aash elf asked, moving down to his right side with the cloth.

Darion neatly folded his traveling shirt before starting to unbuckle his belt. "He bothers me."

"And whom are we speaking of?"

"Craven!" he nearly shouted, throwing his belt onto the table and slumping slightly.

F'Skal nodded as he sat on a stool, beginning to scrub his leg now. "Yes, he does irk me as well, though I am unsure of why just yet."

"Perhaps it is because he seems to know the entire royal family?" Darion continued. "I didn't even realize Marq was the Queen's brother, yet he just knows this upon seeing him?"

"I suppose they have met before."

"Obviously, but how long has he known them?" he asked the humidified air around him as he paced in his underclothes, folding his trousers just as neatly. "He called the Queen by her bloody first name!"

F'Skal stared at him for a moment, then sighed. "Indeed he did, and yet I still believe there is a deep relationship that we are unknowing of, and therefore should not judge or meddle in."

Darion groaned, tossing his clothes onto the table and joining F'Skal in the wash area. "I don't trust him."

"Neither do I," the elf said quietly. "Yet for the time being, I believe we are stuck with him. Perhaps he is just a wary man that prefers to keep his tales to himself."

"Benefit of the doubt?" Darion asked, looking to his friend's crimson eyes.

F'Skal smirked. "Something of the sort, yes. Now clean up before the Inquisitor gets tired of waiting for you."

After visiting the adjacent washroom, Erika and F'Lessa were accosted by a horde of handmaidens, all of which bore dresses that they held up to each of them. Erika was met with grins and looks of approval while F'Lessa was assailed with looks of dismay

188

and resignation. Erika figured it was likely due to the fact that F'Lessa was two or three sizes too large for any dress presented to her, and that her muscled frame would likely rip through any one of them if she were to try one on.

Eventually, the aash elf backed away and started pleading for her own clothing. The maidens seemed undeterred though and after observing her tribal clothing for just a moment, they ran off to fetch a long swath of green cloth. It took four of them and two stools, but eventually they draped the fabric over F'Lessa, making a makeshift robe, a seamstress quickly sewing a few sections to hold it all together. F'Lessa looked to the satisfied maidens with a look of disdain as she adjusted the fabric, tightening it around her bust and lengthening the gap between it and the waistline to avoid overheating her midsection as best she could.

Erika couldn't help but giggle at the sight but was also forcibly dressed in a long backless gown, with a high slit on the right side of the skirt, colored with the Sylvannan royal blue. The hue of the fabric contrasted with her bright hair quite intensely, even after the handmaidens had tied her hair up in a tight twist that left nary a strand hanging.

"We were unsure of how the lady felt about the scar upon her back," the handmaiden beside her said. "We may change if you prefer, but we cannot hide all the scars." The woman's lithe fingers gestured towards her shoulder and neck where the shadow warriors had maimed her.

Erika turned and looked at her back in the mirror. The three claw marks were on full display, as well as her myriad of Ignis markings. The dress accentuated the sway of her back and hips more than she had expected at first, but she smiled at how she looked, kicking her leg out of the slit with a satisfied smirk. She turned back to her front again and brought her fingers to the scars on her cheek and neck that were finally beginning to darken thanks to F'Skal's treatments. "It's fine. I don't mind my scars," she said, catching a glance from F'Lessa in the mirror, who gave her an encouraging smile amidst her own struggle to expose more skin.

20

The Shadesfall Gala

Some time later, the four met back in the hallway, Inquisitor Marq greeting them as they came, with a bit of a lingering gaze towards her. "A beautiful choice, Miss Erika. I believe my sister will approve greatly," he said, kissing the back of her hand gently with a bow. "I understand you have received some strange glances regarding your markings? Worry not, the guests have been informed that they are symbolic amongst your people of the Fjordlands."

"But, they're not—" Erika started to correct.

Marq silenced her with an upraised hand and sympathetic look. "These people are much too busy with their own ordeals to truly understand or care what your markings actually are. Unfortunately, they have a tendency to gawk at things that are different. Thus, they have been informed that your markings are of your heritage and that clothing is uncouth in the aash tribe, hence their... *loose* attire."

Erika looked back to the elven siblings who looked over each other's similar robe-like attire and then to a window drape that was the same color. Both grinned and laughed at the notion that they were wearing curtains, and Erika began to see what Marq was getting at. These nobles cared not for much more than appearances, and even then it did not go very deep.

Darion stepped over a moment later, straightening the collar of the shirt he had donned and giving Erika a warm smile. "I think I may be the first Stonewall guardsman to have an audience in the Queen's ballroom."

"Very likely. Don't let it go to your head," the Inquisitor said with a smirk. "You all look wonderful, nothing to worry over. Now then, back to the party with us, surely Stacia is finished with her questioning of our mutual acquaintance."

As they returned through the doorways all eyes were on them and Erika suddenly felt a chill run down her spine, twisting over each of her scars. Inquisitor Marq quickly offered his arm and helped her down the stairs and into the room as she struggled in the awkward shoes with the rather thin heel to them. Darion similarly offered his arm to F'Lessa, who looked as if she'd punch him at first but then took his arm gently. Despite their height difference, Erika thought they were an adorable couple. F'Skal walked lightly behind all of them, and was immediately taken into conversation by a small group of people upon reaching the bottom of the stairs.

Marq stepped away a moment later, possibly to refill the flask he had drawn from during their first encounter, Erika mused. She had also seen him drinking from it just before they had gotten out of sight into the washrooms. To occupy the time she paced around slowly, looking at all the decorations about the room. Each step was deliberate as she tried to get used to walking in the heels

"Good eve to you Miss, Erika, correct?" a lithe woman said, startling Erika slightly. She was a prim looking woman with short blonde hair that fell around her jawline. Her dress accentuated her rather large bust to the point that Erika found herself forcing her gaze anywhere else other than the deep cleft. Alongside her was a man with a square jaw and neatly trimmed facial hair. Accompanying the both of them were several other couples that all seemed to be wearing similar clothes or had their hair cut in the same fashion.

Erika simply nodded, nervous with all the attention so closely on her.

"I hope you don't mind my asking," the same woman asked. "But do your tattoos really cover *all* of you?"

"Aye," Erika said quickly, resigning to Marq's story. "Sign o' me heritage." Her eyes started to widen at how quickly her accent had thickened, bringing her father's voice to mind.

The people all seemed to be amused by her words, most of them grinning and chuckling. Another woman piped in. "Well, if I may say, I think they are rather fetching. Why, I would have them done too, if they'd highlight my eyes like they do yours. Makeup and powder would be a thing of the past!"

"How painful was all of that to receive?" another, more portly, man asked.

Erika hesitated, as the markings themselves had come with no pain whatsoever, save for the few times she'd overheated. "Less than ye'd think," she answered with a knowing grin.

"I see you have all found my Fjordling friend?" Inquisitor Marq said, stepping beside Erika.

"Of course, and how fascinating she is, Master Marq," the first woman's husband said.

Erika noticed Marq's lips twitch in the barest of scowls. "*Inquisitor* Marq, if you please."

"Of course, Inquisitor," the man conceded.

The woman at his right hand stepped forward lightly, Erika's eyes snapping down to her cleavage again as she bounded forwards. Erika did her best not to let her bewildered expression show.

"And if I may be so bold, are you and her an item, by chance?" the woman asked.

Erika felt her skin get hot suddenly. She started to stammer a reply, but Marq spoke before her. "I'm afraid I am much too focused on my work at this time to be concerned with romance. No, Erika here is just a good friend."

The woman seemed to deflate slightly, thankfully not taking notice of Erika's reddened face. "I see. Perhaps your sister will find a suitor soon?"

"I fail to see the importance," Marq shot back, Erika startling from the aggressive tone in his voice. The group of nobles backed away slightly. Marq cleared his throat and blinked at the front most man who had thankfully moved in front of his wife's plunging neckline. Erika also noticed he had a hand on the hilt of his sword. "Not a wise choice to duel an Inquisitor in any circumstance," Marq warned, putting a hand on Erika's shoulder.

He turned and led Erika away, not giving the group another glance. "Why were they so demandin' of ye?" she asked after they had made some distance from them.

"Plenty demanding of you also, my dear Ignis girl. You did well in repelling their questions," he straightened his jacket and pulled his flask out of the pocket.

Erika watched as he glanced around the room. "But, why were they gettin' on to ye?"

Marq sighed. "Because these political aristocrats think that marriage is of course the only thing anyone truly needs to do in life. That and have heirs. My sister and I are now into our thirties and have neither. Therefore, the rabble of the nobles think we are being irresponsible."

"An' the threat to pull a weapon?" she asked.

"He believed I was being too harsh in silencing his wife and was ready to defend her. Unfortunate that he would have lost, had it come to that," he answered.

"Doesn't help 'is case that it was an ornamental blade. Wouldn't' ave lasted long against yers in a fight," she added, glancing at his practical sword that he wore on his hip.

Marq chuckled, and turned to her. "That's right, you used to be a smith. Figured you'd notice something like that."

"How did ye know I was a smith?"

"Most women don't have arms the size of yours," he said plainly. "That, and a multitude of burn marks. Not that they detract from any of your physical beauty of course, rather I'd say they enhance your looks." She laughed, causing the slightest of smiles from the Inquisitor. He slowly raised his flask, looking away from her eyes as he spoke again. "And if you were not already spoken for, I would likely ask if you would be available for a nice dinner."

Her laugh faded, her gaze lengthening into the floor as a forced smile sprouted on her face. "Ye're a perceptive one, I'd say ye'd give F'Skal a run."

"So, you are spoken for then," he said somewhat quieter, rubbing at his eyes. "That was more of a guess really."

"Ye seem a wonderful person Marq. Inquisitor Marq," she attempted to rectify quickly, though he waved her correction off. "I am searchin' fer someone I lost."

"Who are you looking for? Perhaps I can help find them?"

Erika hesitated. "I am unsure o' where to look myself. He was taken from this world abruptly, though I believe he's not dead."

"I see," Marq sighed with a slow nod. Something in his expression struck her as strange in that moment, like he was hoping she had said something differently, but like he also knew that the answer was coming. "It appears that this is beyond my expertise then, and I have little more to offer you than well wishes."

She smiled at him and nodded. "Thank ye fer that at least. I appreciate it."

Just then, they both looked to the side to find Darion and F'Lessa being taught to dance by an elderly woman. Erika smiled at the display, and though the movements were much more smooth and careful, she reminisced to the dance she shared with Irvine at her town's final Harvest Festival. Her eyes began to water slightly, Marq proffering a small cloth to her. She nodded to thank him, but he said nothing as he simply stared ahead and drew from his flask again. Erika was unsure of how to speak to the thin man suddenly, simply wiping at her eyes and straightening her back as she stood beside him.

A short time later, Queen Sylvanna returned with Craven down the stairs just to their left. Craven seemed somewhat perturbed, while the Queen simply looked angered. Her hair looked disheveled, as if it had been hastily tied back up.

"If you ever find yourself with some free time, and things are more open, I truly would love to invite you to that dinner," Marq bowed before stalking away from Erika. She hesitated for a moment at his words, staring at his back as he walked towards his sister. Eventually, she found herself trying to watch Craven and the interaction that followed between the two siblings at the same time, but she found the task difficult.

Craven walked straight across the ballroom floor past several pairs of dancers to the makeshift bar that had been erected. He tapped his fingers on the wood, offering several gold coins and was given a spirit bottle quickly after. Marq and his sister seemed to enter a heated conversation, though both seemed plenty able to quiet their voices well enough to avoid any eavesdropping. However, they did draw some attention at the Queen's arms waving frantically around and the crazed look in her eyes.

F'Skal suddenly leaned over Erika's shoulder. "It appears that the Queen's dress has been marred ever so slightly."

"How do ye mean?" Erika asked, raising an eyebrow.

"The cloth just under her left shoulder, right side of the breast, and the skirt in several places have been cut, I'd assume with some kind of blade. Although she herself does not appear to be wounded—or even scraped—in the slightest," he answered.

She looked to the aash elf just as the emerald dust around his eyes began to dim. "Master Craven on the other hand, hasn't a single hair out of place it would seem." They both turned to their newest companion as he downed a full glass of the liquor and quickly refilled it. "Though I worry for his liver," F'Skal added.

† †

The rest of the night moved by rather slowly, Erika noted. She assumed that it likely passed quickly for F'Lessa and Darion, both of whom had barely left each other's side for the entire festivity. She and F'Skal sat at a table on one end of the hall for most of the night, F'Skal enjoying the variety of bite-sized foods that were on parade, while Erika slowly nursed at a second glass of deep blue wine with an appealing enough taste. They were visited occasionally by other nobles or by Marq who—much to Erika's appreciation—brought a third glass when she was nearly finished. Craven seemingly avoided them, content in drinking through three full bottles of the particular spirit that he had originally purchased. F'Skal did not mention his lack of drunken stupors, his eyes narrowing each time the man took a calculated step to avoid another inebriated party goer.

"How is it that you stay sober so easily?" he asked quietly to no one in particular.

As time passed, the nobles trickled from the hall, each bidding farewell to the Queen and the other aristocrats. Some also bade farewell to the guests of the night, still commenting on Erika's markings or the curious nature of the aash's clothing. Erika noticed that Marq was pointedly absent for nearly every goodnight, except for when the noble couple that had spoken to her before came by to wish her well. He almost seemed to stand guard behind her as they approached, his arms neatly behind his back but his stance wide. Erika recognized the demeanor in memories of Irvine's late uncle, Feldran. He would adopt that same kind of stance and expression whenever he knew there was a possibility of a fight and though he looked calm, he was ready to strike at a moment's notice.

"Inquisitor," the same man that had held the hilt of his weapon said flatly as they approached. Marq simply nodded. The woman at his side stepped forward to Erika who was still seated and knelt down, causing Erika to choke slightly at how precarious the front of her dress appeared. The alcohol she had enjoyed seemed to make it even more difficult to maintain eye contact with the woman, especially as she leaned her torso forwards, her tight bodice drawing even more of Erika's attention to her intense cleavage than before. She had the briefest of thoughts that she was glad her own dress showed as much skin as it did, or she would be burning up from how flushed she felt from the wine.

"I do hope we did not offend earlier, miss. We are simply curious about things we do not understand. And quite frankly, your tattoos are very interesting, nothing quite like what is normal around Patrias," she said, a vulnerable look in her eyes.

Erika nodded in reply, unsure of what to say in the moment.

She reached her hands out and took Erika's in hers. "I realize I had not introduced myself, I am Dyla Fargeal, and my husband is a Count in this fair city. Perhaps we may meet again sometime and start off on a different foot."

"Erika Ildherre. Wonderful to properly meet ye, Miss Fargeal," she replied, gaining more confidence, though she wondered if it was simply the alcohol.

Dyla stood then, smiling at Erika. She took her husband's arm, who once again regarded Marq coldly before leaving.

"Well, that went somewhat smoother," she mused as they departed.

She turned to find Marq still watching the two leave, the Count's eyes locked with the Inquisitor's. "Unfortunately, I do believe the good Count will want a word with me or my sister before the week is out. I'm afraid I have transgressed in his business a tad too much as of late, and my aggression earlier was simply the final straw."

"Ye've been investigatin' him? Is he tied to some crime?" Erika asked as she stood from the chair, stretching her arms over her head. Her shoulders felt tense from how she had been sitting.

"I do not believe he is directly, however one of the killings I've been looking into occurred in his courtyard. One of his maids," he looked over while her arms reached upwards, smiling warmly at her. Erika suddenly wondered how much skin she was showing in that moment, feeling a draft of air across the side of her breast, and quickly lowered her arms. Marq looked off and shook his head. "Grim talk for a festive occasion, perhaps a change of subject?"

Erika settled her stance before standing and walking beside Marq, gladly taking his arm again as she started to feel even more unsteady on her heels. "Actually, I had been wonderin' about that. Had ye gained any leads? Was it the same killer as the elf that ye questioned us about?"

Marq sighed slightly, but shook his head with a resigned smirk. "No, not your Hargreave character. Actually, we had been tracking that one shortly after we had spoke that day. I had even gotten reports of him making his way through the city, charred face all down the left side. However, all sightings suddenly were lost and we haven't found him since." The two continued along the wall closer to the back of the great hall. "The other killings I believe are two separate culprits, one very methodical and able to remove heads with no trace of blood—or the head for that matter. The other is much more savage and destructive with their victims."

Erika felt a chill down her bare back at the mention of the former methods, but she did her best to quickly disregard the feeling. She took a few deep breaths to fend off the visions of that night, unsure about telling Marq about her witnessing of that particular death. "Which happened to the maid? And do you have any major leads on either o' those?"

"The more brutal killer it seems, poor girl. Sadly though, we have very little to go on. And the killings have actually stopped, which leads me to believe the culprits have left the city," he said dismally. "I suppose with Hallowden though, anything can happen."

Erika smirked at his attempt at a jest, but her anxious feeling would not subside. A moment later Darion appeared beside them. "Sorry, I didn't mean to eavesdrop, but I wonder about something."

The two looked up at him and F'Lessa who still seemed chained to the young man's hip. Marq nodded for him to continue.

"The night before Erika and I departed my hometown, we were assailed by strange creatures. Erika here definitely proved her worth and had nearly slain two of them single-handedly. My father and I taking another," he began, motioning to the scar on his head from the bladed whip. "One of the guardsmen who suffered the initial attack was very badly wounded, and another who had seen the thing attack him said it did so horridly and without pause. Like a wild animal gone mad."

"You think these events are connected?" the Inquisitor asked.

Darion shrugged. "I think that those shadow creatures were much too early for Hallowden. And frankly, strange things happen around us."

Marq stood silent for a long while, F'Lessa eventually piping in. "Are you forming your own connection Inquisitor? You share a similar look with my brother when he is realizing something."

"Reports did come in of strange people shrouded in darkness. Witnesses and sightings began popping up all across the city not long before the killings began, but have now gone quiet," he said, his foot tapping furiously on the ground. "You lot are heading northwards correct?"

Darion nodded, slightly looking to Erika and Craven still standing at the side of the room. "Craven mentioned a port called Darktide, I believe."

"Then please, stay the night here. You'll have full accommodations," he continued. "Before I retire, I'll reach out to my men on the eastern garrison, see if anything strange has happened up there. I'll have my answers by morning hopefully, and we'll see if you are correct in your theory. Perhaps these strange creatures cloaked in shadow are following you north, or maybe preceding you."

Erika nodded her understanding. "If there's more o' those things, I'd be happy to burn 'em away 'afore they hurt anyone else."

"It seems we've all reached an understanding then," Queen Sylvanna said, gliding into the conversation and lightly tugging at the tear in her gown, frowning when it ripped more. She turned to them, lightly holding onto the fabric as it looked ready to fall free from her body. "I'll arrange the rooms for you, how many are you needing?"

"Perhaps three, Queen Sylvanna?" F'Lessa said. "My brother and I can share a room easily, and I'm sure Erika and Darion would value their privacy for a night."

"I'm sure they would. I likely believe that you and your brother would enjoy a spot of privacy as well, so five rooms it is. Including Master Craven, of course," she said, her final words attached to a slight glare towards the man in question, though Erika saw no real malice behind her eyes. She could only guess at what happened between them while she was off in the bathing rooms. She watched the Queen as she left the room, allowing the ripped garment to drop to the floor as she walked through a doorway in her underdress before a call for a small dinner distracted her thoughts. The Queen joined them a short while later dressed in a much simpler dress, although it was towards the end of their meal. A small group of servants arrived shortly after to show them to their rooms.

21

Nightmares

Craven was glad to be away from everyone, taking the first chance available to slip into the room prepared for him. He closed the door quickly after the steward finally finished speaking to him, and leaned up against it with a heavy sigh. He envied Vaerisa, likely still slaying orks in the Fjordlands as he was running away from his own past here. He had hoped to fade through Sylvanna in less than a day with no one the wiser of his presence, but he had not counted on Stacia Sylvanna to be stalking the streets herself at the same time as his new party.

"Damn my luck," he said to the empty room.

"Damn thy luck indeed," a feminine voice giggled coyly, causing a chill to run down his spine.

The Lady shifted out of nothingness in the middle of the room, the temperature dropping starkly until Craven could just start to see his own breath hanging in the air.

"The Inquisitor speaketh true, my love. Thy quarry hath left the city," her words continued, though her thin lips did not move.

Craven walked around her to the back of the room near a small bedside table. He set his hat gently on its wooden surface and dropped his jacket from his shoulders. "Yes, I can feel the disturbance in the Veil still and I know the source no longer remains in this city. I believe he is moving to Darktide, hence my reason for going there."

"And thine deception of thine companions? Why tell them that Fjordsgate is impassable?"

"You're the Goddess," Craven said with a slight annoyance showing through. "You tell me, Matron."

"Perhaps thou knoweth not thyself?" she replied to his comment, running lithe fingers across his shoulders. Craven did his best not to shy away from her touch, though it chilled him to the bone, even now after all this time.

"Whatever do you mean, Matron?" he said, trying to hide his crass tone.

"Move into the Veil, dear Craven. I bade you observe the young woman thy travel with. She bears the seeds to thine answers."

His eyes narrowed as he turned his head to eye the small-statured woman as she moved towards the door. "Inside the Veil itself, Matron? A rather dangerous overstep into things, don't you think?"

She looked over her shoulder at him. Her dark lips began turning to a frown. "Do not feign innocence with me, my dear love. I understand that with a Shade as old as thee, experimentation is to be expected."

Craven couldn't help but smirk, knowing that the Matron had assuredly known of his independent power for some time. However, admitting that he was bending the rules himself was another matter entirely. A moment later he focused his mind, the world around him becoming unfocused in turn. Color drained and the detail of the room faded away until he could only see the outline of the room. Around him and through the walls he could see the servants making their way through their corridors. The people he saw appeared naked, save for ghostly outlines of clothes, though their bodies only had the physical details of a mannequin. The barest representation of the souls around him.

He raised his arm, grimacing at how the Veil showed him for what he truly was. The bones of his forearm, wrist, and fingers moved with no flesh or sinew; no soul outline like the people around him. Reminders of one's being were not always pleasant.

He glanced over as a smooth movement caught his eye. A young girl drifted along the hallway, looking at him with curiosity.

Every detail of her could be seen as clear as Matron Mortia herself in this state, though she did have a discoloration to her flesh. Her hair drifted around her as she cocked her head at him. He offered her a simple wave of his hand, but the lost spirit seemed intimidated by him and opted instead to quicken her pace away from him. He shrugged and continued on.

Through the wall and into the other room he could see a masculine shape diligently cleaning a blade, Darion practicing his guardsman duties. Just after, he set the blade to the side and retrieved other objects, his whittling knife and wood, Craven assumed. The Matron led him further still. Through the walls he stepped lightly, watching with some amusement as Darion glanced around and shuddered at the dropping temperature. In this state, Craven was little more than a ghost, moving unseen through any surface that he chose. The experience was taxing, but the information that could be gleaned was truly worth it at times.

Next he passed through the room that was to be F'Skal's. He was surprised to find two figures in that chamber, masculine and feminine, both tall and muscled. The muffled sounds of their voices echoed through the space, bouncing from the stone and finally arriving at Craven's ethereal ears.

"Please allow me this, brother," F'Lessa said, a pleading sound in her voice.

F'Skal seemed amused. "Trading rooms is a hassle, you'll need to explain why."

"You are going to make me say it plainly aren't you?" she replied with exasperation.

Her brother simply nodded, Craven only guessing at the smile across his face as it appeared like a blank slate to him through the Veil.

"I'd like to be closer to him. I really enjoyed the night, and I believe I am beginning to make a connection," she finally said after a long pause. Craven turned around, to look at the form of Darion now turning the wood piece in his hand for an inspection. He found the elf's sentiment endearing, even if the guardsman would likely never know of it.

F'Skal shouldered his belongings and looked at her once more before leaving. "I believe you've had a connection for much longer than you believe."

Craven smiled, seeing the budding relationship between her and Darion reminded him of happier times. However, he could not stay and muse on the topic, which he figured to be a good thing.

He continued through F'Skal's replacement room before the elf got there himself, and finally into the fourth room from his own. Inside was a feminine shape, shorter and less muscular than F'Lessa. As he expected, Erika's primordial heritage shone in the form of bright red lines that painted her body. Her dress appeared as a completely transparent shift, so he could see most every detail of her shape, including where her flames had not touched on her upper thighs and hips. He eyed her, knowing Matron Mortia was nearby and watching as well. He turned his back when her form shrugged off the dress she had been wearing onto the ground. Craven turned away from the now nude woman, feeling the need for gentlemanly courtesy despite being unable to see more intimate details from the Veil.

"Surely this is not what you meant for me to see Matron, or is your sense of humor growing more childish?" he said to the empty walls.

He caught just the slightest glimpse of her as she stepped easily through the walls and back again. "Coincidence, my dear. Thou art to move closer whilst she sleeps."

"Firstly, that sounds to be in even more poor taste. Secondly, I am afraid I cannot hold this form for long, and I doubt she will be asleep for a while longer still," he called back.

"Whilst I am with thee, thou may stay for eternity. Patience is key, and thou shall have thy answers to thy mystery," the ghostly woman said, giggling strangely at her rhyme.

Craven shook his head as he stood near the inside wall of her chambers, watching the ground as she stretched her limbs and began to move around the room. Her routine seemed erratic, lacking any substantial actions like F'Skal's preparations of supplies or maintenance, or even hobbies like Darion. Instead, she laid out her traveling clothes for the next day before peeking out of the room and into the hallway. Craven gave her a confused look as she had still not put any clothing on. After she seemed satisfied with whatever she was checking for, she returned to the bed and opened a small book with a pencil. What she drew in the pages he could not see, but he could tell she did not scrawl words.

Perhaps it was some kind of artistry that she had neglected to show her companions, or Craven at the least. After that, she pulled another small object from her satchel, which appeared to be a small box or container, and simply sat with it for a while. She did not open it, she just looked at it. The sound was too soft to come through to him, but he suspected the bobbing of her shoulders indicated she was crying.

Strange, such a strong young woman to be weeping, he thought. He knew everyone had their reasons to shed tears sometimes. "What is it that you want me to see, Matron?" he asked, beginning to wish he could leave Erika in peace. He hardly expected a reply, and wasn't surprised when one never came.

A short while later after she had begun shivering at the lowered temperature, the young woman climbed into the bed, covering herself with the sheets and rolling over to face the wall. She seemed to fall into sleep easily, but he wondered how quickly she could wake. He waited a time later for her to reach a full slumber. Eventually the Matron bade him further.

"Place thy hand to the top of her spine," the familiar voice called from all around him. "Things are, that even thee do not know, mine eldest friend."

With hesitation, he did as she commanded, reaching forward until his fingers just barely brushed against the back of her skull. His consciousness was suddenly thrust from the room that he stood in. Across the city and through to the forested paths just outside he was flung, finally coming to rest on a lone Haranian man sitting beside a calm campfire. A peculiar blade rested at his side with swirling sands in the handle, and in this state Craven could see the ghosts of wars past raging through the forests around him. The man from the far south said something in his native tongue, looking up towards Craven with a bewildered look, as if he could see him. Craven knew that this was the man he must find. He could feel the sentience of the weapon beside the Haranian start to stir, but before it could notice him, another force yanked Craven away.

He was then thrust far from the world that he resided in. Through the vastness of the cosmos he felt himself flying uncontrollably, until he came to rest in a strange place. Sand and rock as far as the eye could see, the stench of unchecked death all around. Before him he saw the most curious of companions. A young man with a jagged lance and armor, the likes of which Craven had not seen in quite some time. Behind him, was a skeletal thing by the name of Zyrxak, though that had not always been his name.

"Why am I witnessing this Matron? I realize what I needed to see, but this... I do not know what I am looking at, save for Vergil's ghost," he called out, but no answer befell him. "Wait," he uttered quieter, turning around and observing the bleary landscape around the two that he had found. "This is the Sands of Conflict. This is Erika's quest? This young man? That is impossible..."

Zyrxak turned, looking directly at Craven, just as the Haranian did before. Instead of bafflement though, the thing Craven once knew smiled wickedly with his shattered skeletal face. "Interesting..."

The sight of that creature's face was just as unnerving as he remembered it to be.

He was then ripped from that reality and returned to the Veil, although he surmised that was thanks to the Matron. Erika awoke with a sudden scream that curdled his blood, even if it were hushed by his current state. His eyes narrowed and watched as all manner of individuals, including her companions, rushed from their rooms to then knock at her door. Craven decided now was the time to vacate the area himself. He made his way through the walls once more before the featureless shapes came through the door at Erika's muffled call to enter.

He returned to the material realm once he arrived in his own room, nearly falling onto the bed with the fatigue that washed over him as he shifted back to the mortal plane. The implications this held for him and the four companions he had stumbled upon were staggering. Now he had no choice but to accompany them to Darktide. Surely Erika knew who the young man in the Dragoon armor was, considering her sudden awakening after the vision. Perhaps she could see what he was seeing as well, or at least to an extent. He stepped lightly to the door, opening it just enough to listen down the hallway. What he heard made his stomach drop. The anguish that he had caused.

He could hear naught but Erika's continual sobbing, along with occasional shouts. "I have to find 'im! Zyrxak's got 'im, I've got no time!" she screamed between labored breaths.

Craven composed himself and walked into the hallway just as Inquisitor Marq rushed down the stairs behind him only dressed in a loose pair of trousers. "What's happening?" Marq demanded as he made eye contact with him.

Craven put a finger over his own lips to quiet him. "I believe Erika has just awoken from a nightmare."

Darion waited anxiously outside the room, his back to the wall as several servants crowded the doorway. Marq asked them to clear the way, he and Craven entering the room as they moved. F'Lessa sat on Erika's bed while F'Skal knelt next to it, both wrapped in their bedsheets. Erika clutched to F'Lessa's chest in a tear soaked fit while the elf tried to keep Erika's sheets covering her similarly bare skin. F'Skal's emerald dust flared brightly around his closed eyes as he ran fingers up and down Erika's arm, pausing at her neck, her chest, and other specific spots.

"Erika, are you alright?" Marq asked quietly, kneeling next to the bed alongside F'Skal.

The young woman attempted to compose herself, visibly trying to take deep breaths with difficulty. She tightly clutched the sheets over her chest, hardly managing a nod to the Inquisitor as her eyes became more bloodshot. Craven started to feel the guilt come in again. Visions of a water nymph and more unintended tears filled his mind.

† †

The night seemed to last forever, but eventually the dawn came. Erika found little sleep besides the scant hours before the nightmare. It was the last thing she expected to see. Irvine, nearly exactly as she had seen him last, battered armor and all, sitting across from that horrible Daemon that burned her home. She had given up her attempts to run from the room and the grand Cathedral as a whole, her new friends finally managing to convince her that there was nothing she could do that night.

Something kept tugging at her and she believed that time was something she did not have a lot of. Irvine seemed more visibly scarred than she had seen him before, several new ones on his face and a particularly concerning mark across his throat. In a way, they made him more handsome in that rugged kind of sense, but in the same breath made her worry horribly over him. Perhaps it was all just a nightmare, with no truth to it. She had a hard time accepting that rationale.

She arrived in the dining room after being led through the maze-like halls of the Cathedral, finding F'Skal, F'Lessa, and Darion already there awaiting breakfast. Across the room, Queen Sylvanna stepped down the steps from the higher floors, looking still incredibly regal even in her thin nightgown. Her long hair drifted free around her shoulders, beautiful in how the blonde mixed with the silver. Alongside her was a rather wrinkled bulldog with a golden-brown coat speckled with white, whom she introduced as Winnifred the previous night before they had all retired. Craven had seemed less than thrilled to see the canine, responding to her resounding growl towards him with a flat tone. "I see you still have a dog." Erika and her friends all had a laugh at his discomfort, but she wondered now if he would show up for breakfast.

Arriving shortly after Erika and Queen Sylvanna was Inquisitor Marq, already dressed in his uniform. "Good morrow to all," the Queen said, nodding and smiling to everyone in the room. She took a seat at the head of the table—the bulldog laying at her feet—but Marq looked much more hurried.

The Inquisitor bade his sister farewell and came alongside Erika a moment later. "I'll get word from the north as quickly as I can, I believe the couriers should be nearing the city again. Please, make yourselves at home, and take care of yourself," he said, raising her hand in his and lightly kissing the back of it before rushing out of the room. Erika watched him leave, thinking about the multiple mentions regarding dinner invitations from him.

"A busybody, that one," Queen Sylvanna said absently, motioning for Erika to join them at the table as she rubbed at Winnifred's jowls.

Erika accepted the invitation, and sat at the relatively small table between the Queen and F'Skal. "I'm sorry fer last night," she said after settling in.

Darion smirked and shook his head while he whittled wood shavings onto a cloth. "I told you all she'd apologize."

F'Skal answered Erika's leery look. "There is nothing to express regret for, dear girl. You had a moment of weakness, and we are here to aid you through that."

"Any help we can offer, we are happy to give," F'Lessa continued, placing her hand over Erika's from across the table. Erika found herself amazed at how quickly these people had become like a second family to her. She was grateful for them, knowing that she'd likely be much further behind had she still been alone.

"You all seem like a tight knit group," Queen Sylvanna said, a warm smile spread across her thin face. "I am curious though, what is your reason for coming all this way? As I understand, Erika is coming from the Region to the south, and Darion is from my own."

Darion nodded. "F'Skal and F'Lessa are from the forest just east of here as well."

She smiled warmly. "Ah, yes. I know of their tribe well. I am not like most of the nobles, disregarding them as savages. I've actually done a fair amount of research into their culture and otherwise."

F'Skal sat back in his seat slightly. "Interesting, and what have you found? If you don't mind sharing?"

"Well, I understand that you wear less clothing than your sol cousins or humans because of your natural body heat," she began, grinning at the elf's seeming doubt of her. "I also came to find that the higher internal temperature leads to a faster rate of healing than us as well. Meaning that idle scrapes and bruises heal in a manner of hours, rather than the days it can take us humans."

Darion looked to the two elves. "Is that why F'Lessa's wounds disappeared so quickly?"

They looked to him in confusion, to which he clarified. "She fought that big man, Bull was his name. Before I went to find Fink, I saw her take several punches to her sides, and I believe she was even bleeding from the mouth slightly? Later that night before we all bedded down, the bruises she had at dinner were already greatly diminished."

F'Skal applauded with a laugh. "Very perceptive! More than I had you pegged for Darion."

Darion's eyes widened as F'Lessa's hair began streaking pink for a moment, trying to stammer an excuse, but F'Skal continued. "But yes, that is indeed why my sister's flesh returned to its normal color before the night was through. Though we are not immune to grievous wounds."

His last statement seemed more pointed to the Queen, and she nodded slightly in reply. "Of course. Unfortunately, you are no more immortal than we humans. I honestly find it amusing that your cousins are known as 'sol' elves, after the sun. I would have once assumed your people would bear a name in regards to the moons."

"A simple misunderstanding from the ancient days I suppose. We aash have skin like dark ash, and the sol have hair like the blazing light above," F'Skal answered. "I hardly mind though. We generally prefer the lack of publicity."

The Queen smiled again. "Of course, and I am also aware that the sol were once referred to by a forgotten name before the Mad King Kaelis' reign. Now then, to my original question, what brings you all through my city?"

Everyone suddenly turned to Erika, who felt her face get hot with embarrassment at the attention. "I just need to get northwards. There's answers I'm needin'."

"Answers about what? I am dreadfully curious," Sylvanna pressed, leaning forward and walking her thin fingers across the table absently.

"A good friend o' mine went missin'. I have reason to believe I'll find 'im further north," Erika said, beginning to feel even more uncomfortable.

This seemed to satisfy the Queen, and she then turned to Darion at the other side of the table. "And you? A guardsman from Stonewall, why come all this way in such a trying time?"

Darion's casual demeanor vanished and he stood up straight suddenly. Erika assumed it was due to his sworn allegiance to this woman, or at least her Region. "I was sent on my way by my own parents Your Grace. Guard life didn't seem right for me, so I decided to lead Miss Erika to Sylvanna to aid her quest. I hadn't thought much about what comes after until we met the aash elves."

F'Lessa glanced up from the table at his words with a kind of hopeful expression, but Sylvanna frowned slightly. She rested the side of her head on her hand, her fingers idly draping across her face. "So you abandoned your post?" she asked flatly, her tone darkening. "During this of all times, you leave your position to help a traveling girl who has nothing to do with you, or your duty as a guardsman?"

F'Lessa's chair flew backwards, slamming loudly on the stone floor as she shot up and brought her fists down on the table, rocking it violently as the ruby designs on her ribs flaring brightly. "How dare you scold him! He helped save my village!" Winnifred began barking at her sudden outburst, but the aash hardly seemed to notice.

"I do not believe you understand the implications, F'Lessa," Queen Sylvanna called back to her harshly as she remained calm in the face of the aggression, draping one hand down to calm her dog with gentle squeezes to the back of her neck. "We are currently at odds with the Region to our direct east, and are likely on the verge of war. Abandoning a post at such a time is treasonous at best."

"Damn your Regions!" F'Lessa screamed, causing several servants to flinch, including the ones who had just begun to bring in the breakfast platters. "I hardly think one guardsman miles away from the border will change a single thing!"

The Queen sat back more easily now as a wry smirk crawled along her lips. "Indeed. One guardsman changes nothing."

F'Lessa's gem dust dimmed, returning to its reflective dark crimson, her face twisted in confusion as her breast rose and fell with her frustration.

"I understand that you hold no allegiance to me, nor my Region, Miss F'Lessa," she began, her tone brightening once more, "but you are absolutely correct, one single guardsman from a small town to the south does frankly nothing to defend my Region from the opposing forces of Tarkal that have been more aggressive than ever."

Darion seemed to finally breathe again, his eyes no longer darting between the two women.

"Then again, what Darion has done would be considered treason by several ranking military officers. Which is why I will personally sign a letter of sanction, to support his ongoing quest with you and your companions."

F'Lessa looked incredibly vulnerable suddenly, as if she had fallen into a trap laid carefully by the Queen and had no way of climbing back out. "Thank you, Your Grace," Darion said quietly, F'Skal noticing the glisten in his eyes that he was fighting back.

The servants finally continued with their march, bringing in the breakfast platters to the delight of most of the table. F'Lessa looked at the dishes with some disdain when she realized the foreign foods that steamed on the plates that also bore the colors of Sylvanna.

"Now then, perhaps the fascinating aash elves will enlighten me of their reasons for travel?" the Queen inquired as she took a small bite from her fork.

F'Skal seemed lost in thought for a moment. "We have both had a certain wish for a pilgrimage from our village since we were young. These two simply offered an open pathway for us to do so," Queen Sylvanna nodded slowly as she buttered a slice of bread. F'Skal continued a moment later. "In addition, our village elder and seer, F'Tara, bade us on this quest to aid Miss Erika."

This brought the Fjordling's attention sharply up, F'Skal meeting her gaze only slightly. "It seems something very important is tied to our friend, and we have been tasked with aiding her on that journey. Still, we both would have been ecstatic to join her, even if it were not for the quest given by our shaman."

"Ye said she just wanted ye to travel," Erika sputtered, unsure of how to take the explanation. "Not that there was somethin' important about me."

"We have our own personal reasons as well, Erika," F'Skal said in an attempt to calm her. "I know F'Lessa is where she needs to be right now, as am I."

F'Lessa seemed to be resisting the urge of looking to Darion in that moment, and Erika understood what F'Skal meant. She started fidgeting with her fork in her thoughts of what would be important enough that the elder would send her niece and nephew with her.

"Wonderful. It seems my brother and I are in an advantageous position to help you along that path as well. If you are heading northwards, perhaps Fjordsgate?" the Queen offered.

"Craven informed us that the ports were closed there, as he was attempting to gain passage as well," Darion replied, still keeping his eyes forward, unknowing of F'Lessa's glances.

The Queen furrowed her brow. "Are they now? I suppose I cannot know everything that goes on in my Region. Perhaps this warrants another investigation from my brother."

"Craven had suggested Darktide," F'Skal said, though he noticed the doubt in her words.

"Darktide is a lawless place. It is outside the boundaries of the Sylvannan Region as well as those of Tarkal, whom we are currently at odds with in all cases," Sylvanna explained. "It is effectively a no-man's land, neither Region ever able to gain much ground due to the less than friendly terrain, and outright hostile locals."

"What sort of people make their homes there?" Darion asked, finally making eye contact with the Queen again.

"Ruffians of all kind. Pirates and thieves. It is a port town itself, and a major reason why a trade route between Sylvanna and Tarkal was never established. Neither nation could ever travel through without being raided by the various vessels bred for violence."

F'Skal chimed in next. "How is it that they stay afloat though? Such a limited area, surely their supplies run low?"

"They survive off banditry and piracy for the most part. They send parties out to claim trade caravans or ships that dare run through or even remotely close to their territory. They mostly target unaffiliated merchants and shippers, but they still carry precious cargo."

"Surely the caravans and ships have stopped by now?" he continued. "Their reputation must precede them after a while, so merchants would stop using that byway. Wouldn't they simply find a different route?"

Sylvanna frowned, roughly skewering a piece of egg with her fork. "Unfortunately, when coin is involved, risk is a secondary thought. It is the fastest route and when it comes to the shipping business, as they say, 'time is money'. To them the risk does not outweigh the payoff, even if it does get them killed in the end."

"And thus the pirates thrive," F'Skal concluded.

"Indeed. I envy their delegation of resources if anything," she answered, sitting back again and shrugging. "You may be able to garner passage north through there. Craven of anyone should be able to get you that much with his wiles. I'll arrange for some warm clothes for your journey into the Fjordlands as well."

"We appreciate that," Darion said, glancing to F'Lessa and making brief eye contact with her. "I wouldn't mind you finding something. I worry about your well being in that cold of a place, even with your heritage." The elf shrugged, still not having touched any of the food. Darion met her eyes again and scooted his chair closer after some unspoken agreement between them. Quietly he went over each of the foods with her, just as he had at *The White Carmino,* as well as the previous night's dinner.

Erika continued eating, listening to the conversation and watching Darion and F'Lessa's interactions, not missing the latter's sly smile at Darion's closeness. The thought of the Fjordlands sunk in even more, along with her seemingly imminent return to a homeland that she's never truly known. "Speakin' of 'im, where is Craven?"

"Likely off stalking around, or still in bed," Sylvanna said. "He used to stay here occasionally when my mother was still alive. Was once a mentor to me and my brother when we were younger. He rarely shared breakfast with us though, or any meal for that matter."

"Seems you have a complicated history," F'Skal dared to say.

She sighed in reply. "An understatement, I assure you."

F'Skal smiled at her usage of the same expression as Marq, seeing the family resemblance strongly in that moment.

She continued after a deep sigh. "Frankly, I used to believe myself in love with the man. However, after as many years away as he's been, I have grown past that."

The group sat in silence, unsure of how to reply to her sudden confession. F'Skal was not the only one who could see the sadness in her eyes.

22
A Matter of Pride

nquisitor Marq was never a fan of the major streets of Sylvanna. It was no secret to the read populace that he was brother to the reigning queen, and as such he was often hounded for news surrounding the goings on in the Cathedral. Thus, he usually kept to the back alleys of the cities, learning them from an early age of delinquency and hiding from his mother. Even if the streets were slow in the morning, the back passages were more like home to him than the mainways of the city. Part of him regretted his choice to not bring along Viktor Carmine, his close ally in his investigative duties. Although he would likely become annoyed with the young man's chattering about their current visitors. He could almost hear the big man's voice despite him not actually being there. 'Gods and that Fjordling girl is just gorgeous. Don't you think so, Inquisitor?'

Marq put his fingers to his eyes, trying to rub away the image of Erika. She was beautiful. Although he knew no amount of attraction would stop her from continuing her quest, not when she had come all the way here from Sildenfeld.

A familiar voice caused him pause. It was just a mutter and, in his hesitation, he failed to see the gleaming metal. A pain like fire exploded through his right leg as he felt the blade tear through his flesh. He looked up to find Count Fargeal standing over him as he knelt in pain. The sword driving through his thigh was not the ornamental weapon he wore the previous night, but a much more functional and deadly weapon.

"Dammit, Fargeal, what are you doing?" he demanded, reaching for his own blade. His fingers brushed the handle when the count kicked his side and threw him to the floor. The metal wrenched through his flesh with a sickening *squelch* of lifeblood and sinew, the ground flooding with crimson that quickly found its way into the spaces between the cobbled stones. A memory of Grandmaster Celine reprimanded him for his lack of focus. Sadly she wasn't there to help him either.

The man seemed unwell, he noticed, sweating profusely despite the sleeveless undershirt he wore and the cooler weather. "You damn Inquisitor. You cannot get away with your insulting behavior!"

"What in the Hells are you talking about, man?" he plead through his struggling breaths.

"My *pride* demands it!" Fargeal growled, making Marq cock his head in confusion at him.

The man clutched a hand to his forehead as if fighting an intense headache. Marq saw this as his opportunity, kicking his still good leg outwards to trip the Count onto the stone below. He finally drew his sword, flinching when his ribs flared in pain. Despite both now being prone, Fargeal easily blocked the halfhearted strike Marq made.

"Damn!" Marq hissed, trying to regain his footing to no avail.

Fargeal started to stand using his weapon as a crutch, but Marq slid his own across the back of the Count's leg, severing tendons and drawing a splash of blood onto the ground. Fargeal groaned, but did not react as Marq expected, instead swinging his sword around and narrowly missing the Inquisitor. He let out a string of curses as Marq rolled along the ground, finally gaining enough distance and momentum to stand once again, but he was quick to realize any weight on his right leg caused him to stumble violently. Warm wetness flooded down his trouser leg and into his boot, his vision starting to shake slightly. Luckily, he had a moment when the Count started trembling in a bout of hysteria. Marq quickly leaned his back against the wall, and his weapon against his good leg before wrapping his belt around his thigh to try and slow the blood, knowing that it would only serve as a temporary tourniquet.

Fargeal charged forward after recovering from his apparent delirium, tripping on his own wounded leg and flailing his arm wildly. Marq snatched his blade up and parried the weak strike to the side. With a quick twist, he raked his sword downwards across the Count's back and forced him to the ground again.

He had no wish to kill this man, instead landing a swift kick to the side of his head with his right boot, sending a shooting pain through his hip and side as he did so. He seemed out cold after a moment, and though it hurt to breathe, Marq was finally able to gain a respite. "What is going on?"

His confusion was only increased as a group of thugs, acting similarly erratic as the Count himself, appeared at another alleyway in the small crossroad he found himself in.

"Damn it all!" he growled, taking the small chance, running as best he could down the opposite way while tearing down a stacked crate as he ran in an attempt to escape them. He started regretting the alleys.

† †

The day moved forward and still no word from Inquisitor Marq had come. Erika was beginning to become anxious, though she wasn't sure if it was merely because she wanted to get back on the road or if she was concerned for the Queen's brother. "Do ye think he got held up somewhere?" she turned and asked, all of them now sitting in a comfortable living room. F'Skal took full advantage of the furniture by laying back on the couches and leaning chairs leisurely, looking as if he were half asleep at the time. Conversely, Darion sat rigidly on a simple wooden chair across a small table from the Queen. F'Lessa was watching the game of Regicile the two played with interest. Erika had sat in a plump lounge chair by the window, which she quickly learned was the favored seat of Winnifred, who took no issue in claiming Erika's lap as part of that chosen place.

Queen Sylvanna removed her chin from her hand as she looked at the pieces strewn across the checkered board between her and Darion. "Marq? Likely. He makes himself very involved with the city's happenings, and probably got caught by a store owner accusing their neighbor of unfair business practices or something of that like." She groaned slightly when Darion moved one of his pieces, eliminating yet another of hers from the board. "Damn, I am out of practice," she said with a smile towards the guardsman.

Erika returned to looking out the window, F'Lessa shifting in her seat as she continued spectating the game between the Queen and her dear friend, though she seemed confused by the rules. Outside, the world was still hazy and overcast. Hallowden was in full swing and the dreadful anniversary of her birth crept closer. She issued a puff of air, resenting the fact that Darion and the others had learned of it and were adamant about throwing her some kind of festivity. A brief conversation regarding it in the hallway earlier that day made her grimace as the three of them buzzed with infectious grins that twisted their hushed tones ever so slightly in the direction of mischief. The thought of the day without Irvine filled her with a dour feeling that made her sick to her stomach. She had spent her birthday completely alone the previous year, locked in her bedroom in the second floor of her father's new house in Sildenfeld. It had not even been a month after Irvine's disappearance, and she was still worn ragged from the tragedy. Her new family of companions had every right to celebrate the day she knew, considering she would wish to do the same for them. It still did not make the emotions any easier to deal with.

Her musing was interrupted by a strange sight outside. A mob of people carrying all manner of weaponry, improvised and conventional. A nearby guard rushed forward but was thrown to the side by the crowd and a torch thrown into the building behind him. Erika's eyes went wide, not understanding what was happening. "Queen Sylvanna? There's something wrong."

Just then the door burst open, startling F'Lessa into knocking over the game board and scattering the pieces. A knight stood in the open portal. "Ma'am, a large mob is outside. Riots have broken out across the city. I'm not sure what has happened, but everyone's gone mad."

Queen Sylvanna let out a deep sigh and looked to Darion with a coy smile. "I suppose we'll have to have a rematch later then." F'Lessa eyed the woman with streaks of green in her hair as the

Queen turned back to the knight. "Ready my raiment. I'll be out directly."

"With respect, my Queen, I don't think that is the best idea," the man replied. "They seem to be rather violent already, and our forces are spread thin with knights all over trying to contain the crowds."

"Which is why I'll have the *armored* raiment specifically. Our new friends will be able to help as well, I'm sure," she said, looking around at the party, who all nodded in response.

Inside the main hall of the Cathedral a while later, Erika and the others were instructed to stay just inside the entrance and out of sight until they were signaled to help. F'Lessa seemed suddenly very excited, bouncing on the balls of her feet and smirking ever so slightly. Erika assumed it was likely at the prospect of being able to hit something. Conversely, F'Skal was silent and calm, observing the mounting crowd with interest, while Darion simply stood with a nervous demeanor.

Moments later Queen Sylvanna quickly walked through the massive doorway. She was clad in a beautiful flowing gown of green and blue adorned with armor plates around her chest and sides as well as shoulders and hips. Her presence was met with screams and shouts, the knight at her side deftly shattering a thrown bottle out of the air with his shield. Erika quickly began to realize the weight of the situation and the bravery of the Queen who seemed the target of the crowd's anger and rage.

Darion appeared even more anxious than before, quickly looking around as the Queen began to speak to her people, likely in an effort to learn the source of their turmoil. Eventually, Darion locked on to another knight that was standing just off from them.

"Pardon, Sir!" he said, quietly enough to not interrupt the Queen. "Which direction did Inquisitor Marq leave this morning?"

The knight seemed hesitant to answer, but eventually spoke. "The northeastern tower. He was awaiting a courier from last night, due back early today."

Darion set his jaw, his three companions looking at him with confusion.

"There's only so much she can learn here," Darion answered them, nodding towards Queen Sylvanna. "I'm going to try and track down the Inquisitor and try and get an outside understanding of what is happening."

"I'll go with you!" F'Lessa quickly volunteered, but Darion held up a hand.

"You need to stay here. I can move through side streets easier on my own, and quite frankly I think they may need you and your beautiful muscles here," he said with a wary nod towards the crowd outside.

F'Lessa's hair flashed pink in a frenzy at his remark.

"In that case, I'll climb to the top of the Cathedral and scan over the city. My eyesight can surely help somehow," F'Skal said, nodding towards his sister and Darion.

The aash was off with haste, making for the higher floors alongside a young maid that he recruited to guide him. Darion started to make for the rear entrance himself, before F'Lessa grabbed him by the arm and roughly stopped him. "Be careful. I don't want you getting hurt," she said, showing a little more vulnerability than she intended.

Darion smiled at her. "I'll be fine, F'Lessa. You and Erika hold the line."

She let him go and he was across the room in moments, the aash elf returning to Erika's side. Both of them stood in silence, before F'Lessa looked to her with a wide grin. "He called me beautiful."

"Aye, that'e did," Erika said with a returned smile.

† †

Darion had known how big Sylvanna was even before he and Erika arrived for the first time together. He remembered his trips here with his father during his younger years, always thinking that the buildings looked impossibly tall. Trying to navigate the place was sometimes difficult when you had time to spare, but now that he was in a hurry and dodging gangs of rioters it was a complete nightmare. He kept his compass out, keeping the correct heading and avoiding any blocked streets. He hoped Thrane was alright in his tavern, but figured that man could fight off any unruly patrons with his gaze alone. He shook his head, knowing his concern should be on himself as he was walking alone through such a hostile area.

Around a corner and into an alley he went after nearly being spotted by another mob, nearly running straight into another man. He took a step back, looking up and recognizing him as one of the nobles that Marq and the Queen had briefly spoken to last night while he and F'Lessa were learning to dance. The man had a strange fogginess to his eyes that Darion hadn't noticed at the ball.

"Sorry, I didn't see you," he apologized quickly, as he started to move around the man. He stopped in his tracks when he saw the considerable bludgeon wound on his head and the bloodstained blade in his hands.

"Where are you going?" the man asked, leering at him with an odd look in his eyes. Darion looked down when the man stepped with a limp, finding a considerable amount of blood on the cobblestones below.

"Where I am going is my own business," he answered, trying to ignore the lurch in his stomach. He put a hand on the hilt of his own weapon. "Regrettably, you are in my way. Let me pass."

The man's head twitched awkwardly to one side. "Let you pass? Are you trying to insult me boy?"

Darion backed another step, bringing his off hand to the left side of his belt.

"I think you're out of line here," he continued, the tone of his voice growing deeper and more aggressive. "You think you can insult my *pride* like that? I'll have your head!"

Just as the noble started forward in a wild swing, Darion pulled his hunting knife from the left side of his belt, holding it in a reverse grip and diving towards the man's left side. Before the oncoming swing could make it down to him, he jabbed the small dagger into his thigh, eliciting a pained scream from the man. Using the momentum of his flight and his opponent's weakened stance, he rammed the man with his shoulder into a nearby wall. Darion quickly recovered, grabbing the man's sword as it fell from his hand and obscured it behind his own back. "I need you to stay down. I have to find someone, and I don't have time to fight you."

The noble's head spilled another gout of blood, dripping down the back of his neck and onto his shoulders. Darion had to hold his stomach as he tried not to think about how the new wound would look. He began backing away, not wanting to drop the sword for fear that the man would retrieve it and chase him.

However, a quick glance around told him that he was running out of time here also, as another group of people had just noticed him and started rushing down the alley with cudgels and variety of craftsman tools.

He broke out into as fast a run as he could manage. Into an alleyway he went, his eyes bolting for a moment to the pooled blood on the stones, before jumping over a broken crate and onwards towards the northeastern wall. The group and eventually the noble all chased after him, their angered cries echoing off the buildings. "Damn city's gone mad," he hissed as he sucked more air into his lungs. He knew he couldn't keep this up forever, his mind racing to find a way to slow the mob.

He whirled around a corner and crouched down, waiting for the group to reach him, not noticing the extra shadow that seemed to follow him. Just as the group passed he swung his leg out hard, slamming his greave into the shins of the first two. They tumbled head first into the street and Darion was up again in a flash, still unsure of what to do with the noble's apprehended weapon. One shot a fist out towards him and he dodged to the side, moving around the two still standing while jumping over the two recovering from their fall. "I don't want to fight any of you, please, stop!" he shouted.

One of the men looked around at him as he whirled for a swing of his cudgel. "It's a matter of *pride* for us!"

There's that word again, he thought, remembering the noble's use of 'pride' just before he attacked. He couldn't really ponder the significance of it, having to duck under the swinging bludgeon. He failed to see the noble throwing a punch of his own in time, the fist connecting squarely on Darion's jaw. The strength of the blow was incredible. He flew through the air several feet, coming to a rough landing on the stone street and immediately pressed a hand to his face. Pain radiated through his entire head and neck.

The world stopped spinning after a moment as he watched the group regain their lost footing and ready themselves to move in towards him. He started to try and stand up, realizing that he had lost his grip on both his knife and the noble's sword, knowing that one or both would likely be rushing for him soon.

As he reached a knee, the group stopped suddenly and began to back away slowly, their eyes to the ground. Darion heard the clanking of metal and heavy footfalls coming from another street corner not far away. With a fearful gaze, he watched for the source to show itself.

A massive creature likely more than fifteen feet tall hulked around the corner. Its body was wrapped in thick armor from head to toe, the polish causing it to gleam brightly in the sunlight. From the top of the jagged helmet that looked akin to a crown were a pair of thick black horns that curled around the brow of the creature.

"Gods..." Darion breathed, though it came out distorted.

The creature laughed a thick hearty laugh, the sound echoing from the metal of its helmet. "A common saying among my kind is: 'The Gods have nothing to do with me'. You seem a strong-willed soul, and someone who appears to be on a mission."

Darion fell back into the wall, trying to make distance between himself and this monster, but he could not find the strength to stand.

"Do not worry human, I am not going to devour your soul. Not yet at least," it said with a sickening chuckle.

The shadow in the alley faded as the creature gripped Darion's skull within its massive hand.

† †

F'Skal leaned against the tallest spire at the peak of the Cathedral, his emerald dust markings flaring around his eyes and ears as he looked over the city. The screams and shouts permeated the air around him as he fingered at his bowstring. He had hoped things were a simple misunderstanding, but he could tell by the sounds that people were dying.

The city seemed to be divided into two factions from what he could tell. One side was completely sane and simply defending life and property, while the second had gone mad and had begun attacking with rampant aggression. What was causing this, he could not tell, but he did understand that the latter people were under some sort of trance. His vision was enhanced by the magic of the crystals, enabling him sight as if used through a spyglass, he could see an apparent ailment in the people's eyes. They were glassy, as if under the effect of some kind of drug. This was obviously the case with the crowd below him who were still engaged with Queen Sylvanna.

He started to settle in to his position, not seeing any real semblance of organization to the rioters and thus unsure of how to help the knights in returning order, until he looked to the northeast and saw fortifications being set up. Further still, he caught a glint of light from an armored individual, much larger than any he had seen before, outside of adult ogres. He peered closer, invoking his magic again and nearly fell from his perch when he saw Darion being dragged along by the head by the same armored creature.

He cursed in his native tongue repeatedly as he deftly made his way back to the closest window into the Cathedral, startling the nervous maid who had guided him up. On his way back down the many stairs, he was joined by a man in thick robes carrying a tome that on a quick glance F'Skal could tell contained information on drugs and toxic herbs that could conceivably cause such afflictions. He and the man were apparently going to the same place and as they arrived in the Cathedral hall, the Queen was making her way back in amidst a rain of missiles from the crowd, her shoulder pauldron was muddied, her cheek cut and bleeding.

"Scholar Ghill, what have you found?" she asked sternly of the robed man who had joined them.

The academic stuttered for a moment, stopping when he caught a look at the Queen's intimidatingly stern face as she seemed to not notice the blood that dripped down her jawline. "Nothing makes sense, my Queen. None of these herbs could have possibly caused such mass hysteria in such a short amount of time nor could have any drug."

She looked to F'Skal next. "You appear to have learned something, go ahead."

"Darion has been captured," he said flatly, his sister screaming in protest from the side of the hall.

"Captured? By what? Where is he?" she yelled as her hair intensely streaked red and orange, the colors alternating down her braids. Erika struggled to keep pace with her as she stormed across the room.

He took a breath and then continued, describing the creature he saw in detail. "It was dragging him further towards the edge of the city. I believe this may be an actual attack."

Erika and the scholar's eyes widened in realization, both speaking in unison. "Pride Daemon."

The scholar looked to her with puzzlement, but quickly returned to the task at hand. "A Pride Daemon makes complete sense. The tales from the Chaos Age speak of them having a unique effect on creatures around them, making them more prone to taking insult and reacting in aggression."

"Why are there so many damned Daemons?" Erika hissed, bunching her hair in her hands to tie up only to let it down a moment later—then doing it over again—in her usual stress habit as she paced through the hall.

F'Lessa looked to be in shock. "If a Daemon has Darion," she began, the tears rimming her eyes obvious for all to see.

"Then we don't have a lot of time," came the voice of Craven, who stepped through a doorway at the side of the room.

Queen Sylvanna groaned, rushing forward before her knight attendant could stop her. "And where the Hells have you been?"

Craven stood fast against the advancing woman, until she came to stop directly in front of him. She looked ready to strike him, but he simply raised a hand and brushed an errant lock of hair from her face and drew it behind her ear. "I have been gathering information."

Queen Sylvanna's shoulders shuddered as she stifled a scream of anger. "And *what* have you found?" she said through gritted teeth, slowly regaining her calmness.

"It is a Pride Daemon, unfortunately. And more unfortunately still, it has gained control over nearly a third of the city," he explained. "From what I could see, it captured Darion, but plans to use him somehow. It will not kill him yet, so we do have some time at least."

Now F'Lessa ran over to him with an aggression matching that of Sylvanna's. "You witnessed it happen?" she shouted, her hair and gem dust lighting a brilliant red, nearly in unison. "And you did nothing to save him?"

Craven turned on her and though no one else could, she saw a different side of him. His face transformed into the visage of a skull as he moved and the world darkened into blackness for only a moment. She blinked as she stopped her approach, the room back to normal once again. Craven's handsomely shaved face looked at her from under the brim of his hat. "If I had attempted to stop the beast, then I may have joined him. If you are so keen on making sure your sweetheart stays alive, then we must mount a counteroffensive against them posthaste."

F'Skal's eyes narrowed as he watched F'Lessa's face, paling ever so slightly. Her hair had just briefly flashed black, so quickly that he wondered if anyone else had taken notice of it.

"What rank do ye think it was?" Erika asked.

Craven spoke without looking away from F'Lessa. "A Greater, likely. Considering the amount of people it has infected and the apparent strength of it."

"A Greater Daemon?" Queen Sylvanna asked. "I am not familiar with the ranks."

"Ye remember the scar on my back?" Erika asked her.

The Queen nodded in reply. "It looked quite the grievous wound."

"That was a Greater. Me and my best friend fought it ourselves and barely killed it. Sildenfeld's wall was partly breached, and I nearly died," she continued with a grim tone. "A Greater Lust Daemon also removed the leg of a close friend not long after, nearly killin' her as well."

The Scholar exhaled deeply. "I had heard the rumors that Daemons had attacked Sildenfeld, but I had not considered them to possibly be true."

"Five Daemons actually, and an Angelus," Erika corrected.

"Surely the Angelus helped you slay the Daemons then?" Ghill asked, almost pleadingly.

"The Angelus did nothin' but kill innocent men and women. He only added more misery to the day," she growled. "The most misery, in my book."

The scholar balked at her answer, his eyes twitching back and forth as he processed the information.

"Well, on the bright side, this is just one Daemon," F'Skal piped in.

"Indeed," Craven said with a brief pause as he crossed his arms over his chest. "So, we can still kill it. We are only hindered by the time limit of his whims and how long he wishes to keep the young man captive, and not dead. As an added incentive: we kill the Daemon, the infection will cease."

Queen Sylvanna called for a meeting to be held with her headmost knights, and for the doors to be barricaded. Erika watched Craven as he moved into the adjacent room behind the knights, with the scholar following close behind. "How does he know so much about Daemons?" she couldn't help but wonder aloud.

F'Lessa began pacing, and F'Skal began to walk towards the side room as well. Erika approached her, the elf's hair streaking orange and red. As soon as she made eye contact with Erika, all of her silver hair suddenly flushed a stark black.

She remembered a conversation with F'Skal before they had met Craven, when he had said. "Of all of the colors, I have only once seen my sister's hair turn black. Black is her color of fear."

Erika paused for just a moment, before making her way to F'Lessa's side.

"What if we're too late?" F'Lessa asked, the tears returning to her eyes.

Erika did her best to put on a brave face, placing a hand on her arm. "We'll find 'im. We have to." F'Lessa could only nod weakly in response, putting a hand to her mouth like she was feeling sick. "Do ye want to head in to hear their plannin'?" Erika asked.

F'Lessa shook her head, her now black hair looking strange on her ebon skin. "I just need a moment."

They took a seat on a bench to the side of the hall. Her hair stayed black for a long while. F'Skal gave the two of them an odd expression that struck Erika as concern but also suspicion. She wrapped her arm around F'Lessa's shoulder as her brother disappeared into the chamber behind them.

23
Faxxyl's Offensive

Darion awoke slowly, his vision blurry and his head wracking with a sharp ache, only outmatched by the numbness in his jaw. He found that he could not shut his mouth and any attempt to do so led to a horrible pain in the left side of his face. He was bound, wrists behind his back and legs tied to the limbs of the chair that he sat upon. The room he was in was lit only by the outside sunlight, which was starting to fade with the day. Around him were several normal looking townsfolk, besides the crazed looks in their eyes and the blood caking their forms. Each of them simply loitered with angry faces, none of them seeming to realize that he was awake again.

He glanced around as carefully as he could, unsure of how they would react if they did discover his consciousness, finding no trace of the massive creature that had grabbed him before. He tested the restraints and concluded that all of them were plenty tight to hold him. The chair was not bolted down by any means, and he considered toppling himself, but he reasoned that likely wouldn't lead to any advantages unless he could manage to break the chair itself somehow. Even then, he couldn't do much against the five people in here with him.

An opportunity came when he heard the loud footsteps again and a booming voice beckoning to them. The citizens left Darion alone in the room, allowing him to freely look around the room and search for some way out of the situation. It appeared to be a normal living room, at the front of a small house from what he could tell. Behind him was a dining table and three unoccupied chairs. The room otherwise held only two small loungers and a fireplace with a painting of a young couple on the mantle.

The red splashes across the portrait made Darion worry for the true occupants of this house, but he couldn't concern himself with that now. Outside, the people seemed to have moved on but he could see the silhouette of the creature through the window. To his dismay the door opened shortly after. The armored giant crouched and squeezed almost comically just to barely make it through the door, and even then had to walk on its knees to move over to him. Its size was greatly diminished from the first time Darion had met it, but it was still massive.

"Wonderful, you are awake," it said in that strangely smooth voice. "I was worried you were dead already."

"Wha' are 'ou?" was all Darion could manage, his lower jaw unable to move properly.

The creature cocked its head. "That's rather rude, don't you think? In normal *polite* conversation, you would say 'who' are you, not 'what' are you."

Darion stared at him in silence, incredulity halted any more attempts to speak more than the agonizing pain that came with it.

"My name is Faxyyl, Daemon of Pride," it continued after an annoyed groan, Darion's eyes widening at the revelation of the creature's origin. "Interrogating you is obviously not an option. Your mouth appears badly damaged and I haven't a clue about human physiology unfortunately, so I won't try to fix it myself. However, as I said upon our first meeting, you appeared to be on a mission of sorts. Perhaps I can lure someone out with you as bait? I understand there is a human monarch here of some import."

Darion's world became cold. This Daemon's words causing an intense anxiety to rise inside him at the realization that his friends could be hurt because of his failure. The Daemon tapped a clawed finger on his chin, seeming to consider other options.

"Come now, you could at least nod or shake your head," Faxyyl sighed, his breath moving through his helmet and blowing onto Darion's broken face. "Then again, the day is growing late, and I have quite the force amassed here. Maybe I'll just leave you as a meal for later."

A long silence followed as Darion stared at the helmeted face with as passive of an expression as he could manage, unsure of what was going on behind that mask of metal. Finally, Faxyyl gave a resigned shrug before backing up to squeeze out the door and into the street once again. He stretched to his full size in the open air, bending back down and looking through the doorway. "Be a good little house pet while I'm gone, alright? I'll be back again after that Queen's head is on a stake."

Darion started bouncing his leg in nervousness as soon as the thing had left the house, his gaze snapping all around for anything he could use to escape. This creature was certainly not like the survatri, or even the thief, Metlox. He wondered if something more similar to this creature was why Erika was so adamant on violence towards Metlox, suddenly starting to understand her mindset a bit better.

† †

Through the darkening streets, Inquisitor Marq limped. The bleeding from his leg was staunched with a torn part of his uniform, his belt holding down the makeshift bandage. Several more open cuts and scrapes lined his arms as well, but he hadn't the time to tend to them. His blade hung from his hand idly, dripping with crimson on the blade and the handle. He had to fight through several more of the mobs, unfortunately having to grievously wound several townsfolk, but he couldn't do much to save his city if he was incapacitated or dead.

He peeked around the corner and saw the armored giant leaving a small house as it said something into the open doorway before stalking off with a group of citizens. Marq had heard some of the people mentioning such a creature and quickly surmised that it was the root cause of all of this.

What was it talking to? he wondered, taking a chance and moving as quickly as he could to the doorway. Thankfully it wasn't locked and he was able to slide in and close the door behind him with careful ease.

"'arq!" came a strange voice, the Inquisitor turning to find the source.

"Darion?" he said in surprise. "What the Hells are you doing here? Where is everyone else?"

Darion began to try and explain but his words came out hardly intelligible. Marq quieted him seeing the pain in his expression each time he tried to speak.

"You can explain later, for now we need to get out of here," he spoke hurridly, moving in and cutting through the ropes that bound his wrists and ankles.

Darion rubbed where the bindings had been and began looking around for his own weapons. Marq gained his attention after a moment. "Were any of the others with you?" he asked.

Darion shook his head in reply, holding his lower jaw so it wouldn't waggle painfully.

The Inquisitor pushed up against the window frame, peeking outside to check for any townsfolk passing by. Darion found his blade—miraculously not stolen by any of the Daemon's minions—and started to strap it to his hip, though his movement seemed slowed because of the pain in his jaw and throughout his body.

"Looks like we're in similar situations," Marq said, motioning to the bloodstained cloth around his thigh.

Darion gave him an apologetic look, but he waved it away, motioning for them to await a chance for their escape. Soon enough, an opportunity arose and they took it, dashing as quietly as they could between the groupings of rioters.

† †

The party moved swiftly over the cobblestones. Erika, F'Skal and F'Lessa, with the accompaniment of six knights. Ahead of them, the lower ranked guards and soldiers worked together with large shields to clear a path through the raving townsfolk.

"We're starting to enter the district that they control. Based upon the information gained by our sources and the keen eyed aash," one knight said, motioning to F'Skal before drawing his sword.

The three companions took this as a good time to ready their own weapons as well, though their previous discussion called for as little lethal force as possible to be used with any townsfolk.

Erika worried about F'Lessa through all of it, as her normally brilliant silver hair had not reverted from black since the Cathedral. F'Skal voiced his concern as well, pointing out that every single strand had turned dark, instead of just a thin streak of hair as was normal with her unruly emotions. The elf woman's face was a picture of determination, making Erika wonder how well she would adhere to simply subduing any in their way, but was glad she hadn't just run off in pursuit of Darion at least.

Fortunately, their progress was unimpeded, the scattered forces of Sylvanna doing a good job at making a path for them. Unfortunately, they were not the only ones using the clear avenue.

As they made their way down the street, two knights moved ahead to check the street corners. The rest of the group could only watch in horror as a blade swung in an uppercut from a crossing street, slicing directly up the middle of the first knight and separating him in two. Blood splashed onto the ground in a massive gout, the other knight baring his weapon in a flash and barely dodging a second horizontal strike. The other four knights rushed out and assumed a formation to cover the retreat of their comrade.

Around the corner the Daemon stepped, his metal boot landing on the right half of the knight's corpse and crushing it with a sickening sound. Faxyyl laughed heartily, waving his massive double-edged sword through the air as he traded it into his left hand while raising his right towards the group.

"It seems I have met my first foes," he called out to them with a strangely giddy tone to his voice. "This initial one was unimpressive, though I suppose he didn't see it coming!"

F'Skal called so everyone could hear him. "That's the one. He's the source."

"Faxyyl! Greater Daemon of Pride, a pleasure to make your acquaintances!" the Daemon roared in response.

"Seems Craven was right," Erika muttered as she sidestepped to try and distance herself from any of her allies, knowing that the monster's blade could easily strike through several of them in a single swing.

Faxyyl brought the handle of his blade into both hands, holding it in an upraised salute before him. "You know, it's considered rude to accept an introduction and not offer one yourselves."

As he spoke he wrenched the handle in two, separating the blade into two single-edged but equally deadly weapons. Erika unintentionally let out a rather foul curse as the metal rang in unison and the lead knight screamed for them to scatter.

Forward Faxyyl charged, both blades whirling furiously before him. His initial strike cleaved through another knight and cut into another, sending her flying into a wall with a shrill shriek. The remaining three knights worked in tandem, expertly watching his strikes and moving in for attacks of their own but the armor the Daemon wore was thick and none of their weapons penetrated.

"Get me an openin'!" Erika yelled. The lead knight nodded and directed his warriors into positions.

Two knights drew the blade in the creature's left hand, while the other two—including the wounded woman—drew his right, dividing the Daemon's attention and distracting him from the other combatants. Erika flushed both of her arms into flame, the immolation turning her flesh black as coal with the magma lines cracking down from her shoulders to her fingers. Forward she rushed as she slammed her hammer with all her might into the side of Faxyyl's knee, causing the creature to lurch in pain.

Down one blade came, straight above Erika. She started to attempt a parry but two axes sailed over her head, slamming into the flat of the sword. She looked up to find F'Lessa, her ruby markings flaring brightly as she used all her strength to divert the blow which went crashing into the stonework below.

The knights took the slight opportunity to breach in closer as well, rushing for the Daemon's legs and slicing into the gaps in the armor. Faxyyl seemed to react less to the strikes of the blades than he did to Erika's hammer blow though, and was able to retaliate much faster.

F'Lessa threw Erika to the side roughly, wincing from the burning flesh brushing against her arm. Erika dropped her immolation a moment after realizing the burn on her ally as both of them ducked down from the Daemon's attacks. Above them, the Daemon's blades whirled in a sudden storm of lethality. Three of the knights turned and dove into the ground, while one was stuck backpedaling futilely. He brought his blade up in an attempt to block, screaming his defiance. Erika tried not to watch as the Daemon's attack severed his sword and his torso from shoulder to ribs.

As soon as Faxyyl slowed, Erika took her chance. She angled herself underneath F'Lessa while pressing her shoulders against the elf's midriff, and kicked her feet into the monster's shin. Just before the impact, she immolated her lower legs and feet, burning her boots to cinders and singing her skirt, but blasting herself and F'Lessa all the way to where F'Skal was positioned. He narrowly dodged them and drew his bowstring back while he searched for another opening in the armor.

Erika landed roughly, rolling three times before finally landing on her chest. F'Lessa fared much better, using her strength to her advantage and only skidding back a ways on her feet, one axe sparking on the stones to slow her. Erika stood a moment later, noticing the multitude of arrows protruding from various gaps in the Daemon's armor. From each shaft, a small gout of blood the color of platinum came forth. The attacks of the knights unfortunately did not seem to have the same effect, much to the frustration of the three remaining.

"The knights are doing next to nothing with their strikes!" F'Skal called back just as Erika was realizing the same. "We need to make a new plan, I don't want to watch all these people die needlessly!"

"Neither do I!" F'Lessa called back, sheathing one axe and holding her hand out to Erika. "Do you trust me?"

Erika looked from her hand to the Daemon, not completely sure what she was doing, but believed herself ready for whatever ploy F'Lessa had come up with. "I trust ye!"

She grabbed hold of the aash's hand, and with a blinding flash of the ruby dust, the elf's arm muscles rippled and corded more than Erika had ever seen them. She pulled violently on her arm, slinging her outwards and towards the Daemon. Erika let out a scream of surprise and fear at her sudden flight, but understood the gambit.

While Faxyyl was preoccupied with the knights at a lower angle, Erika was coming in from much higher up. As she mounted the apex of the throw, she immolated her arms and grabbed hold of her warhammer's shaft with both hands. Faxyyl didn't notice her, still pirouetting in place and holding the knights at disadvantageous distances. Her hammer's head collided squarely on the side of his helmet with a cacophonous ring and crash, sending the Daemon falling to the ground. Erika was just barely able to grab ahold of the top of his breastplate to brace her own fall.

"All of you, retreat! Your weapons are having no effect, we need to regroup!" F'Skal yelled, nocking another arrow and readying his aim for when the Daemon recovered. At his direction, the knights fell back towards him but his sister had other ideas. She sprinted for the corner that Faxyyl came around initially, F'Skal calling for her frantically.

She seemed even more desperate though in her words and expression. "He came from this way! Darion must be somewhere nearby!"

Erika watched her go around the corner and was unsure of which way to run, though her time began to dwindle as the Daemon started to stir beneath her. She took her chance, swinging her hammer in a full arc around her back and over her head, crashing it down on Faxyyl's breastplate. After the impact she immolated her legs again and kicked off of the beast, following F'Lessa down the street.

F'Skal groaned, urging the knights to make their way back to the defense line with haste before clambering up the side of a building in a flash. Across the rooftops he ran, his bare feet slapping against the shingles as he eyed the Daemon heaving himself to his feet again. The side of his helm was cracked, and F'Skal could just barely see the side of the thing's horrible face as he continued making distance from him.

"Where is Craven when you need him?" he hissed through heavy breaths.

† †

Craven stalked through the streets with a scowl. Despite how he wished to pass through Sylvanna without being noticed by those he knew, he still had a particular love for this city. He was always happy to see how much the settlement had grown each time he made his way through and hated to see such mayhem and destruction on the island he once called home. He rounded a corner and looked down the street to see a group of Daemons, one ripping a man's chest cavity open by prying his ribs apart and taking twisted pleasure in its victim's garbled screams of agony. Craven's scowl deepened as he continued down the road towards the creatures. The one torturing the man awaiting Mortia was a Wrath, another was a Sloth, and the last two were Prides. One thing Daemons could be admired for is how well they could work together beyond their Circles, at least under the right circumstances.

"*Klush mal set?*" the Sloth said slowly, each syllable drawn out.

The others perked up at his words, the Wrath dropping his plaything and turning towards Craven. The dark man drew his rapier with a methodical swipe to the side, issuing an obvious challenge. One of the Prides nudged the Sloth forward, who shrugged and began lumbering forward to meet the waiting Craven. The Daemon was around twelve feet tall with an odd helm about its head and ill-fitting trousers around its waist. The thing's arms nearly dragged the ground with massive fingers hanging open and limp until it grew closer to Craven and then they started to curl into fists.

Craven spared a look past the beast towards the others, a smirk growing across his face as he threw his rapier over his shoulder with a flourish. The Sloth gained confidence at the baiting action and flew into surprisingly swift motion considering the Circle it hailed from. On all fours the Daemon barreled forward, issuing grunts with each impact against the cobbled stone. When it was within striking distance it rose back up on two legs, its arms coming out wide to grab Craven and snap him in two. Only it didn't have the chance to do so. With a kick far stronger than the Daemons were expecting, the Sloth's legs separated from its body as if by the sharpest of blades. The creature fell to the ground howling horribly at its lost limbs while black sludge-like blood oozed from its severed knees. The other three Daemons flinched just slightly as they fell into readied stances. Craven began sprinting with preternatural speed towards them.

Next out was one of the Prides and the Wrath as they attacked in tandem. The Wrath held a wickedly jagged blade while the Pride had something akin to a halberd. Craven dropped to the ground as they approached, sliding between the two of them while their weapons rang uselessly on the stone behind him. He popped up from the ground, punching the Pride in the side with such force that it caved its armor and sent the beast careening into a wall, shattering the stone with a loud crash. He twisted and caught the wrist of the Wrath as the horned creature attempted a bare-handed strike at him. Craven gripped harder, and the beast screeched as he crushed the bones between his fingers. The second Pride Daemon backed away as Craven's form melted into shadow, formless and chaotic. The Wrath Daemon was too preoccupied with cradling its ruined arm to retreat.

"Soulless beasts with nothing to do but kill," Craven's voice was distorted, terrifying even to the otherworldly creatures that faced him. He was beyond them. The Wrath Daemon screamed in horror mirroring that of the man he had just tortured as Craven slid jagged shadowy fingers through its breastbone, cracking its ribs apart. "Writhe for a while, wretched creature."

The second Pride recovered its confidence and ran forward thinking to catch Craven unaware, but pain was all that met it. Arms, legs, torso, and head all hit the stonework in separate pieces. It realized its own death as it melted into a light that extended into the sky. The next flare of brightness was the Sloth. After it had tried to regain some kind of stance, its head came off with another of Craven's savage kicks. The Pride with the dented armor crawled free of the building, trying to quickly determine where the man had disappeared to and which direction he would attack from next. However, the Daemon had no hope of keeping up and quickly fell to its knees while its torso above its shoulders hit the ground separately in gouts of platinum blood.

The Wrath watched on in horror as Craven assumed his human shape once more, only to stalk closer. It let out a garbled scream as Craven grabbed its two horns, pulling and twisting as muscle and sinew ripped and popped. It gave one last splashing choke of orange ichor before its head tore free of its neck. Craven dropped it to his side as the rest of the creature joined its brethren in dying lights. He snapped his fingers and his rapier returned back to his scabbard. Mortia had finally claimed the dying man, his spirit not noticing the vengeance that Craven wrought on his behalf. The dark man hardly minded. He had his own reasons for killing Daemons, and resolved to kill many more this day.

Few watched the skyline of Sylvanna that violent day. Those that did would tell of the flaring light columns that rose into the sky throughout the northeastern quarter, despite most others waving them off as having imagined it. Some of them would wonder if they truly did hallucinate those pillars in the heat of the crisis, or if that many Daemons truly did die in the chaos.

After his task was done, Craven found himself at the gates that led onto one of the great bridges to the mainland. A trio of individuals were leaving the confusion of the city, seemingly unaffected and uncaring to all the carnage around them. Something else beyond them made a chill crawl down his spine.

A ghostly hand fell on his shoulder. "Thine quarry is ahead of the Hands."

Craven's eyes widened. "So close..."

"Pursue, and thou may return to thy wanderings."

Sounds of battle rang out in the distance. His companions battling a Greater Daemon. "I cannot leave them."

"Thine hunt has more import."

Craven's fist squeezed harder. "Not after we put that poor girl through the nightmare of seeing her love in the Sands of Conflict. I cannot abandon her now."

"Craven..." Mortia's eerie voice warned.

He ignored her, turning away from the three and leaving them to their fate. There was still one more Daemon to kill.

24
Battle for Sylvanna

Through the streets F'Lessa ran, her axes stowed and the handles bouncing on her thighs as she hurriedly glanced around every street corner. She did not need her brother's enhanced vision to see the crushed stones where the Daemon had walked, but she could not surmise where he was keeping Darion. Her hair finally returned to its normal silver luster as she started to hope. The strands began to pull loose from her neat braid, falling over her dark shoulders and flying into her face every time she came to a halt. Ahead, lay a building with a wide open doorway. Inside was a chair that had cut ropes and bindings around it and her heart skipped a beat. "Clever boy, you got out, didn't you?" she said quietly to herself, excitement building in her chest.

She knew this was where Darion was, she was sure of it. She just had no clue where he could be now. She turned around quickly, her hair now whipping nearly completely free of its ties, twisting around her neck as she looked around frantically.

Finally, Erika caught up to her, her breast heaving with labored breaths. "Gods ye run fast, and I'm not as good at runnin' without shoes as ye," she said, briefly inspecting the bottom of her feet for any open wounds.

"You shouldn't have come!" F'Lessa said in a panic, her arms raising as she pushed her hair over the top of her head. "I meant to find Darion on my own and bring him back while I was free of that Daemon!"

Erika looked at her in disbelief as she stood to her full height, although it was still considerably shorter than the elf's stature. "Are ye serious?" F'Lessa seemed taken aback, actually retreating when Erika stepped closer to her. "Ye left the Daemon to yer brother and I while ye went to find Darion?"

"I need to find him Erika!" she said, tears beginning to form in her eyes again.

"Ye need to help us kill the damned bastard that's doin' all o' this, F'Lessa!" Erika screamed back at her, startling the tears free of the aash's crimson eyes. "We'll find Darion! I promise ye that, but first we need to kill the thing that took 'im in the first place!"

"Now would be a great time for that!" F'Skal called out to them from the rooftop across the street. "Here he comes!" He loosed three arrows in quick succession as Faxyyl came crashing around the corner, his blades cleaving through several buildings as the arrows ricocheted from his armor. One however, did find purchase between his shoulder and breastplate.

Erika gave F'Lessa one more infuriated look, harrumphing back towards the monster and flushing her arms into flame. F'Lessa watched on, the realization of her emotional outburst setting in. She began to wonder if she was truly helping her comrades or if her feelings for Darion were nothing but a burden on all of them.

Perhaps she should have stayed in the village. But she feared what her life would have been without Darion now that she had grown so attached to him.

Her thoughts were interrupted by her brother, landing roughly on the ground beside her and violently slapping her ribs, yanking her back to the present. "Get the helmet off. Its already cracked on the left side, if you can get it off, I think we have a chance."

F'Lessa nodded her understanding, looking back as Erika screamed in rage, slamming one blade to the side with her hammer and reversing the strike into the Daemon's ankle. She dashed off as her brother began pelting the creature with more arrows, climbing up one building and sprinting her way closer. She leapt across the gap as soon as Faxyyl came within range and grabbed hold of his helmet, her feet landing on either shoulder. He started to shake and raise his weapons to rid her, but Erika continued her own bombardment on his legs, drawing the attention of his blades. Erika had to block a slash with her immolated forearm, which thankfully seemed to glance off with no issue.

The aash elf whipped her axes from her belt, jumping up onto the helmet and leaning over with her feet planted firmly as she could. She hooked the beard of each axe into the lower crack in the metal, near where she assumed his jawline was, and invoked her gem dust. The designs flared to life and caused her musculature to swell beyond their normal limits, visibly increasing in size as she pulled with all her might. The sinew and tendons strained and she felt an acute popping sensation accompanied with a numbing pain as she continued.

The helmet only seemed to move the barest amount.

⸸

Erika's yelling was familiar and Darion recognized it easily. He led Marq back to the place of his imprisonment, both of them watching as the battle played out, feeling rather weak and helpless given their current situation. He watched F'Lessa adamantly as she shot off from the rooftop and onto the creature's head. Marq drew his attention as he pulled a wooden object with a metal barrel like a small cannon from his coat.

"I'd wager that this'd hurt that thing," he said, checking the side of the item as if for damage. "Latest weaponry from across the Leviathan Sea, been saving it for an emergency as I can only use it once."

Darion could not reply, but from what he could see of the battle, he believed that the possible damage to the creature was well worth it. He nodded to Marq, who took it with a grim nod of his own. Darion looked back around the corner, realizing that if the helmet did not break or release, then F'Lessa was likely to rip her own arms asunder.

The Daemon whirled in circles trying to rid himself of F'Lessa and Erika, but failing in both as his vision became obscured. The helmet was fracturing and lifting, but not well enough. Darion looked up to find the flesh bruising around F'Lessa's upper

244

arms. Shit, just a little more, he thought to himself, wishing he could call out to her.

"That might be enough!" the Inquisitor called out, rushing around as quickly as he could, Darion close behind.

Neither of them expected the dark shape that flashed across the rooftops, as it landed on the Daemon's clavicle. Craven was silent as his rapier dove underneath the armor. The ornate guard clashing against the base rim of the helmet as the blade tore through the flesh of the creature. Faxyyl let out a scream of rage and pain, platinum ichor spilling down Craven's shoulder. He glanced back and nodded at the two as they rounded the corner. "F'Lessa, dear girl! Time to vacate!"

Before F'Lessa could understand his words, she released her strain out of necessity. Her arms were numb, having barely any feeling below her upper arms. She had a hard time simply holding her grip on her axes. She looked down, her vision bleary from the effort and sweat dripping into her eyes, but she could see Darion. She grinned as she struggled to maintain her balance, beginning to slip backwards before she could utter his name, and then she fell. Darion let out a cry and rushed forward, despite his painfully bouncing loose jaw. Marq stepped out and raised the weapon towards the Daemon's nearly fully exposed face, jagged teeth, and glowing silver eyes.

He pulled the trigger.

The echoing blast, like a hand-held explosion, rang out through the street and likely the whole city. Darion arrived to catch F'Lessa but his weakened state could not support her muscular frame or her crashing descent, simply crumbling underneath her to break her fall. Her weight slamming him down knocked the breath out of him, but hands on her sides confirmed that she was still breathing.

Erika watched the Daemon's head jerk backwards horridly from the impact of the metal ammunition, but still it stood. Faxyyl's expression went blank partially, the right side of his face going limp, though his left eye still held the cunning look from before the strike. "I refuse to die so easily!" he screamed, but his one good eye widened when he looked up to the rooftop and stared straight down the arrow of F'Skal. " *Viskla mrael*," he hissed, an aash death curse.

Erika flushed her legs into flame and leapt with all her might into the air, coming level with the Daemon's head just after the arrow sprung into his eye. She brought her hammer down into the monster's forehead with a finality, crushing his face inwards. Back he fell onto the ground next to Darion and F'Lessa, his form quickly beginning to melt and fade into a silvery white light that extended into the skies.

⸸

Three cloaked individuals departed Sylvanna's northeastern bridge after the chaos had subsided and the whole city seemed to breathe a collective sigh of relief. The Daemon called Faxyyl had been slain and the city was safe once again. Those three were hardly relived at the good news. One even was actively groaning. "Do you think that girl was the one who helped in the south? Wasn't it a Wrath Daemon that was destroyed before he even got to Sildenfeld's gates?" she said, her voice whining.

"I don't know," the man replied bluntly.

The woman shook her fists up and down, obviously more flustered than her small frame could handle as she cursed. "Black gods! How many red-haired women with fire magic are in the west? How many could there possibly be?"

"I don't know, Kena," her companion's voice grew more angry with each syllable.

"Faxyyl was supposed to be it, Tarol!" she cried. "He would take over Sylvanna and pave the way for the Veil to open fully!"

"Shut your mouth!" Tarol snapped at her suddenly. "Do you want everyone to know that we are responsible for the scores of dead in Sylvanna's capital?"

Kena motioned to the empty roadway around them, nothing but a marker flag flapping in the breeze. The effect was not lost on her companion, who simply stood and seethed at her. She wasn't the only one who was angry at the situation. Faxyyl taking Sylvanna as a seat of power could have led to him summoning in the Pride Elder and possibly even more Daemons from the other Circles than he had come from, further weakening the boundaries between realms and allowing them a chance at their real goal. *I wonder who that man in the dark clothes at the gate was,* he

242

wondered to himself. *Was he responsible for the Lesser Daemons' deaths?*

Very few within the Abyssal Hand actually knew the complete picture of what they were trying to achieve, while the lower ranking members simply knew that it would lead to the recreation of the world as they knew it. Although Faxyyl taking over Sylvanna was still not their true goal in the City of Water, their real task had been successful and their tracks were thoroughly covered.

Their third, Dieran, had been lagging just behind them. He was the newest of their group, having the least knowledge of their objectives. He simply shrugged, pushing past both of them and putting his hands on his hips as he walked. "I don't know what you two are so worried about in any case. Things don't always work out the way you want them to, so you just try again. I know it was really taxing and difficult to summon Faxyyl in the first place, but there's six whole other Circles. I'm sure we'll be able to figure something out."

Both of his companions glared at him from behind, but their expressions quickly changed to surprise as a figure leapt down into the road ahead of them. The white robes trailing above him hardly having time to fall before he flashed forward with inhuman speed. Dieran's hands dropped from his hips just as the two felt a rush of wind blow across their faces. The figure came to rest just in front of them with a blade out to the side, a small section of his sword with the edge on the inside curve dripped a dark liquid that fell upwards, a section just about the same width as Dieran's neck.

The two of them burst into action when their companion's head fell free of his shoulders, turning black rapidly and starting to flake into particles before it even touched the ground. Kena shouted a curse, though it was just a curse of surprise and anger rather than anything with any real magic behind it. Tarol however, had the presence of mind to actually say something worthwhile, his words creating a bolt of purple energy before him and launching it towards their assailant. The newcomer dodged around it much too easily, simply standing in the middle of the road as Dieran's body fully fell to the ground, his head completely dissipated. "*Abyssal Hand scum,*" the man growled in Haranian.

Tarol broke away further, foregoing any more complicated vocal spells and concentrated on quick bursting ones with hand gestures instead. Black shards of energy flung free of his fingertips at fast intervals, while Kena mimicked him on the opposite side. They were both careful to aim lower so as to not hit each other with the crossfire but high enough so the volume of magical bursts would eventually hit their attackers legs.

Kharim could not be hit with such trivial things. He simply moved out of the way, the power of his blade pulsing through him, the voice bidding him onwards.

That soul of the first was a wonderful appetizer. Now let us sample the main course. Perhaps the woman first? it cooed greedily.

Next the man on his right tried to provoke him with words. "You must be the one we've heard about, assassinating former members," he yelled over the sound of the crackling magic. "You're doing us a favor really! None leave our ranks alive, our plans forbid it!"

"You should do the world a favor and simply take your own lives then!" Kharim barked back as he flashed out of sight. Kena yelped at the sudden motion, though she wasn't the target. Luckily for Tarol, he had the reflexes required to throw up a quick shield, but he was horrified at the results. Kharim reappeared just to his side, slashing his reverse bladed sword downwards in a deadly arc. The slightly opaque shielding spell manifested over his shoulder with his arm motion but the wicked blade carved straight through his defense. It at first seemed like it had ignored the magic barrier completely, but as time briefly appeared to slow, Tarol could see the fractures in the shield like shattering glass, before it caved away completely. Each of the shards disappeared into nothingness before they touched the ground. Kharim let out a curse in his native Haranian tongue as the spell did manage to divert his attack at the very least, which was all that saved his quarry.

Pain flooded through his left shoulder as a bolt of force from Kena—whom he had foolishly ignored for too long of an interval—slammed into him. His robes smoldered where the impact was, and he lost feeling entirely for a moment as the evil magic took its brief effect, necrotizing the flesh where it hit. So, he reacted by flashing to Tarol's side, opposite of Kena so she couldn't hope to get another clear shot at him. Once there, he executed a furious series of stabbing motions, each one met by another of the desperate shielding maneuvers. The air was filled with consecutive shattering sounds as each barrier was broken one after another.

"Move him!" came Kena's call from behind, but Tarol was running out of stamina quickly. No mage wanted to be in this close of combat for this long of a time. Kharim's endurance was far higher, exponentially so, considering his wicked weapon that fed him continually. Tarol did the only thing he could think of in that moment, loading one of his shields with a reactive tinge of energy, which activated as soon as that blade pierced through it. With a deafening crack, Kharim's arm was blown out to the side. Tarol made his move, filling his fist with magic and readying himself for the strike.

Kharim only grinned at him. Tarol's stomach sank. In the blink of an eye, the man in the white robes was gone. "Kena!" he shouted the warning too late, turning as quickly as he could while trying to transfer the magic in his hand to a projectile instead. Kena's scream of agony broke through the air as the blade drove into her back and out of her chest. Tarol paled as she seemed to age rapidly, her skin turning a dull grey and her hair thinning before his eyes. The wound on Kharim's shoulder stitched and healed in an instant, and with a flourish he removed the blade from Kena's torso and her head from her shoulders. Just as Dieran's before. Her head melted into nothingness, her soul consumed by the evil weapon.

"Damned luck, eh?" came a voice from Tarol's side. He turned to see a horribly disfigured man standing with arms crossed, a sickening grin over his smashed and charred face. "Bastard's good with that sword, I'll give him that much." Hargreave was amused by it all.

Kharim stalked towards his distracted foe, whipping the black liquid from his weapon as it fell upwards just as before. "The only pleasure I take in this, is the vengeance for my fallen brothers," he said solemnly. "The blood debt to Haran is closer to being paid with your sacrifice."

The energy in Tarol's hand dissipated with his distraction between the two men and Kena's headless corpse. "What are you talking about?"

"My homeland was butchered by your cult and their experimentation with that which is forbidden," Kharim said plainly. "Thousands dead to your reckless schemes, upsetting the balance of worlds."

"None of our sect have ever been to the southlands!"

"You're not getting through to this one, mate," Hargreave drew his attention again. "Blind justice, eh?"

Tarol saw little more than Kharim over him then, and then strange sensation of seeing his own body standing above his head as he fell. Until finally, there was only darkness.

"You are much too talkative for a dead man," Kharim glared at Hargreave.

The once-mercenary simply laughed. "Distracted him long enough for you to get the job done with, didn't I?"

Kharim looked to the bodies and shook his head, taking the time to drag them off the road to avoid upsetting travelers. As he left the area, he uttered a prayer of repentance, pointless as it may be. He knew he was far past forgiveness at this point. He simply did his best to ignore the blade's comments on the taste of the souls, as well as what his fallen brothers would possibly think of a priest taking so many lives. Tears came down his cheeks at that notion, knowing that he would never see them again, in this world or the next.

25
Healing Waters

As the Daemon's corpse melted into nothingness, the group caught their breath. Erika had landed roughly to the side of Craven and immediately fell backwards and into the wall of a neighboring building. F'Skal sat back on the rooftop while Marq leaned against the same household underneath him.

Craven simply observed the scene, congratulating Erika on a job well done, then looked back to the final pair. F'Lessa lay unconscious but breathing, cradled in Darion's arms. His jaw hung awkwardly to the side as he looked down at her with concern in his eyes.

F'Skal made his way down a moment later, stepping up to Darion. "Appears you have a dislocated jaw, my friend. Hold still, this will not be pleasant," he warned, gripping the young man's face firmly and cracking the loose mandible back into place. Darion let out a pained scream, stretching his newly set mouth briefly before closing it again.

"Talking will be uncomfortable for a while," F'Skal informed him. He then folded F'Lessa's arms, pulling Darion even closer around her and firmly setting his hands against her. "Hold like this. She needs to be kept stable, but I need to help the Inquisitor first."

Darion looked into the aash's eyes, seeing a seriousness in them that he had not seen since the village. Almost as if he was demanding him to care for his sister. Then he was off, commending Marq on his self-bandaging and helping him across the street to the rest of the group. He followed the Inquisitor's concerned gaze and found Erika gripping her left arm where the Daemon's blade had struck it, a deep cut bleeding down her wrist and dripping from her fingertips onto the stone.

"I'm fine. Had worse," she said, waving off his investigative glance. F'Skal didn't listen to her, taking her arm despite her protests and stuffing some of the black moss that he had on hand into the long wound before wrapping it in a bandage.

"You would have lost this arm, were it not for your abilities," F'Skal scolded her. "You shouldn't try to just block things like that."

She nodded solemnly, glancing over at Marq as he sat back against a building, looking even more weary than she felt. Part of her wanted to check on him, but decided to let him rest for the time being.

Shortly after, Erika accompanied Craven back to the defense line, the townsfolk in the streets all either unconscious or delirious, as if waking from a trance. The city was a mess. Broken windows, smashed doors, and cracked walls. Worst of all were the bodies.

"So where were ye durin' all that?" she asked Craven, futilely attempting to avert her eyes from an older man laying beneath a splash of red against a building.

Craven's face was firm, his gaze unwavering from the path ahead. "Doing my part."

Erika sighed. "Not a very comfortin' answer."

"It is the only answer I am willing to give. And I implore you to trust me in the matter."

Silence fell between them after that, Erika glancing up at his handsome face set in a grimace. Further they walked, eventually coming upon a group of soldiers flanked by three knights, wheeling a cart, and collecting the dead. Erika felt tears in her eyes as she clamped a hand over her mouth at the sight.

Craven said nothing, standing still with his hat respectfully in his hands until the convoy moved from their path.

"Does it not upset ye? To see all o' this?" Erika asked him, again staring at his unflinching gaze as she felt tears dripping down her cheeks.

Craven took a deep breath, the light making his hair seem more grey than she remembered it being. "After a long life of seeing so much death, one becomes somewhat callous towards it." He looked down at her, finally meeting her eyes. "I have done things that I am not proud of, dear Erika, and I have seen more death than I care to admit or ponder on. One day I may find the time to tell you of myself fully, so that you may understand my motives and reasonings, but today is not that day. For that, I apologize. All I can say now is that I have done the best of my ability in the situation we just experienced. I am sorry I could not do more."

He then stepped away from her and towards the Cathedral once again. She waited behind for a long moment, watching him cross the street as it started to fill with citizens and soldiers alike. After a while, she saw the knight who had been wounded by Faxyyl, her cuirass removed and a cleric digging deep into the tear in her tunic and flesh. The woman's face contorted in pain as she gripped hard onto another knight's hand. Erika made her way over to thank her and her two surviving comrades, as well as to offer condolences for the three that had fallen.

The woman, Maria, seemed glad for the momentary distraction. "We are all sworn to protect our city and Region," she said solemnly, the three dead knights having been close comrades. "I thank you for your aid, Erika. Your abilities are a marvel to behold."

Erika smiled and took Maria's hand in place of an embrace, bidding her farewell before heading towards the Cathedral to rest.

† †

Soon after, her friends were delivered to the makeshift medical ward inside the Cathedral's massive foyer and grand hall, while clerics and doctors were hard at work checking on all of the patients.

F'Skal personally took responsibility for his companions, though he was asked to concede care of the Inquisitor to one of the clerics of the city. F'Lessa and Darion were set into cots neighboring each other, the former still unconscious with her arms held in place to promote internal healing, while the latter simply sat watching her sleep with a cooled bag of water against his jaw.

Erika refused a bed, instead sitting or standing against a pillar not far from the pair. F'Skal came to check on her periodically, watching with great interest as one of the clerics administered his own healing to stitch the rent flesh of her arm back together. The clerical magic was strange here, Erika mused. In her home Region they used golden miracle magic. 'Borrowed from the Gods,' as Valk had said back in Sildenfeld. The cleric here told her that they drew their magic from a source much closer to her own heritage. "You yourself are an Ignis Blood," the cleric said. "As such, you were born with your power granted from one of the four great Primordials, known as Infernas. We draw our healing energy from Leviathan, the Primordial of Water. As we are the City of Water."

"So, ye know about Elementia Blood then? I was believin' that we were more unknown than that," Erika asked as she and F'Skal watched the flesh slowly pull together through the crystal clear water that was held suspended over the wound.

The cleric nodded. "Indeed. Many do not know of the Elementia, chosen beings of the Primordials, but we still worship them. It is an honor to serve a child of the Firefox."

She smiled at him as he stepped away, F'Skal observing the new scar that had formed on her arm.

"Impressive how quickly the magic heals you," he said, gently running his fingers along the sensitive scar tissue, adding with a smirk. "If only you could heal like we do."

"Well then I'd be as hot as ye are all the time, and couldn't wear any pretty dresses," Erika chuckled with a sway of her hips that sent her tattered skirt flaring lightly.

"Perhaps you *should* wear less. Lest you burn all your clothes off," F'Skal replied coyly, motioning to her still bare feet. "You saved my sister by sacrificing those boots though, so I will find a way to replace them personally."

Erika waved him off as he departed to assist with other wounded, looking over as F'Lessa began to wake.

⸸

Slowly, the world came into clarity around F'Lessa. Her arms were bound in thick cloth over her torso to dissuade movement. She started to struggle against it at first, but stopped when she felt a cool hand on her shoulder. She looked over to find Darion, shaking his head slightly. F'Lessa nodded her understanding, and narrowed her eyes at him. "Why is that bag on your face?" she asked.

Darion lowered it, the flesh underneath very red and inflamed. He retrieved a small booklet of paper and a pencil, taking a moment to scrawl on it before holding it up for F'Lessa to read.

I got my jaw knocked out of place. and just below that: *How are you feeling?*

"My arms hurt, frankly," F'Lessa replied. Her chest tightened as she thought about what had happened. "I'm afraid I made a mistake during the battle. I lost my focus and left F'Skal and Erika in a terrible situation."

Her words were interrupted when Darion tapped his fingers on her again, motioning to new words in his booklet. *It's alright, I know what happened.*

She looked at him, worry in her eyes as her hair streaked an alternation of orange and pink down the loose strands that fell around her shoulders. "You know?"

He nodded.

F'Lessa's eyes started to flood again, her voice wavering. "I'm sorry, I didn't mean to put them in danger, I just—" She paused when Darion started writing, giving him a moment to finish.

You were scared. I understand, and it makes sense now, all of it. I am sorry for worrying you.

F'Lessa felt a tear fall down her cheek, unable to find any words. Darion began to scribble again.

Everything is alright now. Although, I think Erika is more than a little angry at you.

"I would be surprised if she was not," she replied, glancing over and finding the intense but remorseful emerald eyes of Erika as she leaned against the pillar. "She saved me, and then I just ran off on her. I'm not sure I'll ever forgive myself for that, even if she does."

She knows how you feel. She is searching for someone too.

"I am aware. In hindsight, I feel more connected to her emotionally in the sense that we both lost something we care about, unsure if we would ever see them again," she said, glancing towards Erika again. The Fjordling had turned just before that, looking off elsewhere in the hall. A moment later, F'Lessa realized what she had just said, her hair streaking pink and her face becoming even hotter than usual. Darion smiled at her, though his expression seemed pained from the facial motion.

I understand. I wasn't sure if I'd lost you either when I was trapped by that Daemon.

F'Lessa's eyes lingered on the page for a long while after she had finished reading it, her mind still racing even after Darion took the booklet back.

You don't have to say anything. the next page said. *Perhaps we can go somewhere once we are both well again, inside the city, just the two of us?*

F'Lessa read the last line over several times, her dark eyes darting over the paper more rapidly each time. Finally, she looked up to Darion, his eyes seeming vulnerable and sensitive at her expression. She searched for the words needed, her mouth opening and closing with no sound, much to her frustration. He waited for her patiently, his leg not even bouncing in his nervous habit. Eventually she met his eyes again and spoke through the lump in her throat. "Of course. I would like that very much."

Darion brought his hand to her face, tentatively wiping her cheeks dry. He slowly picked up the pencil once again and held up the paper where her tears had fallen onto the page from his fingers. *Get some rest. Your arms need to heal.*

Erika couldn't help but smile, understanding what was happening even despite not being able to hear their conversation. F'Lessa put her and F'Skal at risk during the battle, but Erika could see herself doing something similar in another situation. It was foolish and impractical, but fueled by emotion, and she could not blame her for that. Truly her entire journey was likely looked upon as foolish and impractical by many and she could see that now. This odyssey was fueled by her own emotion and she couldn't stop until she found her answers. She knew Irvine was still out there. She refused to believe him dead and she wouldn't go home without him. *I just wish I didn't have such a hard time remembering his face,* she thought, bringing a hand to her head as a tear came to her eye. She didn't use to have this much trouble with the memory, did she?

† †

"Do you ever forget what someone looks like?" Irvine asked, staring at the sand that fell between his fingers.

"I forget what you look like every time I look away from you," Zyrxak said sardonically, looking back towards him and feigning surprise. "Oh! Look at that, you're still just as dull and generic as the last time I saw you!"

Irvine glared at him.

"I am not your friend. Any philosophical musings you have are wasted on me," the Daemon continued, huffing air that whistled through his broken bone.

The young man let out a sigh. "Wasn't trying to be philosophical. Just asking a question, for comparison."

"Wondering if you are going mad? Likely, in all honesty. How many deaths have you experienced now?"

"More than I care to admit. I swear, this place is more a prison for me than you," he replied through gritted teeth.

Zyrxak rose and began floating in a lazy circle around him. "I'm not exactly having the time of my life here. Keep in mind, we've already discovered that I cannot leave you. What could be worse for a Daemon really? Constantly being chained to you, having no freedom whatsoever. Pathetic."

"And yet, I am the one who dies and I am the one who has to listen to your grating voice," Irvine remarked, starting to walk down the hill they rested upon.

"A prison for us both then?" Zyrxak offered, almost sounding whimsical. "Or perhaps sick irony against the combatants of endless wars."

"Your meaning?"

"I know of many Daemons who were whisked away in a flash by the Dragoon Knights," the specter continued. "Understand that many of us wished the war to end as well, even in that time."

"Stories always told of your kind starting the war of the Chaos Age," Irvine said in an annoyance.

253

Zyrxak shrugged. "I hardly remember who made the first strike, being locked in that prison for so many centuries. I wasn't even with the Daemons when the wars started."

Irvine shot a curious glance at him.

"Regardless of who swung the first blade, the Dragoons commonly struck at Daemons, even when they were not attacking others. Assumedly they imprisoned them here, as you have done to me."

"Perhaps we will meet one of them here then? Anything to pass the time I suppose," Irvine said, slumping his shoulders and marching on through the sand, another piece of the Dragoon armor falling away from his hip.

Part Three

I am dead.
I still remember the beginning of the Daemon War.
I still remember the smell of burning corpses.
I still remember the sound of a Dragon's death.
*I still remember the shock at the revelation of the Angelus'
lies.*
I still remember the sting of the blade.
I still remember the softness of her hair.
*I have been dead far longer than any creature still in this world,
and I have no right to still be walking around.*

*The Matron teases me in cruel ways at times. Reminding me
on a constant basis, that I am dead and have been dead for over a
thousand years. Things can never be the same. But why does
Stacia look so much like she did? Why must Marq bear such a
resemblance to the man that was to be my brother by marriage?
Why does fate torture the lost?*

*Still, my purpose is clear and now that the Necromantic blade
is in the grasp of the Matron, I can turn my attention to this world,
so close to burning once again. The Daemons crawl from the
depths, the Angelus march from above. And the Dragons . . .
have finally returned.*

War is on the brink of the horizon. I will be ready to meet it.
This time, I will be ready.

This time, I will fight for true justice. For the safety of those touched by my damned fate and all the rest.

The people of this world are not ready for what comes. Garreth has shown me that. They focus on their bitter and petty squabbles. Tarkal wishes for wider territory, Sildenfeld slowly shuts itself in, Sylvanna attempts to garner aid from the Region Council. None, however, are preparing for what is coming. They do not remember the chaos that befell them so many centuries before. Not even the sol elves remember, though they know their society to be so shattered and broken due to the Mad King.

Yet, I believe there is hope. Not because Garreth, Vaerisa, and I stand before the tides; but because their is hope in the hearts of those who defend this world.

I caught one glimpse of Erika before the end of Faygil and Tormis. She smiled. Brighter than any smile I had seen grace her beautiful face.

So full of hope.

Despite the odds and the foes that still stand before her, she smiled.

This world still has a chance.

-Craven,
Lord Wraith of the Shades of Mortia

26
DREAMS OF FLAME

Erika tentatively walked into the large room. A fountain of water poured into a stone tub that looked nearly the size of her old bedroom. Queen Sylvanna had offered her own private quarters for her to bathe, as the washrooms they had used previously were being utilized to treat the wounded downstairs. Despite the invitation, she felt somewhat awkward, walking around the room as if she were sneaking around while taking in the lavish comforts that she never imagined possible. The smell from the water was like the sweetest flowers and the temperature of it was so warm that one could simply rest forever in it. The room was decorated in draperies, blue and green as the city's standard, while flowering vines accompanied them in a pleasant display of natural beauty mixed with expertly carved architecture. She ran her finger tips across the surface of the fragrant water, her entire hand driving in when a voice called from the entrance and startled her.

"Feel free to get in," Queen Sylvanna said with a smirk. She wore a simple dress, no longer bearing the armor pieces she wore before. The cut across her cheek remained, albeit mostly closed from natural healing, making Erika wonder why one of the clerics hadn't healed her by now.

Erika glanced around again, then looked back to the regal woman. "I'm not sure I feel comfortable here. Ye offer such unimaginable things."

The Queen let out a laugh. "Such unimaginable things, in a simple bath?"

"A bathroom the size of my old house," Erika said with a disbelieving stare, only lightly exaggerating. "What 'ave I done to deserve this?"

"More than you know dear girl. You have saved my city from a Daemon, and I can truly do nothing to repay that," she replied, stepping closer to her. "If you are weary, I would be happy to help you in?"

Erika held up her hands at the offer. "I am doin' just fine, thank ye. But killin' a Daemon is nothin' truly to commend so much. My own hometown was destroyed by one, an' I couldn't stand by while another did the same to yers."

Despite her declining, Sylvanna began gently pulling off Erika's tunic until Erika surrendered and began to disrobe. "I also thank you for your expertise in fighting the creature. You and Craven both were essential I feel."

"And does Craven get full reign o' the bath too?" Erika asked, trying to fold her skirt with the same neatness that Sylvanna folded her tunic, with little success.

The Queen took the remaining clothing from her and gave them to a maid just outside the door to be washed. "Craven has been offered many more comforts here, but always declined them. Tell me, what is your opinion of the man?"

Erika carefully stepped into the bath. The water rising up over her legs and sending chills up her spine. She looked back slightly and noted that Sylvanna seemed to be looking over her body. It was likely due to her Ignis markings, but still made Erika's face run warm from the scrutiny. "He seems a good person, if that's what yer meanin'," she said as she sunk down to her waistline in the water. "Though he is a bit odd and I can't quite understand his intentions."

Sylvanna watched her with interest as Erika did her best not to shy away from the woman's gaze. She nodded in response, sitting next to the bath and idly dipping her fingers into the water. "And what are your intentions, Erika?"

Erika paused, not quite submerged down to her neck, looking at the woman as her gaze had drifted down to where her fingers made ripples in the liquid. "Are ye questionin' me fer a reason, Queen Sylvanna?"

"Answering a question with a question, very interesting I must say," she said with a smirk. "I suppose I don't possess my brother's penchant for interrogations."

"So, there is a reason?"

"Of course there is. I apologize for my methods as well. I had planned on offering my personal bath to you regardless, but I find people are easier to talk to when their clothes are out of reach," she continued with her almost salacious smile, now looking Erika in the eyes.

Erika glanced over the Queen's shoulder, remembering that she had no longer had clothes in the room. Although she had no true intention of trying to escape, the thought of running naked through the Cathedral just to avoid the Queen's prying questions was an amusing one. She laid back in the water, turning her back to the older woman and stretching out in the expanse of water. It was an incredible feeling to lay out fully with every inch of her body enveloped in pleasantly hot water.

"You are a curious young woman, Erika. Fjordlings are less common in the Patrian Regions, and one with such an interesting ability such as yours, even more rare," she said, pointing idly to Erika's markings. "I am simply curious about you more than anything. What are you traveling for? What can I help you with?"

"I don't think ye can help me with anythin' Queen Sylvanna. I have new friends that are helpin' me plenty, even if I'm wantin' them to pursue their own goals," Erika replied, taking a breath and submerging completely for a moment, rising back up and clearing her auburn hair from her face.

Sylvanna sighed, pulling her hand from the water and sitting back. "You seem a stubborn girl. I can respect that, though I do wish you would just speak to me. Why are you so reluctant to accept aid when you are so quick to offer it yourself?"

Erika sat on the ledge at the side of the tub, leaning closer to the Queen while still staying comfortably under the water. "I appreciate yer concern, I do, but I am doin' alright and I appreciate all ye've done fer me already."

"Do not worry, your friends will be offered the bath as well," Sylvanna added. "Though, again. I believe Craven will likely decline."

Erika nodded with a smile. "Thank ye. And, since ye're bein' so rewardin'," she paused a moment, Sylvanna leaning in slightly to listen, her expression darkening with Erika's. "I am travelin' because the Daemon that attacked my home town, stole somethin' from me. Someone, more so. I am lookin' fer a way to get him back."

"A lost love, perhaps?"

Erika couldn't hide the smile. "Aye. Just when I thought things could change between us, after all that tragedy, he did somethin' stupid and made both 'imself and the Daemon disappear. All that was left was the body o' the Angelus, melting away on the wind."

"You mentioned the Angelus earlier today, with my scholar."

Erika nodded again. "It joined the battle towards the end, but it wrought nearly more havoc than the Daemons themselves. Irvine seemed to 'ave killed it, but I don't know what truly happened to him an' the Elder Daemon."

"I see. Irvine seems like a brave soul."

Erika flushed suddenly, realizing that she had just said his name.

"And I'll wager that you haven't told any of your companions this full story?" she asked.

"No. I haven't told anyone other than yerself. Given my dream last night as well, I worry that I'm runnin' out of time," Erika admitted.

Sylvanna nodded. "They seem fully willing to help you, despite not knowing all of that. I'd be happy to offer any aid I can as well. Fresh traveling clothes, weapon and armor repair, wagons of supplies. Sadly I'm not sure I can offer an escort considering the climate."

"And I'd ask fer none of it. Ye need yer people here."

"I can insist on the basic supplies at least, for everything you've done," Sylvanna pressed, standing from her seat and beginning to leave. "Also, please call me Stacia. It is dreadful to hear 'my Queen' all the time."

Erika nodded and smiled as the woman left the room. She leaned back on the side of the tub, floating slightly as she relaxed her entire body. She hadn't realized how weary the day had actually made her and she began to fall into a light sleep. Despite barely being able to recall the sight of Irvine from the previous night in her strange dream, a vision of him came to her again.

It was unbelievable. He was every bit as handsome as she remembered, even if he looked a little worse for wear. What made her chest constrict was how sad his eyes seemed. She couldn't even imagine his smile anymore, as if he was incapable of the facial motions. The armor of the Dragoon was broken and torn, but he still held the lance strongly. He had more scars than she remembered, some of them deeply concerning. Her gaze tore away from his eyes and onto his throat, where a thick scar could be seen just under his jawline. She wanted to run to him but couldn't move her legs. His eyes closed and he fell into a black nothingness. She wanted to scream.

From her raging emotions came fire. She could feel her body burning in immolation, granted by her Ignis heritage. She knew she couldn't just burn her way to him.

You are lost, a voice called, both masculine and feminine at the same time. Disembodied, yet close. Alien, yet familiar.

Find me, the voice said again. *Find the city that burns with no remorse.*

She was thrust northwards to the Great Rift that separated the continent from the Fjordlands, though she didn't understand how she knew that. An island became apparent, billowing black smoke towering high above it as massive buildings stood in contrast to the natural beauty of the water and cliffs.

Atop it was a mountain, fire and magma burning within. Eyes watched her from that blazing peak, ancient and knowing. The gaze, like the voice, was familiar. Like a mother that she never knew.

Then darkness.

She felt as if she was falling, sending waves of panic through her body, no longer burning. She came to rest in a place of nothingness, a great surface like a dark mirror below her. She could see herself, her naked form covered in the Ignis markings all glowing like the embers of a forge. Power surged through those lines, filling her with a strength unlike anything she had ever known. She held one arm across her breasts, her other hand carefully exploring around her for something tangible other than her own body.

Her attention was drawn to the distance. A fox, bright orange and white, with shining eyes that pierced through her. Nine tails flicked idly behind the creature, while its fur seemed to blaze like an open flame. She felt drawn to the creature, as if it was a piece of her.

Infernas, Erika said, though her lips did not move.

The fox nodded slowly, the tails flitting even faster now as a sly smile seemed to curve her snout. She turned and began to run, Erika feeling compelled to chase after her. She stood on that rippling reflective nothingness and ran. Strong arms outstretched towards the creature as she disappeared from sight.

Erika sprang upwards from the bath, whispering the name. "Infernas…"

"Are you alright?" F'Lessa said from behind her.

She turned in a panic, finding the aash woman gently closing the door behind her.

"Erika?" she asked. "Is everything alright? You've been up here for some time."

Erika steadied herself, standing waist deep in the water now. She roughly ran her hands up her waist, breasts, and shoulders, half expecting her markings to still be glowing. They held their normal crimson color, making Erika let out a slow breath to steady herself. "Aye. I'm fine." She looked to her friend, her arms no longer bandaged as before, but still bruised heavily. "Do ye need help gettin' in?"

F'Lessa smiled. "No, my legs work just fine. I appreciate the offer though. Will you stay awhile?"

"If ye'd like me to," she offered.

F'Lessa nodded as she disrobed slowly to not aggravate her injuries, stepping into the water and beginning conversation with Erika. She remained silent about the strange dream she had just experienced, instead trying to focus on the aash as she spoke. The elf seemed perfectly happy to talk about Darion's invitation, serving as a distraction to the young woman's errant thoughts.

27
COURTSHIP

F'Lessa carefully made her way down the stairs of the Cathedral. She had been so excited talking to Erika the previous night in the bath that she had lost track of time and actually slept much later than she intended.

Around the corner she whirled in her hurried steps, but immediately halted. With a jerking motion, she swung back around, slamming her back into the stone with a dull *thump*. Darion was already at the doorway, leaning against the Cathedral just outside and looking down at a piece of paper, twiddling a writing stick between his fingers.

Her hair flashed pink, even more embarrassed now that she realized just how late she was. She hadn't even had time to braid her hair, the silver strands falling freely over her shoulders. She buried her face in her cloak that she draped over her forearms in front of her and stifled a scream. Eventually, she steeled her nerves—as best she could—and stepped carefully around the corner. Darion looked up to meet her eyes when she was halfway across the foyer and smiled, making her stomach swim.

"Everything alright? Your hair isn't braided."

She brought a hand up, trying futilely to cover the streaks of pink. "I wanted to try something different," she lied, not wanting him to think her lazy, even if they'd spent the better part of a month traveling together already and she usually awoke before him. "Have you been waiting long?"

Darion shook his head, folding the parchment before she could see what was on it. "Not at all." A large part of him wanted to say that the wait was worth it, but he wasn't sure he could choke that out or if she would choke him for saying it.

"Where are we going today?" F'Lessa asked, glancing out the door at the warm sunlight in the plaza as she straightened her cloak to drape over her shoulders.

Darion shrugged, watching her dark eyes light up with the sun. "I have nowhere particular in mind. It's been a long while since I was last in the city, so I'm frankly not sure where anything is."

She risked a smirk at him. "So you're going to get us lost."

"More than likely," he said with a laugh. F'Lessa tried to control her breathing better, but could feel her heart pounding from her chest. Darion paused before they stepped out and lightly brushed the cloak back and leaned towards her. "Your arms look better already. I really am jealous of that."

She flushed at his close inspection of her still discolored but mostly healed upper arms, trying not to pull away in shyness as his fingers grazed her skin while her nerves jolted at his cold flesh. Her gaze turned slightly somber though, seeing the still intense bruising around his jaw and cheeks. He did seem better overall after having to go through the uncomfortable experience of the cleric's water flowing through his mouth to heal his jaw further. "Are you alright, Darion?"

He glanced up at her worried expression as he put his hand on the door and smiled. "Oh, I'm fine. It is sore, and I have that booklet just in case my jaw starts hurting, so we can still talk."

F'Lessa smiled back, and shrugged her cloak back over her shoulder as Darion led the way into the streets.

Despite the previous day's immense violence, the city was back to normal—in appearances at least. The section that Faxyyl used as his base of operation was still blocked off with barricades, knights and clerics combing through the section for any still trapped or injured, accompanied by workers who had already set off to repair the buildings. The pair instead made their way to the southwestern section, finding more festivities as the month of Hallowden and Shadesfall continued. Darion laughed each time he looked up at

F'Lessa wearing a wary expression and smiled when she was simply curious as he explained the month-long holiday to her. "Shadesfall is synonymous with Hallowden. We revere any who have died and guard against any who may return unwanted."

She looked down at him as he explained, following his extended arm to a grouping of gourds with strange faces carved into them, lit by candles within. "The lanterns serve as guides to those who have passed and warnings not to turn back. It is said that the guardians embodied by the lanterns will defend against rogue spirits who try to defy death."

"How do the guardians know who to guard against? And who are the guardians?" F'Lessa asked, looking from the wicked-faced lanterns to Darion and back again.

He shrugged slightly. "No one really knows where they come from, but we believe that the more we carve for Shadesfall, the more will come." They began walking as Darion continued. "When I was younger, my sister, Jess, and I would carve at least five each. I always wanted to make mine look fierce and scary, with sharp teeth and angled eyes, but she always made them rounder and friendlier looking."

F'Lessa looked down to him, noticing the difference in their own eye shapes as she brought a hand up to the corner of her's. "Do you think my eyes are fierce?"

Darion paused, looking up to her and stammering slightly. "Well, I think they are plenty fierce."

F'Lessa's hair shot orange, her eyes widening considerably.

"Not scary!" he said quickly, throwing his hands up to calm her. "I think they are absolutely gor—" his speech cut off as he halted suddenly, gripping a hand at his jaw.

F'Lessa darted back to him, her hair firing a continuous orange now. "Darion! Is your jaw hurting? I'm sorry I'm making you talk so much!" She grabbed his shoulders as gently as she could and leaned down, trying to look at his face, even if the injury was internal. They froze in place, both realizing how close they were, their eyes locked on one another. Darion backed a step and waved his hands as her hair streaked pink, stretching his mouth open and closed several times. "I'm alright, it just surged for a moment."

They looked over to see a group of young children dressed in funny costumes and masks, staring at F'Lessa with wonderment.

She shot upright, making sure her cloak was covering her body and quickly drawing her hood over her head. Darion grimaced at the action, walking behind her and tugging the hood off of her head. He stepped over to the children as she let out a petulant "Hey!" and placed a few silver coins in the bucket that they all seemed to share.

"She's so big. Is she a giant?" a young boy asked.

Darion shook his head. "No, she's an elf. An aash elf."

One of the others, a girl, stated with a smile that was missing a few teeth. "Well, I think she's beautiful!"

F'Lessa's ears perked and her hair flashed pink when she barely caught Darion whispering back to the small girl. "I think so too. I think she should keep her hood off too, can't see her pretty hair if it's up, hm?"

All of them nodded in agreement as he patted them gently on the heads and ushered them along their way, no doubt pulling Shadesfall pranks.

F'Lessa smoothed her hair from her face as Darion approached her with a smile, saying. "How about we find a bakery and get some spirit bread?"

The aash slightly grimaced at the thought of new strange food, but couldn't help but smile at Darion's excitement. Her heart nearly leapt from her chest when he suddenly grabbed her hand so they wouldn't get separated in the crowd. Darion's heart similarly raced, especially when he saw her endearing smile, one of her upper canine teeth poking out over her lower lip.

† †

"These should be the right size for the young lady," the cobbler said with confidence, despite the sweat on his brow.

"Three pairs then," Queen Sylvanna said firmly.

Erika whirled on the stool. "Three? Stacia, really, I'm not needin' three pairs o' boots."

"So you'll burn through one pair in a fight and have a backup, but then what if you burn through those as well?" the Queen asked, tapping a finger on her lower lip.

The cobbler nervously glanced between the two women, racking his brain and trying to deduce who this strange auburn-haired girl was who called the Queen by her given name.

"I'm only just recently immolatin' my legs, I don't use it often."

"But you do use it. So, three it will be," she said with a finality. "Next up is the tailor, best in the city. We'll have you extra tunics, perhaps even some with *sleeves* for the colder weather?"

Erika rolled her eyes at the obvious jeer towards her tendency to not wear sleeves. "And what would I be needin' all the tunics fer?"

"Why, if you immolate your entire body of course," Stacia commented as if it should be obvious. "Gods, we can't have you running around naked after reducing your entire wardrobe to cinders. Attractive as you are dear, you'd freeze in the coming months unless you kept yourself burning all the time."

"Understandable," Erika conceded, but continued to plead. "I've lasted this long in these clothes though, I don't think I'm needin' so much."

Sylvanna spun around suddenly, the cobbler jumping as if the Queen was about to yell at him. "That reminds me! Your birthday is this month, yes?"

Erika narrowed her eyes. "Which o' those damned fools told ye? Better yet, I'll beat every last one o' 'em."

"Now now, I won't be telling you who informed me of your big day, but I do insist you let me treat you. Favorite food, favorite music, and favorite color?" Stacia listed expectantly, her eyes wide with anticipation.

Erika stared at her blankly. "Color?"

"The color for your gown of course. You can't go to your own celebration without a dress as beautiful as you are," she laughed with a coy smile. "Come on, let me treat you like the little sister I never had. Marq is no fun when it comes to these things. Sometimes, I truly wish he'd been born a girl."

"Is it really that important to ye?" Erika asked, fearing the answer somewhat.

Sylvanna simply nodded, smiling and waving to the side as townsfolk noticed that their Queen was among them.

Erika groaned slightly. "Fine. Though I don't know we'll be in the city still for the actual day of."

"When is it, exactly?" Sylvanna asked, leaning in.

"The fourteenth of Hallowden. *Four* days from now. A long while fer us to tarry."

"Of course," she conceded. "I can throw you a party before then. Though I would be delighted if you'd stay just awhile longer."

Just then, the two noticed F'Lessa and Darion walking along the street opposite of them, the two seeing them and making their way over. F'Lessa was covered in her cloak, but Erika spied a small bag clutched to her breast.

"Ye two seem to be doin' well," Erika observed, not having seen either of them since the previous night.

Darion nodded, but F'Lessa smiled widely as she leaned in whisper towards Erika. "I can't remember the last time I was this happy."

"Perhaps you'll join us for lunch?" Sylvanna asked, the two accepting tentatively.

Shortly after, they made their way to a nearby tavern that had seating under an awning outside the building, a wonderful smell emanating from the inside. They took their seats as a young waiter stumbled back into the establishment, reemerging a moment later with a portly cook that looked as if his eyes would pop free of his skull upon seeing the Queen of Sylvanna at his establishment. After introducing himself to the group and personally taking their order, he went frantically back into the tavern. Stacia offered a shrug and a sigh to her three companions who looked on the verge of incredulous laughter.

On the rooftop of the Cathedral, F'Skal watched with his enhanced vision. He smiled for his sister, glad that she had finally made some progress towards her own happiness.

"See anything interesting?" Craven said from behind him.

F'Skal turned slightly, unsure of where the man had come from but deciding to ignore the surprise. "Plenty of things. None that particularly concern you though."

"Plenty of things concern me," Craven replied, straightening his coat and crouching next to the aash. "For instance, the fact that this district of the city is nearly untouched." He extended his hand out to accentuate his point.

"A sign of a job well done. The knights and soldiers are capable individuals."

"That, and the Daemon probably came in from the northeastern side, yes?"

F'Skal eyed him, wondering where his point was. "That seems likely. Unfortunate for the northeastern section of the city."

"Indeed. Do you not find that strange though, that the Daemon appeared from the northeast? The direction we are planning on going?" Craven led on.

"I hadn't considered the significance."

"Have you ever heard of an organization known as the Abyssal Hand, F'Skal?"

The aash elf shifted slightly. "They killed my uncle without reason, so yes, I am somewhat familiar."

"My condolences," Craven wore a saddened look for a moment, and for the first time, F'Skal did not question his authenticity. "As you may know then, they are a group that partakes in Daemonology, and the summoning of Daemons under the attempt at controlling them."

"The point, Craven? I tire of your endless ranting," F'Skal said bluntly.

"Some of the bodies that came up under Inquisitor Marq's prior investigation were former members of the same cult. The other bodies, were not. Do you think it probable that a cult would send an errant Daemon to muddle the waters?"

F'Skal remained silent, as Craven continued his explanation. He narrowed his eyes in thought. "You think the Abyssal Hand sent a Greater Daemon to distract the city from whatever is killing their ranks?"

Craven held up a finger. "But most of the bodies were 'former' members. So why would they care if they died or not?"

"Unless they have reason to be afraid of this killer?"

"My thought exactly. I do not believe their murderer is in this city any longer, though the cult may not know that. Perhaps the Daemon was sent as a distraction, for the Hand to investigate things themselves?"

F'Skal pondered a moment. "Perhaps we should meet with the good Inquisitor? Pay a visit to where they are keeping the bodies?"

"Sounds like a wonderful idea, my friend," Craven affirmed with a smile.

28
Retribution of Haran

You hear?" said the first man, sitting near the bar. "Sylvanna was attacked by something."

The second grunted into his drink. "You actually know what it was? I figured it was Tarkal mounting an offensive."

"That's stupid! I heard it was a Daemon," the first replied, drawing the attention of the stranger in the tavern.

"A Daemon?" his drinking companion scoffed. "And you said what I heard was stupid. You believe in those ghost stories?"

"More than you and the ghosts of Shadesfall!"

The stranger leaned slightly to the side, glancing over to the two men in their banter. His robes shifted slightly, allowing only a small sliver of his dark skinned face to be seen.

"What? You think you heard different?" the second man said, taking notice of his eyes.

The stranger shook his head. "Just interested is all. Where I come from, stories of Daemons are not too far from the truth."

"And where is it you come from exactly?" the first man asked.

"Far to the south. Haran and its desert cities."

"Haran?" both men said in simultaneous disbelief.

"Lotta stories about that place circling around too," the second said.

Kharim shifted again, not allowing his hood to fall from his face. "Stories interest me greatly. Perhaps you could tell me more of this Daemon that just attacked Sylvanna?"

"Buy me a drink and I might think about it," he flouted, turning towards the bar.

Behind it was a man in horrible shape. The side of his face scorched and burned, missing one eye while viscous blood dripped from his grinning jaw. "Better to just tell the man."

The man spit his drink out and nearly fell from his stool, looking up to find nothing facing him from behind the counter.

"Seems you've had a few too many already," Kharim offered, the first man laughing at his friend's fearful outburst. The second man stammered, pointing to where he saw the wounded man with a shaking finger. Kharim stood easily, leaving coins of silver on the table with his empty cup and plate, seeming to glide over to the two men. "You look like you've seen a ghost, my friend," he said, putting a hand on the man's shoulder and steadying his shaking.

The first seemed to take offense. "I think you need to get away from him! What do you think you're—"

He stopped suddenly, feeling the tip of a blade under his jaw. He hadn't even seen this stranger move, his eyes still looking at his friend but his arm was raised with a thin curved blade poised to his throat. He wondered why no one else was stepping in to stop the man with his weapon bared in the middle of the tavern. He glanced around, but no one was there besides them. The room appeared darkened, like all the candles and chandeliers had been dimmed.

"Now then, where could a Daemon have come from around here?" Kharim asked, his voice calm and low.

The first man didn't dare move with the tip of the curved blade pressing into his neck, the second man trying to calm his own breathing as he replied. "I don't know anything! I can't help you."

"You realize he's going to kill both of you, right?" said the horribly wounded man, appearing again yet disappearing in the blink of an eye.

The man's eyes widened at the sight, looking over to the Haranian who held his shoulder as sweat dripped down his face. The stranger was smiling behind that obscuring hood, his eyes closed and head tilted slightly to the side, as if nothing strange was happening at all. "Anything odd in the nearby area you feel the need to tell me about?" Kharim asked.

"There's a town," the man said quietly, "just outside the Sylvannan border, but not past the Tarkalian border. The no-man's land."

"Yes?" Kharmin cooed.

The man swallowed hard. "They ain't affiliated with anyone and refuse to answer any call to arms. They're strange people, I don't know what goes on there!"

"Any of the citizens have six fingers?"

"I don't know! I swear, that's all I know about the place!" the man practically screamed.

He and his friend blinked hard. Noise erupted all around them, and when they opened their eyes the room was no longer dimmed. Patrons talked and laughed and drank, and the owner stepped over to the table behind them to collect the dishes and currency. He looked at them curiously for a moment, before shrugging and sliding the coins into his apron. The two men looked all around the tavern but found no trace of the Haranian.

† †

The Inquisitor stared at the two over the small reading spectacles he wore at the edge of his nose. The story they proposed was odd, but oddly made sense.

"Thus, the Abyssal Hand would send a creature to try and neutralize the threat to them at best; distract from their activities at worst," Craven finalized.

Marq removed the glasses and gently set them on the desk with a sigh. "And you want to examine the murdered corpses to see if it supports your theory?"

F'Skal nodded slowly. "Admittedly, Inquisitor, I do not particularly care for Craven as a whole."

Craven smirked and shrugged, but stayed quiet.

"That being said, I believe he may be on to something here. Any information we receive in this regard could possibly help," he said, giving Marq a genuine look of concern.

"Very well." Marq stood from his chair with an effort, grabbing the cane at the side of the desk that he was forced to use and starting from the room. "I'll assume my sister is in good hands wandering the city streets, as both of you are here."

"Erika is with her and last we saw they were about to share a meal with Darion and my sister," F'Skal answered.

The Inquisitor paused at the first name, but quickly returned to the topic at hand. "Wonderful. I hope things are going well between those two, after the tension that anyone and everyone could find between them. I hope you both have strong stomachs, or you may want to skip your lunch after seeing the bodies," Marq said, halfway between amusement and irk.

"I believe them to be doing quite well," F'Skal replied, "and I am an experienced healer, so I believe I shall be fine."

The two arrived down the final steps below the guardhouses, Marq slowing them with a hand signal. F'Skal immediately smelled the reason for his halt and Craven seemed to understand as well. Just around the corner was a pool of blood puddling around a single body.

Marq drew his blade as he carefully stepped over the liquid and into the cold room. F'Skal and Craven followed suit, both having weapons drawn. They found nothing in the room besides the fresh corpse.

"Damn it all," Marq said, sheathing his blade. "Always figured Huron was the safest all the way down here."

Craven eyed the lifeless body of Huron for a long moment. "F'Skal, do us a service and turn the body over?"

F'Skal glared at him slightly but obliged, straining slightly to turn the heavyset man onto his back. They found the blood to be dripping still from his eyes, nose, mouth, and ears, but no outward wounds to speak of.

"What in the Hells?" Marq cursed under his breath.

Craven sighed. "As I suspected. A curse was inflicted upon this man, which means a ranking member of the Abyssal Hand was already here. Where are the corpses?"

Marq looked over a document on the small podium next to Huron's body, avoiding the blood splattered on the papers, and found what he was looking for. He stepped over to the wall opposite of them and opened two drawers, one labeled *Delron Slare*. From the inside fell piles of ashes and soot, causing the Inquisitor to stumble back on his cane.

"Damn it all," Marq said again. He looked at Craven blankly, taking a long draw from his flask. "I truly hate it when you are right."

††

The sun began to set on the mountains in the distance, flooding the landscape with an eerie light that seemed to have no true source. The two moons above shone brightly, the second smaller one showing a particularly bright red this evening. Kharim watched the small village. People in varying degrees of armor patrolled the outside of the wall, but none of them quite seemed to be fighters. Torches came out as the darkness fell but none saw the Haranian man swiftly dashing across the field, as if made of mist. To the top of the wall and then the peak of the highest building he climbed easily, remarking that these Patrians made things so easy with their square and angular architecture.

From the vantage of the three-story building, he found what he was looking for. In the center of the village was a large crater in the ground, in the process of being covered by dirt and soil hauled in from elsewhere.

"Now what could have caused that?" the ghostly voice of Hargreave called.

Kharim smirked. "You seem to be much more cordial now."

"Just you wait. As soon as I find a way to get out of your otherworldly clutches, I'll kill you," the mercenary growled with conviction. "And after that, I'll find that girl and I'll skin those damn tattoos from her body."

"So violent, and just the reason I cannot let you go. That girl has harmed no one. By my judging of her, she has been hurt in a similar way as I have," the foreign man replied, causing Hargreave to snarl at him. "Long as the young woman stays from my path, I will have no part in harming her."

Hargreave scowled still. "Yet your paths may cross, and that righteous bitch will have plenty issue in your ways and methods."

"That may be true, but for now this village is our next quarry. Go, tormented soul, have your fill of violence," Kharim said, slashing his wickedly curved blade through the ghost of Hargreave before raising it to the sky. "*Come, souls of departed warriors, aid me in the deaths of those who have wronged us all,"* he uttered in Haranian as the sword dripped black sand.

Out of the forest came hundreds of shadows. Some bore armor and weaponry of the Patrian Regions, others of the Haranian oases, more still of the Fjordland crags, and even some of the women warriors of Sukaira, all with a blood lust unrivaled.

The guards patrolling the walls had only seconds to bare their weapons before they were set upon by the shadowy creatures. Blades pierced flesh and screams were cut short as the short stone wall was splashed with red. Other warriors made their way into the town, smashing through doors and windows and slaughtering all they found with their insatiable rage.

Kharim easily slid into the window of the building he sat upon. Inside was a frail man with six fingers on his left hand. "It seems I was right to besiege this place," he sighed calmly. "I do so like when I am correct in my suspicions."

"Who are you? What is this?" the man called back, his head whipping around at every scream that rang out.

"I am the retribution of Haran. Your organization wrought havoc against us with no consequence, but now I come bearing that punishment."

The old man seemed confused. "No, you've made some mistake, I've never been south of Myrefell!"

"Your people have however, and I am afraid your entire organization is guilty by association!" Kharim said, mounting into a shout before flashing forward and ramming the man against the wall, blade edge pressed against his neck.

"I don't understand!"

"My people are dead because of your Daemons!" Kharim screamed at him, pulling the man's shoulder right and his blade left.

The body hit the floor while his weapon consumed the head, adding to its toll.

One hundred and seventy-four. Progress to peace is furthered.

Kharim no longer shuddered at the voice that called from his blade.

More blood will be spilled this night. I will rest happily afterwards.

Hargreave sat back on a chair outside a small home, watching as shadowy specters dashed through the streets. It was entertaining at the least, but he had no stake in this. "I have my own feelings about fate," he said calmly as one shadowed figure with a large axe hacked down a fleeing woman on the house's porch directly next to him. He looked idly at a cigar that he was able to pick up from a dead man's grasp, wiping blood from it before lighting it in a nearby lantern. "And I believe that Spitfire will find us again."

29
SYLVANNA'S MUSINGS

The skies above Sylvanna turned grey and overcast, issuing foreboding signs of rain with a near constant cold breeze from the north. Stacia decided that the weather had turned much too ill for the party to head out and instead invited—bordering on ordered—the group to stay within the Cathedral until the weather passed. Erika asked Marq of it one morning when they were the only two remaining at the breakfast table and he said that the next leg of their journey would likely be permeated with the freezing rain and possible snows, musing that his sister was simply invoking a ploy to have them stay longer. Erika huffed at the notion, but the Inquisitor could only shrug in reply. "You do have other companions who may wish to stay for a respite before a long trek north. A couple of them were wounded as well." He bade her to join him on a walkabout, leading her through the corridors of the Cathedral. Erika walked closely beside him, taking his arm both as a polite gesture and to help him when he would grow weary of his cane, which she often eyed with concern. Eventually they arrived at the relocated infirmary where F'Skal was diligently aiding those still sick or wounded from the Daemon attack. "He has quite honestly doubled the speed that the clerics estimated for recoveries," Marq said, causing Erika to pause with a remorseful expression.

She watched for a time, mirroring F'Skal's friendly wave as he worked while Marq idly stood just outside the doorway. When they turned to leave Marq proffered his arm for her again, which Erika took with hardly a second thought. They walked further through the Cathedral, Erika walking patiently with his slowed pace and only lightly scolded him when he threatened to throw the 'damned cane' away. Along the way, Marq commented on various paintings, sculptures, or stained glass that adorned the interior. Finally, they arrived at a sunken room with seating on either side. Erika realized quickly that the chamber was an arena of sorts, as she found two fully armored individuals circling each other before coming together violently with a deafening clash of dulled blades. Around halfway down the stands sat F'Lessa, resting her elbows on her knees and her head in her hands watching the sparring pair intently. Erika noted that her arms appeared almost fully healed and surmised quickly from her intense gaze that the shorter of the armored figures was Darion.

"Sir Viktor Carmine," Marq explained, still holding her arm in his and pointing to the opposing knight with his other hand. "He's one of our best, and is my partner in my investigations after the death of my previous, Sir Karrigan, last year."

"Sorry," Erika uttered quietly, Marq nodding his head appreciatively.

Erika watched the two men bat each other's blades back and forth, before Sir Carmine made a sudden rush offensive and caught Darion on the side of the neck where his helmet sat. F'Lessa jumped, but quickly quelled herself as Darion recovered. He and Carmine removed their helmets and the knight began talking to the young man, using his gauntleted hand to show Darion the angle of his strike and to explain how to counter it.

Erika recognized the tutoring. She used to sneak outside of Valen while her father was busy in the forge to watch as Feldran taught Irvine sword practices in the fields. Erika glanced over at F'Lessa, remembering her similar reactions when Irvine's uncle would suddenly get the best of him. She could recall several times that Feldran would lecture Irvine after knocking him to the ground, while Erika watched from her hiding spot with so much pent-up anger that she'd often start crying.

"F'Lessa has already lined up sparring matches with half of our First Chapter of Knights," Marq said. "Celine even said she'd take her on if she beat ten of her best."

"Is Carmine on that list?" Erika asked.

Marq nodded with a smirk. "He was the first that F'Lessa challenged. No doubt due to his 'poor' treatment of Darion. If I'm honest, Viktor is a much better fighter than me and likely the reason I'm still alive today. But, if you ever consider telling him of me saying this, I will vehemently deny every word."

Erika giggled, looking over at Marq's face. She had come to realize that he had very subdued facial expressions and that this was his version of near absolute joviality, which was strangely endearing in a way. Soon after, they departed for the corridors again. The rain began to come down in a torrent, audible even within the stone walls of the Cathedral. They paused before a wide stained glass depicting a fierce looking serpent with six pairs of wings down its body, coiled in a large circle. Marq explained that it was the visage of the Leviathan, patron of Aqua bloods and the Sylvannan Isle.

"I'm needin' to tell ye somethin', Marq," Erika said slowly.

The Inquisitor stared at the glass Leviathan, waiting for her words to come. Erika gently removed her arm from his and started scratching her fingers together, feeling the nervousness and fear well up inside her breast. "I wasn't completely truthful with ye."

"Oh, so you're rethinking leaving and will take me up on a dinner sometime?" Marq commented with a grin. He met her gaze before closing his eyes with a shake of his head.

She looked away from him. "No, it's about the killin's."

He sighed heavily. "Yes, I know."

Erika's head darted up in surprise. "What do ye mean ye know?"

"You witnessed the first murder. Delron Slare, technically homeless, living in *The White Carmino* for some time, apparently as a favor from Thrane from some past event," he answered plainly, looking directly at her though she found she couldn't meet his eyes easily.

"How do ye know that?"

Marq held a finger up to his eye. "You remember in the guild house? When I asked you a direct question and looked you right in your eyes? You couldn't look away, could you?"

She nodded, glancing up at him now.

"I have an ability, passed down from my ancestors, that allows me to briefly see inside someone. Their mind, spirit, intentions," he said, pulling his flask from his jacket. "You were an interesting place to explore. Very endearing if I am honest. I saw the killing and that it happened when you were just talking to him in the alley. I also saw Hargreave, cutting your fingers, stabbing you."

Erika nodded slowly. "So ye could see my past?"

"And your emotions, your character. Lots of things. It's... difficult to explain."

"What else did ye see?" she asked, almost not wanting to hear the answer.

Marq paused, taking another draw from the flask. "Irvine. Zyrxak. Teria. You were a noble person, helping Irvine when he was bullied as a child."

Erika watched the sadness overwhelm his face. She suddenly felt like she would burst into tears.

"I understand your journey better than anyone else can Erika, because I looked inside it. I am sorry. Sorry I partially lied at the gala as well, about guessing after your relationships. I knew you were spoken for, but..." His words seemed to die before reaching his lips.

Erika turned towards the Leviathan again and fidgeted with her fingers continually.

Marq offered her his flask and she took it reluctantly before taking a deep pull from it. "I hope you don't feel ill of me now."

Erika exhaled sharply from the strong liquid. "Of course not. Ye were investigatin' murders, and I was a prime suspect."

"Part of me wishes I hadn't."

"Why's that?" she asked, looking to him again.

"It's more fun to learn about a person through their own words and experiences with them. Although I understand you better than anyone else could because of that power, I would rather learn about you from your friends, and yourself," he said, not looking away from the window.

She nodded again. "I suppose that's a drawback, then."

Marq chuckled. "That, and the burning sensation and worsening vision," Erika looked back at him sharply. He grinned sardonically back at her. "The more I use it, the higher the chance of blindness."

Her eyes widened and she took another draw from his flask after a brief pause. He started down the hallway, leaving her with the stained glass and calling over his shoulder. "If I were to go blind though, I couldn't see those beautiful eyes of yours, so that's an incentive not to overdo it."

"Dammit, Marq..." she muttered, wiping her hands at her face. Only one other person ever talked about her eyes that way. She drank again from the flask, holding it close with shaking fingers as she realized the container had the faintest trace of the Inquisitor's scent.

Erika stood before the stained glass window for a long while. She gripped the metal vessel, resting her cheekbone on the knuckles of that same hand. With her hand occupied, she could not engage in her usual picking and pinching at her bottom lip, so she took to chewing on it instead.

"Why'd'ye have to be so bloody sweet to me, ye daft bastard."

30

Pretty Dresses and Noble Knights

The morning came, Erika rolling out of the comfortable bed and straight onto the stone floor with a *thump*. More accustomed to the wood floorings in her old home in Valen, the cold shocked her awake as it gripped her naked flesh like a skeletal hand. She squealed and wrapped the blankets around herself tighter, groaning at her old habits and longing for the warmth of the bed. Once the surprise wore away, she sat up, rubbing at her eyes and stretching her arms high, the sheets falling to her waist. Her drowsiness was ushered away even quicker by Winnifred licking her face from the side of the bed. The surly bulldog had developed quite the liking for her, even choosing to sleep in her room. The last several mornings had gone just the same as this. She stood a moment later, deciding to brave the cold as she cast the blankets off herself and onto the bed again, before beginning her morning hunt for where she had set her clothes.

After a while of pacing around the room on bare feet, she finally found them laying over Irvine's satchel on the desk for whatever reason that she could not remember. The mirror in the corner of the room caught her eye and she looked over herself, tracing how far along her body the Ignis markings had traveled, finding them to end just above her waist and around her upper thighs, her lower torso mostly untouched by the power. She drifted a hand over the last of her unadorned skin before tracing the lines over her curves with a finger.

Strangely, she felt incomplete. It was as if the crimson lines were a part of her truly natural state, and she wouldn't be whole until they did cover her fully. She remembered the multiple times that her father had offered to take her to a secluded place where she could immolate for the first time, joining him in their family heritage. Irvine's fear of fire always stopped her.

She considered fully immolating now but thought better of it, not wanting to have to explain scorch marks on the floor to the maids or to scare poor Winnifred. She barely saw her scars in that moment, only thinking of Irvine from her multiple dreams and wondering if his appearance was at all accurate, or if her mind was playing tricks on her. She wouldn't be surprised, considering how she couldn't even sketch a rough portrait of his face in her notebook anymore. It was like he was being erased from her memory. The notion made her furious.

She had once again returned to her comfort of sleeping in the nude, not having to share her room with anyone besides the soft plush of Stacia's dog. Despite that luxury, she was actually happy at the prospects of being on the road the next day. She smiled as she pulled her skirt over her waist and slipped her strapless tunic over her torso. Deciding to enjoy her last day of not having to use her boots, she left them by the bed and made her way down the hall to the dining chamber. Her bare feet tapped lightly on the stone floors with her canine bedmate quick on her heels.

None of her companions awaited Erika and Winnifred. A senior servant dropped his book to the counter when she arrived and quickly procured a platter of breakfast foods just for them, offering to keep her company while she ate.

"Where is everyone?" she asked, her mouth half full of bread as she looked around.

The older man, Joffes, replied after a hesitant pause. "They ate breakfast some time ago, Mistress Erika, and have gone about their daily duties."

She winced at being called 'Mistress', not quite liking the sound of it, but ate the rest of her breakfast quietly and settled for Joffes' amusing stories of Stacia and Marq when they were children. After she finished, she and Winnifred went along at a bouncing pace through the corridors, realizing just how late in the day it was when she would pass the occasional window. She let out a scowl as she thought about having to give up that particular sleeping habit as well when they were on their way, lest her companions decide to leave her behind and continue on.

They passed the infirmary, however F'Skal was not in attendance among the clerics and doctors within. Their next stop was the training arena, F'Lessa and Darion sparring alongside each other against a pair of knights. Darion was more dressed as he would be for traveling, albeit using a shield and a blunted sword, and F'Lessa similarly used blunted axes rather than bare knuckle brawling as she had the days past. Their opponents were a woman with short hair known as Grandmaster Celine—leader of all the knights in Sylvanna—as well as a gruff, dark skinned man named Sir Heden. Both of her friends seemed much too preoccupied by their match and Erika worried Darion would get the flat of Grandmaster Celine's blade to his face should she call out to him, so she decided to leave them in peace.

Next, she bobbed down to Marq's office, but found the place vacant. She was glad to see that he had not left his cane behind, as he had commonly done only to nearly fall a few paces down the corridor. She smiled at the empty room nonetheless, glad in the close friend she had found in the Inquisitor, even if he was impossibly cynical. She took a moment to walk silently around his office, her thoughts wandering to how things might have turned out under different circumstances. She hopped up to sit on his desk facing his chair, kicking a leg up onto the seat and taking a deep breath. Her other foot came to rest on the top of his desk and she propped her elbow on her knee, picking and pinching at her lower lip. She had been involved with only a few other people throughout her life, but no one had ever made her feel like Irvine.

Marq came close.

She had heard through idle tavern talk in years past that love was a wonderful but also painful thing. Irvine's disappearance, and the thought of what could have been with the Inquisitor, showed her that clearly. Her strangely waning memories of her childhood friend made it hard not to imagine another life where she had come to Sylvanna under less pressing happenstance. She felt like her strange dreams had actually given her proof that Irvine was still alive, and that she had a chance to find him. So why did her heart hurt so much when she thought about Marq?

She glanced to the side at Winnifred who gave her a funny expression with her lower canines jutting out over her top lip. Erika giggled slightly when she made a pitiful whimpering sound, remembering the dog wasn't technically allowed in Marq's office. Something about torn papers. "Shouldn't leave yer door open, love," she teased to his empty chair.

She flushed briefly at the sound of footsteps down the corridor, dreading how the position would look to anyone who stumbled upon her as she realized how much of her backside was pressing on his desk, the wood cool against naked skin. She slid off the desk, her breath quivering lightly. She quickly trotted from the room, calling Winnifred with short, quiet whistles so neither of them would get into trouble.

Down the hall they went to the sitting room where Stacia and Darion commonly played Regicile in continual rematches since the day of Faxyyl's attack. F'Lessa had finally started to understand the rules, and even F'Skal tried his hand at the board game, defeating Erika, Darion, and Stacia each on his first try. Ever humble, he simply claimed it to be beginner's luck.

The rest of the day went by similarly, eventually eating lunch again accompanied by Joffes. From there she and Winnifred repeated their rounds around the Cathedral, this time not even finding F'Lessa or Darion. As the afternoon wore away, Erika became increasingly perturbed, especially at being barred access to the main hall and the absence of nearly all the familiar faces.

Later in the afternoon, she was accosted by a veritable army of handmaidens and maids who practically dragged her to the lavish bathroom. There they quickly undressed her and scrubbed her head to toe, despite her many protests and threats to immolate. Once they were finished, they wrapped her in a towel and ushered her through the hallway, Erika flushing and screaming about her abandoned clothes as she became increasingly self-aware of her near nudity through some of the usually more public walkways, until they arrived in a room ripe with fabrics and sewing materials. Across the room stood the personal tailor of Stacia, who smiled warmly at Erika while standing behind a gorgeous green strapless dress with silver accents.

"Damn it to shite!" she cried suddenly, causing the handmaidens to flinch around her. "It's my bloody birthday, isn't it?"

The tailor couldn't find any words but nodded in confusion at her outburst before he motioned all of them forward. The handmaidens tentatively guided her to the podium where they helped her into the dress, despite her outward fuming. The tailor made last moment adjustments to the gown and turned her around to look in a mirror. Erika's breath caught. "Gods, it's beautiful."

She smiled at the look, admiring the work of the dress. It was a similar color to her traveling cloak, with a very flattering corset sewn into the bust leaving her shocked at how accentuated her own curves looked under her exposed collarbones. The skirt draped down to her upper calves, with a slit up her left leg, flaring out brilliantly with even the lightest of twists in her hips. She bent at the waist, continually amazed at how womanly she looked. "Bloody Hells, Marq's gonna faint," she muttered to herself with an amused snicker.

The group of attendants sat her down in front of a mirror, brushing out her long auburn hair as she declined to let them use any makeup save for a thin dab of kohl around her eyes. Within minutes, they had tied the majority of her hair into a single braid similar to F'Lessa's normal style, with the remaining strands into a crown braid around her head. Erika giggled lightly, draping the thick grouping over her shoulder and running her fingers along it while the tips tickled her chest.

The room seemed to darken around her for a moment. *Is this really alright?* she idly thought to herself. Irvine's face looked like an inkblot in her memory.

"No tears now, m'lady, you don't want to be smearing," one of the handmaidens cooed at her, blotting at her eyes lightly with a kerchief. Another attendant had just finished tying a pair of boots with green laces matching the dress over her feet, the high heel to them a far cry from the thin things she had worn to the Shadesfall Ball. Erika looked around, feeling as if she had missed something. Two of the women took her hands and guided her from the room.

They led her downstairs to the doors of the foyer as the sunlight over the city dimmed and Erika's face twisted back into a scowl. The wide doors opened from the upper great hall and she stood at the top of the stairway above the lavish party. The walls were decorated with streamers and curtains of green, the multitude of tables set with various food and drink. Stacia and Marq stood at the base of the stairs awaiting her descent with pleasant smiles. She quickly twisted those expressions to surprise.

"Ye two blasted royals!" she called, storming down the stairs. Winnifred ran after her, barking happily the whole way in excitement. "I was lookin' fer both o' ye all day, and what do I find? Nothin'!"

The servants at the edge of the party wore shocked expressions, while Grandmaster Celine, clad in a long silver gown, poorly stifled a laugh. She quickly cupped her hand to her mouth and turned away, her shapely shoulders bobbing with unrestrained cackles.

Marq began to speak but Erika shoved her hand out and put her fingers over his lips, which twisted into an amused grin under her touch. "No! No excuses from ye, Inquisitor! I had to endure Joffes callin' me 'Mistress' all day, while all o' ye were off plannin' whatever the Hells this is!" She glanced over to the servant in question. "Sorry, love."

The older man met her apology with a raised hand and a nod before she continued to accost the two.

Her outburst was abruptly interrupted when she was jostled and nearly toppled with tackling embraces and shouts of "Big Sister!" as survatri crowded around her. She looked down at all the small red-skinned creatures in surprise, unsure of how to react. She looked around to find many members of the Shalti tribe also in attendance, all meeting her with wide smiles.

"They of course wished to celebrate the birth of Erika, our honorary tribe member," F'Skal said with a grin. "We just had to make sure all of them put *something* on to not offend you humans." He himself was dressed in a silver ankle-length skirt piece, with ornate cuffs of matching color around his upper arms.

Erika laughed, her infuriated facade quickly melting. She gave in to the innocent greetings of the survatri, crouching down to embrace each of them. Little Vati lingered for a moment, hesitating before kissing her on the cheek and running away towards Darion and F'Lessa like a child retreating to his parents. Darion was dressed in a similar suit as he had worn to the Shadesfall Ball. F'Lessa wore a better tailored silver robe-like dress that still exposed her midriff—with a thin silver chain wrapped around her waist as ornamentation—but definitely looked more cohesive as clothing on her. Surprisingly, her hair was not braided, but instead lay curled and wavy around her shoulders.

Stacia hugged her gently as she stood again. "Happy birthday, Erika." She waved her hand for the bards to begin their music. Erika couldn't help but smile as a small procession of people came to bid her well wishes, including the recovering Lady Maria who walked with a crutch held beside her tight dress and a surgeon close by. Darion and F'Lessa shared a dance now that they were both more proficient in it and Erika mused at how happy both of them seemed. The only one not completely happy was the young elf, Y'Skara, who stood at the edge of the dance floor and watched the two with a flustered expression.

F'Skal was the first to ask for Stacia's hand in a dance, to which the Queen accepted with a suspiciously giddy grin. The aash again showed that he was a great visual learner, just as he had been with the Regicile game. Erika just wondered at their expressions as they spoke softly about something, her curiosity piqued even more when Stacia laughed and briefly put a hand on F'Skal's bare chest.

Eventually Dyla Fargeal made an appearance as well, Erika musing that she was the one showing more cleavage out of the two of them this time. "Inquisitor Marq, I would like to formally apologize for my husband's appalling behavior during the recent crisis. If there is anything we can do to make up for his atrocious actions, please, do not hesitate to name it," she said from a deep curtsy.

Marq waved her off. "It's fine, truly. I know he was under the influence of the Daemon at the time and was not in control of his own actions."

Dyla seemed mostly satisfied as she turned to Erika and embraced her. "Happy birthday, dear. I do hope we may get to know each other better some time, and you can tell me more of your heritage. Perhaps you can tell me of the clothing fashions or some such. Oh, I'm so sorry, is that offending in some way?"

Erika laughed. "It's quite alright, Dyla. Truthfully, I've lived in Patrias my entire life. Never 'ave I been this far north since I was a wee thing. I'd love to chat with ye about what I know about my ancestral home though. Perhaps when I come back this way one day?"

"Thank you, dear, that sounds lovely. Er..." she glanced to the side at Marq, where Erika failed to see his insistent expression. "The happiest of birthdays again, I'll be off to learn about the aash people and their curious little red friends."

Erika found herself truly enjoying the festivities, and resolved to bring Irvine next year rather than being distraught over his absence. She was sure Stacia would want the excuse to throw her another party.

"May I have a dance?" Marq called from over Erika's shoulder. She looked over at him before giving his leg a doubtful look. He smirked. "It is healed enough, I can manage a slow bit of movement at least."

Erika turned to Marq and took his hand gently, feeling his fingers on hers. Part of her wondered how Irvine would react, but she knew that Marq was a good man and believed Irvine would have seen that before her. The music slowed as they moved to the center of the foyer—the bards likely instructed to do so for Marq's injury—and he turned to her with a raised hand.

"I'm not so practiced at this kind o' dancin'," she said nervously.

He just nodded slowly to her, gently directing her left hand to his shoulder as he lifted her opposite hand in his. They swayed gently back and forth to the soothing sound of the instruments and she felt her face flush slightly as his finger tips stroked gently at the naked flesh between her shoulder blades.

"Nothing to be embarrassed about," he encouraged. "I would have asked for a dance even if Irvine was here."

"He would've allowed it fer yer station regardless," she shurgged, trying to breathe steadily while also attempting not to stamp on his shoes with her boots. Her stomach swam, and she suddenly wished she had gotten a glass of wine or something before they had come over here.

"I would hope he would have allowed it regardless of anything. It is just a dance after all."

She smiled and fell silent, knowing that he was right. Irvine was just that good-hearted after all.

Their dance carried on and he pulled her gently closer. She rest her chin on his shoulder, trying not to let her whirling emotions get the better of her. Thankfully, he began softly speaking to her; lamentably about grim topics. "We have found that the killer has left the city—all of them, most likely—but Craven fears that you may yet meet again."

"Does he know who they are?"

"Unfortunately, we have no conclusive evidence, but Craven always knows more than he lets on."

She giggled lightly at his annoyed remark, and she felt his cheek stretching into a grin against her neck.

"I just need you to be careful. All of you. The world is getting dangerous, between the near war with Tarkal, and the Daemons apparently on the loose."

Erika nodded. "Of course. We'll watch out for any Angelus as well. Don't ye worry."

"I'll arrange an escort to the border towns tomorrow morn—" he began.

"We'll have no such thing," she interrupted in a singsong tone

Marq smiled again. "Then I will always worry."

His hand rest on her hip as he kissed her on the cheek and spun her into a twirl. She laughed at the motion, but when she slowed down he was halfway to the drink table again and the music resumed a more upbeat tune. She fought back the threatening tears as she raised a hand to her cheek where his lips had touched with a bittersweet smile.

Craven offered a dance shortly after, which Erika—glad for the distraction—obliged just the same. Thankfully, the dark man quickly educated her on the upper tempo movements, which she started to take to after a few repetitions. Erika found herself glancing around as they moved, trying to determine where he had been the entire time but figured he likely had just arrived from wherever it was that Craven went all the time.

After he bowed to her and tipped his hat gently, F'Skal requested a dance after he departed.

She smirked at him. "If everybody keeps askin' me to dance, I won't be walkin' tomorrow."

"You can always ride on F'Lessa's back," he replied with a laugh.

Furthering her point, Stacia herself approached after F'Skal gave her a bow. Erika grinned at her. "My legs are startin' to get a bit shaky, love."

The regal woman curtsied to her and returned the smile. "I promise a rest after mine."

After their dance had finished, Erika retreated to the drink table and into a chair. She grabbed a thin glass of lightly colored bubbling liquid and took a drink, nearly gagging at the flavor. Luckily, Marq was nearby, quickly offering her a stemless glass of dark amber liquor matching the one in his hand.

"Oh, thank ye, love," she said, realizing just how out of breath she was. Although it was such a euphoric kind of weariness. Erika sat back, enjoying the much better taste of the whiskey, while the heavy rise and fall of her breast began to slow. Unfortunately, the alcohol did little to settle her nerves with the Inquisitor standing by her chair.

Stacia called for attention at the base of the stairs a short time later. "Tonight, we celebrate the birth of Erika Ildherre. A wonderful young woman that I have grown to love dearly. She is a savior of Sylvanna, and will always be remembered as such."

Erika felt Marq's hand settle on her bare shoulder as his sister spoke of her. His fingers were cool and rather nice on her flushed skin. She placed her hand atop his and leaned her head on his knuckles. He gave a slight squeeze and started to slip away, but something made Erika grip at him harder, bidding him to stay.

"I wonder how many rumors will be started after tonight," he said quietly.

She grinned mischievously. "No matter to me, I'll be leavin' in the mornin'."

Marq chuckled, settling beside her chair more comfortably as his palm seemed to melt into her skin. Erika let out a small sigh of contentment. The circumstances were wrong, but she could at least enjoy this moment.

"I also have another well-earned celebration to be marked," Stacia continued.

The grouping quietly awaited her announcement, the survatri seeming to fidget in nervousness.

"Darion Woodsmark, please step forth," she said clearly.

Erika looked quickly across the room, where Darion's face paled to a ghostly white. Grandmaster Celine, despite her feminine dress, gave him a stern look that caused him to stand quickly. Over he stepped as Stacia was given a beautifully ornamented rapier, silver with set emeralds and sapphires in the guard. At Celine's quiet instruction, he knelt before the Queen. Erika heard F'Lessa hold her breath sharply as Stacia removed the blade from its scabbard.

She placed it gently over his left shoulder and spoke again. "I, Queen Stacia Sylvanna, formally dub thee, Knight of Sylvanna." She raised the blade and placed it again on his right shoulder. "Thy instruction: Shield thy companions valiantly, and fight for the glory of Sylvanna with thy blade."

Erika could only guess at Darion's shocked expression.

"Now rise, *Sir* Darion Woodsmark," Stacia declared with a finality, leading to the survatri to suddenly burst out into excited applause and cheers for 'Brother Knight!'. Even Y'Skara applauded politely, despite her pouting expression.

Celine said something to Darion that Erika couldn't make out, but her stern expression gave her the impression that she ordered him to continue training. Darion turned away from the two, his hands shaking slightly as he returned to his companions.

"Well, I'm sure F'Lessa would like a dance with *Sir* Darion," Erika said almost teasingly. "Though now I think I should be havin' a dance with 'im too."

He gave a wide but nervous smile, nodding at her. "I think I need a moment before any of that, the world is spinning suddenly."

Marq raised his glass, his hand still resting comfortably on Erika's shoulder. "A drink might help with that, lad."

They all laughed and the night continued on. Erika was able to enjoy her twenty-fifth birthday and was able to forget about the rest of the world, if only briefly. Her bed felt strangely cold that night as thoughts swirled her emotions, but tomorrow they would be back on the road and heading further north once again. Far from the comforts and allurements of this Cathedral—and the people who lived there.

† †

The day began early, Erika forcing herself to awaken sooner than she would have liked, dressing and bidding her comfortable room in the Cathedral a fond farewell. The group all stood in the great hall, packed and ready once more for the road ahead of them amidst the lingering decorations of the previous night's festivities. They awaited the monarch and her brother to see them off, comfortable with their fresh traveling clothes and well stocked supplies. None of them seemed happier to be on their way than Craven. He ran his gloved fingers through his long dark hair before donning his wide-brimmed hat, tapping the toe of his boot on the stone below him the whole time.

Stacia arrived, starting down their line with Darion. She dusted off the side of his new Sylvannan shield and the shoulder of his tunic before presenting him with a broadsword ornamented with the flowing designs of the city. "A knight needs a sword worthy of his name," she said, to which Darion bowed and accepted, holding the weapon reverently while looking like he was trying not to cry.

She stepped to Craven next, the two holding each other's stare for a long while before she moved to F'Lessa without a word to the dark man. She hugged F'Lessa and whispered something to her that made the aash's hair run pink for a moment before stepping to her brother. She gave F'Skal a kiss on the cheek, putting one hand on his broad shoulder and her other on the side of his neck. She smiled at him in such a way that made Erika wonder again what she may have missed between the two. Her thoughts were interrupted as the Queen finally stepped before her. She took the Fjordling into a tight embrace. "Thank you for all you've done here, Erika. I hope you've come to see me like family, as I have come to see you."

Erika smiled and returned the loving embrace, thanking her for the gifts and hospitality. "I hope to be back soon."

Stacia moved to the side and Inquisitor Marq stood before the group and nodded to each of them. He lingered on Erika for just a moment longer than the others, his eyes falling to the floor before addressing them all. "Your services to this city will be remembered, and you all will all be treated as honored guests throughout the Sylvannan Region. I understand your journey takes you outside of our boundaries, and I wish you every luck and expediency in that trek."

Craven smirked at the brevity of the man's oration, but wasted no time in making his way from the Cathedral.

"Oh, Marq, yer flask, I never gave it back," Erika blurted, fishing the container from her satchel and holding it out to him.

He looked at it for a moment before his eyes came up to hers. "Hang on to it for me. My sister and Celine have been trying to get me to drink less for years anyway."

Erika turned hesitantly, Marq giving her a smiling nod as she did. Her stomach swam as she ran her fingers on the outside of the smooth vessel, bringing the side of it to her lips briefly before placing it back into her pack. Her step was almost distressed as she rushed to catch up with Craven, whispering curses to herself.

The rest of them finished their goodbyes, whirling to catch up with Erika and Craven into the overcast streets of Sylvanna. "And to think, if Craven had not returned, we would not have met them," Stacia mused. "Or at least, I would not have met them."

Marq chuckled. "Indeed, although I did suspect them of murder upon our first meeting."

She smirked slightly, watching them until they disappeared from sight. "I do hope we'll see them again."

"I'm sure we will. Now, what was it that you and Craven spoke about in private the night of the Shadesfall Gala?" the Inquisitor asked, turning to his sister.

She stared off at the door, now closed behind their new friends, sighing deeply. "I wanted to know what happened to him, where he had gone."

"And what did he say?"

"Cryptic words and beautiful bladework, as to be expected from my teacher," she answered. "He is not for us to hold, or to judge."

Marq sighed now, looking down at the floor and gripping his cane to walk to his office, several knights stepping forward to escort him. He thought on the time when he was much younger and had attempted to Delve into the dark man as he had Erika. That particular invocation of his ability had led to nothing but the visage of a coyly smiling woman in black, and abysmal nightmares for a month. "I can only wonder, what does have the right to judge him?"

Outside, Craven paused a moment at the statue of the nymph atop the fountain, looking up at the woman's carved face for a long while. Water streaked down her face, as if his presence made her weep. He moved on to catch up with his companions who had started down the stairs towards the city streets.

Few words were shared between the companions as they departed. Each of them lost in their own thoughts regarding the home they had found, and were now leaving.

31

Good Intentions

The wilderness was a welcome sight to many of them. Erika pondered at how she preferred living in a smaller town than the cities like Sildenfeld or Sylvanna as they grew further away from the long bridge. The air seemed so much more open and the colors so much more vibrant. Even still, she imagined the possibility of opening her own blacksmith shop and living in Sylvanna close to her newfound family, regardless of if her quest was successful or not. She wondered if she could handle seeing Marq on a more regular basis. At the thought, she suppressed the urge to smash her warhammer into a tree.

Blessedly, the mood of the entire group seemed to improve as they made distance away from the city under Craven's guidance. None of them shared much conversation though, even when they made camp for the night, each of them absorbed into their own tasks or tinkers that passed the time before they bedded down for their rest. F'Lessa did seem to take more of an interest in Darion's whittling, often trying to lean in to peek at his work.

The landscape itself flattened more as they closed distance to the border settlement. They had stopped once to watch a herd of wild cerotae making their way across a field, the singular cobalt blue horn at the tip of their noses contrasting with their heavily silver furred bodies. Presently, they paused at a large lake in a forest with a stream running through it. Darion nearly screamed when F'Lessa and F'Skal—coming winter or not—simply stripped off the little they had on for a short swim and bath in the clear water. Erika simply laughed at them, while Craven seemed distracted by something else off to the side of the clearing.

"A refreshing swim is good for the mind you know," F'Skal said, stepping from the water some time later and drying with a cloth from his pack despite his hot flesh steaming the moisture from his skin plenty quickly.

Darion looked sharply away as F'Lessa made her way from the lake, making no attempts to hide her nudity. "Mixed company, however," he reasoned.

Erika noticed F'Lessa to seem put off suddenly, the elf beckoning for her just a moment later. Her hair flashed orange and light blue as her face shifted to confusion and slight frustration. "Does he think me unattractive now? He says I am beautiful days ago, but now won't even look at me."

Erika nearly laughed again but caught herself, understanding the elf's misunderstanding. "No, he's just shy. Plenty o' people only see the opposite sex naked when, well... sex," she explained.

F'Lessa's hair streaked an impressive amount of pink, muttering something about the natural form and 'irritating human sensibilities'.

"Are they done yet?" Darion asked, going so far as to cover his eyes with a hand in embarrassment.

"Aye," Erika said coyly while trying to hide her giggles. F'Skal looked at her with an amused grin. The knight started to turn again, but quickly looked away as he caught even more of F'Lessa's nude form, his eyes widening as he whirled. The aash woman put her hands on her hips and stared at his back while her silvery hair danced with blue and indigo. Erika and her brother shared hearty laughs at Darion's fluster. F'Lessa indignantly threw her arms in the air before bending down to retrieve her loincloth.

"I'll have to start calling you Erika the Liar!" Darion called back at them, starting to pace.

Craven almost managed a smile at the exchange but turned away from the group again, their mirth and laughter beginning to fade out of his mind. He felt a chill in the air and could smell the particular smell of decay. "Busy times for Matron Mortia," he noted quietly, sniffing the air and finding the direction of the scent. The source still lay far northeast of them, but was definitely there in their path. The stench of death and the stench of unrest. He arrived back just as the two aash elves finished dressing again. "Everyone fill your waterskins, we need to keep moving."

F'Skal watched him as he crouched next to his pack, standing a moment later. "What's the rush? Can we not have a quick bath? Perhaps some fun with our companions?"

"That was fun for you, eh?" Darion said incredulously, though neither heard him.

Craven stared into the red on black eyes of the elf. "I have allowed for your bath, and your fun. It seems prudent we leave before we run out of sunlight, yes?"

"Indeed. Unfortunate you humans lack the eyesight that we aash have in the dark of night as I understand," F'Skal continued. "Curious, you seem just fine in the dark, Craven."

"I have had a lot of practice in many different situations, F'Skal," he retorted back with the same annoyed tone.

"What are ye two arguin' about?" Erika demanded suddenly, both of them startling at her annoyance. "I'm just about as worried about time as any o' ye, but ye don't see me rushin' anyone." The two looked at her after her outburst. "I got somethin' I'm needin' to find, an' I'm thinkin' the more time I lose, the harder it'll be to find it. Yet I'm alright givin' everyone the time they need. I'm not the only one on this journey now," she continued, the words making her think of Marq again.

"I apologize Erika," Craven said. "I understand your rush, and I will do everything in my power to help you find him. I am simply concerned that we are lingering here for too long. If you think differently, perhaps we should rest here?"

"Honestly, why don't we?" she asked. "We've a nice lake and stream fer drinkin' and swimmin' as we like, even if it is a bit cold. We can get an early start tomorrow."

"As long as we all wake up on time," Darion said towards her with a smirk, which Erika answered with a glare.

Craven held up his hands in surrender. "Very well. We will follow your judgement."

"So, another swim?" F'Lessa asked.

Darion turned sharply on his heel and walked into the forest "I'm going to get some firewood."

Erika turned to the elf woman. "There ye go, now ye're gettin' the humor!"

F'Lessa looked at her with purple streaks matching her confusion. "What humor?"

⚔ ⚔

Darion idly stepped through the forest, looking around every so often, but mainly looking below and around his feet for good branches to be used for firewood. He was still unsure of the situation as a whole. He and F'Lessa had a nice day exploring Sylvanna and her interest in all of the human concepts and traditions made him think that what he believed to be her interest in him was still there, but nothing more had happened save for the two of them attending Erika's party as a sort of couple. He had planned on telling her how he felt during their city explorations, but could never work up the nerve to do so and she had kept conversation specifically on their current activities. After that, they saw little of each other, besides watching each other's sparring matches. He had to admit her fighting still frightened him some. She never seemed more animated and excited than when she was battling someone. Some of the bulkiest fighters had to resort to dodging her powerful blows, though she reacted to any hit that was landed on her similarly to if someone had nudged her lightly—often with a laugh that showed just how much enjoyment she had in the sport of it.

"She must've fought people three times bigger than me," he said to himself as he walked. "How could she be interested in someone who wouldn't ever dream of competing with that physicality."

He wondered if that was what she looked for in a partner and was suddenly very conscious of how he had not as of yet gained the muscle of his father. He groaned and leaned against a tree, realizing that he wouldn't be in this situation if he had just stayed home in Stonewall. There, the biggest of his worries would have been which older guard would bully him at best, the sad glances of the Mason family at worst. Now he was left with how he would talk to the beautiful elf that he couldn't imagine a day without. He rubbed at his eyes, memories of Ryla Mason flashing through his mind. He felt tears when he imagined the blood. "Shit," he breathed. "I'm not deserving of anyone, am I?"

His thoughts were sidetracked when he heard a sudden puff of air, turning slowly to find a massive cerotae staring down its singular cobalt horn directly at him. He crouched down slightly, setting his sparse gathered wood on the ground next to him and putting the other hand on the hilt of his knighted weapon. He nearly fell over when the creature issued a deep guttural bellow, though he recognized it not to be specifically aggressive, but more defensive.

"Easy," he said, putting his free hand out to the animal slowly. "I didn't realize I got in your territory, I'll back away now."

He started to do just that, but twitched when he heard heavy thumping sounds. The cerotae grunted and started into a charge, Darion cursing and ripping his sword from its sheath. He readied himself to leap to the side and out of the track of the beast, but was again caught off guard when F'Lessa appeared in front of him and threw both hands onto the creature's horn. Her ruby dust shimmered brightly with power as it flowed through her muscles, allowing her to stop the animal. Its legs came free of the ground with the momentum it had gained and F'Lessa groaned loudly as she threw the beast over her own head and onto the soil down the small hill from them. Darion moved to the side as it fell, sliding down the opposite side of the knoll and wincing as branches and brambles scraped at him. He looked up to the elf woman, her breast heaving with the effort, her muscles still fully corded with tension.

She's so beautiful when she's like that, he thought to himself.

"Are you alright Darion? I came as fast as I could when I heard the beast," she said, worry and sympathy in her dark crimson eyes, her silver hair flashing orange again. He had slowly begun to understand her colors, knowing that orange signified distress of a sort.

Darion set his jaw firmly at her words. He started to wonder if she saw him as just something to protect. "I'm fine," he said bluntly, blinking his eyes hard as they started to sting. He just hoped she didn't notice. He started off, snatching up the few pieces of wood that had snapped from her offensive sprint as he walked away in frustration. F'Lessa backed away from the cerotae as it started to regain its footing and followed after Darion in a light jog. "Darion?"

He kept walking, now more focused on picking up dead branches and piling them into the crook of his arm. The task helped bury the sense of worthlessness.

"Darion?"

He paused a moment, looking up at the treetops and regaining his direction. He turned so that he would be heading back for the camp, pointedly putting her behind him as he kept walking.

"Darion!" she finally cried, grabbing his shoulder and forcibly turning him around.

He whirled on her with an aggressive expression in his reddening eyes, causing her to jump back slightly. "What, F'Lessa?" he asked more angrily than he had meant.

She retreated another slow, nervous step as he held her gaze. "Did I do something wrong? I'm trying to learn about humans, but I am very confused right now."

"What were you doing back there?" he asked, pointing a branch back in the direction of the cerotae that they could still see slowly walking away around the bend in the hill.

F'Lessa stammered, feeling her throat constrict. "I... I was helping you."

"You were provoking it!" he yelled back, causing her to take another step back with a suddenly very vulnerable expression. "I was fine, really! It was protecting its territory, possibly even some calves, but your hard footsteps scared it and made it charge."

"I was only trying to—"

"I understand, F'Lessa, but," he said, his voice quieting again, "I'm not helpless, despite how I look. I understand how to do some things right."

"But you scared me!" F'Lessa screamed back, now causing Darion to take a step back. Her hair flashing red and orange. "You ran off again, just like you did with the Daemon in Sylvanna. I was terrified that something would happen to you!" she continued, tears starting to rim under the blacks of her eyes.

"This was just a wild animal though, not a Daemon," he reasoned.

She stamped her foot down with a *thump,* her ruby markings flaring with the impact. "That doesn't matter!"

"Yes, it does matter!" Darion yelled back. "In the city, yes, I made a mistake and almost paid very badly for it. This time was just a wild animal and I knew what I was doing!"

"It still could have hurt you!"

"Stop acting like I'm not capable of defending myself!" Darion continued, advancing on her.

She retreated another step, pressing her palms into her eyes.

He advanced again. "I am not helpless! You don't have to protect me at every turn like I'm a child!"

"Stop it!" she shouted, throwing her arms out. With another flash of her markings, her fists made contact with Darion's chest. He flew backwards, slamming into a tree and crumpling to the ground. F'Lessa looked up with shock and horror in her eyes. "Darion!"

She sprinted to him, sliding on her knees to where he lay motionless. Blood dripped onto his neck and shoulder from his hairline, causing F'Lessa's heart rate to quicken sharply. She raised him up in her arms. "Darion? Darion, please!" she pleaded. She started panicking, her hands shaking and tears falling onto his still face.

His breathing was there, but terrifyingly light.

The wound on his head bled onto her dark hands.

"No, no..." she muttered breathlessly, her vision becoming bleary as a lump rose in her throat. She feared moving him, instead looking to the campsite and calling out her brother's name. She rocked gently, holding Darion's face to her breast. Haggard shrieks were the only thing to break her weeping.

Eventually, F'Skal and Erika arrived at the scene. "What 'appened?" the young woman immediately asked in a panic, causing F'Lessa's stomach to turn knots.

She wiped her face, not realizing the blood on her fingers. "He's so cold... I didn't mean to..." she said quietly.

F'Skal wore a grim expression, a thin streak of yellow passing down his silver locks as he carefully took Darion from her grasp. His eyes looked disappointed, making F'Lessa start to cry even harder.

"Take care of her," F'Skal said firmly to Erika as he quickly walked away with Darion, his hair returning to its regular color once he regained his emotions.

Erika stepped over to F'Lessa, who, in Darion's absence, had wrapped her arms around herself. She knelt down, pulling F'Lessa's head to her chest in the only way she knew how to comfort someone. Warm tears washed down her tunic as the elf wailed and held her bloodied hands outward.

Eventually she calmed, content with where they were and shaking her head when Erika asked if she wanted to go back to camp. "It's all my fault," she said, her voice still very small. "Darion was completely right, and I couldn't accept what he was saying to me."

Erika stayed silent, simply watching the aash woman with a sympathetic gaze as she explained what happened with a quivering voice.

"What do I do from here?" she asked, rubbing at the drying blood on her palms.

Erika thought for a long moment.

"I 'aven't talked to Darion very much about this," she admitted, "but I do believe he feels fer ye in a very similar way."

F'Lessa looked to her with a slight hopefulness in her eyes.

"However..." Erika continued, the look fading from the elf's eyes. "I think ye've seriously hurt 'im here. In more ways that physical."

F'Lessa started to tear up again. "But after what happened in Sylvanna, I'm always just so worried over him. I can hardly stand it when I can't see him. What if he gets hurt again? And now I've hurt him," she fell into blubbering sobs with those last few words.

She buried her head in her forearms, Darion's blood getting into her silvery hair as it ran with a myriad of colors that Erika had trouble keeping up with. Erika placed her hands on the aash's shoulders. "I once had someone that I see in the same way as ye see Darion," Erika said, drawing the elf's gaze again. "Growin' up, 'e got bullied a lot, but I was always there to protect 'im. One day, he started goin' away a lot, an' one night when 'e got back, I went to visit 'im. Planned to give 'im a big hug cause I was so happy 'e was home."

She paused, F'Lessa nodding for her to continue. "He had this 'orrible wound, like nothin' I'd ever seen. Somethin' just ripped 'is back open. I nearly screamed then an' there. I stayed home and cried all night. I just couldn't stop. I tried my best to just forget about the worryin' fer a long time, until I traveled with 'im and saw just how capable 'e was."

"So, what am I to do now?" F'Lessa asked.

Erika looked at her for a long while. "Give 'im a chance to prove 'imself to ye."

"He doesn't need to prove anything to me!" she protested.

"Doesn't 'e?" Erika snapped back sharper than F'Lessa expected, making her flinch. "Ye came rushin' to 'is aid blindly, twice now."

F'Lessa started to speak again, but Erika stopped her. "No, I 'aven't gotten over it yet. I am still upset with ye, but I can't say I wouldn't 'ave done the same if it were the one I cared about. But Darion is the one ye need to be concernin' over now."

The big woman's voice was so small in that moment. "So what do I do?"

"Give 'im some space, and let 'im prove 'imself," Erika reiterated.

They eventually arrived back at the camp, F'Skal sitting back from Darion who now wore a bandage on his head as he lay unconscious still. Craven arrived a few moments later with a bundle of wood for a fire, carefully setting each branch in a circle. F'Skal and F'Lessa shared a long look while Erika sat next to the wood pile and immolated her hand inside it to start the fire. The aash woman avoided eye contact with any of them after that, simply cleaning her hands as best she could and sitting down away from the group. She hugged her knees tightly to her breast, trying to hold back more tears.

32
REVENANTS

The night pressed on in silence. Each of the companions ate their dinner while simply looking at the fire or their quiet surroundings. Occasionally F'Skal or Erika would glance back at Darion just to make sure he hadn't woken up yet. Craven often scanned the forest around them, seemingly looking for something, though he would not volunteer any further information. F'Lessa kept her eyes to the ground, occasionally looking towards Darion, albeit never directly at him. She seemed like she was holding in tears still, often wiping at her dark eyes or nose to clear them as she turned away from the group. Her sniffling was the only constant sound save for the crackling of the fire.

Eventually, the two women laid over for their sleep, leaving F'Skal and Craven alone to their watch, despite both of them insisting on taking the lookout themselves.

"Is your sister alright?" Craven asked after a while, doubting that F'Lessa was truly asleep.

"She is shaken," F'Skal answered plainly. "She is unused to humans and has severely overestimated how different our cultures are."

Craven sat back slightly, holding a hand up and offering. "To be fair, from what I understand of your people, you value kinship throughout your tribe. That there is much different than humans in most capacities outside of actual blood or chosen family units."

"Indeed, and she does realize this. Still, as I said, she overestimates that," F'Skal glanced down at his sister's steadily rising and lowering form as he paused. "She would likely strike me for going into such detail."

"I'll say I forced you," Craven said with a grin.

F'Skal shrugged. "I'm sure you've noticed, as Erika and I have, that my sister is trying extremely hard to court Darion."

"I'd say Darion himself is the only one to not have noticed fully," Craven smirked.

The elf nodded his agreeance to the possibility. "The reason for her trying so much, and so forcefully, is that she believes humans collectively to be very cautious with new individuals."

Craven scratched the edge of his thin beard that had begun sprouting, speaking with some sarcasm. "So, she is trying to earn the elusive and coveted 'human trust'?"

F'Skal chuckled slightly. "Precisely. Which is why she is leaning so hard into this endeavor, trying to ingratiate herself to him. However, I fear that she has leaned too far this evening, and in her outburst, pushed the young man further away."

Craven made a long *hmm* sound, looking to the bandaged man across from him. "Thankfully, I do know of one thing that humans have that elves do not have in the same capacity, or at least in my experience."

"And that is?"

"They forgive easily," Craven said, making sincere eye contact with the aash. "They may not dwell on their shorter lifespans much, but they do remember that they will die much sooner than their elven neighbors."

"Live and let live, I believe the saying goes," F'Skal offered, only just slightly perturbed at how Craven did not acknowledge himself as human.

Craven smiled at him warmly. "Just so. I have hope for your sister yet."

"And what of you? Any special woman in your life?"

"Once," the man muttered, darkening slightly. "I'm afraid I've left that part of my life far behind."

F'Skal spoke quickly. "I apologize, I did not mean to dig up any sore memories."

Craven managed another smile. "You are much too worried over my feelings, friend."

"'Friend' may seem a bit forward for our relationship," F'Skal replied with a smirk.

Craven shrugged to concede the point. He started to lay back, but snapped his gaze to the side quickly. F'Skal also paused his medicinal fiddling at the sound, his emerald dust lighting around his sharp ears to amplify the sense. He nodded to Craven, but jumped when another noise sounded from much closer behind him. Craven whipped upwards with a speed that surprised the elf, pulling a thin dagger from his boot and deftly throwing it straight past F'Skal's long pointed ear. The blade impacted something near a tree, causing it to fall with the crashing sound of a body onto the soft ground below.

"To arms!" Craven bellowed, waking Erika and the barely slumbering F'Lessa. "Revenants! Sever the heads or damage the spine, all else will fail to kill them!" he called as he leapt into the forest behind F'Skal. The elf watched as Craven raised the head of their stunned assailant in his arms, brutally twisting the neck with a *snap* and dropping the corpse into a melting pile of fine sand, black as the creature.

Erika was up after just a moment, lamenting that she would not be able to don her armor in time. She raised her left arm high, immolating it in a bright flame that illuminated the area around them. Craven cursed in unison with her as they looked around to find nearly a score of shadowy warriors that surrounded them.

"Fight with all you have, they will not relent!" Craven screamed as he drew his rapier and dashed into a grouping of them.

Erika groaned, remembering her previous encounter with these creatures. "Excuse the immodesty," she said, knowing that neither of the elves would care at the least. She swiftly pulled her tunic from her torso with her other arm and tossed it to the ground, exhaling as the brisk cold air enveloped her naked torso. With a thundering open flame, her body immolated from the waist up, her blazing hair exuding a light far greater than their campfire. She gripped her warhammer tightly and threw herself forward, immediately crashing her fist into the first adversary she found.

F'Lessa's head whirled with the action, struggling to her feet and to find her axes.

"Stay and guard Darion, I'll be nearby," F'Skal said to her.

She felt tears rimming her eyes again. "I can't!"

Her protest fell on nothingness as her brother quickly scaled the tree they rested beneath. She found one axe, reactively swinging it towards an advancing revenant. The shadowy warrior simply leapt out of range of her attack though, baring its thin curved blade as it slowly came in again.

The thing was like a moving silhouette. There were no real visible features besides the occasional edge of an armor piece or tunic, save for how this particular one seemed oddly feminine with a rather pronounced bosom. Similarly, you could see no eyes or facial features, and yet F'Lessa noticed when it looked towards Darion.

A rage filled her. Darion may have been angered by her trying to safeguard him from any threats, but what else could she do? "I can't just not protect that which I love," she growled, planting her feet over his unconscious body.

The creature pressed forward again, its wicked blade slashing fast.

† †

Erika dashed through the forest, whipping around the trees with her hammer bared. She could see the creatures all around her, some of them seemingly waiting for her immolation to die down. She had not used her fire across her body like this in more than a year now. She couldn't have felt better. Her muscles surged underneath the hardened and burning flesh, blood felt like boiling lava through her veins. It was intoxicating. She grinned wildly at the exhilarating rush of it.

Around another tree she came, directly into one of the revenants who swung a curved blade down at her. She ducked, spinning the butt end of her weapon upwards and slapping his blade to the side, continuing the momentum around and bringing the head of it crashing into the warrior's helmet. She silently thanked Irvine, Teria—and even the odd ranger, Farris—for teaching her how to use the warhammer for more than just reckless swings.

The thing crumbled to the ground in a pile of black sand, the other revenants deciding that this was their chance to advance on her. She welcomed their charge. The forest flared to life in a million flashes as she twisted and turned betwixt the surrounding force. Her fists blasted gouts of flame, some severing appendages or heads, while her hammer spun in a chaotic dance of death for her adversaries.

She felt so in control. Her weapon crashed through the creatures, while theirs glanced off her naked skin as if she were wearing the thickest of armor.

If Irvine could see me now, she found herself thinking, though she did wonder what he would make of her. More unbidden thoughts came at how he would react to the Ignis markings covering nearly her entire body, especially now that she felt the power crawling further down to her hips, threatening the waistline of her leggings. She felt more akin to flames than she did as a child, even when working in her father's forge, and learning about her heritage from him and his mastery over the power. An animalistic urge washed over her, wanting to embrace her fire fully. She could burn away the leggings too and meet these monsters as a pure elemental being of flame...

Would Irvine's fear of fire drive him away, if she ever found him again?

She lost her focus. A hard blow came across her jawline and broke her immolation for a moment. She fell onto the ground her flesh naked again, feeling the soft and damp soil on her bare back as she glanced up to her newest opponent. The tall creature that looked to have once been an elf slammed a pair of metal caestus gloves together with a loud bang and slight spark. He started in again and she curled her left arm into a block. She heated the entire left side of her torso until blazing flames exuded from her, yet still the revenant came.

The warrior's boot went crashing into her bare ribs from underneath, knocking the breath from her and rolling her on the ground. Her immolation broke again as she came to rest on her back, struggling to suck air into her lungs. It was so cold suddenly. Survival instincts kicked in, heaving herself quickly to her feet, the soil sinking under her heels. Her warhammer felt heavy in her hand.

As the pounding footsteps approached for the next strike, she immolated her torso again with a groaning effort. She looked to the side, spotting her assailant. She threw her hammer out in a feint, the motion causing the revenant to pause and allowing Erika to duck to the side, swinging her weapon around with the back spike leading. The warrior tried to back away, holding up his left hand to block, only for the spike to drive through his palm, halting on the inside of his caestus.

Erika heaved with all her strength on the weapon, twisting it up and around, taking the warrior's limb with it to the ground. She closed the distance quickly on his back side, driving her right hand onto his neck and flushing more heat through her palm, gouging a deep ravine through his neck. She could feel the spine under her hand, gripping it hard and severing it with her fire. She heaved with labored breath as the creature melted into sand. She raised her hammer back into both hands, backing against a tree for a respite. She extinguished her body, save for her arms, as to not to set the old oak ablaze, the rough bark prickling against soft skin.

† †

F'Skal watched as Craven led the other major half of the force away from the camp, easily sliding his blade between armor to sever spines with brutal efficiency. He could not help but be impressed with the man's finesse, though he still wondered how he was able to see the first revenant in the darkness. There was more to this man that he did not understand, and could not bring himself to fully trust. He glanced back, watching Erika's blazing glory as she knocked aside opponent after opponent, knowing that she did not need his help right then. He loosed several arrows, understanding that his quicker shots would not damage the creatures enough to slay them, but that they would distract them and slow their attack on his companions. He spotted one approaching from a distance and drew his bow to its full length, releasing the arrow a heartbeat later. The shaft drove straight through the thing's spine and sent it to the ground in a cascade of black particles.

Craven finished a pirouette, three of the warriors falling at his feet. F'Skal noted the look of rage upon the man's face. He slung his left arm downwards, a shape moving from his shoulder to his outstretched hand, gaining the elf's interest even more. Craven raised his arm with the dark shape in his palm and said something to it that he couldn't make out, then the shape flew from him like a bird of shadow. It quickly went out of sight through the trees.

F'Skal narrowed his eyes at the man, unseeing of his sister's plight.

† †

Below the tree where her brother perched, F'Lessa desperately fought off the last few warriors that did not chase after Craven or Erika. She hacked her axe through one's neck, only for another to appear behind it and nearly score a strike on her neck with a blade. She narrowly dodged, the edge instead drawing across the soft flesh under her shoulder, drawing a splash of her steaming lifeblood. In came the revenant again, locking its sword against her axe, taking all her strength to hold it off and nearly causing her to bend a knee from its force. Another rushed in sharply and she grabbed onto the first warrior's shoulder to kick her leg upwards and into the oncoming second. She sacrificed her footing with the move, falling to the ground with them. She looked back up to a third revenant coming from behind the tree that Darion had rested against.

She screamed in protest, not even realizing that Darion no longer lay where he was, until the young man's blade cascaded through the third warrior, cleaving the head from its shoulders. Before F'Lessa could register what was happening he rushed forward, blocking an oncoming blade over her head with his shield and striking the creature's spine through its chest.

She tried to speak but he made a grunting noise to stop her, offering his arm to aid her in getting up while holding the shield against the remaining three foes.

Scared to even touch him, she regained her footing on her own and retrieved her axe. She lost track of any enemies around them, all she could see was Darion. He glanced back at her briefly, registering her expression. "Later," he said shortly before backing towards the tree as one of the revenants charged in. The attack grated across his shield, Darion using the moment to jam his own blade through the creature's side and ram it to the ground. F'Lessa looked up as the second came in a breath later, dodging the mace that it swung. With a lunge, she closed the distance and slammed her axe sideways into its neck. She wrenched the weapon from the fading creature, looking back in terror as the final shadowed warrior kicked Darion from his feet and back into their campsite. She struggled to break into a run, knowing that the revenant would be on him before she could intervene but stopped sharply when the warrior jolted. A second strike hit it, lopping its head to the side but not cleanly. Darion shoved it to the ground, holding F'Lessa's second axe in his hand after losing grip on his own sword.

"Why was this all the way over here?" he asked incredulously, holding the axe in the air.

F'Lessa could only laugh as her knees gave out from under her. Tears of joy rimmed her eyes at Darion's vigor as she wiped at the side of her mouth with her wrist.

† †

Eventually, Craven and Erika arrived, the latter sheepishly covering her breasts with one arm. She dropped her warhammer unceremoniously beside her bedroll and bent down to retrieve her tunic, turning away so she could slip it over her head.

"Your side is bruised, do I need to take a look?" F'Skal asked as he landed with a soft thump out of the tree.

She waved him off with the tunic still in her hand as she struggled to get it the right way. "Nah, I already checked like ye told me. No tender ribs, just the bruisin'. Guess I'm more thick skinned than all that."

F'Skal nodded approvingly, still touching warm fingers to her skin to double check.

"Dammit, F'Skal, ye don't have to press so bloody hard," she said, her hissing tone turning to a friendly laugh. She pulled her tunic over her head finally and sighed. "Ye alright, love?" she asked F'Skal, reaching her arms up to hug the tall elf as he nodded and returned the embrace.

Craven watched the young woman make her caring rounds to her companions, hugging F'Lessa as well before leaning down to kiss the top of Darion's head as he was already sitting. "Good to see ye're back in the realm o' the livin'," Erika said to him, ruffling his hair gently.

Darion gave a half-hearted salute, scratching his arm slightly where his shield had rubbed on his bare skin. "Just a splitting headache, but I'm fine."

Erika glanced to F'Lessa as he spoke, the elf woman looking down at the ground a bit at the mention of her inflicted wound on him. She looked back to Darion, who seemed to be holding no grudge and Erika nodded resolutely between them, then looked to Craven. "Ye too, love, give us a bit o' sugar," she grinned at him, pulling him into an embrace as well. She didn't notice F'Skal's scrutinizing gaze of the dark man.

"So, what d'ye know of these creatures?" she asked, releasing him and adjusting her tunic to be more comfortable. "F'Lessa, love, would'ye sit close? I'm a bit chill from the half-naked walk back."

Craven set his jaw, glancing around the perimeter one last time as everyone settled around the fire. F'Skal knelt behind his sister to attend the shallow gash she had sustained as Craven spoke. "Revenants are what they are called, as I had called out before. Undead warriors raised from the grave due to a grudge in this world that they still hold onto, commonly being towards what killed them in the first place."

"So, you're saying the ghost stories of Hallowden are true?" Darion asked sardonically, with a teasing glare to Erika.

She sneered at him just as mockingly before they both shared a smile.

"Not exactly," Craven answered with an effort as he lowered himself down into a sitting position on his side of the dwindling fire. "The month of Hallowden is said to lessen the gap between the realm of the living and the dead, but revenants can crop up anywhere under the right circumstances."

"So, you're a hunter of Daemons, and now a hunter of the undead?" F'Skal muttered with some obvious contempt, taking his previous seat.

Craven eyed him suspiciously at the tone, while everyone else just seemed confused at their silent exchanges. "I simply battle against injustice and imbalance," Craven said shortly.

"And what side of that balance do you fight for?" F'Skal pressed still.

"The side that is getting overzealous," Craven said with a grim finality, his eyes unblinking.

F'Skal held his gaze for a while longer, the other three companions glancing between the two, all of them suddenly afraid to utter a sound.

"As I was explaining," Craven finally continued. "Revenants are exceedingly rare, and the fact that we have slain damn near a score of them here tonight is very concerning."

Darion raised his hand as if he were a shy schoolboy, the group turning to him and causing him to shrivel slightly. "Just wanted to add: the night that Erika came to my town, there were three of those creatures that attacked the wall guard."

Craven lingered on him for a long while, his eyes still unblinking. "Did anything strange happen the day before that? Any odd occurrences or strange characters?"

"Nothing completely out of the ordinary," Darion said with a shrug. "I was on South Gate duty, which is where I met Erika towards the end of my watch. My over-paranoid partner was turning away anyone that came by, 'due to the war' he said over and over." Darion rolled his eyes at the irritating memory of Jhon.

Erika took a short breath, narrowing her eyes toward the ground. "I believe there was another oddity besides me around that time." Darion looked to her in confusion, she nodded at him as if trying to jog his memory. "Y'know, that strange fellow from the south lands, far south he said."

"Oh, the Haranian?" Darion asked.

"Aye! That's the one!" she perked with a gentle slap on F'Lessa's thigh. "Strange merchant type, tryin' to sell me clothes an' such from 'is homeland. Didn't seem to get my apprehension about 'em when the skirt 'e showed me wouldn't 'ave even covered my ass," she laughed. "Oh, he did give me this little trinket fer free."

She dug a moment in her satchel, producing the bracelet of stones that Kharim had given her so long ago. "Was a bit worried I'd break it if I actually wore it," she added with a chuckle. Craven motioned to see the bracelet, thanking her when she handed it to him. He turned it over in his hands several times, holding it up in the air and spinning each individual stone several times. "What're ye lookin' fer?" Erika asked in confusion.

"Anything strike you as odd about this Haranian man?" Craven inquired, not looking away from the bracelet. "Anything he was guarded over, or didn't want to speak with you about?"

"As much as I'd expect o' foreigners in a strange land, though he seemed to regard me in a similar way," she shrugged, pausing for a moment before speaking again. "Now that I'm thinkin', he was a bit off about 'is weapon. Seemed less than proud o' the thing an' not wantin' to talk about it more than 'is clothes an' other wares."

"Describe the weapon to me," Craven bade her, still inspecting the bracelet.

Erika made a slight face while everyone else around the smoldering campfire looked on in interest and confusion. "It was strange, had no scabbard, metal was just naked. The blade looked a bit similar to a few sickles that Papa or I 'ad made back home, cuttin' edge on the inside curve, but straighter an' longer. The handle looked like it was made o' glass, with sand or somethin' inside." She cast a sidelong glance to the dark forest around them, thinking about how the revenants had died in gouts of black sand. *Just a coincidence, right?*

"What kind of weapon has a glass handle? You'd shatter it in your hand and be in poor straights yourself," Darion added with a look of disbelief.

Craven finally lowered the bracelet. "Magic weapons are, at times, hard to believe."

"True magical weapons are incredibly rare as well," F'Skal added sternly. "No dwarves remain to make them, and the remaining ones from their reign are sparse at best. One is more likely to have a weapon enchanted by a reputable mage or druid, but those belong in other groupings entirely."

"Not impossible to find though, and not all made by the dwarves," Craven said softly, his expression looking almost angered. "Thank you, Erika and Darion. I believe you've just given me the answer I need."

"What was the question?" F'Skal asked, leaning forward. "What are you looking for Craven? And does it involve dragging us into the line of danger?"

Craven looked to him again, still unblinking and looking more unnerving by the second. "I swear to you, if at all avoidable, I will handle my own business alone. However, our quests take us to a similar destination and I plan to help you all reach the Fjordlands whilst pursuing my own quarry."

"Your quarry being the Haranian?" Darion asked.

Erika seemed conflicted, putting her hands to her arms and squeezing herself slightly. "Kharim was 'is name. He was perfectly personable though, I can't see 'im bein' a bad sort."

Craven gave her a sympathetic look. "I can only hope that is the case, my dear. Time shall tell though."

F'Skal sighed deeply. "We should rest while we can, I fear for more of those creatures and believe we should make distance with expedience in the morning."

Craven glowered slightly, considering his suggestions earlier that day. "My thoughts exactly."

33
Echoes of War

The morning arrived earlier than any of them would have liked. The weather had taken a turn for the colder just as they bedded down after their battle, sending chills through even the hot-skinned aash elves. Craven stalked around the camp quietly, his outward gaze falling inwards as Darion awoke huddled near F'Lessa for her warmth. He smirked as the young man grew red in the face, realizing that he had been curled into her chest before he began shyly moving away from her, appearing thankful that she hadn't awoken.

Erika grumpily packed her bedroll and satchel, having gotten little sleep that night after the physical exertion and the pain from her bruised side. She missed Winnifred greatly, as well as the soft mattress at the Cathedral. She gave a shake of her head, knowing that if she had stayed any longer, she would have stayed forever.

Eventually the companions were off and back on the road leading to the border town. Erika wrapped herself in her gifted ranger's cloak that offered some magical heating in the dropping temperature as well as the ornate scarf that she was given by Sárif, after the aash twins declined her attempt to give it to them.

Darion hugged himself in his thick clothing and stared at the still scantly clothed elves incredulously. Occasional steam would rise from their ebon flesh as sparse snowflakes started to fall, instantly melting on their skin. Soon enough he found himself staring in a less negative way, his eyes tracing the lines and curves of F'Lessa's shoulders and sides as she walked. F'Skal's suggestive grin towards him at one point made his face flush and his eyes go out to the landscape. The rest of the group gave F'Skal odd looks when he suddenly laughed as if he was the only one to hear a joke.

Erika and F'Skal started their own conversations over various things while Craven led the charge, Darion and F'Lessa held up the back of their convoy though they did not speak for a long while. Occasionally he would glance up at her, her hair sometimes slowly streaking an appealing purple color that complimented her silver locks and ebon skin beautifully.

"What does purple mean?" he asked quietly.

F'Lessa briefly glanced down at him in a slight panic. She did her best to hide it, but her ever traitorous hair flashed pink and orange alternate of the purple. She stammered for a moment, looking over as Darion shook his head.

"It's alright if you don't want to tell me. I was just curious. Frankly I think it a nice color on you, but I suppose I'm just being strange. I apologize for asking," he stammered, waving his hand over his face and beginning to increase his walking pace past her.

She was quiet for a long time, staring at his back as he walked with his gaze downwards or to their sides. His head bandage was lightly stained in the back, making her chest hurt. "It goes purple when I'm confused," she said nearly quieter than his original question.

He nodded slowly, turning his head back towards her but not making eye contact. "I see. Same as me then."

"Darion, I—" she started, but stopped abruptly when he held up his hand behind him.

"I know you didn't mean to," he imparted slowly. "Do you remember when you asked back in your village if I was afraid of you?"

She nodded, reddening at the memory of cornering him in the small room.

"Quite honestly, I think I may have been."

F'Lessa lowered her gaze, looking at the ground under her bare feet even as Darion continued. "However, I don't think I am anymore. I know how to take a punch from you now."

She glanced up to see him grinning at her, causing her to smile despite herself. "Not something I want to make a habit out of."

He nodded again. "Me neither. Say, next time I go get firewood, what do you think of coming with me? I'll show you how to read the animals you may not be familiar with a bit better, and without as much aggression."

She smiled even wider now, though Darion did not see her as he still kept pace in front of her. She reached her hand out and nearly touched his shoulder, but pulled away. "I would like that very much."

A while later, Craven stepped off ahead of the group as he commonly did during their marches. F'Skal leaned closer to Erika. "I do not trust him."

Erika scoffed. "I hope ye don't think ye're hidin' that well, love."

"Of course not," F'Skal huffed, straightening again as Erika looked up at him with an amused look. "I simply want you to know that I'm not sure I *can* trust him."

"And why is that, exactly?" she asked.

"He is strange. More strange than I find most humans, or at least differently," he replied. "I've never seen him rest, he always asks peculiar questions, and he always seems to know more than he lets on."

"But he doesn't seem to mean us any ill will. Even if he has some concern about Kharim, that shouldn't involve us," she reasoned, although she herself didn't wasn't completely satisfied with that notion.

F'Skal twisted his face in disagreement. "However, if it comes to light that this Kharim is innocent, then we may be leading to him a dangerous man who means him harm. And worse, we could end up in the middle of their conflict, however it may unfold."

Erika sighed. "What do'ye suppose we do then?"

F'Skal shook his head, looking completely perturbed by the issue.

"He's bein' more useful now than Darion, as we're beginnin' to reach the end o' his home region. Not sayin' we should get rid o' Darion either mind ye. All I'm sayin' is he's helped us plenty in the past, even if he is a bit odd."

"Very well," F'Skal said with a resignation. "I trust your judgment."

Erika laughed. "I only just turned twenty-five, love, don't ye put too much faith in my wisdom."

"You've more wisdom than I think you realize. Even if you are only barely in adulthood by aash standards," F'Skal said with a smile, rubbing a comforting hand on her shoulder.

She returned the gesture, wrapping an arm around his waist and hugging him close. "Everythin'll be alright. We just have'ta keep goin'."

††

Craven moved just off the roadway. The terrain had begun to level again as their altitude dropped into the northern plains of the continent. The forestry around them only thickened however, giving him plenty of cover from his group of companions as he summoned the dark entities that constantly stood around him, normally invisible to the naked eye of normal folk. One strange looking creature with a large gaping maw but no visible eyes stalked towards him with a low stance. "What do you ask of us, Lord Wraith?"

"Where is the scout that was sent late last eve?" he inquired.

"North and east from us, Lord Wraith," a larger and bulkier shadow creature with one eye spoke.

Another slithering one came to the side. "He believes to be close to your target, Lord Wraith."

"Good. Tell him that this is the signature he is seeking," Craven said, holding down the bracelet from Erika to the creature that seemed nothing but mouth.

"The message is received, Lord Wraith, your will shall be done," the big one-eyed one said gleefully.

"Thank you, all of you." Craven gave a sympathetic smile. "You are all so helpful. Now, be scarce, I do not wish my companions to think you enemies."

All of the creatures made bows to the dark man, stepping and slithering backwards and out of sight.

†† †

Winter chill filled the air more and more with each passing day and sent shivers up Kharim's spine. He knew the icy season would be a trying time for him when he came to this land, but now that it was starting to set in, he dreaded the weather it would bring. The open fields to the east of the Sylvannan borders did nothing to ease him, except for the fact that it gave him a break from the claustrophobic feeling that the tight forest trees filled him with. Ahead of him past a few rolling hills, was a curious little hamlet, much like one other he had seen during his travel through Patrias.

Gaia elves.

They were an amusing sort, short of stature with wildly varying hair and skin tones that mirrored much of this continent's verdant landscape. They also had a strange culture that seemed to revolve around bathing, although Kharim could appreciate the enjoyable sensation of being enveloped in water. He had never heard of such creatures in Haran, but they had been friendly enough to him each time he had spoken with them. Some in the previous village had even purchased some of his wares, when he still had wares to act as a merchant. He suddenly wondered how the would-be slaves he had freed were managing, and if they had kept the Haranian clothing he had given them.

So lost in thought, he nearly ran clear into one of the diminutive elves as he hurried down the street, shouldering a pack that seemed even more comically sized than Kharim's old thing that he used to carry. He had since traded it out for a much smaller bag after nearly emptying the contents for those freed people.

"Oh, beggin' yoor pardon, sirs!" the small male said, his green tinted mustache bouncing with his panicked bows.

Kharim cocked an eyebrow at him. "*Niae*, little one. It is I who should apologize to you. I was not watching where I was going, my mind drifting with the winds."

The little elf kept glancing over his shoulders and all around, as if he was terrified some beast would leap out and kill him on the spot.

"Are you well?" Kharim asked, looking around with him and seeing nothing in the way of danger. It seemed like a perfect late autumn day, by Patrian standards anyway. "Is there some kind of attack on your village?"

He shook himself back to Kharim, like he suddenly remembered the much taller Haranian was right in front of him. "Oh, no's, not yet anywho. There's'a somethin' in the air though, so we're all packin' up and leavin' the place for now's."

Kharim could barely understand the poor creature with how quickly he spoke and his peculiar manner of speech. A glance upwards helped fill in the gaps in his understanding. The village seemed to be evacuating in a mass, all moving somewhat southwards. Many children were hoisted up onto parent's hips, while others sat nervously in little carts that were pulled along by donkeys or pygmy runner birds. Not a soul had a bare back, their packs and bags overflowing with supplies, handles of cookware and other utensils hanging out of the flaps.

"Will you come back to this village?" he asked, suddenly feeling a pang of sadness at the exodus.

"Oh, aye. After the danger's been passed an' all," the gaia replied after a moment. "Where are yoo's headin'? If ye don't mind my askin' o' coorse."

Kharim felt bad for the length of time that it took him to answer, but the strange accent was truly difficult for him to understand, especially with Patrian being a second language to begin with. "Oh, I am heading east at the moment. Why do you ask, good elf?"

"Ooh, yoo's might not want to be headin' east rightabout'a'now, sirs. Beggin' yoor pardon again o' coorse," the elf started waving his hands frantically towards the eastern horizon. "Mayhaps yoo'd come with us? Safer in numbers they say."

"Many thanks to you, kind soul. I have urgent business though. Is there perhaps a different course I could take, rather than directly into this dangerous direction?"

The elf stroked at his mustache a bit, and Kharim noticed him eye the blade at his side warily. Gaia elves were also not particular fans of weapons as he understood, even if they could appreciate the need for such implements on a longer journey. Even still, Kharim's sword seemed to leave a particularly sour taste in his mouth from the way his wide nose scrunched up. "There is a seaside docky type place a ways a' north a' here. Dangerous typers there'n though."

"I assure you, I can handle dangerous types," Kharim said in as comforting a tone as he could manage.

The elf nodded, looking back up at his face. "Aright, if you's insists. North'n'east a' here, throo a cave doorway. Darktow's the name o' the haven. Just you'n be right careful, aye?"

Kharim gave a bow and stepped to the side to let him rejoin his neighbors, who waited at the forest edge for him. A small girl smiled at him as he grew closer, giving a friendly wave toward Kharim. The gaia turned again and called out to him, Kharim turning to hear him. "That swoord a' yoor's, good sir. There's bein' a lake just a bit western a' where yoor headin'. I say you's should chuck that blade into it. Deeper'an it looks, I tell you's. Bad luck'n that hunka metal."

The gaia held his gaze for a long while, giving him a solemn nod after having clearly read the look on Kharim's face. Soon after, the little gaia man and his daughter were out of sight. The Haranian wished he could do as he had advised, but had come much too far to stop now. For that, he shed a few tears as he walked through the eerily empty village.

†┠

As the group neared the border the two elves donned their obscuring cloaks. Both complained some, but did admit the cloth was not as bad with the dramatically lowered temperatures from the last time they had worn them. Just the same, they could all tell that F'Lessa was less comfortable than F'Skal as she was already rubbing at her arms where the cloak draped. The snow had begun falling harder, making way for an early winter as far as Erika was concerned, though Darion informed her that they would experience somewhat earlier snowfall the further northwards they went.

Shortly after, they paused for a long while at a grim sight. A ruined battlefield with a great number of corpses wearing both the Sylvannan colors of green and blue, as well as the red and silver of the neighboring Region of Tarkal. Darion stepped forward slightly, observing the wasteland of scorched ground and trampled soil.

F'Lessa looked to Erika and F'Skal as if to ask permission. They both nodded to her. She stepped forward and gingerly put a hand on Darion's shoulder, to which he gave a warm smile but still kept his gaze to the sea of dead. Craven looked on, crossing his arms and wearing an expression of disdain, as if he had tasted something foul. F'Skal ignored him for the time being, figuring no one enjoyed such a sight.

"So many dead, and for what?" Darion uttered quietly, his voice quivering. "All because Daemons were rumored to have returned to the world, and suddenly everyone goes mad?"

"Queen Sylvanna is directing her troops in the interest of defense and the safety of her people," F'Skal offered. "I admit this is concerning though, as we are still a good way from the proper border between Regions, if I am correct in thinking."

"You are," Darion said grimly, looking to F'Lessa's hand still on his shoulder. "I am sure the soldiers at the border town are aware, but we should inform them that the Tarkalan forces are pushing further in behind the Sylvannan lines."

"Indeed," Craven commented darkly. "My guess is that this was an insurgent group that crept around the main force. I count more Sylvannan dead than Tarkalan. Does not bode well for your side of this conflict."

"Who's side are you on?" Darion asked, not looking away from the scene.

"The side of balance, as I said before," Craven replied, almost sounding remorseful as he walked away with his boots crunching on the charred ground. "This war, however, is not balanced."

Darion sighed, beginning to turn away but accepting the consoling embrace from F'Lessa before moving on.

Erika stared at the battlefield for a moment longer, wishing there was more that she could do to help in this conflict. She wouldn't know where to even begin. She idly wondered if Irvine had ever been involved in such a battle during his travels.

⸸

Into the border town they walked, though it seemed more an armed fort than a town. Darion stepped forth, presenting his shield and sword given to him by the Queen as a sign of allegiance, as he knew his official title as knight would not have reached their ears. The guards readily accepted them inside the high walls upon seeing the crest. The town itself had a strange air to it after being in the relatively peaceful city of Sylvanna for so long. Faces were dour and people moved quickly to and fro in the streets, carting damaged weapons and supplies to smithies and stores.

An older woman wearing a loose shirt with a thick apron paused as the group cautiously made their way through the main street. "Oh, travelers?" she asked, smiling slightly at the nods she received. "Tavern with open inn rooms is just down the way, dears. Seems we've had a lot of travelers these days."

"Any more heading north?" Craven asked, tipping his hat in greeting. "Sorry for the sudden question, I'm looking for someone."

"No problems, happy to answer a strapping man like yourself," the woman said with a wink and an even bigger smile.

Erika stifled a laugh at the exchange, hanging back while the other three moved towards the tavern.

"Anyhoo, we did have a strange man in robes come through not long ago. Traveling merchant I think, sold my neighbor's daughter a jingly skirt, little metal pieces all over it, very colorful. Lass hasn't stopped wearing it since, goes around shakin' her hips to make as much noise as she can when she's got the free time."

Craven smiled cordially. "I see. Did he happen to say where he was going?"

"Unfortunately, I hadn't had many words with him myself. He stayed at the tavern for a bit, but I don't think he got a room there," she shrugged with a frown.

"I understand, thank you for your time, madam," Craven said with a small bow.

"My time is free, long as you keep looking like that," the woman replied as she walked away with a hearty laugh.

Erika smiled at her as she and Craven continued walking. "She seemed the happiest person here yet."

"Just wait until we get to the tavern," Craven grimaced. "War time. Most people out here on the front can't manage a laugh without a belly full of drink. She is probably using her laughter to suppress the sadness."

Erika couldn't find the words to reply, but understood his meaning poignantly when they arrived at the tavern. The interior was nearly full of patrons all in varying degrees of drunkenness, ranging from generously tipsy to falling onto the floor with a crash.

She watched the the scene with surprise and some amusement, as a couple men stumbled past them and into the street. Finally, they spotted F'Skal at the bar side, appearing to be conversing with the owner over rooms for the night. F'Lessa sat at an otherwise empty table resting her elbows on the wood and her hands on her cheeks. Erika and Craven moved further in, the latter stepping over to F'Skal while Erika pulled a chair next to F'Lessa. She sat down, glaring at the group of drunks that were staring lecherously at the elf who had pulled her cloak slightly off of herself.

"It's hot in here," F'Lessa fussed, holding the cloak off of her skin with her arm, not seeming to notice the attention.

Erika smiled at her. "As far as I'm thinkin', all these people'll be too drunk to remember it tomorrow, so I think ye could prob'ly take more off," she chuckled as a few of the men fell face first into their table.

F'Lessa turned to her after draping her cloak over the back of her chair. "You think I could?" she asked in complete seriousness as she tugged at the straps of her halter, one of the drinkers at another table near them spitting his drink in response to the jiggling motion of her breast. Thankfully F'Skal and Craven stepped back to the table, taking seats beside them and giving Erika perplexed looks as she fought to dampen her laughter. F'Lessa eased back into her chair with a slight pout after realizing that her Fjordling friend was joking with her. She started fanning herself lightly with one hand, her expression returning to idle irritation at the stifling air of the establishment.

"Two rooms is all they have," Craven explained. "So men in one and women in the other? Or are we giving F'Lessa and Darion their own room now that they seem on good terms again?"

F'Lessa's hair flushed a hot pink and she nearly slammed the table with her palms, but Erika put her arm across her. "Craven, that's not nice to tease 'er like that. Girls and boys'll be fine."

F'Skal smirked into his mug of mead as his sister slumped back into her chair and continued fanning herself in a weak attempt to cool herself down. "Darion is off speaking with the Watch Commanders by the way, if you were curious," he said.

"Wanted to tell them about the 'possible infiltration', he said," F'Lessa added, looking sad and annoyed all at once.

Erika nodded, flagging down the barmaid as she made her way through and ordering a plate of food for everyone. "Surprised F'Lessa didn't go with 'im."

"She tried," F'Skal said with some mirth, giving his drink an interested look after trying it. "He rightfully assumed that they would be nervous with an aash elf around though."

"I could have helped," F'Lessa complained.

F'Skal tapped his fingers on the table towards her. "Now now, sister, he is a proper member of this region's military. In this situation he knows completely what he is doing and can handle it just fine."

F'Lessa harrumphed back into her chair again, her party members giving her amused looks as Erika asked to try F'Skal's drink. Soon after, a bard began strumming a lute off in the opposite corner, singing a song of a hunter who slew the 'monster of the bog', the lyrics including all manner of innuendo. A short while later, their dinners were provided, one plate being placed at the empty seat awaiting Darion. F'Lessa idly poked at hers with her fork, still unsure of the human cuisine as a whole. Just as the bard finished his second song—a ballad that focused on the legs of a promiscuous dancer—Darion arrived at the table.

"How did it go?" F'Skal was the first to ask.

Darion nodded his head, seeming slightly annoyed. "The shield and sword actually did get me in to see the Watch Commander, but I'm thinking that it's just about the only thing that did. He commented several times on how *young* I was. But, I got the message through. It seems they were aware of the insurgence into the territory, and already have a company and a couple mercenary bands tracking the Tarkalan soldiers."

"Good," Erika said. "That means there isn't much threat then, right?" The barmaid passed by and set a new mug of mead in front of her after she had taken a liking to F'Skal's. "Oh, thank ye, dearie," she cooed with a warm smile before taking a hearty drink.

"It means there is somewhat *less* threat, than we were expecting," Craven corrected. "The infiltrators don't have the days lead on the Sylvannans that they could have, so there is less of a chance of them succeeding in any plans, if they have any at all to begin with besides weakening lines."

Darion nodded, pulling his plate closer while glancing at F'Lessa's mostly untouched plate. He sighed with a smile, his spirits looking suddenly lifted, placing a hand on her shoulder and helping her identify all of the strange human foods, as he had done at nearly every meal they had while in civilization. Erika smirked at F'Lessa's self-satisfied grin, knowing that she had been simply waiting on Darion to dote on her.

Craven slid his chair back and placed a few coins on the table next to Erika for his meal. "I'm going to get some fresh air. Don't wait up for me," he said, making his way through the tavern, dodging two more falling drunks as he did.

"Where is your cloak?" Darion asked F'Lessa, just then looking at her fully. Erika and F'Skal laughed as F'Lessa defended herself.

"This is why you couldn't go to the garrison with me, they would probably be threatened by you! I swear, bloody arms the size of my thighs." He shook his head to the continual laughter of F'Skal and Erika, and the pouting face of F'Lessa.

"You said my musculature was beautiful in Sylvanna," she muttered.

Darion put his hand under the table, resting his palm on her thigh and making her jolt briefly with a flush in her face and pink in her hair. "I'm just joking, F'Lessa. Why don't you try the vegetables next..."

†⸸

Outside the tavern, Craven adjusted his coat as the snowfall began again. The sun was nearly beyond the horizon, and torches were being lit down every street. He backed into an alleyway, shifting his body into the Isles of the Dead. Around him lay a ruined visage of the same town, separated by great glowing crags in the ground. Black ash fell heavily from the sky, mirroring the weather of the physical realm. The streets were populated by perhaps half of the mortal realm's living occupants. Many of the ghostly figures wept while others sat and watched the barely visible shimmers made by the living. Wayward souls who chose not to move past the Gate, or perhaps simply had lingering regrets. He turned to the street where he had just been in the physical realm and found Matron Mortia, her arms held outwards and her face turned skywards, as if bathing in the eerie 'snow'.

"Enjoying yourself, Matron?" he asked as he stepped closer.

She lowered her arms, turning slowly towards him. "To enjoy the snow and rain is to experience one's youth again. Dost thou disagree?"

"I suppose I can see your philosophy," Craven said with a shake of his head. "However, is revelry in youth a loss in dignity?"

She giggled. It was a pretty, yet ominous, sound. "One's dignity cannot be determined but by oneself alone. I may even decide to dance along this precipitation, and retain my dignity with every step."

Craven nodded, turning away from her and looking skywards as the black particles fell around him, it reminded him in a strange way of how the revenants had turned to sand as they died. "Matron? What do you know of this Haranian, Kharim?"

He felt a slender hand on his shoulder and turned away from it. "He hath experienced much death. Death rivaling thine own experience, from the time when I first claimed thee as mine."

"Is justice to be dealt?" Craven asked further, feeling the cold touch on his cheek this time and again turning away.

"Justice is said to be blind, though I hath never queried Iuri of this saying," she answered cryptically, Craven shrugging at the mention of the Goddess of Order. "It is for thee and thee alone, to met out thine justice."

"What is justice when decided by one man?"

"Thou hath lived long enough, to understand *perspective.*"

With her last words, Craven was suddenly back in the realm of the living, falling back against the stone wall of the tavern from the force of a shove. Mortia was feeling coy this evening.

An old man stared at him, too inebriated to fully grasp how Craven had appeared beside him. Craven shook his head slowly and walked into the street again, wishing he could just rest.

34
Accusations

The group gathered well rested in the tavern below, relatively empty in comparison to the night before save for the few late workers that had stopped for a drink before heading home themselves. They learned through morning gossip that a nearby town outside of the borders had been raided just over a week prior, but no one knew if it was Tarkal or another entity that had been the culprit. There had been no survivors of the raid, naught but butchered corpses now. Strangely, no supplies had been taken.

They ate the rest of their breakfast in relative silence after the grim news. Darion leaned his head in his hand after they had eaten, watching F'Lessa as she had her arms up to tie her hair into its customary braid.

"What?" she asked with a timid grin, that same canine poking out over her lower lip in such an endearing way.

Darion smiled back. "It's nothing, just interesting to watch the process that goes into that braid. I don't fully understand how it works, but it's pretty."

The table all had a slight laugh at his expense. "Ye've never braided Jess' hair?" Erika asked.

Darion simply shook his head, starting to feel a bit embarrassed by his lack of knowledge.

Craven took a drink from his flagon with a chuckle. "Even *I* know how to do braids."

F'Lessa's hand fell on top of Darion's opposite hand, warming it considerably. "I'll show you sometime, we can use Erika as a practice dummy," she said, giving the Fjordling an evil smirk.

"Hey now," Erika warded with a returned smile. "I'm not sure I trust Darion not to pull my hair out."

The hour after they left the tavern was spent perusing through the general store—balking at the prices—and purchasing simple supplies for the next leg of their journey. Erika tugged on the waistline of her long-sleeved tunic she had gotten in Sylvanna as they stepped outside. She had neglected to try the garment on in the city, the fabric nearly skin tight around her bust and thick arms while exposing several inches of midriff. She shrugged, throwing her ranger cloak over her shoulders and shuddering as the garment flooded warm air around that bare bit of skin. The temperature was even lower than the previous day, leaving a short layer of snow that piled around the buildings and road edges.

"You look strange with sleeves," Darion jeered at her.

She gave him a mocking scowl. "Maybe I'll get F'Lessa in some, how *salacious* would that be?" she whispered to him, prompting him to playfully slap at her. "Ye don't suppose the snow'll slow our pace?" she asked as they neared the edge of the town, more to the group than any one person.

Darion shrugged. "I imagine the roads close by here are still clear from foot traffic, but we may have to walk through some after that."

"Our larger problem will likely be the fog," Craven said, motioning to the thick haze that permeated the fields that they could see from outside the gates.

"And ye two are sure ye'll be fine without foot coverin's, even in the snow?" Erika looked to the two aash elves, pointedly glancing down to their naked feet and legs.

The two nodded, F'Skal adding. "We are plenty fine, even in snow, but thank you for your concern."

Shortly after, the companions were out of the border town and into the undesirable weather. The fog made it to where they could barely see more than two arm lengths ahead of themselves but they were able to stick to the road beneath their feet.

"The town that we heard was attacked, do you think it was those revenant creatures that attacked us?" F'Skal inquired Craven after a while.

"Possible," Craven said with a scowl. "Considering Tarkal has claimed no responsibility for the attack, but then, why would they?"

"Especially if it was such a slaughter," Darion added grimly.

Craven nodded to him. "My thought exactly. Tarkal would gain more by occupation, not by complete annihilation. It is also strange, taking into account that the attacked town had no allegiance in the conflict, one way or the other."

"Rough place to be though, right outside the front lines of a war," F'Lessa said.

"Between a rock and a hard place," Darion agreed with a shake of his head.

The rest of the day went by slowly, the group eventually coming into a wide open plain where the wind blew hard enough to keep the haze at bay. Still, the horizon was obscured and the road was difficult to make out under the snowfall, but they could at least finally see more around them. They had no real way to track time, as they couldn't see the sun or even really tell where it was between the overcast skies and the foggy atmosphere. Interestingly, they could only tell that the day was coming to a close when the world suddenly became brighter as the clouds illuminated with the approaching sunset.

They found themselves within a gathering of mounds with doors in the side of them, making for odd little natural homes surrounded by small farm plots. "Gaia elves?" Darion asked, drawing curious gazes from the two aash.

Erika nodded though. "Aye, I came across a village o' them on my way out o' Sildenfeld. Kind folk."

Craven stepped to the top of the hill after checking the interior of the abode through a window. "They were smart, as always. They've vacated the premises with only crucial belongings, they know war is coming."

"Friend o' mine used to 'ave a sayin' about gaias. Can't fer the life o' me remember what it was though," Erika said, picking and pinching at her lower lip as she thought.

A short while later and just off from the derelict gaia village, they began to make camp. Darion stepped off to find supplies for a fire with F'Lessa in tow. Erika used her abilities to clear the snow away from their chosen spot. After removing her leggings from beneath her skirt, she held the draping garment above her thigh as she immolated a single leg below her knee, dragging it behind her to melt the snow and evaporate the leftover slush.

F'Skal watched Craven out of the corner of his eye as he found stones to set in a tight circle in the middle of the area. The man was stalking around their chosen hilltop and peering into the whiteout as if he were looking for something, one hand resting on the hilt of his rapier. "What did you send out the night of the revenant attack?" he asked suddenly, causing Erika to pause and Craven to look over his shoulder with narrowed eyes.

"Whatever are you talking about, dear F'Skal?" he replied lowly.

F'Skal stood. "When I was in the tree, I watched a shadowy object roll down your arm. You spoke to it and released it as if it were some kind of strange bird carrying a message."

Erika looked to Craven with a raised eyebrow.

"I am afraid I still have no idea what you're talking about," Craven said, his voice lower than his normal registry. "Perhaps it was a trick of the light? Confusion during the chaotic battle?"

"I know what I saw!" the elf raised his voice in a more accusatory tone, causing Erika to shrivel slightly.

A long pause ensued, Craven staring at F'Skal with a sidelong look. "I say again. Perhaps you are mistaken."

Erika stepped forward, dousing her leg but hopping to keep her bare foot from the cold ground. "Alright, whatever this mistrust between the two o' ye is, I'm needin' it to stop. Or at least cool it down," she pleaded. Both men looked at the Fjordling who jumped back when they snapped to her, yet still she continued. "I understand ye don't trust 'im F'Skal, but I also understand that Craven may 'ave some secrets he doesn't want to tell."

F'Skal started to speak, but Erika held up a finger at him like she used to do to her father when he was being unruly with her or Irvine. "I 'ave things I 'aven't told all o' ye! None o' ye 'ave the full tale o' why I'm makin' this pilgrimage to the north. I 'adn't told any o' ye the details."

"Yes, but—" F'Skal tried again.

"And yet ye still follow me! Fer better or fer worse, ye're all followin' me, or at least walkin' in the same damnable direction!" she interrupted.

Craven stayed silent, still just standing there.

"So please, just *try* to get along," she said, clasping her hands and placing them on F'Skal's chest with a pleading face, only partially using him to balance on one foot. F'Skal looked down at her, seeming ashamed that he had inadvertently pushed her patience. She looked to the gaunt man a moment later. "If Craven wants to tell us somethin', he can. I trust 'im enough. He's a good person."

He lowered his gaze slightly, a sadness flashing behind his grey eyes. "Thank you for that, Erika. F'Skal, I apologize for not being forthright with you, but please understand..."

F'Skal looked to him patiently.

"I am sworn to certain oaths and duties, so please allow me to carry them out."

Silence ensued again, dampened only by the wind through the dale. F'Skal nodded slowly, Craven bowing his head in gratitude.

Still, both men walked off from the campsite to avoid each other, leaving Erika to slump onto the newly uncovered grass and take a deep sigh of relief. "Those two are gonna rip each other's 'eads off by the end o' this," she groaned quietly, taking her straight blade and waterskin from her satchel and starting to shave her legs.

35

LOVE AND LOSS

F'Lessa and Darion walked silently across the low hills covered mostly in just a thin layer of snow, with occasional thicker banks here and there. Darion's steps created troughs at times through the deeper sections. F'Lessa followed closely behind him, marveling at the wide open space around them broken only by the visage of the Crown of Patrias mountain range to their north. She had never seen such a large sky before, besides on the cliffsides of the northwestern isle, though this seemed even grander somehow. Her amazement was interrupted when she quite literally ran into Darion, who had abruptly stopped in front of her. "I'm so sorry!" she started to panic, thinking she had hurt him again.

He simply squeezed at her thigh after balancing, putting a finger to his lips to quiet her and pointing off into the field. She followed his gesture to a grouping of creatures that she had never seen or heard of before then. The largest of the massive deer-like animals were at least six feet at the shoulder, their incredible antlers adding another two feet atop their heads. There were more than a score and a half of the creatures in closely varying degrees of size, some younger ones bounding around the small herd.

"Elgas are such beautiful creatures," Darion said with a smile. "I've only seen them myself once before, when my family visited the far north of the Region when I was small."

F'Lessa found herself torn between watching the animals and watching him as he spoke in such wonderment. He pressed down on her thigh before crouching down and moving closer, gesturing for her to be quiet as she could. They were able to get within a few yards of the creatures as they passed through the area, Darion showing her how to appear non-threatening, allowing them an even better view of the migrating beasts.

He sat back slightly, resting his hands on his knees and staring off at the beasts as they moved past. "I'm glad I was able to see them again," he said, though he seemed not to say it to her particularly.

Now her eyes were on him intently, not noticing the calf that stalked over to them cautiously. She startled when she heard the small thing huff at them but Darion put his hand over her leg to still her, reaching into his pack and retrieving an apple that he rolled towards the small animal. It only came about halfway to them at first, one of the larger of the creatures watching at the interaction, but Darion coaxed it a little closer with the food that had stopped another half foot away from its nose. They both smiled as the young one gently grabbed the fruit and crunched into it with already strong teeth.

He slowly pulled his hand from her knee and looked toward her with a knowing grin. "I am sure you could defeat the big one singlehandedly, but this way we don't have to."

She nearly burst into laughter, realizing that she had just been thinking about fighting the great beast. Darion had so easily read her mind. She had always taken the hard route in her life, learning to speak with her fists more often than with her words, but he had seemingly grown in a much different way. She was frustrated when she couldn't figure out the language part to interact with others, but even still, he had connected with her.

Her eyes locked on his handsome face, watching the curl of his lips as he smiled at the creatures before them. F'Lessa almost didn't realize that she was leaning closer to him as he watched the calf trot back to its family. The hand that she had been leaning on came free of the ground, itching to reach out and touch him. Her face was barely a breath away from his as he turned to her. She barely understood her own actions, but lunged forward all the same, pressing her lips over his.

F'Lessa followed him as he backed away from her, until he was laying in the snow and she was draped over him. She couldn't have imagined anything feeling quite so euphoric, until he put his hands on her shoulders and pushed her back gently.

The act of rejection made her stomach sink, and she worried that she had done the wrong thing without thinking. She stared at him on the ground for the barest of moments before pulling away and sitting down again, the snow cold on her backside.

He sat up, silent for a long while. It felt like a scream was trying to pound its way free of her chest. She brought a hand to her breast and pressed, trying to rid herself of the sudden constricting pain.

"I'm sorry," he said flatly. "I don't think I'm prepared for that."

She looked into his eyes as he spoke and could see a conflicting light in them.

"I really don't know what to say," he muttered shakily, trying to lighten the mood with a slight laugh, reaching up and rubbing the back of his head lightly. Her eyes flinched when he winced, his fingers brushing against where his head was still wounded.

F'Lessa shook her head, starting to move away from him. "You don't have to say anything. I'm sorry. I shouldn't have done that, I just lost myself for a moment." She hated how her voice had started to crack.

Darion grabbed her arm, pulling her back to him. "That's not what I meant."

The elgas were nearly out of sight by then as they sat at the base of the hill.

"That was nice," he said quickly after struggling for a moment. "I just don't think I am in the right place right now."

She looked at him but moved her head to the side, away from his view as she tried to fight the tears. "Because I hurt you."

"Because I am unsure of *myself*," he corrected, as he tried to move into her line of sight again.

F'Lessa wiped a hand across her angled eyes and made a stern face, trying to fight her emotions to no avail. She could only guess at the rainbow of colors her hair was streaking in that moment.

"It isn't something I can forget," Darion admitted. "However, I also know that I was to blame as well."

"You were not to blame at all," F'Lessa groaned slightly, turning to him again. Her expression started to turn to anger, but she could no longer hold back the tears. "I am the one who hurt you, because I was afraid of what you were telling me."

"And I was being too aggressive."

"Your aggression should not have mattered!" she blurted, her voice breaking into a sob and her expression melting fully into sadness. Her cheeks shimmered with wetness and she felt her throat constrict as she fought to choke out the words. "You were telling me how you felt and I was being too defensive about it. I'm sorry that I rushed to you, even when you didn't need me, I was just so terrified of something happening to you."

Darion sat up and wrapped his arms around her, her head resting on his chest. "I know how you were feeling now, and I'm sorry I made you feel that way. I failed in Sylvanna and I worried you for my mistakes."

F'Lessa grabbed at him, toppling them into the snowdrift. She cried openly then, feeling like he would disappear if she let him go for even a moment.

"I'll try not to worry you anymore," Darion said, putting his cheek on her head, her wracking sobs shaking him hard as he stroked a hand over her hair. She was so warm against him, her body heat easily permeating through his clothes.

They lay there for a long while, as the overcast skies became darker around them. Eventually F'Lessa calmed, but still held to him tightly. Darion rubbed his fingers at the small of her back, sending lovely little chills up her spine at his cool touch. "We should actually get that firewood before it gets too dark. I don't think Erika wants to lounge in the middle of our camp as the fire all night."

F'Lessa giggled at the amusing thought, relenting and allowing them to stand again. She wiped at her eyes and nose, before Darion stepped forward and hugged her this time, his head partially pressing between her breasts. He didn't seem flustered by it, just holding her close with contentment. She was still sad that he had reacted so negatively to her kiss, but this was enough for now.

††

The night pressed on, the whole party falling into as restful of a sleep as they could considering the drop in temperature when the sun finally fell fully. Both Darion and Erika found themselves huddling between the aash twins and their unbelievably high body heat despite the biting cold. Craven was the only one who sat away from the group, not sleeping. He watched the four of them pressing together next to the smoldering fire. They looked so peaceful.

F'Skal was right. He had become callous in his duty and was dragging these four innocents into a struggle that they had no part in. He did not wish any of them to have a part in it anyway, although he worried that Erika at least would rush to his aid once he met his quarry. He began to lose himself, becoming distracted with his own thoughts and failing to focus on the watch that he had volunteered for.

He was just so... *tired*.

All he wanted was to rest. No matter how strong that want became, he could not find the respite he so desperately craved. He envied these young people he found himself traveling with, so lively and energetic.

So full of *love*.

He found himself watching them more, until Darion started to stir. He peeled himself from the inside of F'Lessa's shoulder, realizing where he lay and quickly sat back and away from her. Her arm still lay across his legs, which Darion seemed afraid to move. Craven couldn't help but smile at the two, even if Darion looked a little sad.

"Your feelings for each other are very mutual," he said, still trying to be quiet as he could.

Darion gave him a look. "I am starting to finally realize that."

"Then why not act on those feelings?"

Darion sat back, running his hands through his hair and looking at the aash woman. "I don't feel I deserve it."

"Why is that?"

Darion stared at the fire. "Guilt? Is that what it is when you fail to stop someone from killing themself?"

Craven's smile faded. "I believe you are correct in the word. But you mustn't hold on to things like that. You'll only destroy yourself."

"Thank you, Craven, but I don't feel like talking about this right now."

Craven sighed, nodding his understanding as he stood and stared out into the darkness. "Well, I think you two are very good for each other, as little as I'm sure that means coming from me."

Both of them fell silent, Darion holding his arms close for warmth, feeling F'Lessa's breath and soft nighttime moans against his leg. Craven gazed eastwards at the impending dawn. A tremor had them both falling very still. Darion looked up at the dark man. "Did you feel that?"

Craven nodded quickly and set to work packing any items he saw. "Wake them quietly, we need to move, *now.*"

Darion remembered a story his father had told him of the Region Wars that he had fought in briefly, the shaking of solid ground that heralded an approaching force, thousands of men and mounts moving into battle.

He began shaking his friends roughly, placing a hand over Erika's mouth when she started to loudly protest at the interruption of her rest. Once all three of them were roused, F'Lessa and Erika lazily looked to each other as they took over packing their things from Craven. F'Skal seemed alert almost immediately, the emerald dust around his sharp ears lighting in a more dim manner than usual. His eyes widened, appearing to almost glow in the darkness as the realization hit him. "A large force of soldiers is coming, isn't there?"

"We need to leave very quickly!" Craven said as loudly as he dared. "Everyone follow me once you are ready, but please, hurry."

F'Skal looked to Craven, again asking his question with just a look.

"There is," Craven confirmed. "And it's coming from Tarkal. As soon as they see the crest on Darion's shield, they will be on us, thus the urgency. *Haste,* my friends, I beg of you."

The sun began peeking over the eastern horizon, lighting the sky in brilliant colors, dampened only by the cloud cover. As they looked on they found a mass of shapes cresting the same horizon. Poles with flags and blades were held aloft, giving them an eerie visage like naked trees after a wildfire. They all knew that death would soon follow.

"Run, now!" Craven shouted as a battalion broke into a charge, sending clouds of snow into the air.

Darion uttered a string of curses as he fell over himself, F'Lessa reaching a hand under his arm and righting him. The companions pumped their legs with all the strength they could find and more than they thought possible. Yet still the peaks of the mountains to their distant north did not come any closer, while their pursuers closed the distance with great expediency.

Craven began to slow, F'Skal being the first to notice. He waved them on as the rest of them turned in confusion at Craven's abrupt stop. "Keep going" he shouted. "No matter what you see, *keep going!*"

Erika started to protest, baring her warhammer to prepare for a fight but F'Skal gripped the handle between her fists. "We cannot fight them, Erika!"

"He can't do it by 'imself!" she screamed back.

Craven looked to them and called again with more intensity to keep running. Erika felt tears welling in her eyes at the thought that she might lose one of her companions. F'Skal pressed her weapon down and grabbed her by the arm. "We need to go!"

They began their dash again but kept looking over their shoulders at their strange friend. The force came onwards, more than two score soldiers on the backs of large pholido mounts, wrapped in natural armor under their leather saddles. The beasts were not as swift as horses, but several times more imposing once they got into a charge. One soldier raised a long object made of metal and wood, a gout of flame firing from the end of it with a crack that made Erika nearly fall over in surprise. The others all held weapons high, red and silver banners of Tarkal billowing with the motion.

Craven whipped around, slinging daggers outwards. Several flew wide, but many hit between armor plates, causing the riders to fall from their plated mounts. His rapier ripped from its scabbard and he seemed to welcome the oncoming force with a taunting gesture. Another explosion rang out from the strange weapons, seemingly larger versions of the one Inquisitor Marq had used against Faxyyl, and Craven was thrown from his feet. Erika screamed in protest, but F'Skal dragged her further. F'Lessa came in a moment later and lifted the Fjordling from her feet and slinging her over a muscular shoulder. Darion kept his crossbow at the ready for anything that may impede their path.

Craven rose slowly, and even at the distance, Erika could see the red splashing against the snow. Still the dark man fought on.

Another mounted man in robes raised a staff on high and a bolt of energy cracked forth, though Craven was able to dodge the massive splash of melted snow. Darion turned back at the abnormal noise, his eyes going wide at the bright display of magic. "Seven Hells, I've never seen a mage before!" he said in shock. "Why are they here? All the stories I've heard said that Tarkal distrusted arcane magic!"

F'Skal turned and regarded the massive magical barrage as two more mages released gouts of energy. "And to my understanding arcanists have strict rules to abide by. Magic like that should be very difficult to enact without opening a portal to the realm of Daemons. It seems things have changed."

Erika heard the elf's words and immediately thought of the Daemon that had taken Irvine away from her. Zyrxak was an Elder Daemon. Her father, Irvine's uncle, and Sárif had fought Daemons before, but there had not been an Elder in the world since the end of the Chaos Age. Had the Sundering event done something to the nature of the world?

"It appears that magic is flowing more freely now," F'Skal continued, still urging them to move on. "That would explain how our druids were experiencing strange waves in their abilities as well."

Craven dove to the side, rolling through the snow past a fiery wave that left a void in the powder. He came to his feet and slung his left arm out, but no dagger came. Instead, a flowing sash of black energy like a shadow came forth, bolting the arcanist from his mount and onto the ground. They could not hear the ripping of flesh from where they were, only the screams.

Erika wanted to call out to Craven, but she failed to choke out the words as a soldier came from behind him and ran a blade through him. Craven bolted upwards from the strike, ramming his rapier backwards and through the very same soldier who fell a moment later. With great effort, he pushed his hand on the back of the blade and pushed it of his own body, falling to one knee in the obviously excruciating action.

A moment later they were in a great forest. Erika could no longer see Craven. Tears flowed freely from her face and onto F'Lessa's shoulder as they continued to flee. After what felt like hours had passed, they finally halted. F'Skal and F'Lessa barely seemed winded but Darion fell against a tree with an exasperated groan. "I'm not sure I can run any further."

Erika leaned on the other side of the tree, F'Skal coming over to her while F'Lessa bent downwards beside Darion. She put her hand on his shoulder and offered up her waterskin, Darion drinking from it gratefully.

"Are you alright?" F'Skal asked Erika.

She shook her head, her cheeks still slightly wet and frosted from the cold. "I didn't want to lose anyone else," she whispered through the lump in her throat. Her knees buckled and she slid slowly down the trunk and into a sitting position, burying her head in her knees and trying to wrest control of her breathing away from the panic.

F'Skal stood straight, looking around their current area and thinking about what they should do next. Darion glanced to him, taking another draw and swallowing heavily. "We should keep moving, loathe as I am to say it," he managed between breaths. "Tarkal soldiers are not known for letting stragglers escape easily, or at least that's how the stories always go."

"You think they'll give chase?" F'Lessa asked, taking the skin from him and drinking from it as well.

He nodded grievously. "They had to have seen that there were more of us. Even if they didn't see my shield, they have to assume that we are Sylvannans, we're too far west in the no-man's land. And if they assume we're involved in the conflict, they'll assume that we'll loop back and warn the garrison that there's an incoming attack."

"On the bright side, that means the group still remaining will be thinned, allowing the garrison an easier time?" F'Skal offered.

Darion chuckled nervously. "Except that the thinning force is still coming after us. Which I am not keen on fighting, even if I am an assigned knight to you all."

"We may have to," Erika hissed, though no one seemed to hear her.

A few moments later, they gathered themselves and began walking further northwards. It was quieter than ever it seemed, as all of them were scared to even take a breath.

36
MAGICAL RESURGENCE

The sun rose higher in the sky, reflecting off the snow in blinding rays. In the freshly coated dale, eleven corpses lay, their blood darkening the frost around them. One drew breath again.

Craven sat upright, putting his gloved hand to his head to quell the migraine that followed his resurrections. Across from him he saw the visage of Matron Mortia, her body contorted and her face more hideous than he had seen it in a long while. Her features were sunken, her dress and flesh beneath torn hideously. The bones of her fingers jabbed out into grotesque claws and her mouth of sharpened teeth let out a horrifying hiss. The souls she pulled on were resistant to her, however futile that may be. Craven almost pitied them, save for the fact that they had just killed him moments before.

He stood a moment later, dusting off his coat and rubbing at his chest where the broadsword had punctured through. Never would he understand how Vaerisa reveled in that pain. *Then again,* he considered, s*he is burying much more recent anguish than my own.* Perhaps at an earlier time in his existence, he may have done something similar.

With a snap of his fingers, his daggers and rapier returned to their sheaths. He ignored Mortia when she turned to him, refusing to look at her ghoulish form as he began to made his way north again. The marks in the snow suggested the soldiers had parted ways, some chasing his companions with the bulk of them pressing westwards. The armored tails of the pholido mounts made for easy tracking of the splintered men at least and now, Craven knew better what he was dealing with. Magic had returned to the power it had during the Chaos Age, and he had failed to notice it.

However, now was no time to dwell on mistakes. Now was time for a hunt.

⸭

The winds began to howl harder and the uncomfortable sand bit at Irvine's flesh. More of the Dragoon armor had fallen away, and there was still no word from Arce'Thrak. He wondered if the last of the Dragoon's life force had expired when he had transported himself and Zyrxak here but hoped that wasn't the case. How he desperately wanted someone else to talk to other than the Daemon.

He had now died more times than he could possibly count, bearing the scars from every battle. One stretched from his brow to his right cheek and crossed over his eye, which he had lost the use of for a while after. Thankfully his vision returned some time later, but walking and fighting with half his vision proved more difficult than he had imagined and he mentally commended his courier friend Dreyfus for his prowess despite his missing left eye.

Zyrxak seemed more pensive as of late, speaking less abrasively when he did but often not speaking at all. Irvine hardly minded since the mere sight of him reminded him of the situation he found himself in. He rested on a boulder, itching at the scar tissue of his leg where the flesh had been melted by the acidic Daemon he had fought before Zyrxak, before checking the worsening condition of his weapon.

"Company approaches," Zyrxak muttered lowly, his form descending to be more out of view.

Irvine looked up, pulling the spear from the sand and peering out at the two figures that walked towards them. One was a heavy individual with armor of blue and a large axe to match. The equipment looked strangely familiar, Irvine comparing it to the sparse pieces that remained on his own body. Next to him was a lithe form, bearing a strange mix of masculine and feminine features. It walked with an eerie smoothness that made it appear to almost float, though its impossibly thin legs obviously held it aloft.

"Interesting..." Zyrxak said, rising further in the air and drawing a curious glance from Irvine.

The first figure raised his axe high. "Lo, fellow wanderer!"

Irvine nearly fell from his feet in surprise at the non-violent greeting, but held his spear aloft in the same manner. "Hail!" he called with as much politeness as he could muster.

As he approached, Irvine could see that this man was indeed clad in very similar armor to the set he had been shedding, though his was much more vibrant and complete. "Greetings," he said as the stranger came close. "I am Irvine."

The man shook his head. "Names are unimportant in this place, young man."

Irvine recognized the sound of age in the stranger's voice, reminding him of his uncle whom Zyrxak had killed.

"It appears that you have a Dragoon weapon, and pieces, at least, of Dragoon armor," he continued.

Irvine nodded. "I was chosen as a Vessel for Arce'Thrak."

"I knew them," the man confirmed after a long sigh, looking past Irvine to Zyrxak. "It seems you have unfortunately fallen prey to our accursed duty."

Zyrxak grinned wickedly. "I always wondered what happened to Wyxia."

The lithe figure behind the man shifted their weight and looked up to Zyrxak with its featureless face. "Fair greetings, Elder Zyrxak, it has been some time," came a voice both masculine and feminine.

"Over a thousand years, Elder Wyxia," Zyrxak replied.

Irvine stared at the two Daemons during their odd reunion, then back to the Blue Dragoon before him.

"Wyxia is an Elder of the Lust Daemons," he explained. "I trapped it when we were locked in a stalemate, but unfortunately, the sealing magic encompasses both parties."

"What does it do to the Dragoon's spirit? And is there no way out?" Irvine asked, his voice faltering.

The Blue Dragoon simply shook his head, resting his axe on the ground below them. "I am sorry you have been forced to shoulder this burden. As for the absence of Arce'Thrak—which I infer you have experienced—the activation of the seal likely expelled the last of their lifeforce tied to their weapon. We were unsure as to how the Vessel magic would affect the Dragoon undertaking it. Many of us were against the idea, but times were desperate."

Irvine looked down to the lance at his side, and though he felt an incredible sadness, no tears came. He turned to Zyrxak slowly, an incredulous expression on his face. "You destroy my home, kill my uncle and countless others, and to make you suffer for it I must suffer with you."

"Do not forget burning your childhood home with your sires inside," Zyrxak added, scoffing at Irvine's expression. "You think I had not made the connection? I knew I had seen you before I was released fully. It seems we were destined for each other."

The Blue Dragoon reeled. "You destroyed this young man's home from *inside* a Consecration?"

Irvine slumped his shoulders and Zyrxak cackled. "Not the perfect prisons you thought they were, eh?"

Wyxia giggled. "Seems none of their methods are perfect."

The man placed his armored hand on Irvine's shoulder. "This is the best we can do for the world. These Daemons are tied to us here, meaning they cannot wreak havoc on those where we come from."

Irvine had a hard time swallowing his words, turning as Zyrxak looked off in the distance.

"Shame that the Seven Hells will always have an Elder, even if we are gone," Wyxia cooed, drawing a glare from the Blue Dragoon, but a chuckle from Zyrxak.

"Indeed, new leaders will always be appointed," the Wrath Daemon agreed.

Irvine sighed, the stranger saluting him sharply. "Good luck to you, Vessel. May you grow strong enough to forget your woes."

"And may death find you alive," Irvine found himself saying, the courier farewell.

The two parted ways, their respective Daemon companions following after them. Part of Irvine considered trying to walk with the kindred spirit, even if just for a while. However, the Blue Dragoon didn't seem to have any interest in the prospect, and Irvine figured Zyrxak and Xyxia would drive the both of them insane with their possible conversations. Irvine wasn't sure if he would ever find another friendly individual in this damnable place.

37

Massacre and Mercy

The sun began to set and Craven finally found the path nearing his quarry. Nocturne gryphons and the more common owls began stirring in the high treetops. The former of them looked on in interest as he passed, possessing an uncanny intelligence and awareness for what he truly was. The pholido mounts had been stowed a ways back, Craven taking a moment to cut the creatures of their bonds and setting them to the wilds. After they were freed, he moved on to the bootprints in the snow and soil. He recognized the older sets with the larger bare feet as his aash companions. Focusing on the newer tracks, he made his way quickly and silently. Slipping through the trees, he spotted a robed man with a staff and registered that it was likely one of the mages.

He'll be the first.

Craven crouched low to the ground, enacting his own magic and drifting into a formless black smoke. Around him the shadowy creatures that called him 'Lord Wraith' eagerly awaited his command. With unnatural swiftness he was on his prey, reforming above the mage's crouched form and driving a dagger into his right shoulder, wrapping his hand around his mouth to silence the man's cry. Down he sliced, giving the slightest grunt of effort as he snapped through the collarbone and ribs, arcing through the chest cavity. Blood cascaded like a waterfall onto the snow below, the man struggling to breathe as his right lung was punctured and torn. Craven slung his wrist to the side and took the mage's head with it, the neck snapping with a dull *crack*.

He looked to the right and pointed to the archer among the ranks. The shadow that seemed to be all mouth grinned horridly, lunging outwards with unnerving movements. A moment later, the archer's screams were muffled from inside that maw, legs twitching as bones snapped and more blood painted the forest floor.

The other soldiers turned, one of them loudly cursing as a brutish creature with no face slammed its fist into his chest and sent his body careening violently into a tree. His arm separated from his torso on impact, causing another man to fall from his feet in terror as blood rained from above.

More curses rang out, but Craven stayed silent. He moved forward in a flash to the next in line, drawing the terrified soldier's broadsword from the scabbard at his hip and turning it around in a horizontal slash, cleanly removing his helmeted head from his shoulders. The one behind him pulled the trigger on a crossbow, but Craven disappeared, the bolt driving into the headless man's torso. Craven reappeared before the man with the spent weapon, the sword suddenly appearing through his throat. He gripped and grabbed at the blade futilely, as his blood drained from his mouth onto the metal. His eyes were filled with fear in the face of Craven's passively furious expression.

"He's a damned ghost!" another soldier shouted, Craven angling the blade downwards and letting the dead man slide off of it to slump on the ground.

"I'm worse," he said darkly, throwing the weapon with a flick of his wrist. The man tried to dodge but the spinning blade caught him in the side, drawing a deep gash in his flesh through his armor. A larger man rushed to his aid, tower shield upwards and ready for an attack, however it did not protect him from beneath.

To both of their horror, a shadowy mass of tendrils rose from the ground, slipping into seams between their armor and constricting their bodies. Their screams ceased as gouts of blood emptied from the faceplates of their helmets. Craven looked on in grim satisfaction as the last was run down by a winged creature driving through his back and out his chest before continuing upwards as if it had simply hit a sudden gust of wind.

Craven straightened his coat and stepped lightly through the forest. Several trees had been painted a thick crimson, dripping with viscera. The shadowy creatures disappeared from view one by one, each thanking the Lord Wraith for allowing them to join in his battle.

As he moved past the one who had lost his arm, a gauntleted hand grabbed his ankle, Craven exhaled deeply as he looked down at the profusely bleeding man.

"Why were you in this forest?" Craven asked, almost annoyed, as he crouched over the dying man.

He spoke in labored gasps, wet with internal bleeding. "To pursue the scouts."

"There are no scouts," Craven replied, gently pulling the helmet from his head. His eyes were bloodshot and damp from tears. "You saw figures in the dark before dawn and assumed hostility. Yet they were merely travelers." The man stared into Craven's overcast eyes as he continued. "Aggression will always be met with aggression, and thus wars do not end. In this, I am no better."

The soldier looked remorseful now, but seemed unable to find words.

"What is your name?" Craven inquired with a sigh.

"Garreth," he said quietly, the sound coming with difficulty.

Craven took a deep breath, removing the glove from his right hand and dipping a finger into the pool of blood below him. He gently drew an ancient and forgotten rune on Garreth's forehead in the crimson ichor, speaking softly.

"I am sorry for your death, Garreth, but you must understand I was protecting that which I know to be important," he began, though Garreth seemed absent now. "Soon you will meet a woman, her name is Matron Mortia. If you have things you too wish to safeguard, then think of them as you fade. She will ask you three questions."

Craven slowly slid a needle thin dagger of the blackest metal from his coat, nearly imperceivable sigils scrawled on the cross hilt. He put it to the side of Garreth's neck. Craven's face faded away, leaving the expressionless skull of the Lord of Death.

Craven's jaw moved, his voice coming from it like whispers. "Answer these questions well, and she will give you the power to protect that which is worth protecting. Remember always, that *life* must be preserved."

Garreth's eyes looked up at that naked skull above him in sorrow, but also in understanding. He winced as the blade entered his flesh and punctured his spine.

The light faded from his eyes then, while the Lord of Death's empty eyes remained ever watchful.

"Matron Mortia, find this man Garreth with open arms and welcoming spirit. He has regret that he wishes to quell and I believe him genuine," he uttered quietly, lowering the body onto the ground and removing the thin dagger from his neck. He sighed deeply and stood, his face returning to that of a man.

As Craven departed, a spirit stood over his own dead body, looking on with an unsettled expression. He was joined by a woman in black robes and a blinding crown who smiled sweetly. Her voice carried on the wind in silvery whispers that Craven wished he could forget.

Never had he answered her questions, for never had she deigned to ask Craven.

⚔

Through the forest the friends trudged, still unsure of how to proceed with their possible pursuers and missing comrade. Even F'Skal found himself looking back and wishing that there was some way that Craven may have survived. Darion could only think on what he had said to him before they noticed the oncoming soldiers, looking to F'Lessa more often than not. Erika though, wore an expression of rage. Her legs pumped underneath her at a seemingly tireless pace, leaving her companions far behind her at times. She scanned the wooded surroundings and would occasionally catch sight of what seemed to be a person, but would find nothing more when she investigated further. Despite enjoying her pilgrimage again, she suddenly wanted this journey to be over. She wanted Irvine to be with her again, and for both of them to return home.

Except they had no home to return to.

Valen was gone, and she truly had no idea what she would do if she even managed to find him again. That grim thought halted her progress long enough for her companions to catch up to her again. Everything had been a downward spiral for so long and now that she thought of her situation, she was unsure of how to proceed. All she could do for now was to take another step forward. Her melancholic thoughts were interrupted a moment later when Darion exclaimed incredulously from behind her. "What in the Seven Hells?!"

She turned to find Craven stepping easily towards them, seemingly unharmed, as disbelief overtook her.

"Ye were run through!" she shouted, marching on the man sharply, who halted and stood his ground against her. "How are ye here, an' unscathed?"

Craven wore an expression of mock disappointment. "Are you not happy to see me Erika?"

She answered his question by simply tackling him into an embrace, her quivering breath warm on his neck.

"I think all of us are relieved, but confused," F'Lessa added, casually resting a hand on her axe.

F'Skal also stared at him, his face neutral and hard to read.

"You don't have to worry about pursuers," Craven said after a long silence. "We can travel freely once again."

"You killed them?" F'Skal asked. "One man—thought to be dead—slaying a full party or more of soldiers? Single handedly?"

"I have my ways," Craven said with a sardonic smile as he gently pulled Erika free of him. "Trust in me, friends, I have your best interests in mind."

He walked off then, making his way to the north and leaving the group with bewildered looks. Darion shrugged with some mirth. "Maybe he's immortal?" and stepped off himself, following after the dark man.

The rest of the group shook their heads, moving forward and eventually out of the forest. The Crown of Patrias sprawled before them, snow-capped mountain peaks just barely visible through the overcast sky and hazy landscape. Looking up at them, Erika was reminded of the Seraphine Mountains over her old home and felt a strange comfort in the valley. Darion, F'Skal, and F'Lessa all gazed up at the gargantuan display towering above them after so long in the empty fields. Despite them all growing up in areas nearby mountain ranges, this one still evoked a sense of awe at their sheer size. Craven though, marched on, silent as a hawk. He seemed to know exactly where he was going. The others could do naught but follow him.

38
DARKTIDE

The party arrived at the cave entrance of the port town, snow flanking the rough roadway just outside of the gates. The shifty men out front lacked the usual colors and armor of Region guards, Erika and Darion both grimacing in unison at the realization that they had left the society they had always known and called home. F'Lessa, F'Skal, and Craven however had no negative expressions about them, the former of them had very little real knowledge of the Regions, the latter though almost seemed to hold a sly grin at the prospect. He straightened his waistcoat as he led the group towards the great wooden doors, flipping his hat from his head and allowing his mane of raven hair to cascade around his shoulders.

"Greetings, friends. My comrades and I come to ask for passage across the Rift," he said with a flourishing bow to the two rough looking men who lounged next to the gates. Erika found herself gripping her hammer slung behind her legs especially hard, seeing these two with their common naval cutlasses resting across their laps like they expected to hurt someone, and eagerly awaited that chance.

"And what're ya offerin'?" the thin one on the right asked with a raised chin held pompously over the mild-mannered Craven.

Erika set her jaw, desperately wanting to bash in the irritating man's face due to his tone. Craven seemed to sense this and flashed her a knowing smile with a wink. "I apologize dear sirs, but we have no trade to offer, save for a fair amount of coin for the ship that grants us passage."

Now the man sat up, gripping his saber's handle and swaggering up to him. The contrast of their dress was astonishing, Craven's well kempt waistcoat and scarf making the guard's loose tunic and baggy pants look incredibly drab and dirty. "I don't think you're understanding, old man," he said, leaning down to look at Craven threateningly. "What're ya offerin' *me*?"

Craven stood steadfast against him. The rest of his party waited impatiently for his reply, all of them gripping their weapons and expecting a fight. A moment later, Craven's shoulders moved as if he had said something, although none of them heard anything from him. The guard fell over backwards with a stutter. His weapon tumbled from his hand and his partner's face paled as they both rushed for the doors, opening them with all haste. Craven applauded the two with his gloved hands and smiled back at his companions. F'Skal's wide eyes narrowed at the sudden compliance. Erika simply shrugged and followed after Craven as he waltzed through the open doors, the two guards staring at him as if they had witnessed their own deaths.

"Darktide awaits," he announced with an echo in the tunnel.

† †

They walked through a long and straight underpass, lit only by torches every so often and manned by more guards in between. They did nothing to hinder them, simply lounging at different sections of the cavern. Eyes followed them, some suspicious and wary, others salacious and leering. Craven forged ahead stronger still, the others pushing through the uncomfortable air to follow him.

When they finally arrived on the other side, they gawked at the sight before them. The tunnel opened into a massive cavern, the ceiling far above their heads and the yonder side completely open to the water and sky of the expansive Great Rift that separated Patrias from the Fjordlands. All around them was stone and wood fashioning the docks and ramshackle buildings of the independent city. The place was in constant motion, ships of varying size moving out of the harbor and into the waters of the Rift while men and women moved to and fro with crates and sacks. Most wore thin and loose cotton shirts and drab trousers, their boots the only part of their wardrobe that seemed serviced.

Across the jumble of civilization from them, and on the side of a dock hung a massive creature, its tail held aloft from a crane more than twenty feet overhead. It dripped seawater and blood off of its giant fins and strange tentacles as a crew of butchers carved through its rough hide. Erika felt much less out of place here, as she was hard pressed to find anyone that didn't have a myriad of tattoos across their skin. Some depicted sea creatures that she did not recognize, while others bore anchors or swords that seemed to have some significance. Several even had large flowing markings that more so resembled her Ignis tattoos, though not the bright color or covering quite as much flesh.

The veritable town was lit amazingly well, the light from the sky reflecting from the water and giving the entire city a look of waving movement as it shimmered on the cavern ceiling high above. Erika turned and found that her other three companions were just as awestruck as she was, but all of them snapped to attention when Craven called their names one at a time and pulled them into a tight huddle.

"Everyone here is out for themselves and themselves alone. This is one of the most dangerous modern settlements in the realms," he informed quietly, all of them nodding their understanding. "Keep your coin purses tight and your hands close to your weapons. F'Skal and F'Lessa, keep close watch on your clothing straps, lest someone try to cut them as a distracting prank. We are now in the haven of liars and murderers, and you would likely all be appalled by their 'judicial' system."

Darion grimaced at his inflection of the word, raising his hand sharply as he was wont to do. "What are we to do if we are attacked or someone attempts a theft?"

"Lay them low, perhaps a good bash with that new shield of yours," Craven answered bluntly. "Avoid killing if you can, though the city is hardly sore for population."

Darion looked a little sick from that answer.

Erika glanced around them, seeing the point of his statement in the massive sea of people around them. She began to wonder if their private conversation was really so private.

"I suggest if we are to stay here for a night, we share a single inn room," Craven continued. "It will be cramped and awkward, but I would feel more at ease if I could see all of my companions at once, so don't stray off."

All of them nodded amiably, besides F'Lessa, who looked put out by the orders to not wander around. Craven noticed her side glance and offered with a sigh. "If you must explore, take someone with you at the least."

She brightened immediately. "Darion," she cooed in an uncharacteristically singsong tone.

Darion shrunk slightly and gave her a sheepish grin while glancing around.

"I'll go with ye too," Erika added. "Strength in numbers."

Craven clapped his gloved hands sharply, bringing all of their attention back to him again. "Right then, you three go find something to *not get in trouble with,* while F'Skal and I will garner passage for the morning."

F'Skal looked as if he wished to protest, but stayed silent.

"We'll meet at that inn, before nightfall," Craven declared, pointing to a nearby tavern, labeled *The Serpent's Bane.* A line of women stood on a second-floor balcony, lifting thin skirts and pressing up cleavage at passers-by. Darion's eyes widened and face flushed while F'Skal scrunched his nose lightly.

"It's a brothel," Erika laughed.

"It's a central place that we can all see from here," Craven amended with a heavy sigh.

They all nodded and started off in opposite directions. As Erika's group approached a wharf she paused, gazing out onto the water. The towering Fjords were just visible over the horizon, and she felt a sudden fear grip her stomach. She was so close to her ancestral homeland, but was unsure of what she would find there.

"Erika, are you alright?" F'Lessa asked, Darion looking past the aash's shoulder at her.

Erika nodded, shaking her head free of her errant thoughts before following after them.

† †

"We feel the presence, Lord Wraith. He is here," a small bird-like creature whispered from high above. Only Craven could hear it. "Your quarry is at hand."

Craven blinked hard and felt himself taking a deep breath. *Amusing that I should be nervous about this, after so long in my line of work,* he thought.

"So, where are we to find aid in such an apparently hostile city?" F'Skal asked, halting the dark man's private musings.

Craven held up a finger. "When you travel as much as myself, you make a few friends."

"Enemies as well," F'Skal shot back with an annoyed tone.

"Indeed, so let us hope we find the friend first," Craven agreed with a chuckle.

††

Erika, F'Lessa, and Darion found their way to the market area of the city, Darion assuring them that he knew the way back to the inn. Despite his original nervousness, he seemed to be taking fully to the city, looking through several trinket shops before arriving at a food stall with an enthusiastic "Ah!"

"What *is* it?" F'Lessa whispered to Erika, crossing her arms and hunching just slightly towards her ear. The dark elf's hair gently streaked a dull green, suggesting some kind of uncomfortable emotion.

Erika shrugged, pointing to the stall. "The sign on the side says 'squid', but I'm not entirely sure what that is exactly."

Darion returned with three of the arrow-shaped creatures on wooden sticks, offering one to each of the girls. "Either of you ever had squid before?"

Both of them shook their heads, delicately taking the skewers from him and glancing back at the massive monster being butchered by the docks, noting some resemblance.

"Some of the best food the sea can offer!" he said jovially. "We don't get it back home but when I visited Sylvanna, I would always get some. I'd forgotten to look for anyone selling them when we were there, so I'm glad I could get it here."

F'Lessa flicked one of the dangling tentacles with a finger and scowled at the roasted sea beast. "I *love* your enthusiasm, Darion, but this seems... inedible."

"I assure you it is," Darion grinned, biting three of the appendages off at once. "The tentacles are a bit chewy, so don't be surprised by it."

Erika gingerly took a bite of one, her expression turning to puzzlement at the strange texture. She looked at F'Lessa, who stared at her hesitantly. "The flavor is kinda nice," she shrugged between chews.

By the time the two looked back at Darion he had already finished his squid and was nibbling absently on the remaining stick. "Since you two are still eating, I'll make my way just over there. Don't worry, I'll stay in eyesight."

F'Lessa seemed reserved, but Erika nodded at him and he darted off to a nearby shop built into the cavern wall. She glanced between the two, but F'Lessa was surprisingly absorbed by the food she was given.

"I don't want to waste it when he was so gracious to purchase one for me," she said, her voice shaking as her hair continually streaked that same sickly green.

Erika glanced back again to look at the sign outside the store that Darion was in, confirming that they sold jewelry and other accessories. She had to stifle a laugh at F'Lessa's lack of attention, able to pass it off as amusement at their current predicament. She took another bite, nudging her friend to actually try it. She bared her teeth, Erika slightly surprised at the size of her canines, and took the slightest of bites off of the same hanging tentacle that she had flicked with her finger. Her face wrinkled up at the immediate sensation of the texture Darion had warned her about, but she looked at Erika with a surprised look.

"The flavor is *somewhat* nice," she said, echoing Erika's statement with much less enthusiasm, wincing with every chew.

Erika took another bite of her own, watching Darion return with a satisfied smirk on his face, although it vanished quickly when Erika gave him a sly look. F'Lessa was taking another bite when Darion put a stern finger on his lips to silence Erika, who stuck out her tongue at him before giving a quick wink and jabbing at his side with a grin.

"How do you like it?" he asked the elf woman after fending off Erika's playful assault.

She gave him a sheepish smile as she struggled through her second bite. "It is... interesting."

He laughed with a shrug. "It's alright if you don't care for it, I'll eat it if you don't want to."

F'Lessa happily gave the stick back to Darion who let out another laugh and patted her on the lower part of her back. With that, F'Lessa took it as her turn to wander and stepped down the street, leaving them to follow.

"So... what'd ye get?" Erika asked Darion as they walked, F'Lessa a wide elven pace ahead of them.

Darion couldn't help but smile. "I bought some pieces of bone to try out scrimshaw on, and a tool to help with it too. For F'Lessa, I got a chain bracelet that she could wear on her wrist or ankle. I couldn't see her wearing much else."

"Aye, I can agree with ye there," she replied, watching the scantly clad aash elf as she looked around in wonder at the dockside city, both of them idly wondering when she had removed her cloak. "I'm sure she'll love it," she assured him, wrapping an arm around his neck to yank him towards her and pressing her lips to the top of his head.

"Didn't mention before, she... kissed me."

Erika whirled on him. "She what?"

F'Lessa glanced back at the commotion of her friends, but they simply waved her off. Darion continued, suddenly shy under the scrutinizing gaze of the Fjordling that had become a kind of older sister to him. "Yeah, when we went to go get firewood last night. I didn't quite accept it though."

"Too soon after yer injury?"

Darion shrugged, obviously nervous to go into more detail. "Something like that. But, I'm afraid I upset her. So maybe the chain will help?"

Erika nodded. "Anythin' ye do with love fer her'll help. I promise ye that."

Darion smiled back at her before they both quickened their pace to catch up with F'Lessa.

† †

Craven and F'Skal walked along the side of the docks, dodging work hands and guards as they went. F'Skal could instantly recognize that the man had been here before as he seemed to know his way around exceedingly well. He simply followed as best as he could, avoiding the curious glances under his hood. Thankfully, the weather was cooler and the cloak was not as much of a bother to wear. He did fear for his sister, who was generally more hot skinned than he was, he only hoped she wouldn't remove her cloak when Erika and Darion weren't paying attention. He did as Craven told him, keeping a palm on his satchel and the other on one of his shortswords while keeping an eye open for dexterous hands.

Finally, they reached their destination, a dock where others seemed to avoid. Craven greeted a surly man with a thick grey beard, leaning against a large crate beside the gangplank of a ship. His face was tanned from sun exposure and scarred in multiple areas, a cloth over one eye as a makeshift patch. He wore a long grey overcoat, F'Skal noticing the large cutlass blade hidden underneath as well as two of the firearm weapons like Inquisitor Marq had used against Faxyyl.

"Craven," the man muttered slowly. "There's a face I truly never thought I'd see again."

Craven smiled at him. "Wonderful to see you, Jekal."

F'Skal grimaced when Jekal grunted at Craven's greeting, unsure if this was one of the friends or enemies Craven had spoken of.

"And what are you wanting, Wraith?" he asked.

Craven glanced back at F'Skal with an awkward look, then turned to Jekal with a grin. "To hire you and your services of course."

"You can get around the Rift with no issue. I know your ilk," he spat back quickly, lighting a short wooden pipe and blowing smoke out towards Craven.

F'Skal narrowed his eyes at the two of them, Jekal serving to further his suspicion of the dark man.

"But, your friend cannot traverse so easily," Jekal said, looking up at the aash. "Shame he seems awfully wily around you, not that I blame him."

"I have three more companions as well," Craven added lowly,

Jekal grunted again. "What do you offer me? Your head?"

"I believe that is uncalled for, sir," F'Skal interjected.

Jekal scoffed. "False sense of righteousness in this one."

"You could also speak with me as an individual, Master Jekal," F'Skal shot back.

"Hard to do so when I do not have your name to address."

"F'Skal is my name. Now, what can you offer *us*? Safe passage on the Rift?" the aash asked.

Craven wore an expression of annoyance suddenly. "F'Skal, stop this. I can handle the negotiations."

"He obviously seems perturbed by your mere presence, Craven. Not that I can blame *him*, you often irk me as well."

Jekal burst out laughing. It was a raspy, wheezing sound. "Seems like he's got a better head on his shoulders than you, perhaps I should request his as payment." F'Skal gave him another sharp look, to which Jekal rolled his one eye. "Come aboard. We'll talk in the cabin."

They climbed up the gangplank of the ship, F'Skal looking down at the water far below the wood and stone and feeling just a slight bit dizzy. The feeling worsened when his bare feet thumped down onto the deck of the ship, the gentle rocking in the tide causing him to stagger. Jekal gave him a look of near concern before walking into the doorway. Inside was a lavish room with a furnished bed on one side and a full bookshelf on the other. Towards the back, before a great open window overlooking the busy harbor, was a desk piled with papers and inkwells. Jekal stepped around the desk and lowered himself into the high-backed chair, releasing another puff of smoke that lingered in the still air. F'Skal walked to the other side of the room, trying to focus outside the window to subside the nausea, while Craven stood on the opposite side of the desk from the sailor.

"You know I have a reputation to uphold, Craven. And I just returned from carting a group of refugees to the west," Jekal said after a long drawn out sigh.

"As do I, Captain," Craven began, giving the man a more aggressive look now. "And frankly, it is my companions who need the passage, not me."

"Indeed, we have a Fjordling among us who seeks her homeland," F'Skal interjected, looking to Craven in confusion upon realizing his words. "You are not coming with us?"

Jekal leaned in, his eye going between them with suspicion. "What color is her hair?"

Craven sunk a little, F'Skal speaking up after a moment. "Auburn red, why?"

"Radur clan is dead, Craven!" Jekal said in a sudden aggressive tone after his one eye had gone wide at the description. "You didn't think to tell her that her clan has been gone for twenty years?"

F'Skal's expression darkened. "She has no home to go back to..."

Craven shook his head slowly. "I did not wish to sully her plans, only to aid her."

"I do not truly know her intentions, they could lie elsewhere, all I know is that she is looking for someone," F'Skal offered.

"Always thinking of others, aren't you Craven?" Jekal chastised.

"What is it exactly that you do, Captain Jekal?" F'Skal asked, distracting the both of them from what seemed close to being an argument or fistfight, though he could not pinpoint which.

Jekal stood up abruptly, jamming a thick dagger into the desk with a slam, causing F'Skal to jump back slightly. "I'm the most ruthless damned pirate you'll ever meet and don't you dare insult me, boy, lest you escape this place with your life!"

Craven snickered in the corner of the room, drawing further confused glances from F'Skal.

"That's the reputation anyways," Jekal said in a calmer tone. "In reality, I ferry people to and fro across the continent. Though I don't much go to the Fjordlands."

"And what must we actually pay you, for the passage?"

"Nothing, my large elf friend," he said with a sigh. "I do it for charity, and for those who have no other options. You and your companions are welcome aboard in the morning and we'll be underway."

"Thank you, Jekal," Craven said quietly.

"I do none of it for you, Wraith!" Jekal spat with a pointed finger.

"Why do you call him that?" F'Skal asked, drawing a glance from both men.

Craven shrugged at the elf with a wry grin. "Reputations."

† †

Erika, F'Lessa, and Darion sat in the middle of the busy tavern room of *The Serpent's Bane*, each of them shrugging off bumps and nudges from other patrons. F'Lessa grimaced deeply at the seafood stew that was provided to them, picking idly at the shells of the underwater creatures as they poked above the creamy liquid. She smiled quickly when Darion looked over at her, even though he had learned her disdain for unfamiliar food well enough by now. He scooted his chair closer and set to educating her on the different crustaceans within, Erika leaning in out of curiosity as well.

Across the room, they did not see the eyes watching them from underneath a white hood. Kharim stared at Erika with unsure dread, the unseen specter of Hargreave growling intently next to him. It took all of Kharim's willpower to stop the murderous man from lashing out, as a scene would be bad for him considering the number of capable fighters in the room.

The doors opened from the darkening cove, Craven and F'Skal stepping in and making their way over to their companions. Kharim caught the eyes of the shadowy man, who lingered on him for a long while. To his confusion, the man also made eye contact with Hargreave. Kharim looked between the two as they locked eyes.

They sat down a moment later, Craven greeting his companions and pulling one of the cups closer to himself. He looked at the strange pair in the corner again, then turned as if retrieving something from behind his chair.

"Inform Jekal that we may need to leave sooner," he whispered to a shadow.

Darion handed F'Skal the loincloth that F'Lessa had previously been wearing, shaking his head at his confused expression. "She took off her cloak in the market and a kid cut the string before snatching at Erika's satchel. I just want you to check my knot before she puts it back on."

F'Skal laughed, causing his sister to shrink in her chair. She adjusted her cloak under her thighs—which she had been using as a skirt since the incident. Erika leaned in towards him while he double checked Darion's work, listening to his words about the

366

interesting man who would be transporting them until Craven caught her attention.

"Do you happen to know those men?" he asked her, motioning back to the two. "The one in the white hood and the other with the disfigured face."

"I see the white hood, but I don't see the other one," she said, the first man's light fabric mantle angling down suddenly and obscuring her view.

Hargreave made his own eye contact with the young woman who could not see him and Kharim felt a thread suddenly snap. "Damn you Haranian, I'm ending this now!"

"No, stop!" Kharim found himself saying, a little louder than he intended. He lifted from his seat suddenly, his hood falling as he gripped the handle of his weapon hard. Hargreave halted mid-stride, as if he had been frozen by some unseen force.

Erika glanced over again. "Kharim?" she asked with a smile. She started to stand, Craven noticing too late to stop her after fixating on the aggression of the disfigured man.

Kharim stared at her pleadingly, wishing he was anywhere but here. Hargreave turned around slowly, fighting the Haranian's hold on his spirit. He gripped Kharim's hand around the hilt of the weapon and began to squeeze.

Erika stepped over towards Kharim as he winced from the pain of Hargreave's grip. "Run, please..." he uttered towards her, able to speak no louder than a whisper.

His eyes lost focus, as he felt the sting of tears.

The glass handle of the sword shattered.

Craven's shoulders slumped. "Shit."

39

Tides of Darkness

An unnatural shadowy force flooded outwards, sending all within the tavern onto the floor in a sudden wave of pressure. Revenants sprang forth from their shattered prison and immediately let into the tavern patrons with swords, axes, hammers, and spears. Craven watched it all with pure hatred in his eyes.

Erika flew over her chair as Hargreave suddenly stood over her. "Time for revenge, Spitfire!" he cackled gleefully.

Darion got his shield up just in time as a blade tip came over him, but couldn't reach his own weapon dangling from his chair. He quickly rolled over to block an axe away as it came towards F'Lessa. She looked at him, her dark eyes widening as he felt the sting of metal enter his body. She screamed, swinging her own axe outward with her ruby dust flaring brightly. Her weapon broke through the sword that pierced Darion's side, causing him to grunt painfully at the twist in his fresh wound. The revenant above them went flying back from F'Skal's arrows, who had successfully dodged to the side of the tavern.

The elf grabbed as much of their supplies as he could. "F'Lessa, get Darion! Craven, Erika is yours!" he shouted, slinging more arrows outwards and banging a nearby table loudly to garner the attention of the revenants. *"On me, dead ones!"* he screamed in his native tongue as he dashed out the door with several of the shadowy warriors in tow.

Kharim sat in the corner, the glass of the weapon's hilt jutting into his bare hand while the eerily shifting sand within seeped into his open wounds. His eyes shifted from their base brown color to a brightened gold, tears flowing freely from them. Craven stared at him from across the room, creatures of shadow fended the revenants away from him and his companions as he waded through the sea of darkness. He wrenched Darion to his feet with one arm, still watching the Haranian warily. Darion grabbed at the sword tip in his side until F'Lessa stopped him. "Just leave it for now," she urged, as she helped him through the doorway.

Erika rolled over backwards, immolating her forearms and crossing them over her head as Hargreave's blade came crashing down. She gasped loudly at the pain, the metal actually penetrating through her hardened flesh. Bright orange droplets of her molten blood rained down before her and returned to crimson before landing on the ale flooded floor. She threw her hands outwards, catching the side of the blade as it came down again and threw it to the side. She drove her other fist outwards and planted it directly into Hargreave's side, causing him to hunch heavily from the blow.

"Ye're supposed to be dead!" she screamed through the cutting sensation.

Hargreave glowered at her. "I've come back just to make sure you join me!"

Craven knelt in front of Kharim's seemingly catatonic body. "What have you done?"

The Haranian's shining gold eyes looked to him in agony. "I only wanted justice."

"Justice is flawed," Craven uttered, looking to the blade lodged in his hand. "This weapon of Necromancy cannot give you that."

"The Abyssal Hand," Kharim said, now with rasping breath. "They destroyed my homeland with Daemons and murdered my people for sacrifices."

Craven was familiar with the Abyssal Hand's rise in the south, wiping over half of the country from existence with Daemonic insurgences, even despite not knowing the key to the summoning yet. Every Daemon was tied to a cult member and when their time expired, so did their summoner. It was a massacre on both sides. However, the existing Abyssal Hand of the Patrian Regions had little, if anything, to do with it.

Craven tried to take the Necromantic weapon from him but he could not release his grip. Craven saw the change too late. Kharim's hand lifted and Craven was blown through the wall of the tavern with a massive blast of force.

Hargreave ducked in surprise as the blast happened, nearly losing sight of Erika. She had escaped to the street, barely able to grab her belongings as she went, but halted just outside at the violence that surrounded her. Darktide had turned to chaos, revenants flooding everywhere and massacring the people who still fought back savagely. She couldn't see where her companions had gone, only able to focus on Hargreave as he quickly caught up to her. She swung her hammer outwards, smashing it across Hargreave's vulnerable jaw then spun it over and slammed it across again. The Heathen's head snapped to the side violently, only held by a thread of flesh.

Hargreave still stood and, to Erika's horror, simply snapped his head back into position. "Seems I've gotten a bit more resilient than all that."

Erika didn't let up, spinning her hammer back around and continuing her assault. Hargreave backpedaled heavily, unable to retaliate through the force of her blows. Craven started to heave himself upwards from underneath the remnants of the wall, looking on as his companion battled a ghost that she had no hope of defeating. Thankfully he knew Hargreave would not last long either, but he had to get to her quickly.

Up and up came Hargreave again, recovering from every blow and laughing the whole way. He taunted Erika continuously, although many of his words came slurred from the force of the hammer strikes. She stopped a moment later, as the temperature around them dropped dramatically. Hargreave could not feel the cold, but he could feel the dread. His single remaining eye winced as he looked at Erika.

"She ruined me!" he pleaded to nothing. "I have the right to her life, you cannot take this from me!"

Erika gasped sharply as his head flew from his shoulders, disintegrating into dust in an instant. The body similarly dissolved into nothingness as Kharim stood behind it, his eyes ethereally golden but lifeless.

"Kharim?" she asked with a wince, hardly recognizing the man who had shown her kindness outside Stonewall. It felt so long ago now.

The ghostly shell looked down at her and brought the curved blade around in an arcing slash. Erika moved to the side, bringing her hammer up in a hesitant defense. Craven pushed free of the rubble and flashed towards them too late.

The sickle-like blade cut through the metal haft of Erika's warhammer and then Kharim pressed it forward into a stab. The tip penetrated easily through her armor and into her breast. She let out a gasp of surprise and pain as she began to fall backwards.

Craven cursed, catching her as she fell and covering her eyes. Both of them instantly faded into darkness. Several streets away they reappeared, Craven retching loudly as the toll of dragging a living being through the Veil tore violently at him. Erika lay next to him, her eyes wide open and watering as she struggled to breathe. Frost from the brief travel through the deathly realm began to disappear from her cheek as her arms came up towards his face. "Craven, don't leave, please," she pleaded with a weak voice as he stood.

Craven drew his blade, snapping his fingers to a shadow near him to find help. He let out a furious scream at himself and his lack of caution. He readied himself for Kharim's imminent arrival.

† †

Down the street further still and nearly to Captain Jekal's ship, F'Skal loosed arrows endlessly at the revenants as they poured through the alleys and buildings like waves flooding through a labyrinth. F'Lessa carried Darion who clutched at the blade lodged in his side, spreading his own blood as it seeped through his tunic.

"Well, that's not good," he muttered as he lifted his hand and looked at it, his eyes starting to lose cohesion.

F'Lessa screamed back at him, freeing tears from her dark eyes. "Stop talking, Darion!"

371

Jekal stood at the edge of the dock and hurried them down, recognizing F'Skal and assuming the rest. A group of revenants seemed to see what they were doing and changed their course from chasing the dark elf, slamming weapons into the hull of the ship with savage abandon before F'Skal could release more arrows to dispatch them. Jekal let out a curse, firing one of the weapons from his coat and flinging one revenant into the water below.

"Get on board, now!" he roared at F'Lessa, turning to the crew already on the deck and barking orders at them to ready the ship.

F'Skal drew his shortswords after throwing his bow and the belongings he had to the deck, He turned to defend their escape, becoming increasingly worried over Erika and Craven. As the revenants seemed to pool further, a flood of darkness swept through and an army of horrifying creatures took the undead warriors from behind. F'Skal winced at the carnage and fell into stance to defend against these new entities until a winged one landed on a crate next to him, like some sort of strange bat. Its body opened into a massive maw that let out a high-pitched warning. "Craven calls for aid! The Ignis is gravely wounded!"

F'Skal's confusion deepened, before Jekal nodded at him and moved to help the crew begin make way.

"Follow me to the Lord Wraith!" called the disturbing creature and flew over the crowd, the shadowy monsters clearing a path between F'Skal and the street they came in on. On he ran, his bare feet slamming into the cobbled stone below, slashing at the occasional revenant that broke through the tides of darkness. He just hoped he wasn't too late.

The winged creature landed next to Erika on the street and angled its wings in a pointing motion towards her. F'Skal nodded, looking up at Craven who stalked down the street a ways down waiting for the source of the revenants. The dark man held his rapier low, his whole body taut with violent intent. The elf skidded to the ground beside Erika, wincing at the skin ripping from his knees. He quickly and efficiently unbuckled her armor and carefully slipped her shirt from her torso to get at the wound just above her left breast. It seemed to pump blood forth like a geyser while jagged glowing yellow lines radiated across her chest. He tore a section from his cloak and used it to staunch the blood flow and looked to the winged creature. "Can you hold this down?"

The strange entity said nothing, but stepped up onto Erika's right arm and pressed the tips of its wings onto the cloth. F'Skal nodded, and began to ready the black moss from his bag. "Erika, I am not sure if you can hear me right now, but this will be uncomfortable."

Erika looked to the cavernous ceiling, tears falling down the sides of her face as she coughed and wheezed. A woman in black with a strange mask appeared above her, a smile spreading across her dark lips. She simply shook her head slowly at Erika.

F'Skal readied a large wad of the medicinal paste, the creature pulling the cloth out of the way for him to drive his fingers deep into Erika's chest cavity. He carefully spread the moss through the wound, closing his eyes and allowing the emerald dust to guide his feeling.

Erika screamed a moment later, the burning sensation of the moss grafting into her flesh was unbearable even in comparison to the original wound. F'Skal pressed one hand to her chest to keep her down as he added more of the moss. He placed a new section of cloth over it and gestured to the small being once more. "Hold it again!" he commanded the shadowy bat. He shouldered the Fjordling's things, before wrapping her body in his cloak and lifting her in his arms. "Keep pressing!" he urged Craven's bat-creature that still stood on Erika underneath the cloak, balancing against F'Skal's collarbone. She moaned into his chest, tears still flowing forth.

"Craven!" he shouted. "I have Erika!"

Back through the same streets he raced, shadows deftly defending him from stray revenants as he pumped his legs underneath him. Finally, they arrived at the ship and, against F'Lessa and F'Skal's arguments, Jekal set off from the dock.

"We have enough damage as is!" he shouted at them. "We'll be lucky to make it to Mintheras! Craven can handle himself!"

Erika lost consciousness a moment later.

40

Where Titans Wage War

The town quieted as the surviving denizens found places to hide from the ravaging undead. The remaining specter of Kharim called them back, facing Craven.

"You have not the power to fight me, Shade!" Kharim called, although his voice was layered with many, no longer truly belonging to the Haranian. The dark man had fended him off thus far, standing with a steady hand and unlabored breath.

Revenants crowded at Kharim's back, and so too did shadows cling to Craven's sides. Two massive waves of pitch, primed to crash against one another.

"You are merely a blade," Craven said to Kharim's unblinking eyes. "A weapon, who thinks it the master now. Your power wanes with each passing moment as your sand drifts onto the wind."

Kharim's eyes flinched, knowing the truth of Craven's statement. With that slight movement, Craven's shadows flooded forwards, violently crashing into the wall of revenants with a deafening blast of sound and force.

Kharim flashed past the line of battle, crossing blades with Craven in a splash of sparks. Kharim moved the blade downwards and to his right, slinging his left fist outward into a strike. Craven dodged the blow carefully, closing the distance and kicking his boot downwards into Kharim's left knee with inhuman force. The joint snapped and fell backward awkwardly, though Kharim showed no pain. He crossed his curved blade over his chest in a rushed parry of Craven's rapier that left him even more unbalanced.

The waves around them ebbed and flowed with their battle, two creatures of darkness battling on the edge of the world.

Through Kharim's sternum pierced Craven's rapier, shoving him to the ground as Craven deftly moved over his opponent and returned to a standing position. Kharim stood again, his broken leg cracking back into shape with a sickening *snap* before he turned to rush Craven. Just as his momentum began, it was quickly bashed to the side as the edge of a metal shield crashed into his jaw and sent him careening nearly into the water.

The torrential storm of darkness fell suddenly still, the overcast sky becoming visible once more.

Craven looked to the newcomer, a knightly warrior armed with an ornate sword and a shield whose emblem had been purposefully scratched away. The warrior raised the visor over his face and saluted Craven with a raise of his blade. "Good to see you, Lord Wraith, may I join you in this conflict?"

"You already have, Garreth," Craven smirked. "Now pay attention. This is our worst of enemies, the embodiment of Necromancy and the Spirit of Undeath."

Garreth nodded resolutely, slamming his visor back down and readying his stance.

"So, two Shades come to die," the specter that was once Kharim called in its layered voices, raising to its feet again in a single motion. "The Creators shall be pleased!"

"The Creators are *dead*," Craven said through gritted teeth as he rushed forward, Garreth only a step behind.

Craven drew a slash from Kharim's blade, blocking and carrying it around in a thin circle with his rapier as Garreth stepped on the opposite side of him and slashed at his exposed ribs. Kharim lurched in an almost pained expression but made no sound. The specter struck his fist out in a backhanded strike that sent Garreth flying into a nearby wall before crashing to the cobblestones below. He slashed his blade around again towards Craven who disappeared in a haze of shadow.

Garreth returned to his feet and raised his shield to block a strike from Kharim's blade who flashed to him in a lightning fast motion, the momentum driving him into the building again. He grunted as his back slammed against the wall, Craven reappearing at Kharim's side and tearing into his ribs with his blade.

"Go for the weapon!" he shouted, thrashing Kharim with a blinding series of blows from his rapier. Kharim attempted to take charge of the battle, focusing more into an offensive strategy but Craven pulled a dagger from his jacket and wrapped the blade around Kharim's, locking the three weapons together.

Garreth dashed forward and swung his sword in a wide arc, slashing through Kharim's right wrist and separating the hand from his arm. Ghostly energy flowed from the wound as the weapon fell to the ground and began to pull the energy into itself. The few revenants still battling the shadows were flung from their feet as if gravity no longer bound them, each one being sucked into the hilt of the weapon one after another.

Craven grabbed Kharim's body as he fell and lowered him to the ground, the ethereal golden color fading from his eyes and his breath becoming shaky.

"I wanted justice," he said in a quivering voice.

Craven sighed deeply. "The south found its peace long ago. The Abyssal Hand in our lands had nothing to do with the Abyssal Hand of yours."

Kharim's eyes were wide, like those of someone who had seen something unfathomable.

Craven looked to him. "Did you witness the Tree?"

The Haranian nodded, unable to choke words from his throat.

Craven sighed. "I am sorry. No one should have to witness that and return."

A moment later, the revenants had vanished and the blade lay dormant. The severed hand released its grip on the broken handle, shards of glass exited the flesh and returned to the handle of the weapon in perfect order, indifferent to the many lives it had destroyed.

Garreth stood vigil beside the weapon and observed Craven as he consoled the Haranian.

"Did I hurt Erika?" he asked, tears beginning to flow from his once again brown eyes.

"She will be well again," Craven said slowly, although even he was unsure of that statement.

Kharim laughed and then coughed, blood spouting from his lips as every wound he had sustained came forth, no longer sustained by the sentient weapon. His leg fell limp as the broken joint gave way and his robes began seeping with his own crimson ichor. "I never wanted to harm her. I only wanted her to be well. Tell her I hope she finds what she is looking for, please."

Craven nodded, as Kharim looked to the clouded sky again. "Her hair is so beautiful..." he whispered as the life left his eyes. Garreth bowed his head respectfully. Craven breathed a deep sigh, wishing things could have ended differently.

† †

The two Shades melted into the Isles of the Dead. The Great Rift yawned out before them in ethereally glowing water. Garreth was still unused to this place, feeling somewhat jittery as they arrived through the Veil. The spirit of the Haranian had accompanied them, passing through the Gate and walking reverently through the fields underneath the sky-spanning boughs of the Tree of Life. Garreth stood on the banks of the ghostly sea, thinking about how wistful the man had looked as he departed. Even Craven had given the ghost of Kharim a strange look, commenting that he didn't seem entirely whole as he went through the Gate.

"Careful near the edges," Craven's voice roused him. "The water is no place for new Shades. Not until they are ready to accept their Domain."

Garreth looked to him as he approached with the sickle blade that they had fought so hard to obtain. "What is your Domain, if you do not mind my asking?"

"*Death*," Craven replied, dropping the Necromantic blade into the water. It floated for a long while, as if unbound by the pull of the depths. Finally, a shape of incomprehensible size breached the surface, swallowing the weapon into its fathomless maw.

Garreth found himself stepping back in surprise as the eldritch creature dove into the darkness once again.

"As I said, the water is no place for new Shades," Craven intoned again.

The once Tarkalan soldier stared at those ghostly tides. "And once I am ready for my Domain?"

Craven looked to him, Garreth thinking that the dark man seemed even more like Death now than when he had been killed by his hand. "Your Whale must accept you."

An eerie hum drifted from beneath those depths, the collective song of those creatures that inhabited their unknowable secrets.

41
DEATH OF REASON

Rain fell in soft patters against the rooftops in Tarkal, dampening the near constant din of civilization that permeated the wide breadth of the city. Far off rhythmic clangs of a blacksmith came and went, wagons rolling behind the quiet footfalls of pholido, and the loud ring of a pole axe cracking on the cobbled stone. The wielder of that weapon was a massive man in full plate armor bearing more ornamentation than the average soldier or mercenary who would wear a similar raiment.

Many bowed their heads in reverence as he passed, respecting his high position in the city despite the church having fallen out of power in the last few decades. Beside him walked a tall sol woman, who looked dignified despite the thin white dress that she wore. It was rather obviously too small for her, additions had been made to lengthen the skirt, but there was little that could be done for her shoulders, bust, and hips. A sol elf working a position in a clergy was exceedingly rare, and as of yet she had declined a special order from the tailors for herself. Instead, she simply kept her grey cloak wrapped around herself as tightly as she could to cover what the dress failed to. The armored man at least commanded enough of the public's attention to distract from his companion's long and muscled legs, bare under the diminutive skirt.

"I don't think I'll ever be accustomed to the attention you get when you leave the church, Azrael," she said quietly, her bright amber eyes shifting nervously.

They rounded a corner and were faced with the main administrative building of Tarkal, the heart of the Region and their destination. Azrael turned to her as they paused before the doors, his armor clinking with the motion. "You should imagine how I feel," his voice echoed from within the helm, deep and somber. She could still hear the smile he wore. "I swear one little Oath and suddenly people start bowing their heads at me."

"They bow their heads to you," she corrected, wiping a hand across his tabard to rid it of some grime. "Hardly a *little* Oath, anyways."

His pauldron covered shoulders gave a shrug, which was impressive considering the size of them. "Perhaps they are also taken by your beauty, Zylta, radiant as the sun that we so rarely see this time of year."

She blushed slightly, her golden hair gently streaking a few different shades but mostly violet. Azrael was the only one in many years that could make her hair shift colors. "Why did you even ask me to come?" she questioned as they stepped through the doors and walked through the halls of the great building, Azrael now walking with his pole axe resting in the crook of his arm to minimize the echoing noise. "Everyone knows I'm not the most pious of the Sisters under you, I can't even be bothered to get a proper dress. Even the Triumvirate knows my lack of faith, and only one of them even occasionally comes to your sermons.

"You do know your way around a blade though," Azrael said in a hushed tone, but her sharp ears caught it. He turned to her when she paused in the long hallway.

"Azrael..." Zylta muttered quietly. "I can't do that." She startled when he took her long-fingered hand in his gauntlet. She hadn't noticed she was trembling just at the thought.

"I pray fervently to Morian that I will never need you to help me in that way."

The thin fingers of her other hand reached up and gingerly brushed the emblem that hung from a chain at his chest, marking his status as a Paladyn.

"However, considering the state of our world right now, I like to have all the help I can get," he continued, his deep tones helping to calm her. "You know where I keep all of my weapons should you need one, Zylta, both in the temple and on my person."

Her bright hair, slightly damp from the rain, bobbed as she nodded.

"Your hair is getting rather long. It's nice," he said, serving to distract her further before she leaned down to straighten the standard at the Paladyn's hip. It bore the symbol of the God of Salvation, a shield with an ancient rune centered on it. Her eyes flashed to the dagger hilt behind the standard, pausing a long moment. Her throat constricted as she stared at the weapon with a quivering breath before quickly standing straight and clasping her hands together tightly. They continued on their way after Azrael gave her an encouraging smile and light pat on her lower back.

Zylta hugged her arms close to her breast as they passed the administrative workers within, the color of their coats identifying which of the Triumvirate leaders they served specifically: Blue for Lord Pitr, yellow for Lady Jaria, and red for Lord Micah.

One dressed in red approached them. She was a mousy girl with dark skin and darker hair, her eyes the color of sand. "Well met, Paladyn Azrael," she began with an awkward bow, stumbling slightly over her lanky legs as she sidestepped alongside them. "The Lords and Lady are expecting you, as you know, but Lord Micah wished me to extend a formal greeting on his behalf before the meeting."

"Is there a reason?" Zylta asked.

Azrael smiled under his helm, knowing from her tone that her anxiety had passed now that she had a clear path before her.

The girl bowed, but looked around nervously. The Paladyn pulled off to the side and gripped at a strap on his armor, acting as if he were adjusting it. The girl looked confused, but perked up when Zylta nudged her closer from behind. "Lord Micah has expressed some concern over certain behaviors of his two colleagues. Lord Pitr specifically has been acting somewhat suspicious, speaking more openly with shady individuals that leave no trace of their presence or identity. He also seems to be completely unconcerned about the departure of Warden Tormis, despite the many vocal citizens who are afraid of a retaliatory offensive from Sylvanna now that the Angelus has departed for Mintheras."

Azrael nodded, setting his strap back and glancing down at her. "I will keep my wits about me when it comes to Lord Pitr, as I always do. Be sure to extend my thanks to Lord Micah in person after our meeting is through. Keep in mind the Angelus did speak of a threat arising in Mintheras before leaving, so we must keep faith that he has Tarkal's best interests in mind."

The girl moved to the side and Azrael continued his walk down the hall, needing no direction from the workers. Zylta jogged briefly to catch up with him, leaning in closer to him as they went. She felt more at ease in what she considered a hostile place when she was by his side. Eventually, they arrived in the audience chambers. The three leaders of Tarkal sat at nearly identical desks, each spaced evenly from one another. The two of them entered in between Lady Jaria, who seemed distracted by her fingernails, and Lord Micah, who gave them a friendly smile. Azrael brought the end of his pole axe down on the wood floor with a heavy and echoing crack, announcing their presence officially. Zylta had to hide her startle as best she could, even knowing the loud sound was coming.

"Lords and Lady of the Triumvirate. Paladyn Azrael and Sister Zylta, addressing your invitation of council," Azrael's commanding voice carried through the chamber, bouncing off the vacant seats in the wide room.

Lord Pitr looked as if he were about to laugh, his pale face always seeming like he knew something that no one else did. "Always so formal, though it is entertaining."

Lord Micah eyed Pitr, interrupting any further words. "Thank you for coming on such short notice, Azrael. As you know, the Angelus Warden Tormis has departed the city for our island territory of Mintheras. With his absence, you and Father Baris have been reappointed to the status of High Clergy in Tarkal. I would also like to extend our appreciation for your understanding as to why the position was taken from you in the first place."

"Who am I to dispute an Angelus?" Azrael said with a reverent bow of his head, removing his helm in one smooth motion. His shaved head shimmered a bit in the little light that came in from the high windows while his neat beard widened with his smile. Zylta relaxed a little at the sight of his silvery grey eyes.

Jaria leaned forward, after finishing the inspection of her fingernails. "I trust you remember *how* to be the High Clergy, hm?" Her voice always grated on Zylta's ears, with a twisting and pompous tone. "Aiding the city guards with daily duties of course. Those tax aurums won't collect themselves, and having you around makes the process so much smoother."

Azrael turned to her. "That, as well as providing council to the people of Tarkal, no matter their station. Perhaps I will see some of you in our humble temple, to hear the word of Morian?"

Zylta shuffled, glancing to the nearly hidden body guards flanking Pitr. She sincerely hoped they wouldn't. Something always felt off about this city to her and this meeting was a poignant reminder of it. After what seemed like an eternity, they walked out of the building and into the wide streets of Tarkal once again. Despite the increasing chill in the air, Zylta delayed in pulling her cloak over her shoulders, closing her eyes and angling her head upwards as the wind blew around her. She wondered at times if she shared some kind of kinship with her aash cousins, as much as she enjoyed the breeze on her skin.

"Sometimes I wish we weren't so bound by this place," she said quietly. Of course, she was not quiet enough to escape the ears of Azrael, who had yet to put his helm back on.

"One is only as bound to a location as their spirit demands."

"That feels like a stretch," Zylta replied, her shoulders slumping a little as she looked over at him.

His warm smile put her at ease. "I know," he said, stepping forwards and pulling her into an embrace. His armor was cold, but the feel of his jaw against her neck warmed her all the way through.

If only you weren't a Paladyn, she thought absently. *If only you didn't swear your Oath to* this *city.*

"Perhaps we can go on a trip sometime. Take all the Sisters and Father Baris, and Alistair if he's feeling well enough," he offered, patting her on the back. She didn't want him to let go.

"Where would we go?"

"I hear a summer in Mintheras is a holiday worth taking,'" he grinned at her. "Long as Tormis rids it of whatever threat he felt coming."

Zylta returned a weak smile. "If you don't mind the hedonism," she countered sardonically, remembering the one time she had been there, long before becoming one of Azrael's clergymembers. Although she would almost be tempted to pay for the whole trip just to see the Sisters' reactions to the pools commonly with nude swimmers.

Azrael shrugged, replacing his helm over his head and muttering something about new members to come to the temple. "Chill wind today, eh?" he called as he descended the steps down to the street.

Zylta wondered how she might express the bad feeling she got when she looked out on this city that her dearest friend was so dedicated to. "Feels the same as death," she whispered to that wind.

Azrael did not hear her then.

† †

"Daemons have broken free from Consecrations, Angelus have once again turned their gaze towards the realm, and yet," the voice paused for but a moment, the sound of rushing water through the vale becoming the dominant sound once again, "the dwarves are silent."

Xhalia sat back, far out of the way, near a greatwood. Her silver scales and yellow stripes shimmered in the early morning light as she stretched out in the warm sun. She just hoped she didn't glint enough to draw any attention to herself. She was much too young to really have a say in these meetings anyway, she just wanted to keep in the know.

The Dragons of her family, and others, stood around the lake, each many times larger than her. Fashila seemed unconvinced that they should do anything, whereas Morosh was more concerned over their ancient rivals returning from their respective worlds. All the others, including Xhalia's family, were neutral to either side. She however, was very concerned over the state of things.

No living memory remained from the conflict, as the oldest among them had passed to nature not long into Xhalia's life. She could just barely remember the scars of the Great Elder scattering across his body, his eyes unseeing, his wings unable to lift him from the ground. He always spoke his stories, even if no one was around to hear them. She had been present for many, curling underneath him where she hoped he wouldn't notice and scold her. She loved to listen to his stories of Dragoons, Dragons who had bonded their soul to a human, elf, dwarf, or other creature who was usually considered lesser and, in the process, becoming more.

Tyranimeaux was an eloquent speaker, and she often felt as if she could see the tales playing out before her. Daemons of the Seven Circles battling Angelus of the Ten Ideals, whilst the Dragons did their best to defend the weaker races caught in the center. Even now, she often visited his bones. When looking up at his great skull that he had left behind upon his departure to the Lifespirit, she wondered if the world would ever be able to see such beauty again. Her kin were adamant about staying away from the other races.

Xhalia herself enjoyed the company of humans on the rare occasions that she was able to sneak away from her own kind and into the villages and towns within flight distance. The people there knew of the Dragons, but did not approach. She did not know if it was out of reverence or fear that they stayed away.

"It should not matter!" Morosh's aggravated roar startled her from her daydreaming, the sound echoing past their vale and beyond like rolling thunder. "Daemons and Angelus cannot be reasoned with, the Great Elders made as much clear! We should simply raze the areas where their plague has touched and be done with it all."

Xhalia flinched at the prospects. Massive expanses of land, turned to ash and death.

Fashila grunted in an irritated way. "Showing our presence still exists in this world will simply bring turmoil to our home. We have enjoyed this peaceful existence with the local denizens for centuries, why would we jeopardize our convenient abodes for more war and strife?"

"Confinement, you mean," Xhalia muttered, too quietly for even her mother to hear.

Morosh bristled, the sky growing overcast and the lake between them beginning to freeze. Yathil, Xhalia's father, spoke in an attempt to ease both sides of the conflict. "Perhaps we should call a recess for the time being and all have a nice long ponder on the issues. No matter how things are happening on the continent to the south, it will take both of the vermin time to gather their strength fully. Plenty of time for us to decide how to deal with them," he said, looking to the opposite side of the lake quickly. "Or *not* deal with them." The ground beneath Fashila's feet beginning to crack and smolder before his addendum.

Soon enough, all of the Elders departed, retiring to their resting spots in their expansive domain. Xhalia stepped down to the water and laid out on the grass, resting her head on her upturned claw like she had seen so many humans do when frustrated or overwhelmed. Such a gesture would likely have her scolded by many of her kin, as interaction with the lesser species was technically forbidden. She hardly cared. Things needed to change, but perhaps not quite as radically as how Morosh was proposing. A low and comforting rumble drew her attention as her mother, Payisa, stepped next to her. Her scales were of a darker tone, with platinum markings that showed her as one of the Elders.

"What is troubling you, little one?" she asked.

Xhalia shook her head, speaking in a halfway mocking tone. "As I have heard it said, the 'normal problems a hatchling has when they feel they cannot fly free'."

"Fashila is eldest among us, and as such has forgotten what it is to be young," Payisa chuckled. "She does not call you hatchling out of malice, but merely as friendly chastising."

"She is not wrong in that I cannot fly free. I feel trapped at times, like Fashila and the others are simply afraid of the humans and other races.

Her mother's voice flared a warning tone. "Do not let them hear you say 'afraid'. They will burn the human settlements just to prove the opposite."

"Does that not prove me correct? Rather than deal with them in a meaningful way, they simply kill them all and say they've solved it."

Payisa stifled a laugh. "You have a point, but sadly they would not listen to you. I am sorry, Xhalia, for not being able to do more for you. Only time and experience can give you credence to our kind."

The smaller Dragon let out a huff of air, which crackled with electricity. "Which is why they won't listen to anyone who isn't one of us either, even if they are objectively correct and the Dragon is wrong."

"And Pride Daemons are one of our most hated of enemies," her mother said slyly, drawing a giggle from her daughter at the irony. "Perhaps you should go visit with your siblings. You may find some distraction from the politicking."

Xhalia was the youngest of her clutch, having yet to depart from her parents' side for more than a few days at a time. Visiting the others would likely mean months away from them. Before she could express any excitement at the prospect, Morosh barreled back to the lakeside, his heavy steps making waves in the water. "Payisa! A Daemon and Angelus are set to battle on an island in the Great Rift. We must act now, gather the others."

"What about Fashila?"

"Damn Fashila," he said harshly. "She knows as well as the rest of us, whoever the winner is will come here next. A Dragon soul would greatly heighten the advantage for either of them, so let us go end their threat before they can hunt us in turn."

Payisa nodded hesitantly. Within the hour, a score of Dragons were taking flight. Xhalia hurriedly grabbed her satchel that she carried at the base of her left wing and raced to catch up. Even if she didn't participate in the battle, it was important for her to watch and to learn. She spared a glance back at Fashila, who stood on a great rock ledge beside the lake. Disapproval was clear on her face as the water began to boil.

42
Rest and Revelations

Erika awoke slowly, the sound of creaking wood the only accompanying sense before her vision restored. Around her was a large enclosed space with several bookshelves and a desk facing opposite from a curtained window. She sat up slowly, touching a hand to the bandages that wrapped her chest as she gradually took in her surroundings. She wondered where her shirt was as she stood, feeling a bit cold as she was nearly naked to the waist. Her legs were uneasy beneath her and it felt like the room itself was moving. Across the floor she stepped, carefully dusting off her skirt before she arrived at the back of the room and threw open the curtains. She winced at the direct sunlight and gasped sharply. Nothing but water spread out before her. She took a step back, leaning against the desk and taking as deep a breath as she could until her inhaling sent a pain through her chest. She jumped slightly as the door on the opposite side of the chamber opened, F'Skal entering with a bucket of water. Involuntary tears filled her eyes as her coughs sent more pains through her.

"You're awake," he said with surprise in his tone as he quickened his pace to reach her.

Erika nodded. "Where are we?"

"Aboard *The Winged Siren*, captained by a man named Jekal. We sail for the Tarkalan island of Mintheras, for repairs. We are only a few days out I am told," he answered while he gently pressed his fingers over her, inspecting her bandages.

He paused for a moment, the emerald dust around his eyes lighting as he stared at her chest, fingers probing around. "You gave us quite the scare and I admit my own healing abilities were tested with this latest wound."

She gently touched her fingers to the dark stain in the bandages just above her left breast, wincing as she felt the tender flesh. "Is everyone else alright?" she asked after acknowledging F'Skal's cautioning.

The aash let out a deep sigh, Erika surmising that it was more from fatigue than anything. "Darion was stabbed in the side but is doing quite well, with no small thanks to the ship's own medic. F'Lessa and I made it out with little more than minor cuts, scrapes, and bruises."

"And Craven?"

F'Skal fell silent, taking a long and deep breath. This time was not just the fatigue. "We haven't heard from him. Captain Jekal insisted we leave without him."

Erika's eyes burned, her expression turning furious.

"Erika, please," F'Skal attempted to stop her with gentle hands. "Erika, dear, please sit back down."

She strode across the room, throwing a blanket over her naked shoulders and stormed barefoot out onto the deck of the ship, F'Skal just barely behind her heels. Crew members all about quickly averted their eyes from her, the bandages doing little to cover her shape under the loose blanket, as she climbed onto the upper deck and ran up to the man in the coat and hat that she assumed was the captain.

"Ye're Jekal?"

The man turned to her after giving instructions to the helmsman. "Aye, that's me. I'll bet you're our Fjordling guest?" he said with a grin at his own poor humor.

"Aye," she replied slowly, taken aback by his childish smile. She recovered a moment later, throwing her hands up again while being careful not to let the blanket fall away. "Why did ye order to leave Craven at the docks?"

Jekal took a breath, scratching the back of his hand idly. "Well first of all lass, he wasn't at my dock he was quite a ways back still. And, Craven can handle himself. Honestly, he's probably the reason those creatures stopped chasing us."

"Revenants?" Erika asked F'Skal, unsure of how much she could remember.

"Yes. Craven stayed behind to fight that man who unleashed all of them," the aash filled in for her.

"But Kharim wouldn't 'ave done that," she said quietly, feeling confused tears stinging at her eyes.

"Not sure it was Kharim's wishes," came a familiar voice, as Darion climbed onto the deck with them. "As I saw it happen, Kharim was forced into it somehow and it appeared as if he lost his humanity too. Maybe that was just the blood loss at the time, I'm not sure."

Erika smiled and hugged him through his obvious fluster at her lack of dress. "Good to see ye're well Darion. I'd still like to know what all happened though."

F'Skal chimed in. "I think the only one that knows the full tale is Craven I'm afraid. The rest of us were busy running for safety and trying to avoid the revenants. I only went back when a strange creature found me and guided me back to you after you'd been hurt. Little thing is probably still around here somewhere."

"Some of us were trying to make way to avoid any more damage to my damned ship," Captain Jekal cut in. "Original plan was to get all of you to the Fjordlands, but that isn't happening."

Erika nodded her understanding, despite her persistent look of irritation.

The captain looked around for a moment, then started waving his arms at all of them. "Alright, too many bodies on my quarterdeck, all of you off!"

Just as everyone was down to the main deck, a sound of air rushing through suddenly caught their attention. "Well, that was a trip," came another familiar voice.

"Craven!" Jekal bellowed. "See, I told all of you he would be fine!"

Erika looked up at them from the main deck below. "Ye bloody bastard! Get down 'ere," she ordered him, dropping her blanket and wrapping her arms around the man as he descended. The worried ache in her chest overpowered any need for modesty, not that she was very shy to begin with. His hands were cold on her lower back, making her realize she had rarely touched his actual skin.

She turned after releasing Craven to see F'Lessa assisting with the rigging not far off. The aash came over and hugged her silently, before F'Skal requested Craven join their party in the captain's quarters.

"Absolutely, take my private cabin, I've no issue with it," Jekal mocked.

F'Skal waved him off. "You already surrendered it for Erika to use while she recovers, and she is still recovering. Thank you for your hospitality."

Jekal muttered something about guests as the companions shuffled into the room, finishing his conversation with his helmsman before following a moment later. He promptly took the seat at the desk and began sorting through papers. Erika sat on the bed and laid back against the wall to rest at F'Skal's suggestion. F'Lessa sat next to her and helped cover her still mostly bare torso, while F'Skal and Darion stood by the door and eagerly awaited Craven's tale.

Craven suddenly looked sheepish with all the attention on him, letting out an uncharacteristically nervous chuckle before beginning. "I understand that all of you need answers."

None nodded more than F'Skal and Darion, but even Erika joined them with a slight movement of her head.

He took a deep breath and began. "I am not human, as I'm sure some of you have surmised. Or at least, not *quite* human. I am what you might call undead, a Shade more specifically. I work directly for the Goddess of Death, Matron Mortia." He paused a moment, looking around at the relatively unfazed faces of his companions. "Now I plead you, this must remain secret. Shades are not permitted to reveal themselves unless necessary."

"*This* is not necessary," Darion pointed out.

Craven shrugged. "You are technically correct. My assignment when I met all of you was to find an individual using a weapon made by ancient Necromancers. Using its power, he was able to raise undead warriors—which I did tell you about—known as revenants."

"Kharim," Erika said quietly. A tear came down her cheek and her nose beginning to feel clogged.

Craven bowed his head briefly. "And now that I have completed my task my presence here is completely unnecessary, as is my telling you of my true state." The room fell silent, before Craven stepped to Erika and bowed deeply. "My condolences for your friend. If there had been any other way, I would have taken it. He seemed a good man, in the end."

Erika gave him a weak smile, unsure of how to respond. A lump came into her throat as he handed her the small bracelet of stones that he had given her when they had met. "I am sorry I did not return it to you sooner." He leaned in closer for a brief moment and whispered so only she could hear. "I need you to tell me truthfully, Erika, when I carried you away from where Kharim's shell attacked you, did you see anything? A Tree, perhaps?"

Erika thought a moment, unsure of when he was speaking of. She shook her head, unable to recall anything of the sort. Craven seemed deadly serious about whatever he was talking about, but seemed satisfied, putting his cold skinned palm to her cheek with a smile.

"So, why are you here then?" Darion asked, his expression harder than usual. "Your task is finished, your appearance here not necessary. You have no further business with us."

"Apologies are in order," Craven answered. "Fjordsgate was never closed to travelers. I myself came through there from the Fjordlands where I received my task and I met all of you on my way south. I lied to all of you and melded my way into your party in an attempt to guise my travels."

"Yet Stacia still recognized you. Does she know the truth about you?" F'Lessa piped in.

"No. I originally hail from Sylvanna and Stacia and her family hold a certain place in my heart, so I am unable to stop myself from caring for them in my own way. However, she nor Marq know anything of Shades or my allegiance to Matron Mortia."

"*What* are ye exactly?" Erika finally asked, laying her arms on the top of the blanket over her and idly spinning the stone bracelet in her fingers. She sharply remembered that she had been the one to insist on bringing Craven along on their journey.

"A Shade is an individual that has been chosen for life beyond death by Matron Mortia herself. I do not age and I cannot die. Wounds last only so long and severe bodily damage will merely put me into a death-like state that I awaken from hours afterward at most," he explained. "One such instance is when the force from Tarkal attacked and I covered your escape. They managed to 'kill' me, you might say, but Shades do not stay dead for long."

"And these strange creatures? They are under your command?" F'Skal asked, motioning to the winged being that seemed to be sleeping above the bed where Erika had rested. Erika stared at the thing for a long moment, having not noticed it before. "Unnerving as he is, he was very concerned over your wellbeing," he said to her quickly. "Stayed by your side the *entire* time."

"Indeed. All Shades have a measure of shadows that they may utilize, myself having the most as I am the highest ranking Shade known as the Lord Wraith."

Darion scoffed offhandedly. "How do you get promoted to that?"

"By being the first," Craven answered blankly.

The room fell silent at the implication of his age. Jekal spoke up several moments later, adjusting a monocle that he used to file through his papers while the conversation was happening. "I believe the gravewalker is attempting to make amends for using all of you to achieve his own agenda. Not something Craven usually does, being as he is a very detached individual. For as long as I've known him at least."

The group looked to Erika, who stared down at her crossed legs and picked at her fingers between the bracelet. She looked up as they did, her eyes looking bewildered and shy for a moment. She took a deep breath after recovering. "We wouldn't be here if it weren't for Craven. Ye used us, that much is sure. But ye also helped us immensely, an' fer that I'm grateful. I wouldn't be breathin' if it weren't fer ye tryin' to save me from Kharim."

Craven shook his head slowly. "F'Skal saved you. I honestly wished for nothing more than to send all of you off on Jekal's ship and then go after Kharim myself, but the spirit that had it in for Erika had other plans it seemed."

"Hargreave," Erika answered, tasting bile in her throat.

"Hargreave then, is the one that ruined all of our plans. However, I am glad I was able to speak with you all again and explain," Craven finished, stepping back to the corner of the room. "Despite Captain Jekal's ire, I do try to avoid burning bridges when able."

Darion nodded and promptly left the room after waving to Erika, F'Lessa following closely a moment later with a confused look on her face. Erika continued fiddling at her fingers and the bracelet and said nothing. F'Skal motioned for Craven to follow him out of the cabin as well.

The dark man stepped over to Erika again, leaning towards her. "May I, for a moment?" he asked, holding his hands out. She consented and lowered the blanket to her breasts.

He lightly inspected underneath the bandages where the golden lines that had brightly shone beneath her skin had dulled. "Good," he intoned, helping her raise the blanket again and giving her a loving pat on her head before following F'Skal. The aash immediately questioned his inspection but Erika could not hear much of their conversation.

"I hope you don't mind my being here?" Jekal asked quietly after the door shut.

Erika smiled at him. "No, I think I'm just needin' a little time to think is all. Sorry fer yellin' at ye like I did."

Jekal smirked back, waving his hand over his face. "If you need someone to talk to, just ask. These papers are days behind anyway, I don't mind letting them fall back a bit more. Let me know when you want more privacy as well, I'm also not sure where your friends put your clothes."

She chuckled lightly and leaned back onto the bed, letting the events settle in. The strange bat creature leapt down from above her, startling her as it landed on her lap.

"You are alive!" it said with excitement. "So glad we are!"

She giggled as it nuzzled against her, petting its strange feeling essence before it curled up on her lap and promptly fell back asleep.

Erika leaned her head back against the wall, having to remind herself more and more why she was on this journey in the first place.

People kept getting hurt. Even the little companion to a servant of death itself was worried that her latest wound would kill her. She put a hand over her eyes, poorly trying to hide her tears from Jekal. Perhaps she should just turn them around and head back for Sylvanna after they made repairs.

What worried her even more, was how Irvine's face had begun to lose even more detail in her memory...

43

Seafaring Recovery

The days on the open waters of the Great Rift were dull. The weather had cleared, much to the improvement of the sailors' morale, but Erika found herself trying to find anything to occupy the multitude of hours that she found to herself. Looking at her pierced breastplate proved to be a poor choice for her mood, so she left that buried in her belongings alongside her ruined hammer, knowing there was nothing she could do to repair them unless she had the proper tools to do so, if she could even do anything with them at all considering the ancient weapon that had broken through them. It seemed the healthier choice was to assist the crew in any way she could. Unfortunately, between her, Darion, and F'Lessa, there was not much for them all to do. She sharply declined any offer to climb up to the crow's nest, the thought of which brought back vivid memories of her fear of heights. Darion on the other hand had no issue with it and took to the jargon of the sailors relatively quickly.

He found a lot of peace in the raised platform over the ship's deck. The quiet reminded him of guard duty when he was occasionally allowed to be alone. How strange it all was, how not long ago he was a guardsman who regularly received the bullying remarks of the entire guardhouse and now he was an official

Knight of Sylvanna. He wondered if some of the people in Stonewall would be able to accept that promotion if he ever made it back. He himself wanted to decline the honor, the fact that he was faced directly with the Queen of Sylvanna being the only thing stopping him from doing just that.

His thoughts were interrupted when he glanced down and saw silver hair peeking over the edge of the wide bucket, two red on black eyes staring with uncertainty at him.

He smiled, beckoning with his hand. "Come on, F'Lessa. No point in just hanging there."

She leapt onto the yard next to the nest, her hair flashing an appealing golden color as she attempted to suppress her smile. He watched her for a long while before looking back out at the waters around them. "Darion..." she began softly, seeming unsure of how to begin.

He hesitated a moment, but spoke first. "I'm not angry about the kiss. It was very nice, I am just disappointed."

"Disappointed?" She looked at him sharply, her hair flashing orange. "Was there something wrong with my lips? Did I do it wrong?"

Darion threw his hands up, speaking quickly to quell her distress. "I'm disappointed in myself, F'Lessa. Not in the kiss."

F'Lessa breathed a long sigh of relief, her hands pressing on her thighs to force herself to calm and wait for him to continue.

Darion laughed slightly while rubbing his side where his wound was still healing. "It's honestly so stupid. I said I wanted to prove myself, to show you that I didn't need your protection and I went and got stabbed by a revenant."

"Darion, you've never needed to prove yourself to me," she interrupted him. He turned to her with confusion on his face, watching her eyes soften as she spoke. "You've protected me twice now. In the forest when the revenants attacked, you shielded me. And again in Darktide, as the creatures rushed forwards you guarded me valiantly."

Darion chuckled, shaking his head. "That isn't really that big of a thing."

She slapped his arm with the back of her hand as softly as she could muster, though it still stung a bit. "You protected me when I was distraught, and when I was distracted. I believe in you Darion.

You do not have to prove anything to me. And I..." her voice trailed off, like there was more she wanted to say.

He took a slow shaking breath, trying to process her praise.

"That said, none of that is what I came up here to ask you," she began again. "May I borrow your sword and shield? Only briefly," she asked, almost nervously.

He obliged, giving her his sword first which she took gently from him. She dipped her fingers into a pouch on her opposite hip and procured a small stone, pressing it to the blade just over the guard. Darion's stomach dropped as the metal marred. He thought briefly to stop her as she activated her ruby dust magic and carved a line into his weapon with the sharp stone, yet he wanted to know what she was doing all the same. He kept his watch along the horizon while occasionally looking back to her as she worked intricate runes into the metal. He found his eyes wandering over every part of her. Her sharp face and dark eyes, braided hair and hot skin. That same fang that poked out when she smiled was pressed over her lower lip as she focused on her task. Darion smiled at the cute expression, F'Lessa failing to notice how much he enjoyed the sight... Her thick musculature did nothing to detract from her more feminine features, most of which were barely hidden by the little clothing she wore. He looked down at her bare hip as she propped a leg up on the yard, seeing the knot he had tied in the string resting taut over her smooth ebon skin just over from the sensual curve of her backside. His eyes then drifted to the inner thigh of her opposite leg as it hung over the edge of her perch. He realized his staring as she started speaking softly. His breath shook as he turned away abruptly and felt his face get warm.

He started to apologize, until he realized the words were not being spoken to him nor could he understand them. He looked back as the three runes she had carved began to glow slightly with a deep red, light blue, and strong orange emanation respectively. F'Lessa handed him the weapon a moment later, her smile bright and her fangs showing even more prominently.

"What did you do?" he asked, holding the blade aloft and staring at the runes that glowed brighter now, before looking back at her in realization. "Your axes have similar runes."

F'Lessa nodded. "Druidic magic held in permanent sigils and runes that project properties into the weapon, and the wielder."

Darion stared at her in amazement. "You're a druid?"

She shook her head quickly, laughing in what sounded like a disparaging way. "No, not fully. I was training before leaving the village. Wasn't very good at it anyway."

"Why would you leave that?" he asked with a disbelieving chuckle, remembering how she had sat by the druids in her village and watched as they used that fascinating magic. Y'Skara hadn't mentioned that F'Lessa was learning to do that sort of thing as well.

Her hair flashed pink as her face flushed slightly. "I figured you would have known the reason."

Darion realized his words and looked back at her, flushing even more furiously than she did. "F'Lessa... I didn't mean for you to leave your people or your training."

"I *wanted* to go with you," she said sternly, staring into his eyes with an intensity.

He was at a loss for words as she leaned over him, her naked side brushing the back of his hand and arm as she gently took his shield from beside him. She sat back in her position again and began carving into the material. These five runes—after she spoke the soft words—glowed with blue, red, green, golden, and pink hues. All of them lined the inner right side of the shield, just above where his hand rested when he wore it. She handed it back to him and he ran his fingertips along the grooves. "So, what do they mean? Or do, rather?" he asked after securing it beside himself again.

"The three on the blade are for strength, fluidity, and ferocity. To promote the power of your strikes, ease of movement, and your tenacity in battle," she said, holding his hand and tracing his finger to the motions of each rune. "The shield bears runes of protection, health, prosperity, happiness, and..."

He glanced up from the runes as she trailed off, turning back to her. She quickly looked away, her hair streaking pink. "Does that pink rune mean the same thing as your hair when it turns the same color?"

F'Lessa shook her head, avoiding his gaze as she looked out onto the water ahead of them.

"So, what does it mean?" he asked again, leaning closer to her and prodding further.

She shifted on the yard, still not looking at him. " *Vasil.*"

Darion laughed, sitting back again. "Well, I don't speak elvish, so I suppose I'll have to remember that word and ask F'Skal about it later."

F'Lessa looked to him suddenly. "No! Don't ask him!"

"Then what does it mean?" he asked a third time, eyeing her coyly. "You put it on my shield, the least you can do is tell me what it means."

"Are you really going to force me to say it?" she asked, looking vulnerable.

"I could always just try and guess," Darion teased, smiling still. "Is it, *love?*"

She made a sudden squeaking sound before nearly falling from the yard. Darion lodged himself in the nest, reaching out and grabbing her arm with one hand, his other pressing onto her bare side. He laughed the whole time he was holding her steady.

Once she settled again, he sat back into place and looked out onto the horizon. "I won't tell anyone what the runes mean. They'll be our secret."

F'Lessa grinned, and looked off to the clouded seascape with him. "Do you mind if I stay here for a while?"

"I would love that," he replied, drawing a golden streak through her hair.

They stayed for a long while, until night began to fall and the smell of cooking food fragrantly wafted up past them.

"Smells like dinner," Darion said, looking over the side of the nest briefly. "And here comes Waylan for his shift now."

F'Lessa was distracted looking down at the relief, and failed to notice Darion stand. He leaned over and kissed her on the cheek. She sat back stunned for a moment before he smiled and hefted his shield and weapon.

"Thank you, for the runes, F'Lessa," he said, rubbing a hand on her shoulder. "See you down there. I'll save you a seat at the bow."

A moment later he was climbing down the opposite side of the mast from Waylan, who climbed into the nest with a handkerchief filled with food hanging from his teeth. "Oh, hello F'Lessa," he greeted. "Are you alright?"

She smiled up at the darkening sky. "I think I'm finally doing what makes F'Lessa happy."

Waylan gave her a confused look with a mouthful of biscuit before she deftly flipped backwards from her perch and made her way down to the deck.

††

Erika found herself with little to do on *The Winged Siren*. She saw Darion or F'Lessa most often at mealtimes, and almost never stumbled upon Craven. The only one of her companions that she talked to very often was F'Skal but it was never anything of real importance, always just conversation that seemed to fill the time more than anything else. The only thing that he had talked to her about truly seriously was her injury, which still marked her flesh with pale gold-colored veins that spread out from the scarring tissue. The spidery marks climbed up onto her neck, a few even crossing her scar from the revenant's arrow in Stonewall. More still made their way down her left breast, following the swell and ending near her upper sternum. The strike had luckily just missed her heart and nicked past her left lung, which explained her extreme difficulty breathing at the time as well as her tendency to get winded occasionally while on *The Winged Siren*.

The other times she and Darion saw each other was often times in Jekal's cabin to get their wounds checked by F'Skal. "Well, Erika," F'Skal began after looking at the thankfully decreased wound in her chest. "Craven has informed me that the golden lines will be permanent. Although they have dimmed from when I first tended your wound in Darktide." He paused for a moment, watching her for a reaction. She simply shrugged.

"I've already got scars, an' my Ignis Blood marks me plenty. I'm not seein' how this is anythin' worse," she replied, garnering an understanding nod from the aash. She made her way to a mirror in the corner, lifting her breast and tracing the lines over her skin. These and the stone bracelet were the only two things she had to remember Kharim by. One was from pure kindness, the other was from possessed violence. She let out a sigh, pulling her long-sleeved tunic over her head and looking over her shoulder as F'Lessa joined them. The aash woman walked over to Darion and helped him remove what was to be the final bandage from around his torso. She reached her hand around his neck and gently felt along the space where she had harmed him before, both of them locking eyes as she did.

Erika found herself intently staring at them, fascinated in the way they looked at one another. F'Lessa made a slight grimace when she found the scar that had formed, accompanied by a blue streak through her hair. Darion put his hand to her cheek and said something that Erika couldn't make out. She nearly let out a girlish squeal when Darion leaned up and kissed her on the forehead, her hands jittering briefly in the air as she hesitated between hiding her smile and trying to stifle it—she ended up simply biting her lower lip instead. Luckily neither of them seemed to notice her as F'Skal turned and beckoned his sister to help him gather and organize other medicines.

F'Lessa smiled at Darion's squeeze of her hand before leaving him to aid her brother. Erika gave her a giddy grin as she passed, to which F'Lessa simply mouthed *shush* before taking a small bowl of the black paste to Darion.

The only other time that she would consistently see the two was when they would play a game on the side of the deck with a set of cards that Darion had bought in Sylvanna. The entire crew marked when F'Lessa finally defeated the young man with a sudden cheering shout from the elf, as well as a few deckhands that had been rooting for her. Soon after that raucous event, several crewmembers sat down with them and showed them a dice game, which even Jekal joined in for a few rounds. Erika noticed that F'Lessa seemed to exceedingly enjoy the human games, commonly inviting Erika to play or loudly asking Darion when they could play again.

Craven was continually elusive the entire voyage, though Erika was fine with that. She was still unsure of how to approach him, or what they would even talk about if she did. He would simply smile at her as warmly as he seemed capable when she would occasionally find him with Captain Jekal. Other times he would simply be looking off the side of the ship, staring at nothing in particular.

Thus, the days passed until they began their approach to Mintheras.

44
RUINATION OF MINTHERAS

Flotsam on the starboard side!" came Darion's cry from above, causing Erika to startle slightly.

The captain leaned over the side, watching the floating object as someone rushed forward with a long-handled hook.

"Not actually flotsam," Captain Jekal muttered warily. Erika was the only one besides the crewman to hear his uneasy tone. "Good catch!" Captain Jekal called back as the hook dropped the piece of scrap from the water onto the deck.

Erika approached curiously. "What is it?"

The sailor crouched over it and gave the captain a look of concern. "It's a piece of roofing, sir. Shingles."

Erika looked at Jekal, unsure of the implications. She was taken aback by his grim expression, feeling a nervousness settle in the pit of her stomach. "Ready yourselves for anything!" the captain called out to the entire ship. "Something has possibly happened in Mintheras. Considering our trip thus far, I'm not going to hold my breath for anything."

"What do'ye mean, somethin' has possibly happened?" Erika asked, stepping to match the captain's pace as he moved along the deck.

His gaze didn't waver from his path. "Unsure of that, miss. Being on an island in the middle of the Rift, they are protected from most bad weather as it doesn't make it past the mountains in the south and generally fizzles as it comes off the northern shelves."

His words did nothing to help her anxiety. "So, what shears off shingles?"

Jekal nodded. "My thoughts exactly."

"Captain!" came Darion's next warning call from above.

They joined another crewman at the bow as Darion continued his shout. "There's more than just shingles!"

Erika followed Jekal's eyeline off the front edge of the ship and gasped when she looked over the water. The dark surface of the liquid was littered with wood shrapnel and pieces of man-made structures, but worst of all were the bodies.

"Well, that changes things drastically," Jekal muttered, answering Erika's unspoken question quickly. "Mintheras may not even be there anymore."

"Daemon?" Erika breathed, more to the air than anyone in particular.

Craven stepped beside them. "Not sure that was done by a Daemon."

"Your reasoning?" Jekal queried.

The Shade pointed to a few of the bodies. "See how the wounds are spread with black discoloration? That's an Angelus."

Erika's fists clenched as she remembered the Angelus that attacked Valen. "No better than a Daemon." The sight reminded her of Farris, a ranger in Sildenfeld, who had a cut across his nose from where the mere sharp air of the Angelus's blade had blown past him. The wound had yet to heal the last time she had seen his hawkish face, a testament to how dangerous the creatures could be.

"Someone in Sylvanna, that young man in *The White Carmino*. He had mentioned a rumor of Tarkal being in league with an Angelus," F'Skal added as he joined them.

"Looks like they may have had a falling out then," Jekal added, grimly staring at the bodies as they were pushed aside by the motion of the ship. Crew members stood at the edges, lightly poking at the figures in case any were alive. "We're not long off from the island now, so I suggest everyone ready yourselves for the worst. If things are as bad as I am expecting, I'll take a group of men ashore to see what scraps we can find to patch up the ship. You all can try and find supplies, and we'll be back off onto the waters quick as we can. I'm thinking we don't want to linger long."

Erika stared at the water, partially wondering at the names of the people floating by, as she nodded and internalized the plan. She retrieved her pack—broken hammer and armor stuffed inside—and sat with Irvine's sword, staring at the cross guard and trying to picture his hands against it.

Keep thinking of him, a gentle voice cooed to her.

She snapped her gaze upwards. No one was nearby enough to have said anything, let alone any of the few females among the crew. The voice was more familiar than that.

† †

The sky darkened quickly. Black clouds rolled over the sky as bolts of red lightning flashed through them. The world seemed to blacken around the Rift, all but the two aash elves and Craven having to squint to see anything beyond the ship. A single light, like a massive fire shone from straight ahead of them, flickering in and out of the black clouds that billowed through tumultuously. Craven stood, arms crossed at the bow of the ship. He had admitted that he did not know what exactly was happening, but knew that the world itself was not at ease.

"I feel a nervousness in my gut that I haven't felt in several lifetimes," he said when Erika joined him.

"When was the last time ye felt it?" she asked, almost afraid to hear the answer.

Craven did not look away from the light, setting his jaw. "The Daemon War."

Erika found herself holding her breath, staring at the dark man. "So, ye were actually *there?*"

"Incoming!" came a crewman's shout, cutting off any reply Craven would have given her. A massive piece of rock crashed into the water off the port side of the ship, Erika having to hold against the railing for support as the vessel rocked violently to the side. Jekal's boots slammed onto the deck as he barked orders. "Full sail, now! We're making it to that damned island and seeing just what in the Hells is happening! Move, all of you now! Be ready to brace!"

Erika simply crouched where she was, knowing that she would get in the way of anything that she attempted to help with. Craven still stood above her. He stared dead ahead of them, nothing but unbridled rage in his hardened gaze. Another boulder flew towards them, Craven's eyes flashing up towards it. Erika steadied herself again for the impact, but the shadows around all of them suddenly seemed to move and contort until they blacked out the boulder and moved it to the side, landing harmlessly in the water. As they began to pick up more speed, Craven's jaw set again and he muttered quietly. "There's the Angelus."

Erika leaned up slightly, looking towards the island that was now more in view, but she saw no Angelus, only the light. She gasped as her head suddenly racked with pain, her vision going blurry and then dark altogether. In the nothingness she saw a fox, glowing as if made of pure flame. Its eyes were bright and ethereal, staring directly at her. Its single tail split into many and the creature itself grew in size several times over.

You are close. The world is not as it should be. Come to me.

The world came back in a flash, crewmen shouting and running past her. She removed her hands from her head and looked around as the blurriness faded. Craven had his rapier drawn above her with an expression of aggression locked on the oncoming island. He turned to her and his face softened as he knelt beside her.

"Erika, I am truly sorry for everything that I have put you and your friends through. Please know that Kharim passed peacefully," he said quickly.

She started shaking her head. "What're ye doin'? We need yer help!"

"And you will have it," he assured her. "However, I believe this to be farewell for now. Do what you need to do Erika, and I believe you will find Irvine."

Her eyes widened. She had never told him his name.

"Do not give up. The Sundering has begun a cycle, one that I believe *you* can break," he continued, his voice beginning to trail off in her mind. "Goodbye, Erika. I am glad I was able to know you."

Before she could reach out to him, Craven leapt from the edge of the ship. His form instantly vanished in a puff of black smoke that faded with the wind. She searched the perimeter around them, even knowing he would not be there. The island was even closer now and she could finally see the Angelus. It was larger and more thickly armored than the one she had seen in Valen, gold and silver plates stacking over one another. It carried no weapon but its arms were the size of her father's entire body. It looked away from them and Erika caught a glimpse of a shadow that seemed to lure the creature away, its six wings folding to allow it to turn sharply.

Jekal called out after a pause. "This is our chance! Move while the thing's distracted!"

Erika barely heard him, her eyes drawn higher up the central mountain of the island. A catastrophic volcano belched smoke and ash. Molten rock and pieces of buildings flowed into the water as the eruption intensified with a deafening blast. The air became thicker with soot all around them and in the city approaching ruin. People in extravagant but scant clothing were screaming, running, and diving into the water. At the opening of the peak she could just make out the visage of a massive entity, familiar and alien all at once to her. Darion flew down the rigging and landed with a *thump* on the deck beside her. F'Lessa and F'Skal joined them promptly.

"I can't leave with the ship," Erika said, unsure of her own words even as they left her lips. The companions all looked at her sharply and she met every one of them. "Funny as it sounds, I think destiny's callin' me."

F'Skal smiled. "Then we run with you. Lead the way."

To her surprise, Darion and F'Lessa both nodded firmly at F'Skal's declaration.

Darion spoke up a moment later with a grim smirk. "We can't leave you alone, you'll get hopelessly lost without us. How long did it take you to get to Stonewall from Sildenfeld?" he chuckled before looking to her again. "So, we'll just go with you."

Erika felt a tear well up in her eye, but F'Lessa knocked it away with a resounding slap on the back of her shoulder. "Our shaman said you two were important. Let's go."

Jekal saluted towards them as they made it closer to the land. The companions thanking the crew quickly for their hospitality before grabbing ropes and leaping down onto the remnants of a dock. They pulled their weapons as they stood, looking up towards their gauntlet.

Before them was the ruination of a once great city, compact and layered on the side of the island mountain. Shining architecture was marred by burning flames that spread like wildfire. Demolished pillars marked the graves of untold hundreds. Broken statues that spoke of history were lost to destruction. There was no clear path through the once pristine city. Daemonic creatures snarled in the streets while terrified civilians ran blindly through the chaos.

Without a word the companions started their ascent.

45
Destiny

Irvine slashed savagely through the neck of an oncoming opponent. He began to see any and all individuals in this horrible place as just another enemy, not even registering if they were human, elven, orkish, or otherwise. Zyrxak floated close behind, watching his progress as he tore a bloody swath down the center of the roving band.

"Left!" the Daemon shouted, prompting Irvine to snap to the side, parrying the oncoming strike with the butt of the spear before spinning it around and severing bodies with the full length of the blade.

On and on he fought, with no end in sight.

More and more he killed.

Erika would be appalled at how much blood was on him.

If only he could remember the particular shade of her hair...

Over three more combatants he broke, not giving full breath to his internal thoughts. The world became hot, scorchingly so. The flames burned from the Dragoon lance once more, Irvine smiling wide at the elemental power that once frightened him so much. "Yes! Finally, you show yourself!"

But the world around him grew hotter as well, and it was quickly made obvious that it was from more than just the

Draconic magic. All around him the world became distorted and blurry. He gasped for air, suddenly finding it hard to breathe. More enemies came, some fighting each other in the chaos of the battlefield, yet all of them began falling to the sands under agonizing pressure. Conversely, Irvine's steps felt lighter, as if he was losing the pull of gravity in the realm. The sensation sent him off balance and he had to readjust. Using the knowledge of the lance's powers that he had gained from the Arce'Thrak, he thrust the blade downwards. A blast of fiery energy exploded from the tip, sending himself careening over the mass of warriors. With an awkward twist and stab he landed back onto the sands and slid a short distance, thankfully away from the ongoing conflict he had found himself in the middle of.

Zyrxak slowly descended next to him. "Something's changed."

Irvine fell to his knees, his vision growing even more bleary from the strange lack of air. He gripped at his neck, the angry scar across his throat rough against his fingers.

Zyrxak floated upside down and inspected the young man's face. "What awaits us next, eh, friend? Perhaps we're leaving soon after all." The Daemon cackled as the draping cloths around his waist drifted lazily to his chest, exposing his distinct lack of legs. "Maybe the next world will have a nice beach, hmm? Somewhere we can get our feet wet."

Irvine's boots slowly came free of the sand beneath him, trailing small cascades of the fine powder as he hovered upwards. The heat became overwhelming as walls of fire started to tear around the world around him. Warriors in the field screamed as they were incinerated, but not a single flame touched him.

† †

Creatures familiar to Erika broke out around them, skeletal thralls of a Daemon crawled through the shattered buildings. Unlike the flaming red ones that Erika had seen previously, these dripped in bright green ichor that gave them a look of acidity. They fell all the same, several sprouting arrows and falling to the broken stones with dull thumps. Others slammed more violently to the ground as F'Lessa dashed ahead, separating limbs and heads with her axes.

Several times, the group came across terrified people, cowering in fear of the destruction. All they could do was tell them to flee to Jekal's ship, each time giving them approximate directions of where they had come from, hoping that the way was still clear of monsters.

Death was all around, bodies littering the streets in all manner of states, but rarely ever whole. Darion had already vomited twice, the rest of them doing their best to warn him of worse sections before he saw them. Their trek to the top continued on, past rivers of magma pouring from the peak, over demolished buildings where society had once thrived, and through hordes of Daemonic thralls that weakly attempted to halt their progress. They could see the end of the buildings up and ahead of them. It was still a daunting climb, but one that they could all make in a relatively short time if given enough leeway by their adversaries. Erika knew that was where she needed to go.

They pressed on up the crumbling streets, Erika and Darion sharing a brief nod when they approached a small group of the Daemonic creatures. He bashed one to the side with his shield and Erika swung around him to cut through a second with Irvine's sword. She drew back violently as green slime splashed onto her and scalded her skin like acid. F'Skal had called out a warning at the nature of the substance early on after seeing it hit a doorway, all of them doing their best to avoid the scalding ichor. Erika immolated her arm to burn the rest of it away and looked back to her friends.

Her eyes widened as she saw the buildings next to F'Skal shift and shatter. She couldn't choke out any words before the real threat made itself known. A horrid creature with elongated limbs crawled out with a screeching hiss. It bore eyes all along its skull, with a gaping maw of teeth hanging below them, a long tongue lolling about as it moved dripping the same green ooze. The Daemon of Envy slammed its hand over F'Skal's eyes, drawing a pained scream from him as he was lifted from the ground in its tight grip.

Erika flushed her legs into fire, incinerating her boots as she launched herself into the creature blade first. The weapon drove through the Daemon, causing it to howl in pain and swing wildly around. F'Skal was thrown up the street towards his sister, his face blackened across his eyes and sizzling where the claw had gripped him. His agonized scream caused Darion and F'Lessa to pause briefly. Erika immolated her body where the acidic blood of the Daemon splashed her flesh, quickly burning the substance away but not without a scalding sensation on her skin where it had made contact with her.

In the back of her mind, she felt the creature at the peak of the volcano taking notice of her. As she continued to immolate more of her body, it seemed to look in her direction further. The familiarity grew and she thought of her name.

Infernas.

The Firefox Primordial called her as well, and she felt drawn to her ever more intensely, distracting her from the dazed Daemon. Darion rushed past and slammed his shield into the Daemon with a screaming curse, sending it tumbling down the sloped street as it struggled to get its gangly limbs underneath itself. "Come on! We have to keep going!" he yelled over the chaotic din that surrounded them.

F'Lessa had F'Skal on her shoulder, having quickly washed his face with water. His eyes were still shut tightly, his hands grasping around for his supplies. Around the bend of the island, Craven suddenly came into view along with the hulking Angelus that gave chase.

Erika looked to the peak and pleaded silently.

Closer, the voice called to her.

Craven looked to them after dodging a fist that cratered the street below and nodded to Erika, insisting that they keep moving. She stared at him for a moment before turning around a building, leading her companions out of the direct violence. She hurriedly girded her skirt about her waist, her burning legs propelling her powerfully across the intricate stone streets that cracked with every footfall.

The Envy Daemon recovered from Darion's bash, shaking its ugly head free of the ringing it likely experienced before letting out a hissing snarl. Instead of giving chase to the four that it had originally attacked, it turned to the Angelus and the Lord Wraith. It leaped onto a neighboring building, skittering inhumanly across it and cascading down onto its ancient enemy. The many-winged Angelus was too preoccupied with Craven to notice, as the acidic monstrosity landed on its back kicking and biting. The feathers and flesh of the wings began to melt into bone and sinew, but the

Angelus simply turned its hand over its back, grabbing the wily beast and slamming it to the ground just in time for Craven to pierce through it with his rapier.

Darion managed a grim smile at the glimpses he got of the battle before catching up with F'Lessa and F'Skal. He hung onto his sister weakly as she fully carried him on her back now, blinded by the acid. Darion retrieved F'Skal's bag and bow, nearly running into a pair of civilians as he shouldered them. He shouted brief instructions to get to *The Winged Siren* and warnings of the Daemon and Angelus fighting not far away, before running to catch up with his friends.

Erika's immolated legs pumped underneath her, sending her strides ahead of her companions. She slashed through Daemonic thralls as she went, hoping it would clear the path for F'Lessa as she carried her brother, her axes stowed on her hips. Darion started to become unsure of how all of this ended for them, cutting down another of the skeletal beasts as he began to look around for an escape route. They had to have somewhere to go after Erika found what she was looking for.

Up and up Erika went, hardly noticing the resistance against Irvine's former weapon as it slashed each monster. She could almost hear his voice again, almost see his face again. Yet all she could rationally see was the gigantic spirit at the top of this mountain that she scaled.

The voice called in her mind again. *I shall give what is lost, but you must aid.*

She neared the apex of the ruins now. No buildings remained, only barren rock and stone. Around her lay the waters of the Great Rift. The distant shelves of the Fjords seemed closer than ever, towering unfathomably high above their already staggering altitude. The Crown of Patrias on the other side came up short in comparison but made up for it in its imposing appearance, rocky claws scratching defiantly at the sky itself.

Above her was the Firefox, looking down as the island around her crumbled to ash and dust. Erika stood before what appeared to be a crack simply standing in the air, like a glass pane that had been struck with a rock. Flames seemed to seep from the voids between the fractures. Infernas looked to Erika as her many tails flitted about in agitation.

What was lost is near, but your power must bridge the final gap. I may only weaken the Border, you must pry the rest.

Erika immolated her arm fully and reached out to the spirit. Infernas bent low and touched her nose to her palm, despite still seeming so far above her. The sensation guided Erika's arm into the glowing fissure that hung in the air.

With huffing breaths, her companions reached her finally. F'Skal sat on the ground, one blade in his hand and held close. F'Lessa and Darion stood abreast of each other, using the practice they had with the Sylvannan Knights to repel the Daemons that encroached on their standing. They were beginning to look weary. Darion fell to a knee briefly before F'Lessa picked him back up again. F'Skal's blind panic sent waves of guilt through her. Erika wondered if they'd ever forgive her for guiding them into this.

Now dig, Infernas' voice brought Erika back to her task. *Pull. Rip. Tear away the walls until you find what you are looking for.*

Erika's other arm flashed into flames, her fingers moving into the crack and prying at the edges. Her arms ached with the effort, tears falling down her face from the pain that she felt as the barrier fought her.

† †

Zyrxak looked around at the blazing walls of fire. His one remaining eye watched the otherworldly flames as they consumed everything around them. Something settled in his ribs, something he had not felt even ages before the nothingness that was his only companion in the Consecration.

Awe and dread.

This power was beyond anything that any Daemon had ever attained. Simply from the force of the walls, he could feel that it was from something far older, far more powerful than anything he had ever known. The flames were beautiful, swirling with colors so vast. He had once witnessed a power so incredible that it had driven him to madness. He had strived to gain the fires of destruction that Wrath Daemons wielded, given up everything to hold that power in his own hand, just for a taste of that incredible power that he should never have even seen. The fires before him now made him realize his folly, to realize that he had given up on everything to chase after a foolish ambition.

414

These fires of creation, hot enough to melt existence itself yet warm enough to give life to all it touched. His efforts were a proven mistake in the face of their majesty. Through the waves of heat, he began to feel again. Pangs of anguish, pain, sorrow, and misery flooded over him. He would have wept if he still could, as he felt the warm touch of humanity once again.

His eye was drawn to the shattered sky above him where a blazing hand ripped through the swirling clouds of sand that turned to raining glass in the heat. Unconsciously he raised one skeletal hand to those outstretched fingers, brushing the tips just barely before shying away. He realized himself again, drawing his own hand back and close to his breastbone. *It is not for you,* he chided himself.

Zyrxak's gaze lowered to Irvine, still struggling to find a breath in that stifling swelter. Irvine called out briefly in protest when that same skeletal hand gripped at his collar, lifting him up.

"Time to go," Zyrxak said quietly.

Irvine did not hear him.

† †

The ground shook and rattled as a shockwave of heat blasted from the fissure as Erika pulled something free of it, throwing F'Lessa and Darion from their feet and instantly disintegrating the horde of Daemons that overran them. *The Winged Siren* departed quickly, pushed on a large wave that rippled through the waters towards the west. Ash filled the sky and magma rolled from the Firefox's feet. The volcano under the Primordial gave another rumble and blast, sending boulders sailing through the sky and crashing back onto the island below. The Firefox nudged Erika's back.

You must go, quickly. In purging this island of the Daemon and Angelus that mean to resume their ages long war, I have sealed its doom. Quickly now. The Dragons come.

Erika let out an involuntary gasp as the words entered her mind. She stared at the ethereally glowing creature as it looked to her in sadness and hope. The Firefox began to vanish, although the volcano continued to erupt. Erika sucked air through her lungs, her breast heaving from the effort she had just exerted.

She looked around as if she had been in a trance, then glanced down and screamed in shock and elation. Irvine lay in a curled heap, the Dragoon spear clutched in his hand. He was ragged and thin, bearing many new scars that she was not familiar with as well as a beard that had fully grown in around his features. He awoke slowly and Erika fell to her knees, dousing her flames and wrapping her arms around him. Tears flowed down her face as she sobbed openly for the return of her love. He seemed dazed, unsure of where he was or what was happening. He returned the embrace, feeling the warm skin of her back. Irvine nearly cried at the simple fact of having someone to cling to after so long. He felt the softness of her hair and the strength in her arms as she started to lift him from the ground.

Darion and F'Lessa walked over to them, unsure of how to interject into the heartwarming scene. Another resounding crack from the volcano returned them all to reality.

The island burned around them, rubble and magma cascading down the steep incline and into the water with a constant hiss. Far below, Craven easily fended off the Angelus and Daemon. He looked as if he had done it before. He looked as if he was enjoying it.

A deafening cacophony of roars sounded from above and the ash was cleared from sections as the beating of massive wings flooded the area with new air. Hundreds of gargantuan winged creatures dove from above, their jaws billowing gouts of flame, frost, lightning, and various other elemental blasts. The very ground below them melted and tore asunder with the strength of the mythical creatures as scores of them glided down the mountain and began tearing into both Angelus and Daemon.

The companions could not see where Craven had gone, but could easily surmise that the Dragons meant to destroy the island and everything on it. Darion turned sharply to Erika, stopping short when he realized that she held the newcomer in a deep kiss. He stepped forward, putting his hand on Erika's shoulder despite the latent heat from her immolation. "We need to go, Erika, I saw a cave in the mountains to the south that I think we can get to."

Erika pulled away from Irvine, who still seemed lost staring at something to their side. She acknowledged Darion and stood, pulling Irvine's thin form up with her. "Come, my love," she said with a wonderful ache in her heart. She was right, he *was* alive.

Irvine gaped off to the side, overwhelmingly happy to see Erika again but horrified that Zyrxak was still with him. The skeletal being floated only a few feet from the charred ground observing his restored form, no longer shattered and broken.

"This is peculiar," he muttered, though not specifically to Irvine.

No one else seemed able to see him.

The five then made their way down the side of the mountain. They scrambled to stay upright, F'Lessa once again carrying her brother on her back as Darion led them. The streets were clear of Daemons, only the sickly green ashes of their forms remaining after the wave of energy had washed over the island. Eventually they made it to the shoreline and Darion ushered them all onto a nearly destroyed boat. He quickly got the rickety thing into motion with a groaning push, F'Lessa grabbing his hand and pulling him in to the vessel with them. He worried they would capsize before long, as they barely fit on the rotting hunk of wood, but another shockwave came from behind them. They all gripped onto whatever they could find with whitening knuckles as the wave of water pushed them nearly all the way to the cave entrance Darion had seen and almost crashing them into the rock face.

Moments later they crawled onto the cold stone just as the volcano exploded again, sending entire sections of the island into the Great Rift and bathing Mintheras in magma. They all breathed heavily, staring at the chaos. The Dragons lifted from the island, trumpeting triumphantly as they raised into the sky on their powerful wings. They disappeared into the heavy ash with a resounding chorus of roars before the world went quiet once again. The crackling of the island in flames and the sizzling of the magma reaching the water was the only sound, save for their labored breathing.

F'Lessa smeared the black ointment on F'Skal's face. "Sister, stop," he pleaded. "The medicine doesn't do anything for blindness!"

She kept fighting him through tears until a resounding slap startled them all. All eyes went to the twins, where F'Lessa held her reddening cheek with shock on her face. F'Skal's eyes had opened again, white and unseeing. He gripped the hand that he had unintentionally struck his sister with, his face painted with horror. "I didn't—" he whispered quietly.

Darion met F'Lessa as she ran to him, cradling an arm around her as they walked to the cave's entrance. F'Skal's shoulders drooped lower with each of her sobs. Darion stared out at the island as a towering building crumbled into the roiling waters. His shoulders were stiff and he felt more drained than he had ever been in his life, physically and emotionally.

Erika watched her companions with sadness before looking back to her returned love. She ignored her own pain, skin red and irritated from a near overheating immolation. She fell to her knees next to him, grabbing him and holding him close to her. Irvine stared with wide eyes toward the entrance of the cave from her breast, where only he could see Zyrxak.

"They cannot see me," Zyrxak said slowly, almost amused as Darion walked through his form.

Irvine watched on as he realized that where he once had Arce'Thrak tied to him, he now had his family's murderer.

The small boat they arrived on sank below the surface of the water, abandoning the group with only one option forward. The caves underneath the Crown of Patrias loomed before them, no light to guide them and no way to go back. For now, they simply rested, all of them exhausted after the events they had just experienced.

After a while, Irvine was able to tear his eyes from Zyrxak and looked to Erika. She looked older, weary. His fingers drifted over her hands and arms where her body was covered in crimson markings like her father's. Her skin felt so soft and smooth after so long of nothing but sand. He couldn't help but smile at the sight of his sword on the ground beside her, but worried over the broken warhammer that had fallen out of her pack. Similarly, he noticed scars that he didn't remember her having and the distinct puncture hole in the middle of her marred breastplate that lay beside the pieces of her warhammer. From there he looked out across the water that he recognized as the Great Rift, the distant Fjordlands far above them. He surmised that the island they had just escaped was Mintheras, although it was little more than bare volcanic rock now. His eyes widened as he realized the distance that Erika had gone.

"What happened?" he finally asked her.

She beamed at the sound of his voice, all the memories of her best friend flooding back to her. Before she could answer, Darion piped in from the mouth of the cave as he gazed out on the destruction with crossed arms.

"More than you can imagine."

Epilogue

I miss Erika. I miss my dear friend. I have failed to write her since she left, and I know not where she is to even attempt to send a letter.

Everything in Sildenfeld has been fine, her father is working hard and Sárif is adjusting as well as he can. The artifact that protects Sildenfeld from the inclement weather has experienced a change, beginning to lock out objects and even people as well. Sárif was thankfully able to calm it with the help of Jericho, Selbor's little sister. She's become a kind of crutch for me. Although she can help with my missing leg, she still cannot fill the void that Erika left behind in my heart. I see her as often as I can at the bakery she works at, as well as in Sárif's sanctum. She makes me miss Erika less, but I'm unsure if that's a good thing or not. I miss hearing her voice, seeing her smile. Her warmth radiates to all those around her, and the Gods know how selfish I am being for wishing she was here with me still. I know she has things to do. I know her heart already belongs to another...

Farris has gone somewhere as well, although I do not know if he is alright or not. He was quieter before leaving. I believe he blames himself for much of what occurred last year. I tried to talk to him, but he's always been the people person so I'm not sure if my efforts are having any effect. Selbor has gone after him as well, which Varia is furious about. Farris made it clear that he wanted to get away, but he just left without so much as a word to us. I think

Selbor is angry with Farris and means to drag him back to us. I only hope they don't kill each other in the process.

Erika, I hope you'll find Irvine quickly. I need you back here where I know you're safe.

-Teria Wyldsbane,
Honored Willow Ranger of Sildenfeld

Selbor is angry with Farris and means to drag him back to us. I only hope they don't kill each other in the process.

Erika, I hope you'll find Irvine quickly. I need you back here where I know you're safe.

Twenty-Eighth Day of Hallowden, Year 1127

Xhalia looked down on the annihilated island. The Daemon's corpse had exploded into a column of verdant light that disappeared into the clouds. The Angelus reached out futilely while his body slowly chipped into particles that floated away on the winds. That island was once a human city, she had seen it before. People laughing, singing, dancing, all in lavish decadence that the people of Máðir would consider frivolous. They were happy though. Could that not be enough? Was that such a sin for which they should be reduced to ruin?

She glanced away as her kin turned northwards, going above the clouds and returning to their home. Xhalia was too small to be noticed by any but her direct family in most cases, and none had noticed the leather bag she kept strapped at the base of her left wing. They didn't seem to notice her failure to follow the group either, even her parents surprisingly—too caught up in the victory to take stock.

She felt a hesitation deep in her chest.

Return, and nothing would change. Leave, and maybe she could make a difference.

It wasn't so hard a decision in the end.

South and west she flew, coming to rest on the neighboring continent of Patrias. She focused on her body, willing herself to change, to shrink, to morph, until she stood in the wide forested valley that now seemed much bigger. She appeared as a human woman as she looked around, taking in her surroundings. She picked up her leather bag where she had dropped it and slowly walked away from her landing, smiling at the creatures that stopped and looked on at her. The soil under her bare feet was cold, damp, and alive. The chilled air swept around her naked flesh and through her black hair that bore a single gold streak towards the front, filling her with an excitable sense of adventure.

She stepped out of the forest and into an open field that rolled down to a roadway, before coming back up into towering mountains far to the south of her. A shrill cry rang through the air as an adult royal gryphon came down upon her, landing nearby with precision and tucking its wings inwards. Its eagle face eyed her as it circled, but froze when she turned to look at it. The civilized races could not recognize her for what she was inherently but animals had an instinct about these things. The gryphon stalked around, keeping its distance even while Xhalia padded out further into the field, before seeming to give a kind of deferential bow. She simply smiled at it as it leapt from the ground and spread its great wings, propelling itself into the sky and away from her. Another motion caught her eye shortly after it had gone. On the road far down the way, she could see a caravan. Four legged creatures with natural armor and long flat tails pulling wooden carts along the path, humans and elves going about tasks beside them.

"Good a place as any to start," she said aloud, dropping her bag atop a boulder and retrieving her human clothing from within. They were various pieces she had picked up along her excursions in Máðir, which she liked to think made her look like a wandering warrior similar to stories she'd read. It wouldn't do to approach the caravan while still unclothed. Humans especially seemed to take that kind of thing strangely, Xhalia found. After a few moments she was dressed, adjusting her leather armor and sword belt before making her way down to intercept the caravan.

Xhalia wondered how long it would take her kin to realize she was gone.

††

Garreth stood on the precipice of the Fjordlands, overlooking the vast expanse of water between him and the home he had always known. Craven stood beside him, his coat billowing in the wind. The 'shadow step' as Craven called it, came in handy when he needed to cover long distances. He never would have thought it possible before becoming a Shade, even in the magical prowess of sorcerers he had met, teleportation was thought to be a forgotten art. "What happens from here?" he inquired of the silent man he now called leader, and Lord.

Craven took a deep breath and turned to look at Garreth and the woman that stepped up behind them, her visage even darker than Craven's. "The Chaos Age is attempting a return, and we must stop it."

The woman glanced between them briefly, hardly acknowledging Garreth. The whites of her eyes shone past the black paint across her upper face, making Garreth shudder slightly. "So, you were right after all?" her voice sounded irritated.

"One thing I hate to be correct about, Vaerisa," Craven replied. "The Daemons have made their full presence known, and the Angelus are retaliating."

"Would that not be a blessing?" Garreth asked earnestly, flinching when the strange woman began cackling with laughter.

Craven turned to him. "Unfortunately my new friend, it is not that simple. Angelus are just as bad as Daemons, despite how much modern history attempts to say otherwise."

"But the Divine Decree—"

"Is a sham!" cried Vaerisa, suddenly ceasing her laughter. "The Angelus lie to mortals just like any 'higher' being. The only honest one is Matron Mortia."

"No lies in death," Garreth breathed quietly, reciting the creed of the Shades which he had recently learned. Craven nodded to him.

They all turned to look at the scorched earth of the island far below them, the desolation razed by an Angelus and a Daemon warring in the streets of that once paradise now threatened to spread across the world. Craven had experienced it once already.

"We are with you, Lord Wraith," Vaerisa said solemnly. Garreth could have sworn he spotted a tinge of anxiety on her features at that pledge.

Craven smirked as he gazed down. "Is that so? Not too busy massacring orks in the Fjordlands?"

She clicked her tongue sharply, seeming to bite back a retort as her gaze fell to the Great Rift below them.

"And what of you Garreth? Do you wish to aid us in this endeavor? I will not force you."

Garreth could not take his eyes from that ruined island. "I seek truth, Lord Wraith. From you, the one who has slain me, and from this world, the one which has lied to me. Tarkal may be my home by birth, but I hold no allegiance to them in death." He turned to face Craven resolutely. "I am with you, Lord Wraith."

Craven smiled. "Well then. With all that settled, it is time to depart. Let us find both Angelus and Daemon to vanquish. Their ilk has stained this world for far too long."

Moments later, the three Shades vanished in black smoke and mist that was quickly carried off into the wind.

——————— End of Odyssey ———————

Characters and World of Odyssey

Erika Ildherre

Erika is a young woman who once fled from her hometown of Valen with her best friend, Irvine. After his vanishing she set off on a journey northward, both to search for any whereabouts of her missing love, as well as to distance herself from the grief she felt in her home Region.

The crimson lines that cover her body are left by her natural magic tied to the Primordial Firefox known as Infernas. No longer fearful to be marked by this magic, she wears the markings with pride and uses the gift often.

Despite the struggles she has endured, and the seeming impossibility of the quest she's put herself on, she keeps an optimistic attitude on her travels.

Darion Woodsmark

Darion is a young guardsman hailing from the small town of Stonewall in the southern portion of the Sylvannan Region.

Living in his hometown with his parents and little sister proved to do little for his own morale and well being, after a grim occurance that left him feeling responsible for another's death. Thus, when given the opportunity to leave alongside a strange girl with red markings, Darion eventually jumps to it.

He enjoys traveling, but struggles with the necessary violence that he sometimes needs to take part in. If given the choice, he'd rather come to a peaceful resolution, although he quickly learns that sometimes words are not enough.

F'Skal

F'Skal is an aash elf that lives among the Shalti tribe in a forest east of Sylvanna. He is primarily a healer among his people, using a vareity of techniques and knowledge to treat a myriad of wounds and afflictions, even to individuals not of his race.

When forced to engage in violence, he tends to prefer using his trusty bow, but also uses a pair of short-swords when needed.

Using the dust of a crushed emerald that was grafted into the skin around his head and neck, F'Skal can enhance his senses, allowing him to see great distances or hear even the lightest of sounds. Mostly he uses these abilities to aid in his medicinal duties but also employs it to look closer at the people around him, hoping to gain a better understanding of their character and culture. He joins Erika's party along with his twin sister at the insistence of their aunt, the village shaman and leader.

F'LESSA

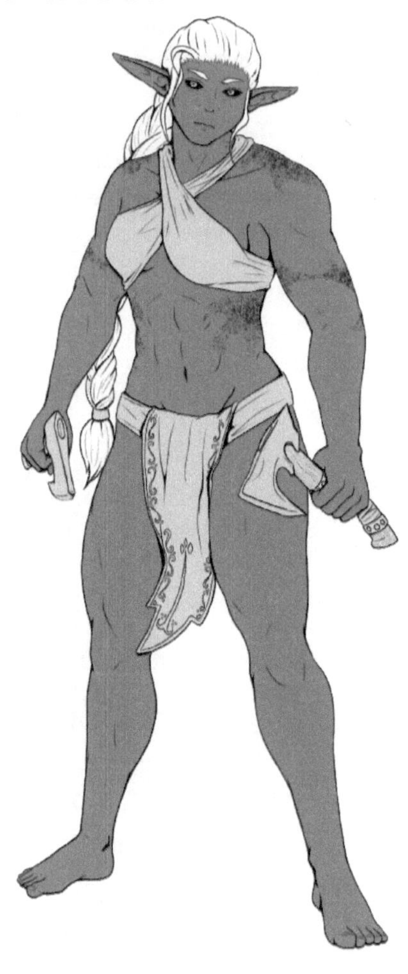

F'Lessa is an aash elf that lives among the Shalti tribe in a forest east of Sylvanna. She is a warrior among her people, defending the village against external threats with strong spirt and body, as well as a pair of keen axes. She is often distrusting of outsiders, but is usually tempered by her accepting twin brother when it comes to strangers.

Using the dust of a crushed ruby that was grafted along her shoulders, upper arms, and ribs, F'Lessa can enhance her strength, allowing her to lift things much greater than her own body weight, and strike with devestating power. Unlike her brother, she has never found a way to use these abilities to aid her in social situations and struggles with many interactions.

Like sol elves, aash have a trait where their hair color may change depending on their mood or emotions. Many elves have an astute control over this, hiding their unique colors from those around them. F'Lessa, however, has nearly no control over her hair colors, her normally silver braid streaking with a vareity of shades.

CRAVEN

Craven is a mysterious man who wanders around the world, doing things outside the purview of mortals.

In actuality, he is the loyal Shade of Matron Mortia, the Goddess of Death.

Having been with her since the very beginning, Craven possesses a knowledge far beyond any living being. He fights against anything that would defy the natural procession of life and death, particularly the continual plague of weapons and objects created by the ancient Necromancers.

He is first and foremost of the Shades, having command over all the legions of shadows as well as any other living Shades that still walk the world alongside him. He remembers a time when many more Shades walked the same path as him, but many have chosen to sleep everlong in the beyond, a luxury he cannot indulge in himself. The only other Shade that currently dwells near to him is a Fjordling woman named Vaerisa, rebellious and unpredictable as she is.

KHARIM N'ASHEZNEMON

Kharim is a man who hails from Patrias' neighboring continent in the south known as Haran. His former home is a dangerous place of deserts and oases, with a far different culture to that of Patrias.

His own trek northward was spurred by the mass genocide of his people at the hands of the Abyssal Hand. After discovering an ancient sentient sword, he has made his way into Patrias where he crosses Erika's path.

Kharim is a good man who means well, but is driven by a vengeful goal.

Appendix

Here, I'll compile a few things that might interest you, or aid you during your stay in Fædin. I myself certainly find them interesting.

If you have any questions regarding the information contained herein, you may always ask the mortal in charge of getting this story to you. Although, he may not know all of the answers, and unfortunately does not know how to get ahold of me when I don't wish to be bothered. Oh well...

-Kharazim Nazir,
Lich of Many Worlds

Calendar System of Patrias

The calendar set in place long ago by the Paladyn Order of Ten. Despite the fall of the Order at the hands of the Mad King Kaelis, the calendar is still in use in the modern era, even by neighboring continents who adopted its use somewhere in the early 1000's to aid in trade between nations. Makes everything easier for everyone involved when you can actually bloody agree on what day it is.

The calendar is split into twelve months, with thirty days each, and seven days per week.

The months:

Novus
Heartsbane
Rainsall
Fonsifal
Geolis
Aestal
Draconis
Solus
Commemorant

Hallowden
Wintershold
Veteris

The days of the week:
Morias, day of Salvation
Persenas, day of Growth
Hepis, day of Trade
Selunes, day of the Moons
Thalias, day of Luck
Galantis, day of the Sun
Phanes, day of Remembrance

† †

Magic

Magic in Fædin comes in several varieties all tied to different aspects of the natural world and reality around them.

Elementia-

The four Primordials responsible for the creation of the world itself are tied to the four primary elements: Fire, Water, Earth, and Air. Certain individuals throughout history have been chosen by one of these Primordials to carry a piece of their power within themselves and their bloodline, leading to a hereditary elemental magic.

Infernas, the Firefox, was responsible for giving life itself to the world. From her flames, souls were created and life was allowed to thrive.

Leviathan, the Serpent, filled the world with water, which nourished the life that was given. From his scales and wings, rain blessed the land.

Gaia, the Mammoth, was given charge with raising land for life to take root on. From his tusks, the gaia elves were given shape as the first life, and the ones with the strongest connection to the four elements.

Tempest, the Stormbird, gave the blessing of wind across the world. The cycle of weather and seasons begun with the first gust of her great wings.

Elementia Blood, or the individuals blessed with the touch of these ancient beings, are able to create their element from nothing, as well as control and direct it to their will. They can also change their physical body into their given element, giving them an array of talents provided by that element.

Each Elementia Blood will be marked by their heritage upon using their magic, which is represented by a series of unique lines on their flesh. The color is dependent on the element: Red for Ignis, blue for Aqua, green for Terra, and light blue for Ventus.

Arcane-

Arcane magic is one of the more well known magics, drawing its power from extraplanar realms—most commonly the Seven Hells. It can be a powerful force, but can come at a terrible cost.

Arcane users have, in the past, pushed past their limits and opened gates to the Seven Hells, allowing Daemons to wreak havoc in the mortal realm.

Other mages have torn their physical bodies asunder in their pursuit of power, many mages holding a belief that these mages are shunted into the plane of magic by the pressure, but many scholars believe this to be no more than a comforting story told to young mages and the family of the deceased. I happen to fall under that latter camp as well, as I have never seen any of these poor bastards wandering around anywhere besides the Isles of the Dead.

Divine-

Divine magic is believed to be given by deities on high to devout clerics and warriors to their cause. The effect most commonly comes in a golden light, but can be changed by the source of the individual's belief, as shown by the clerics of

Sylvanna who revere the Primordial Leviathan above all other Patrian deities.

It should also be noted that there have been cases of Divine magic being used in other continents across Fædin, such as in the tribal Máðir, the monotheistic Haran, the intensely matriarchal Sukaira, and beyond.

It is interesting to note that I have found precious few who use this magic for anything other than healing and bolstering of allies. When it is used in an offensive manner... well, few can stand before it.

Druid-

Druidic magic is derived from the natural world, often being used to guide flora and fauna along a desired path, but can also be used in astounding feats of healing.

The aash elves are the only known practitioners of this unique magic, having learned it from the mythical dryads long ago. Although there have been cases of humans, sol, or other races having grown exceedingly close to an aash individual or tribe and learning it for themselves.

Druidic magic is often practiced skyclad (or naked, for those of you who don't like fancy words), with only body paint to represent runes that help enact the effects. I personally believe this is one of the magics of Fædin that has the most untapped potential, although I myself am not able to use it. If it were not such a closely guarded art, I wonder if it would be able to shake the very foundations of the world itself. Although, what better reason to make it so closely guarded in the first place?

Dragoons-

The Dragoons were an exceptional group of people. Warriors unlike anything this world has seen since, and I doubt will ever see again. Being able to not only earn the surface trust of a Dragon, but the Soul Trust of a Dragon as well. Using the bond between their very souls, the mortal and the Dragon were able to combine their essences and make something that is no longer just one of them, but both of them.

It is an incredible symbiosis between two beings, which allows the users to slay Titans. Sure, they are most well known for their war against the Angelus' and Daemons during the Chaos Age, but that was simply a shadow of the greater conflict.

Shades-

There is no true term for the magic that the Shades of Mortia use. Given to them directly by the Goddess of Death herself, the magic envelops them in a perpetual darkness that few can perceive outside of higher beings such as Dragons.

In addition to their army of shadow creatures and versatile magic, these individuals are nearly unkillable. Shades can only truly die to certain weapons and higher creatures, or by surrendering their souls to their Matron Mortia herself.

Interestingly enough, the eldest among them is unable to surrender his soul, as the Matron is particularly fond of him. Last time I saw the wretch, he looked as if he'd resort to anything to end his days.

Witches-

Few know of the Arboreal Sisterhood of Witches, and they would gladly keep it that way. I, however, am a blabbermouth as well as being the universe's prime scholar.

The witches of Fædin are a staggering force that may be found in nearly all of the world's conflicts through its history, if only one looks closely enough and knows where to look in the first place. Their magic is unique and strange, from blood magic to the ability to touch the very weave of a person's essence, the witches are not a force to be trifled with.

They work alone primarily, but have a way of constant communication even through most world boundaries (a fact that Katalina learned very poignantly on a trip she took without my aid).

There are only a select few of them at a time as well and when one dies, her power is transferred to another candidate who carries their magic until their eventual death. In a grim twist of fate, when a witch meets the one whom will inherit her power, she actually witnesses the moment of her death in a sudden moment of clairvoyance. Very unnerving, I'm sure.

Abyssal-

A very powerful art indeed, which originates from the little talked about Abyss. The Abyss is a realm beyond the Gods and Spirits of this world, where only the most power hungry or foolish ever seek magic from.

The most poignant example of this in the recent years is the Abyssal Hand. Stupid mortals always meddling in forces not meant for them. Somewhere in their history, an Aspect whispered sweet nothings in their ear about remaking the world anew. I sincerely doubt the horrid thing said anything about what that would *actually* entail.

In most cases, the ones who use Abyssal magic are relegated to simple curses. Most view this as the opposite of Divine magic, and while they are on a close path, the categorization ultimately falls short of the truth.

Gods help this world should one of these damnable idiots manage to summon an Aspect one day. The Shades would have their work cut out for them then.

Afterword & Acknowledgements

What a ride this has been.

Odyssey has been my absolute favorite story I have written. Ever. For a very long time after finishing *Sundering*, this story was my life. Every moment I was doing (almost) anything else I wanted to be back with Erika and her friends on this trek through the world she calls home.

This story was absolutely the most fun I had been on in my entire lifetime of writing and, as of yet, nothing has come close to the level of serenity I felt while writing it. Another upcoming novel did come very close, mind you, but not quite there.

Art is something that we create from our very soul. Some use paint and pencils, others use instruments, more still use various needles or threads. All the same, artists have a need to create the things that they do. This novel is a prime example of that need.

I am sad that my time on this leg of Erika's journey is over, but I am looking forward to seeing where she takes us next, in *Salvation.*

Sundering was my first time writing a full novel, beginning to end, over 50k words, multiple perspectives, deep worldbuilding, the whole "kit and caboodle" as some are wont to say. It was also my first time publishing a book, and—unfortunately as is the case with any "first time"—I got a lot of things wrong. I am incredibly proud of that first book, and thankful that it got me out there.

That book has introduced me to so many incredible people.

C.H. Smith, I met at a local craft market selling his books, which then led me to *The Inkwellians Guild* in League City where I met a staggering amount of people going through the same things I was (am) going through. It was so encouraging, and the friends that I've made with that group have been so wonderful.

As well as all the people that have bought and read *Sundering* since I've started doing this. I've heard of people who read the entire thing in a day, I've had people ask "when is the sequel coming out?", and so many more encouraging things. I hope all of you have enjoyed this continuation of Erika's story and the exploration of this incredible world that I find myself exploring even when not writing.

Thank you to everyone who has accompanied me to this point. Your support really does mean everything to me.

Special thanks to the beta readers. Their support and feedback mean that I can keep doing what I love.

Jaycee

Becky

Joanie

Juleen

Davin

Lisa

Patsy

Trinity

Nina

Nathan

*Additional thanks go to **The Inkwellians Guild**, for their continual support and encouragement, even when they don't know what the hell I'm talking about.*

About the Author

Christopher Stephen Hicks lives in the ever-expanding Houston, Texas. He is joined in daily adventures by his wife Jaycee, their corgi Misa, and their multitude of cats: Tesla, Maxwell, Vierna, and Guenhwyvar.

When not writing, he is reading, watching shows or movies, or playing games to explore even more fantastical worlds.

Odyssey is the sequel to *Sundering* in the *Ignis* series.